LOVE IN DISGUISE

Center Point
Large Print

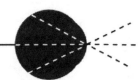

**This Large Print Book carries the
Seal of Approval of N.A.V.H.**

LOVE IN DISGUISE

CAROL COX

CENTER POINT LARGE PRINT
THORNDIKE, MAINE

This Center Point Large Print edition is published
in the year 2012 by arrangement with
Bethany House Publishers,
a division of Baker Publishing Group.

Unless otherwise identified Scripture quotations are from
the King James Version of the Bible.

Scripture quotations identified NIV are from the Holy
Bible, New International Version®. NIV®.
Copyright © 1973, 1978, 1984, 2011 by Biblica, Inc.™
Used by permission of Zondervan. All rights reserved
worldwide. www.zondervan.com

This is a work of fiction. Names, characters, incidents,
and dialogues are products of the author's imagination and
are not to be construed as real. Any resemblance to actual
events or persons, living or dead, is entirely coincidental.

The text of this Large Print edition is unabridged.
In other aspects, this book may
vary from the original edition.
Printed in the United States of America
on permanent paper.
Set in 16-point Times New Roman type.

ISBN: 978-1-61173-489-8

Library of Congress Cataloging-in-Publication Data

Cox, Carol.
Love in disguise / Carol Cox.
pages ; cm.
ISBN 978-1-61173-489-8 (library binding : alk. paper)
 1. Large type books. I. Title.
PS3553.O9148L68 2012b
813′.54—dc23

2012008837

To Dave and Katie,
my constant sources of encouragement—
Your patience and support mean the world to me.

To Kevin, Samantha, Emmalee, and Madilyn—
You bring joy into my life in so many ways.

And to Fayly Cothern—
You may never know this side of heaven
how much your walk with Christ has
influenced me . . . and countless others.
Your life is an example that speaks louder than
words.

Teach me your way, O Lord,
and I will walk in your truth;
give me an undivided heart,
that I may fear your name.
Psalm 86:11 (NIV)

LOVE IN DISGUISE

❧ 1 ❧

Chicago, Illinois
December 1881

"O happy dagger! This is thy sheath."

Ellie Moore gripped her hands together as she mouthed the well-known line from the last act of Shakespeare's *Romeo and Juliet*. The words floated out into the dark chasm beyond the edge of the footlights, and an expectant hush filled the theater, followed by a collective gasp at the moment she plunged her fists toward her abdomen and threw her head back with an agonized grimace.

"There rust, and let me die." Ellie let her head fall to one side and held her pose, silent as the grave, while the Capulets and Montagues reconciled, and the prince delivered the final line.

Not until the roar of applause swept through the auditorium of Chicago's Orpheum Theater did she stir again, ready for the curtain call. Ellie waited for the proper moment, then swept one foot behind her and sank into a low curtsey, spreading her arms wide. Her right hand brushed against the back of the red velvet curtain that screened her from the stage.

11

"Here now. Don't you dare set that curtain to moving."

Startled by the abrupt hiss behind her, Ellie jerked her head around and met the fierce gaze of Harold Stiller, the theater manager.

At the same moment, the actors began to file off the stage. Roland Lockwood, the troupe's Montague, bumped against Ellie's outstretched hand. Arms flailing wildly, Ellie floundered to regain her balance, but to no avail. With a muffled thump, she plopped into an ungainly heap on the wooden floor.

Burt Ragland, one of the stagehands, pushed past, his lip curled in obvious disdain. "That wouldn't have happened if you spent your time tending to your own job instead of pretending you're some kind of star."

Ellie scrambled to her feet, brushing dust from the hem of her skirt and trying to ignore the snickers from the other stagehands who'd gathered nearby.

"At least I intend to make something of myself," she snapped. "You'll be stuck here long after I'm gone." She lifted her chin when she heard the grunts of indignation from the group. *Ha! That rocked them back on their heels, all right. And good riddance.*

Noting the cleaner area on the floor that marked the spot where she'd made her undignified landing, Ellie swiped at the back of her skirt. "I'll think of you all, languishing here in this dusty hole, when I'm sipping tea in London."

Outright guffaws met her statement. Ellie gave up on trying to swat the dust from her backside, finding it too difficult to twist herself into a pretzel shape and maintain her haughty air at the same time.

Let them say what they wanted. It didn't matter anymore. Before the night was over, she would be gone from their midst and on her way to England. There, in the homeland of the Bard himself, she should find many who would appreciate her acting skills, gleaned from years of observation in the theater. Finally people would look past her drab exterior and see the raw talent that lay beneath. All she needed was a chance— just one! Then she would show them all.

While the other actors dispersed to their dressing rooms, one of the crew opened the house curtain one last time, so Magdalena Cole, Queen of the American Stage, could address the audience.

Her voice filtered back into the wings. "Thank you all for being here. Every performance is special to me, but tonight has a significance all its own."

Ellie glared at Burt and the others while Magdalena continued with the pretty speech she and Ellie had worked out the night before.

"This marks my last performance in your fair city, and not only in Chicago, but in this great land of ours." Magdalena paused to let the murmur of surprise die down before she went on. "Tonight I leave for New York, there to board a ship that will carry me away to share my art with the audiences of Europe."

"Don't make out that you're any better than us," Burt growled. "The only reason you get to go is because you're that woman's toady."

Ellie sucked in her breath. "That's *personal wardrobe mistress*—thank you very much."

"Good night, my friends, and God bless you, each and every one." Magdalena glided off the stage to thunderous applause, carrying a bouquet of deep red roses in the crook of one arm. She thrust the flowers at Ellie as she walked by. "Put these in water," she ordered, then gave a quick laugh. "What am I thinking? I won't be here tomorrow to enjoy them, so it doesn't matter what you do with them. Throw them away, if you want." She continued down the hallway without breaking stride.

Burt snorted. "Sounds more like *personal dogsbody* to me."

Ellie tossed the bouquet into a nearby trash barrel and followed in Magdalena's wake, not deigning to give Burt the satisfaction of a reply. She closed the dressing room door, shutting out the post-show flurry.

"Hurry." Magdalena's eyes shone like a child's on Christmas morning. "We haven't time to

14

waste." She spun around so Ellie could unfasten the hooks on the back of her costume. "Arturo will be here any moment. Is everything packed?" Magdalena slipped out of the Juliet gown with practiced ease.

"It's all ready." Ellie draped the costume over the back of a nearby chair and reached for Magdalena's new traveling outfit. She slid the stylish dress over the actress's head and upraised arms and fastened the row of jet-black buttons that ran from neck to hem. Then she stood back to study the effect.

"Well?" Magdalena pivoted slowly. Even in their present rush, she could find time to pause for an accolade.

Ellie reached out to adjust the rounded collar, then nodded. "It's perfect. That cobalt blue matches your eyes exactly. Your couturier outdid himself this time."

"And well he should have. I paid dearly for those new gowns. Even though I'm planning to acquire a whole new wardrobe once we reach London, I could hardly begin my grand European tour dressed like a second-rate bit player, could I? First impressions are so important."

Ellie folded the Juliet gown with care and placed it on top of the other clothing in the costume hamper. She lowered the lid, pressed it down with both hands, and then finally sat on it in order to fasten the latches.

"There now, we're all set. Your new dresses are in the two large trunks, along with your other personal effects. Costumes, wigs, and makeup are here in the hamper. We're ready to leave as soon as Mr. Benelli arrives."

Magdalena cleared her throat. "Ellie, there's something I—" A knock at the door cut her off. She leaned back against the dressing table and struck a pose, then nodded at Ellie. "It must be Arturo. Let him in."

Ellie opened the door to find a small contingent of theater workers gathered there. Harold Stiller stood in front of the group.

"We've come to say good-bye." He pushed past Ellie and walked over to Magdalena, who abandoned her dramatic stance the moment she recognized her visitors. "On behalf of all of us at the Orpheum, I want to wish you a safe journey to England and a dazzling career in the theaters of Europe. We will always treasure the memory that we, in some small measure, played a part in your success."

Magdalena's lips tightened, then curved into an expression that would look like gracious acknowledgment to anyone who didn't know her as well as Ellie did. It was obvious to her that the actress had no intention of giving credit for her success to anyone but herself while she stood on the threshold of her greatest triumph.

Their triumph, Ellie corrected herself. How

16

many times had she heard Magdalena say she didn't know what she would do without Ellie's help?

"Thank you for coming to say farewell." Magdalena's tone held a note of dismissal, but Stiller didn't take the hint. He leaned against the chair as if settling in for a long conversation, ignoring the glitter in the actress's eyes that would have warned a more observant person of a pending eruption likely to rival that of Mount Vesuvius.

Ellie moved between them, ready to intervene, but was interrupted by a commotion at the door.

"Magdalena, my darling." A stout man in a cashmere overcoat swept through the doorway, followed by three workmen. "Forgive me for keeping you waiting, *cara mia*. I had to brave the snow and ice to find the draymen and bring them inside." Arturo Benelli, the famed impresario who would be orchestrating the next step in Magdalena's career, took her hand and kissed it reverently. Then he straightened and clasped her fingers in his. "Your performance tonight was glorious, *magnifico*! Are you ready to take Europe by storm?"

A girlish laugh—the one she'd used when she played Hero in *Much Ado About Nothing*—gurgled from Magdalena's lips. "More ready than you can imagine, Arturo."

"Ah, *perfetto*. Our train awaits." Benelli lifted

Magdalena's cloak from its hook and draped it around her shoulders, then wheeled around and snapped his fingers.

The workmen stepped forward, and their leader asked, "Which of these things do we take?"

Ellie cleared her throat. "Those two large trunks and that wicker hamper belong to Miss Cole." She pointed to each item in turn. "The smaller trunk over there is mine." She indicated the battered case that held her own belongings.

Benelli arched one eyebrow and turned to Magdalena. "You haven't told her?"

Magdalena swung around to face Ellie, all trace of Hero gone. She cleared her throat, and Ellie felt her stomach constrict.

"We've had some wonderful years together, haven't we?" Magdalena murmured with a sweet smile.

Ellie nodded dumbly, knowing in her heart that something dreadful was about to happen but unable to fathom what it might be.

"You've served me well as I've risen in my profession, but now my career is taking a new turn. Arturo has come into my life, ready to lead me to even greater heights. And new opportunities often require us to make some changes." The actress's eyes welled with tears, as they did whenever she wanted to show heartfelt emotion.

"Enough." Benelli's eyes, so adoring when he

18

gazed at Magdalena, held no warmth when he turned to look at Ellie. "What Magdalena is trying to say is that I have promised her the very best of everything on her tour of the great theaters—including the finest wardrobe designers and makeup artists Europe can offer. In short, everything provided for her will be of the highest quality, par excellence—meaning she won't need you."

Ellie's mouth dropped open.

Benelli snapped his fingers again, this time at the man lifting Ellie's small trunk. "Put that down. It won't be going."

"But . . ." Ellie shifted her gaze back to Magdalena, looking for some sign that his words had all been a cruel joke. But the actress's face held no hint of teasing, only impatience, and perhaps a trace of guilt.

"But I'm the one who takes care of you. Who else knows the way you like things done? Your favorite hairstyles, the way you want your pillow fluffed. And what about—" Ellie's voice quavered, and she choked back a sob. She couldn't break down and disgrace herself—not here, in front of an audience of sneering co-workers.

She drew a deep breath, cleared her throat, and tried again. "You can't be serious. You *need* me." This time the words came out with more assurance. Ellie lifted her chin and stared straight at Magdalena, willing her to refute

Benelli's outrageous statement and vindicate Ellie before them all.

Instead, the actress turned to her left and placed her hand in the crook of Benelli's arm. "Let's be on our way." She smiled up at him, excitement shimmering in her eyes. "Europe awaits!"

Together, they exited the dressing room and turned left, toward the stage door. The draymen followed, bearing Magdalena's heavy trunks and the costume hamper.

Ellie shouldered her way through the knot of people lingering near the doorway and stood in the hall, watching Magdalena go. *This must be a nightmare.* It had to be.

"Wait. I've changed my mind." Magdalena stopped halfway down the hall and turned back.

Ellie's heart soared, and joyful tears pricked at her eyes. She should have known Magdalena couldn't go through with it. She took a step forward, ready to forgive.

Magdalena pointed to the man carrying the enormous costume hamper. "Take that back. I've no need for those things anymore." She raised her voice a notch and called back to Ellie. "Why don't you keep them? They can serve as a lovely memento of our time together."

The drayman returned and set the hamper in front of Ellie, then trailed along at the end of the retinue.

In the distance, Ellie heard the stage door close,

signaling Magdalena's final exit from the Orpheum . . . and her life.

A half-suppressed snigger pulled her attention back to the grinning stagehands. Even Stiller wore a lopsided smile.

Ellie drew herself up and glared at them all. "Don't you have work to do?"

Burt Ragland leaned against the doorjamb. "We do. But you don't." The smug look on his face made Ellie want to rip his hair out.

"Of course I do."

"And what would that be?" Burt asked. "Pourin' yourself a cup of tea so's you can pretend you're living it up in London? Looks to me like the reason for all your snootiness just walked out the door."

Ellie bent to grip the handle at one end of the hamper and tugged it back into the dressing room, bumping Burt out of the way as she passed. "Nonsense. I have years of experience as the personal assistant to one of the leading actresses of our day. I'll have no trouble securing another job. And now, I'll thank you all to go about your business and leave me to tend to mine." She moved to close the door, but Stiller blocked her way.

"Not so fast. This dressing room is no longer your domain, not that it was ever *yours* to begin with. Now that Miss Cole is gone . . ." Even though he didn't finish the sentence, his grim demeanor left no doubt as to his meaning.

❦ 2 ❧

Pickford, Arizona Territory
December 1881

Moonlight cast distorted shadows across the silent
landscape near the Constitution Mine. Steven
Pierce edged along the south wall of the board-
and-batten office building, stepping gingerly so as
not to advertise his presence.

Ducking into a pool of shadow, Steven paused to
listen for any sign that his approach was being
watched. Satisfied that he'd made the trip from
his own digs unobserved, he ghosted his way to
the door and slipped inside.

Four fellow mine owners looked up at his
entrance, their grim expressions barely visible in
the feeble glow of a single lantern. A blanket
hung over the lone window, cutting out the light
from the moon.

Steven made his way, more by feel than by
sight, to one of the wooden ladder-back chairs
set in a rough circle in the center of the plank
floor. "Any word yet?" he asked the others.

Tom Sullivan, owner of the Constitution, shook
his head. "Not yet. We're still waiting for Ezra."

Steven closed his eyes for a few moments and

let them adjust to the darkness. A quick glance around the room told him the others weren't in the mood for conversation, so he folded his arms, settled back in his chair, and waited.

The silence dragged on, stretching his nerves to the breaking point. He tried to make the time pass more quickly by studying his companions. Tom Sullivan, Brady Andrews, Alfred Clay, and Gilbert Owens—all of them older than Steven by a decade or more. Did their years of experience give them greater perspective, and more patience as a result?

A sudden scraping outside brought everyone to the edge of their seats. Steven smothered a quick grin at this evidence that the others were every bit as jumpy as he. The door swung open, and the group let out a collective sigh of relief when Ezra Winslow, owner of the Jubilee, entered the room. A blast of night air swirled in with him and set the lantern flame dancing.

"Bar the door," Tom ordered.

Ezra complied, then rubbed his hands together. "It's as cold as the North Pole out there."

Steven bit back another smile at the general murmur of agreement. The night air might seem cold to men who had spent years in the arid Southwest, but compared to the near-arctic chill he'd grown used to at Princeton University, southern Arizona's winter temperatures felt more balmy than frigid.

23

Ezra took the chair next to Steven's and sat in silence.

Brady Andrews and Alfred Clay exchanged glances, and then Alfred leaned forward. "Well? Don't keep us in suspense. Did they make it through this time?"

Ezra shook his head. "Nope." The single word dropped from his lips like a chunk of ore tossed into a mining car.

"What!" Gilbert Owens of the Blue Jacket Mine sprang to his feet and loomed over Ezra. "Don't sit there like a clam, man. Open your mouth and tell us what happened."

Ezra wiped his hand across his mouth, then waved Gilbert back to his seat. "I ain't tryin' to hold anything back. I'm just so bumfuzzled myself, I can barely make heads or tails of it."

Brady pulled a silver flask from his pocket and held it out to Ezra, who accepted it with a grateful nod and took a swig before handing it back.

"Okay, here's what happened. Like we agreed, I was riding half a mile behind Huddleston, off to the side of the road, where I wasn't likely to be spotted. When Huddleston started out in his wagon, he looked for all the world like he was just makin' one of his regular trips to Tucson for supplies. There was nothing to let anyone know we'd loaded the silver onto his wagon and covered it up with a pile of feedbags."

He cast a longing look at the flask, but Brady

24

shook his head. "You've had enough to help you get the story out. Keep talking."

"We were going through that rolling area a few miles this side of Benson, and I lost sight of Huddleston and his team behind one of the hills. Then I heard shootin'. My first thought was Apaches, so I spurred my horse and headed for the fray. When I topped the hill, I saw Huddleston lying on the ground and a group of riders makin' tracks in the other direction."

Tom's face grew stern. "Did they kill him?"

"No, but it wasn't for lack of tryin'. He'd lost a fair amount of blood, so I loaded him onto the wagon and took him on into Benson. The doc there says he ought to pull through, if infection doesn't set in. I waited around long enough to hear that, then hightailed it back here."

"And the silver?" Gilbert asked.

"Gone. Every last bit. As fast as they moved off, they must have split it between them so they could travel light."

Alfred slammed his fist against the arm of his chair.

Gilbert moaned and buried his face in his hands.

Brady uncapped his flask.

Steven felt as though he'd just stepped off a cliff into thin air. He clenched his fists and struggled to keep his face impassive. He'd sunk every bit of his capital into his mining venture, against his father's strongly worded advice. And now it appeared his father's dire predictions of failure were about to be fulfilled. After a series of robberies, sending the silver out of Pickford camouflaged in a rancher's wagon had been the group's last resort. If they didn't figure out how to stop the rash of thefts—and soon—he would be done for.

"Now what?" Gilbert's question pulled Steven's attention back to the moment at hand.

Alfred shot to his feet so quickly his chair toppled over. He paced the narrow room, pounding his fist into his palm with every step. "What else is there? When we sent the silver out on the stage, they held it up. When we hired extra men and shipped it in our own wagons, they picked off our guards. And now this."

"It's a terrible state of affairs." Tom looked as though he'd aged ten years since Ezra's pronouncement. "How are they doing it? How could anyone possibly have guessed the silver was in Huddleston's wagon?"

"They didn't guess. They *knew!*" Alfred's voice rose to a roar. "How's the word getting out? That's what I want to know. Who's giving us away?"

"I don't know, boys, but I think we've hit a dead end." Ezra slumped in his chair, the picture of defeat. "If we could call in the law, this would be a good time to do it."

Brady took a swig from his flask. "We all know that's a bad idea. I don't trust Marshal

Bascomb any farther than I could throw him. I guess we could contact Sheriff Behan over in Tombstone, or maybe the Earps."

Alfred snorted. "That'd be like asking the fox to guard the henhouse."

"Nobody's actually proven they were involved in any stage robberies," Gilbert countered. "So far, it's all been a lot of talk."

"That's an awful lot of smoke if there isn't any fire," Ezra grumbled. "I ain't willin' to trust any of that lot."

"Then where does that leave us?" Tom's gaze measured each of the mine owners in turn. "Are you saying we're all done for?"

"Not me," Steven said with a sudden rush of conviction. "I'm not ready to roll over and die yet." He looked around, willing the others to join him in making a stand.

No one jumped up to lend support. Driven by the defeat he saw in their faces, Steven breathed a silent prayer and pressed his point home. "Let's look at this logically. Tom and Alfred are on the right track. How do these thieves know what we're doing? Where are they getting their information? Those are the questions that need answering."

Alfred slapped his hat against his thigh, and a cloud of dust motes spiraled in the lamplight. "That's what I've been askin' myself for weeks. We've got a rat in our midst, and when I find out

27

who's been giving us away, I know exactly what I'm going to do. There's only one way to deal with a rat."

Brady rocked his chair back on its rear legs and pursed his lips. "I'm all for finding out who's leaking information and then plugging up the hole. I want to keep the Lucky Lucy working just as much as the rest of you want your mines to make a profit. But how do we keep these coyotes from stealing us blind?"

"I agree." Tom got to his feet and ran his fingers through his silvery hair. "We can't keep making shipments, only to have them stolen right out from under our noses. Why don't we stockpile it in one of the unused drifts in my mine until we can ferret out who's behind all this and it's safe to try again?"

"That makes sense," Brady said.

After a short pause, Steven nodded in agreement, and then Ezra, but Alfred and Gilbert did not.

"I think it's best we each take care of our own stockpiling. But I need to get a shipment through soon," Gilbert said. "It isn't just myself I'm concerned about. I have a dozen men, some with families, depending on me for their pay, so we can't take too long to break this open. I'm just a few steps away from going belly up."

"You aren't the only one," Steven reminded him. "All of us are in the same boat."

"But what can we do?" Brady leaned forward, thumping the front legs of his chair against the wooden floor. "This is the craziest situation I ever heard of. We can't find a way to protect the silver ourselves, and we can't trust the law to do it for us. What else is there?"

Silence settled over the group as the men looked at each other in the dim light.

Alfred shrugged his coat higher on his shoulders and stomped to the door. "We're wasting our time here. If I knew who to shoot, I'd take 'em out before the night's over, but that's just it—we *don't* know. What I do know is I can't go on like this. I've had an offer from a fellow back east."

He shoved his hands into his pockets and looked down at the floor. "I've been holding him off up to now, because the Busted Shovel's worth ten times what he's willing to pay. But if hanging on means losing my shirt, I'm ready to call it quits. At least I'll have enough to grubstake me so I can start over again someplace else."

"Wait a minute." Gilbert's voice stopped Alfred with his hand on the door latch. "What about the Pinkertons?"

The name of the famous detective agency lit a spark of hope in Steven. From the flicker of interest that rippled around the room, he could see it affected the others the same way.

Ezra stared at Gilbert as though he'd suggested asking for help from the president of the United

States. "You think they'd send someone clear out here?"

"Why not?" Brady countered. "They've made a name for themselves tracking down train robbers and the like."

The reminder fanned Steven's spark of hope into a blaze. "That's right. They have quite a reputation to uphold. If they take this case on, they'll dig like a terrier going after a nest of rats. If anyone can put a stop to this thievery, they're the ones."

Alfred stepped away from the door, his expression doubtful. "They'd want to be paid, too. Have you thought about what it would cost?"

Gilbert snorted. "It couldn't be more than we've already lost to these bandits."

"What do you think?" Steven asked. "We'll split the cost. Are we all in agreement?"

Gilbert nodded first, then Brady. After a moment's pause, Tom and Ezra murmured assent.

Steven glanced toward the door. "What about you, Alfred?"

The sullen man narrowed his eyes, then shrugged. "I think we'll find ourselves throwin' good money after bad, but I'll go along with it—for a time at least."

Tom rubbed his hands together. "So how do we go about getting in touch with them? Should we send a wire?"

"No," Brady objected. "There's too many ears

listening in up and down the line. We can't afford to show our hand, not when this is our last chance. We need to play this one close to the vest."

"A letter, then," Gilbert suggested. "Who's going to write it? We need to make it real convincing."

Ezra grinned and shook his head. "I'm no good at puttin' words to paper. I'll pass."

Brady pointed across the circle. "Steven, you're the college man. You do it."

Steven glanced at the other members of the group and saw no dissent. "All right. I'd be glad to, if Tom will let me borrow a pen and some paper. What do we want to say?"

Thirty minutes later, he handed around a draft ready for the assembled miners to read.

"Looks good to me." Gilbert picked up the pen and signed his name with a flourish. "Who's next?"

One by one, the others added their names to the letter. Ezra stood back and admired his signature on the page. "This is a pretty impressive moment, fellows. Makes me think of those boys who lined up to sign the Declaration of Independence."

"Just be glad it isn't a temperance pledge." Brady chuckled as he wrote his name below Ezra's.

Tom put his hand on Steven's shoulder. "Make

sure you don't let anyone else see this. We don't want word to spread around town."

Steven folded the sheet of paper with care and tucked it into his coat pocket. "Don't worry. I'll take care of it."

Patting his coat to indicate the letter was secure, he headed back to his horse, feeling the first glimmer of optimism he'd experienced since the rash of thefts began. If only this plan would work. He could picture it now—the Pinkertons swooping into town, ferreting out the gang of thieves, and setting him and the others back on the road to prosperity.

With an effort, he forced himself to tamp down his excitement. They had only taken the first step toward calling in the Pinkertons. They might still have a long road to travel before the problem was resolved . . . assuming everything went according to plan. But Steven knew better than to count on everything going smoothly. He'd learned long ago that things could go wrong even in the best of times.

3

Chicago, Illinois
January 1882

It was the worst of times.

Ellie bent her head and leaned into the bone-chilling wind that blasted along the Chicago streets like a train roaring through a tunnel. She forged ahead, trying to shake off the disappointment of another fruitless interview.

No one, it seemed, wanted to hire a former wardrobe mistress as a secretary or office worker. Her trial stint as a clerk at Marshall Field and Company had lasted only a day—less, actually. Somehow she had managed to alienate four regular customers before her shift was half over. From the way the department manager ranted at her, she must have set some sort of record.

Perhaps she ought to give in and look for a position as a lady's maid. That certainly wasn't what she had expected to be doing at the start of the new year. Only a few weeks ago she'd been dreaming of leisurely walks along the Seine and strolling the sun-drenched streets of Rome, but beggars couldn't be choosers.

Her career in the theater, the only life she'd

ever known, had come to an untimely end. Harold Stiller and the other workers at the Orpheum had seen to that. The world of the theater was a tight-knit community, one small enough that negative word got around quickly, especially when aided by a few strategically placed whispers.

Turning at the next corner, Ellie pulled the edges of her cloak more tightly around her and trudged onward. She had to find some means of earning a living, and soon. Her meager savings would be depleted in a matter of days, and then what? She had nothing to sell to raise more funds, unless she could find someone to buy the cast-off wardrobe Magdalena left behind. Even so, Ellie doubted those items would bring in enough to last her more than a few weeks, at best.

Only half a mile to go before she got back to her rented room. Ellie eyed the leaden sky and hoped the snow it promised would hold off until she could reach shelter. The street, normally teeming with pedestrians, was empty save for herself and two men walking ahead of her.

She plodded on for another block, then two. The men stopped, obstructing the sidewalk. Ellie skirted around them, careful not to step off the curb into the slushy buildup left by the previous day's storm.

"I tell you," the taller of the pair said as she passed, "if we don't find another woman to send along, we're sunk."

Ellie's steps slowed, and she stopped a few paces beyond the men, making a show of adjusting the ties on her cloak. Darting a glance behind her, she saw the shorter man shake his head.

"It's a tough spot, all right, but where are we going to find another female operative? All the others already have assignments."

The tall man flexed his right elbow and winced. "So what options do we have? Refuse to take on the job? The boss wants to use women, and I don't want to be the one to tell him no."

His companion stamped his feet and tugged the collar of his coat farther up around his neck. "I'm not going to risk sending a woman out to Arizona on her own, no matter what he says. To be honest, I'm not sure that's any place for women —no matter how many of them there are. Using female operatives in this case is a bad idea."

"Then let's get in out of the cold, and *you* can tell him."

"Not me. Last time I locked horns with the man, it took hours to sort things out, and I have tickets to the new play opening tonight at the Orpheum."

Without further discussion, the pair brushed past Ellie without a second glance. She followed them toward a building farther down the block and tried to sort out what she'd just overheard.

Arizona! Who wouldn't jump at the chance of leaving Chicago's bleak winter behind for the promise of open skies and bright sunshine? If a job awaited in a warmer clime, she would be willing to tackle it, no matter how menial it might be.

Ellie hurried to the doorway the men had entered, pausing when she noted the sign painted on the window: *Pinkerton National Detective Agency.*

Detectives! Her spirits rose even more. Maybe she would have her grand adventure, after all.

She stepped back a moment to straighten her cloak and pat her windblown hair into place, gauging her chances of winning the job.

Granted, she had no investigative training, but what she had learned through her eavesdropping made it obvious that experienced investigators were in short supply. A job as—what had the man called it?—an operative would surely call for intelligence and courage. Fine, she had those in abundance. And after years spent in the theater, her skills at observation had been honed to a fine edge. Surely that gave her plenty to offer. Squaring her shoulders, she marched into the building.

She spotted the men on the far side of the large, open room, but a heavy oak desk blocked access to them. The gimlet-eyed secretary manning the desk looked up when Ellie entered. "May I help you?"

"I'm here to apply for the job." She projected

her voice as she'd seen Magdalena do so many times. Sure enough, both men jerked their heads around at her statement.

"What did you say, young lady?" The taller man, slender and with a shock of gray hair, approached the secretary's desk.

"I overheard you talking in the street. It's a happy circumstance for us both." Ellie put as much confidence as she could into the words. She lifted her chin and looked him straight in the eye, trying to appear intelligent and courageous.

He looked her up and down, then stuck out his hand. "I'm James Fleming. Why don't you come back here so we can talk privately?"

Ellie followed him, not missing the secretary's audible sniff when she passed the desk. She put the implied slight out of her mind. It didn't matter whether the secretary approved or not. She wasn't the one doing the hiring.

"This is Ambrose Gates," Mr. Fleming said, beckoning to his partner. Fleming led them down a hallway to an office in the rear and pulled out a wooden chair for Ellie before seating himself behind the cluttered desk. Gates set another chair beside the desk, where he had a clear view of Ellie.

Fleming gave her an appraising stare. "You've certainly managed to catch our notice, Miss . . ."

"Moore. Elizabeth Moore," Ellie supplied. "As I said, I overheard your conversation outside.

37

It seems you're in need of a woman to fill a position, and I'm here to take you up on it."

Gates gave a muffled cough and wiped one hand across his mouth. With a quick glance at Fleming, he said, "That's a very enterprising attitude, Miss Moore. We admire your spirit, but you don't have any idea what this job entails."

Ellie sat up straighter. "Not the particulars, perhaps, but I read the sign on the window, and everybody knows what the Pinkertons do. You're the greatest detectives in the world."

Fleming planted his elbows on his desk and tented his fingers. "And what makes you think you'd be qualified for this line of work?"

"Well . . . to begin with, I'm a woman." Ellie hoped her little quip would lighten the mood, but neither man so much as cracked a smile. She cleared her throat and tried again. "I'm resourceful, for one thing. I'm able to think on my feet. And I'm very observant."

Gates nodded. "I'd have to agree. You obviously have a talent for eavesdropping."

Ellie felt her smile begin to slip and anchored it firmly in place. "Isn't that an asset for a Pinkerton agent?"

One corner of Fleming's mouth twitched. "That may be true, but there are other considerations, as well. In different circumstances we might be able to consider you, but not this time, I'm afraid."

Ellie had watched enough auditions to know

when a rejection was imminent. Her stomach roiled. They couldn't turn her down flat. "But you said you need someone to fill this position, and I'm willing to go to Arizona, or wherever you want to send me. I'll grant you I have no experience, but how many trained women detectives do you expect to show up at your door?"

Gates leaned forward, and his expression softened. "I'm sorry. It's nothing personal. You simply don't have the look we need."

Ellie pressed her lips together. So it wasn't only the theater that insisted on casting beauties in leading roles. "I see. I'm not glamorous enough for the part."

Fleming folded his arms. "That isn't the case at all. Mr. Pinkerton has determined that we should send a two-woman team, one younger and one middle-aged. We already have the younger woman. What we're looking for now is an older woman, someone who could pose as her aunt, a well-to-do widow." He smiled as he spread his hands wide and rose to his feet. "Obviously, that leaves you out." He ushered Ellie to the front of the building and bid her good day.

Outside, the sky had darkened, and snow swirled along the sidewalk, creating a bleak setting that matched Ellie's mood perfectly. She wasn't good enough to accompany Magdalena to Europe. She wasn't good enough for any job opening she could find. Was she good enough for anything?

She shivered and set off again, hoping to reach her room before daylight faded completely. Tears spilled, and she dashed them away before they froze on her cheeks.

She'd been so close. Both Fleming and Gates had been impressed by her spunk, even though they hadn't admitted it. And while she didn't know the first thing about questioning suspects or gathering evidence, the roles they discussed sounded like playing a part in a play. It would have been fun to have that connection between the life she knew so well and that of an operative.

And to relocate to a place that was warm. Ellie raised her hand to wipe away another spate of tears. Here she was, perfectly fit and ready to go, and the detectives themselves said they were in dire need of help. Why couldn't they have adjusted the role to fit her?

Her stomach rumbled, and she pressed her hand against it, trying to think how she would assuage her hunger once she got home. Playing detective in Arizona would have been an adventure, but she had more pressing reasons for wanting the job—things like being able to afford a roof over her head. And food, she thought, when her stomach protested again.

One more block to go, and she would be home. Music spilled out of one of the nearby saloons, and Ellie crossed to the opposite side of the street. A clatter of feet caught her attention, and

Ellie looked up to see a young woman about her age staggering across the road. The girl's threadbare cape evidently did little to ward off the cold, for the fingers that clutched it tight around her neck were blue, as was the skin around her brightly painted lips. While Ellie watched, the other girl made her way into the saloon.

Ellie shuddered, from more than the cold this time. What drove anyone to a life as one of Chicago's scarlet women? Being reduced to selling one's body surely required circumstances of extreme desperation. Being destitute, perhaps, or left alone in the world without family or friends to help.

Circumstances very like her own, in fact. Ellie's steps faltered. Would she find herself faced with the same decision that other women made? And what would her choice be, if it came to that?

She would starve first.

And that might very well be her only option, she realized, when she got back to her room and counted the money she had left. If she held on to every penny, she would have enough to pay for another week's rent. But that wouldn't allow for buying any food.

The choice between starvation and degradation might be closer than she thought.

She slumped onto the edge of her narrow bed and buried her face in her hands. There had to be some way to bring in money without dishonoring herself. Once again, she thought of selling some of Magdalena's cast-off clothing. A seamstress might be willing to pay for a dress that was already completed and only needed fitting to a customer. It might garner only a pittance, but a pittance could be enough to make all the difference in keeping body and soul together.

She flung herself on her knees beside the costume hamper and sent up a quick prayer. If God was listening, maybe He'd feel sorry enough for her to grant this one request.

Ellie fumbled with the latches and threw back the hamper lid. Lifting the Juliet gown from the top, she set it aside on the bed. A period piece, it wouldn't be of value to anyone outside the theater. She dug farther down into the pile of clothing and theatrical accoutrements and pulled out the dark gray dress Magdalena had worn in a recent production.

Ellie held it up, wishing the room's solitary oil lamp offered better light. Yes, it would do. With its simple lines, a dressmaker would find it easy to make slight alterations and add some trim to make it a truly elegant creation.

Encouraged, she reached into the trunk again and drew her hand back with a squeal when her fingers encountered something that felt like fur. Ellie picked up one of her boots and used it to push away the clothes surrounding the unnerving object, then let out a relieved laugh when she realized it wasn't some sort of vermin after all, but one of Magdalena's wigs.

She picked up the wig and shook it gently, watching the gray strands settle into place. The memory of Magdalena's pique at playing an older woman brought a chuckle, but the reviews of her performance had been stellar.

As Ellie bent to lay the wig on the bed beside the Juliet gown, a thought seized her, and her hand froze. With her heart racing, she lifted the wig again and held it above the dark gray dress. Together, they brought to mind a respectable older woman. One who might be a widow, judging from the somber color of the dress. One perfectly suited for a woman accompanying her young niece to Arizona.

Ellie rummaged through the costume hamper again, scattering its contents hither and yon until she found the thing she sought: the makeup case she had used to help transform Magdalena into a wide variety of characters.

She held the case on her lap and closed her eyes, taking stock of the things she had at hand and envisioning the task ahead. Satisfied, she nodded and got to her feet, ready to begin.

If Magdalena could play an older woman, so could she.

4

"God hath given you one face and you make yourself another."

The line from *Hamlet* brought a grin to Ellie's face, and she immediately toned it down to a more sedate smile. A quick glance in a storefront plate-glass window reassured her of what her mirror had told her earlier—not only had she created a new face, but she'd done a good job of it, too.

Would it be good enough?

Ellie pushed open the heavy door of the Pinkerton Agency, wincing slightly as the pebble she'd placed in her boot pressed into her heel. Heeding the reminder to alter her gait, she limped toward the oak desk.

The same secretary she'd faced the day before glanced up. "May I help you?"

Ellie pressed her gloved hands together and rounded her shoulders even more. "I . . . I . . ." She put a hand to her throat, pretending to adjust the rows of ruching at her neckline. After all the time she'd spent hovering in the wings, she never thought stage fright would overwhelm her. On the other hand, a quavering voice suited her new character.

She cleared her throat and forced herself to go on. "I'd like to speak with Mr. Fleming. Is he in?"

The other woman studied Ellie briefly, then nodded. "I'll see if he's available. Your name, please?"

"Mrs. Oliver Stewart." With a shy smile, she added, "Lavinia."

"And your visit is in reference to . . . ?"

Ellie pulled a lace-edged handkerchief from her left sleeve and dabbed at her cheek. "It's of a rather personal nature, I'm afraid."

The secretary bobbed her head. "Of course. I'll ask him if he can see you now." She disappeared down a hallway.

Ellie drew in a ragged breath and used the moment of respite to gather her courage. One hurdle had been cleared—the secretary showed no sign of recognition. Now the real test was about to begin.

A moment later, the secretary returned and ushered Ellie back to the same office she'd visited the day before.

Mr. Fleming rose from his chair and rounded the desk to greet her. "Come in, madam." He had replaced the wooden chair Ellie used earlier with a more comfortable padded one. "Please be seated."

He waited until Ellie settled herself, which took several moments. The cloth strips she'd wrapped around her legs to help mimic the stiff joints of an older woman worked admirably—almost too well. When she finally arranged herself, Fleming returned to his chair on the other side of the desk and gave her an encouraging smile. "Now, Mrs. Stewart, how can I help you?"

"Actually, I believe it is I who may be able to help you."

Two quick blinks gave the only indication of Fleming's surprise. "Indeed? Go on."

"My late husband, God rest his soul, made a number of investments that returned even more than he hoped."

Fleming picked up a pencil and made a quick note on the pad before him.

"As a result, I find myself with the resources to embark on a little adventure."

"Mm-hm." Fleming nodded and began twirling the pencil between his fingers.

Ellie sensed she might be losing her audience. Dropping the background story, she leaned forward and rapped the desk with her knuckles. "I intend to visit the West, Mr. Fleming! Its vast expanse has always called to me like a siren song, and now I have the means to fulfill my dream."

She studied his reaction and decided to play a trump card. Covering her mouth with her handkerchief, she gave a delicate cough. "Besides, my doctor says the dry climate should prove beneficial to my health."

Fleming set the pencil aside. "Yes, I see. But, my dear woman, while I sympathize with your aspirations to travel, and I offer my hopes for your health's improvement, I don't quite grasp the reason for your visit. What does all this have to do with the Pinkerton Agency?"

Ellie brushed a strand of gray hair away from her forehead and put on her—or rather, Lavinia's—most beguiling expression. "It is my understanding that you need someone to assist you in an investigation. In Arizona, I believe?"

Fleming's jaw tightened. "How do you come by this information?"

Ellie folded her hands in her lap and peered at him over her gold-rimmed spectacles. "A good operative is able to pick up information in an unobtrusive way."

Fleming's face held the same look of bewilderment Ellie had seen on Roland Lockwood's the night a fledgling actor went up on his lines in the first act of *The Tempest*, thrusting Lockwood into a scene much later in the play. "Madam, are you telling me you are a detective?"

"In the short time we have been talking, I've deduced that the need for a suitable operative has been weighing on you heavily." Glancing at his right arm, Ellie added, "And the bursitis in your right elbow has been acting up lately."

Fleming gaped at her in silence, then shoved his chair back with a clatter and hurried to the door. Leaning out into the hallway, he shouted, "Gates! Come here for a moment!"

When the shorter man arrived, Fleming indicated Ellie with a nod of his head. "This is Mrs. Stewart. She appeared in my office a few minutes ago with a most unusual proposition. She's interested in working with us on that Arizona matter."

"Indeed." Gates stroked his chin as he eyed Ellie from head to toe. "I have to admit she fits the type we're looking for." His eyes narrowed. "Who sent her to us?"

"I have no idea. She said she heard we were looking for someone and thought she might be able to help."

Tired of being talked about as though she weren't even in the room, Ellie cleared her throat to remind them of her presence.

Ignoring her attempt, Gates walked around her chair, inspecting Ellie as though she were nothing more than a mannequin on display. When he completed his circuit, he took a wide stance directly in front of her. "May I be frank, Mrs. Stewart?"

"Please do." Ellie's heart pounded so hard she could barely squeeze out the words.

"You look the part, and you seem like a very nice lady, but appearances aren't everything. This job requires a certain degree of toughness, and you seem far too delicate to—"

Enough. Ellie sprang to her feet. Alerted by his odd look at her sudden display of sprightliness, she pulled herself into character and glared at Gates through her spectacles. "I think you place entirely too much stock in appearances."

He clamped his mouth shut and glowered at her.

Seeing her last opportunity for survival ready to slip away, Ellie drew upon every ounce of resolve she possessed and addressed both men. "What you need is someone with the inner resources to gather the information you're after. Am I right?"

Gates clasped his hands behind his back and glanced at his partner.

Fleming took in a quick breath. "My enthusiasm may have been a bit precipitous. I'm afraid my associate has a point. It's obvious you have an interest in the job, and quite possibly the will to get it done. However . . ." He paused, as if hoping Ellie would take the hint and spare him having to explain her dismissal in painfully blunt terms. When she remained silent, he shot a look of appeal at Gates.

"What Mr. Fleming is trying to say is, this enterprise requires a high degree of stamina. You may have the will to get the job done, but will and stamina are not the same thing."

He was going to say no. Ellie racked her brain for some compelling argument, but all she could come up with was, "Did you enjoy your evening at the theater last night, Mr. Gates?"

Gates's mouth snapped shut like a trap, then fell open again. "Wh-what did you say?"

"I'm sure Roland Lockwood gave his usual brilliant performance, but what did you think of the new female lead? Did she measure up to Magdalena Cole's standard?" Ellie tilted her head and smiled up at him, though her legs were trembling so hard she could barely stand.

Gates shook his head as if trying to decide whether her questions were intended to distract him or merely the ramblings of an aging woman. "Whether or not you saw me at the theater last night is of no importance, madam. And it's hardly germane to the issue at hand. What matters here is—"

"—whether or not I possess the skills needed for this assignment. For your information, I was nowhere near the Orpheum last night."

"Then how could you possibly know . . ." Gates looked at Fleming, who smiled and shrugged.

"She knew about my bursitis, as well."

The two fell silent. Finally Gates drew in a slow breath and murmured, "She really is exactly what we've been looking for."

Spotting a chink in their armor, Ellie forged ahead. "Let me get this straight, gentlemen. You want someone who looks like me and possesses my intuitive ability but has the strength and stamina of a much younger woman. Is that correct?"

Fleming and Gates exchanged glances. Gates had the grace to look mildly embarrassed when he spoke. "I suppose it sounds unreasonable, but that's what the job demands."

"So what you're looking for is a robust young woman with an older woman's exterior. Just how likely do you think you are to find that combination?"

Gates smothered a smile. "I have to admit, it does sound rather ludicrous when you put it that way."

"Then it seems to me you've created quite a predicament for yourselves. Tell me one thing: have you interviewed any other candidates besides me and the young woman you spoke to yesterday?"

Fleming straightened as though someone had shoved a ramrod down the back of his suit coat. His face brightened. "So she's the one who told you about the position."

"In a manner of speaking." Ellie rose and pulled her shoulders back into her usual upright posture. With a theatrical flourish, she took off her spectacles and removed the wax plumpers she'd placed between her cheeks and her gums. Speaking in her normal tone, she said, "Gentlemen, that young woman and I are one and the same."

Fleming and Gates froze in place, like actors in a tableau.

"Good heavens!" Fleming raised a pair of pince-nez to his eyes and peered at her closely.

Gates reached out as if to touch Ellie's padded waist, then snatched his arm back against his side. His Adam's apple bobbed against the knot in his narrow bow tie. "I've been in the field a good many years, but I never would have believed this if I hadn't seen it with my own eyes."

Fleming tugged at Gates's sleeve, and the two men edged toward the far end of the office, where they began conversing in hushed tones.

Gates stared up at Fleming. "You aren't seriously recommending we hire her?"

"Think about it. If she can fool us . . ."

"Even so, she's untrained, untested. Using her could prove to be a complete disaster."

"Or a stroke of genius." Fleming looked at Ellie over Gates's shoulder. "After seeing that transformation, I'm inclined to believe the latter."

"Hoodwinking us for a matter of minutes is a far cry from carrying out a long-term masquerade."

"Granted, but remember, we wouldn't be sending her out there on her own."

Gates responded with a grunt.

Fleming sighed, and they moved back toward the desk, where Ellie stood, barely able to breathe.

Fleming gestured toward her chair. "Please sit down, Mrs. . . . Miss . . . What *is* your name, anyway?"

Ellie unlocked her knees and lowered herself onto the padded seat as quickly as her cloth-wrapped limbs would permit. "My name is Elizabeth Moore, as I told you yesterday." She allowed a smile to play across her lips.

A deep furrow ran from between Gates's eyebrows to his hairline. "Young woman, this isn't a game."

"No, it isn't." Ellie snapped back to attention, chiding herself for her lapse when her goal hadn't yet been reached. "You need the help, and I need the work. So what is your answer, gentlemen?"

Gates eyed her steadily. "Are you a believer, Miss Moore?"

The question caught Ellie off guard. "A believer in . . . ?"

"Are you a follower of Christ?"

Ellie's mind whirled. What reason did he have for asking such a question? She had no way of knowing, but judging from his searching gaze, getting the job—or not—might hinge on her response. Lifting her chin, she forced herself to look him in the eye. "Of course."

It wasn't a lie—not really. She had believed . . . at one time. And she did own a Bible, handed down from her grandmother. She'd even read some of the underlined verses. Surely that counted for something.

Ellie's heart sank when she saw a flicker of concern darken Gates's face.

"In that case, you need to be aware that the job

of an undercover operative, by its very nature, involves deception. As a believer, you may find that hard to live with."

"That won't be a problem." The glib reply brought a sharp glance from Gates, so Ellie hastened to add, "I mean, I'll approach it strictly as playing a role. Lavinia Stewart will be the one doing the deceiving, not I."

Gates turned away and rubbed the back of his neck. "If you want my opinion, it's a bad idea. We're crazy if we go ahead with this."

Fleming nodded slowly. "I see your point. I agree that we may be crazy if we do . . . but I'm certain that we're fools if we don't. I'm willing to take full responsibility if Pinkerton has any misgivings."

A broad smile spread across his face, and he held out his hand. "Welcome aboard, Miss Moore."

Kansas City, Missouri

After leaving all her worldly possessions—namely, her trunk and Magdalena's costume hamper—in the charge of a pimply-faced baggage handler at Kansas City's Union Depot, Ellie strode along Pershing Road in search of the

Imperial Hotel and Norma Brooks, her soon- to-be partner. If all went according to plan, they would spend the afternoon going over information and getting their background stories squared away and leave on the evening train bound for Dodge City, Albuquerque, and points west.

Ellie pressed one hand against her waist to subdue her queasiness and felt her lips twist in a wry smile. Had she bitten off more than she could chew in presuming to play such an audacious role? She pushed the question away as soon as it arose. This job wasn't a matter of choice, it was one of survival. She *had* to be able to pull it off. Besides, she wouldn't be on her own. Her new partner would be on hand to help her make a success of the mission.

What would Norma Brooks be like? Fleming and Gates had given her the woman's physical description—creamy skin, red hair, a distractingly pretty figure—but those details gave no clue as to the inner person, the woman Ellie would be working with daily until their investigation ended.

Ellie spotted the brightly painted sign for the Imperial across the street. She waited for a phaeton drawn by a striking pair of bays to pass by, then crossed the road, reveling in her freedom of movement when she stepped up onto the boardwalk unencumbered by Lavinia's more limited gait. For this leg of the trip, she had chosen to travel as herself, knowing it would be the last time she'd be able to do so for some time. Once she boarded the train to Arizona, she would have to become Lavinia Stewart whenever she went out in public.

Ellie huffed out an impatient sniff. If only she'd heard about the investigation earlier, she might have been able to snag the part of the younger woman herself. Instead, she would have to spend her time in the public eye encased in the wig, padding, and cloth leg wrappings that made Lavinia so believable. Not to mention those cheek plumpers. She had to admit they did a first-rate job of changing the shape of her lower face, even adding a lovely hint of jowl along her jawline. But having the wax disks wedged inside her cheeks for hours at a time proved to be far more taxing than she had expected.

Ah, well. How many times had she heard Magdalena bemoaning the necessity of suffering for her art? Apparently it was Ellie's turn now.

She pushed open the hotel door and stepped inside, pausing to let her eyes adjust to the relative dimness after the glare of the midday sun. As her vision focused, she scanned the lobby's interior, looking for her partner. An elderly couple occupied a settee in front of the large window, and two businessmen conversed in hushed tones over in one corner. Ellie caught her breath and surveyed the room again, more slowly this time, but she saw no one who fit Norma Brooks's description. *What now?*

A balding man peered at her over his pince-nez from behind the L-shaped front desk. Ellie smiled at him, then strolled over to a grouping of over-stuffed chairs and perched on the edge of one that faced the doorway, trying to look as though she had every right to be there. Her heart beat double time, and her toes echoed the rhythm against the Oriental rug. Where was Norma?

Avoiding the desk clerk's gaze, Ellie opened her reticule and pulled out several folded papers, the notes she had scribbled during her all-too-brief training session at the Pinkerton office. She could use this time to refresh her memory of her mentors' rapid-fire instructions and be ready to fill Norma in on the details when she arrived.

She unfolded the papers and, smoothing them against her knee, reviewed her notes. According to the Pinkertons, several factions existed in Pickford—mine owners, saloonkeepers, plus the usual assortment of businessmen and trades-people.

"Don't rely on outward appearances. There's no telling who might be involved. Under no circumstances are you to reveal your true identity or your connection with this agency to anyone in Pickford."

Ellie could almost hear Fleming's dry tone as she read the inked words on the page. *"We have no idea who is behind these thefts, so trust no one, not even the miners who asked for our help."*

When Ellie looked at him in astonishment, he'd added, *"It wouldn't be the first time a miscreant has attempted to divert suspicion from himself by calling us in."*

Ellie frowned and tucked that snippet of information away in her memory. She would ask Norma for clarification on this point. Being an experienced investigator, her partner would surely understand the behavior of the criminal element.

The desk clerk polished his pince-nez with his handkerchief, then set them back on his nose again, never taking his gaze off Ellie. Pushing herself farther back in the seat of the chair, Ellie ignored him as she folded the papers and placed them back inside her reticule. She lifted her head at the sound of footsteps coming down the stairway adjacent to the front desk and swung around to see who was descending.

A stocky blond woman who looked to be in her midforties stepped off the bottom stair of the stairway leading to the hotel rooms and crossed the lobby with determined strides, barely slowing when she pushed open the heavy door and went outside. Ellie let out her breath in a disappointed sigh and slumped against the chair back. Even if her hair had been as red as a strawberry, Ellie would never have suspected the other woman of being Norma Brooks. There had been something in Gates's voice when he spoke of the senior operative, a tone that made Ellie feel sure Norma was a highly attractive woman.

Besides, she must be relatively young, probably not far from Ellie's own age, since the Pinkertons had been looking for a woman of Lavinia Stewart's advancing years to play the role of her aunt . . . and to be by far the less actively involved investigator of the team. Ellie pressed her lips together, remembering the sting she felt when the men told her the role would be primarily a matter of window dressing, giving Norma a necessary chaperone. On the other hand, they also implied that Ellie stood a good chance of future employ-ment with them if she proved herself by learning the ropes quickly.

She needed to look on the bright side and view her role as something like being an understudy, learning the lead character's lines and stage business while carrying on a minor role of her own. Frustrating for the moment, but with the possibility of bigger opportunities to come. She would fix her hopes on that consolation.

The door to the street swung open, and an attractive young couple strolled into the lobby. The dark-haired man was handsome enough, but Ellie's gaze—like that of every other person in the room—was drawn to his dazzling companion. Ellie realized her jaw was sagging and snapped her lips shut. *Could this be Norma?* The

Pinkertons had led her to believe she'd be meeting a stunning redhead, but she hadn't expected anything like this gorgeous creature with her blooming cheeks and air of vitality.

With a show of reluctance, the man moved to one side and stood near the coatrack while the woman stepped forward, glancing from face to face as though searching for someone.

Searching for her! Scrambling to her feet, Ellie tried to collect her wits. This was no time to demonstrate her lack of experience. Plucking up her courage, she approached the other woman and offered a polite smile. "Excuse me. Are you Miss Brooks?"

The exquisite redhead blinked twice before an amused expression spread across her features. "Don't tell me you're my *aunt*."

So it *was* Norma. Ellie tried to match the other woman's easy grin in spite of her pounding heart. "I'm Ellie Moore, at least I am for the moment. But by the time we board the train this evening, you'll be traveling with your aunt, Lavinia Stewart."

"Well, well, well." Norma surveyed Ellie with a long, appraising look, then nodded. "You aren't at all what I expected, but I know Fleming and Gates well enough to be sure they wouldn't send along someone they didn't feel could do the job."

She tilted her head, then added, "They made a good choice. With your nondescript looks, you'll be perfect at fading into the background. Nobody will even remember you were around."

Ellie's heart leapt up at the initial compliment, then plummeted at Norma's casual dismissal of her appearance. Of course she was plain. Hadn't she been told so all her life—by her parents, by Magdalena, by every director she had approached about casting her in even a non-speaking role?

She covered her wounded feelings with practiced indifference. "Tell me about the role you'll be playing. I've worked out most of Lavinia's history, but I'd like to know more about her relationship with her 'niece.' "

Norma twisted a red curl around one gloved finger. "I planned to go as Jessie Monroe. That's a name I've used on several occasions. But I came here to tell you—"

"Monroe should work," Ellie murmured, committing the name to memory. "After all, Stewart is Lavinia's married name, so she and Jessie wouldn't have to share the same surname. Right?"

The curl sprang free from Norma's finger and formed a perfect tendril along her creamy cheek. "True, but that doesn't matter now. There's something I need to talk to you about."

A sense of having heard these lines before swept over Ellie, and she tried to shake off the feelings of foreboding it evoked. Images of her last night in the Orpheum Theater flashed through her mind, leaving her breathless. An imminent journey and the anticipation of a grand adventure just ahead. Magdalena's evasive behavior and the words "There's something I—"

A feeling of doom rolled over her. *No, no, no!* This couldn't be happening again. Ellie clenched her hands into fists within the folds of her skirt and searched Norma's face, trying to reassure herself the other woman's expression didn't harbor a revelation that would shatter her hopes.

"I expected to head back to Chicago as soon as I wrapped up this last investigation. Without another female operative available, it looked like the home office was ready to turn down the Arizona case."

Ellie nodded and forced her hands to unfold. Norma was only giving some personal background, trying to get acquainted and put her at ease. "Yes, that's what I overheard the day I listened in on their conversation." She laughed at Norma's startled expression and quickly outlined the events that led up to her being hired.

One corner of Norma's lips quirked upward. "In other words, you eavesdropped your way into a job? Very enterprising of you. You have the makings of a fine operative."

"That's my hope. In fact, they told me that if you think I show promise during our time together, they'll consider keeping me on permanently."

Norma's look of amusement faded, and Ellie felt

a knot form in her stomach. Taking Ellie by the arm, Norma led her over to a small nook formed by an upholstered wing chair and a potted plant. "That's what I started to tell you. I had my bags packed, and I was ready to head back to Chicago when I got a wire from Gates saying they might have found another agent after all. They told me to stay put and wait for further instructions."

Ellie nodded, trying to look as though she followed Norma's line of thought, although she had no idea where the woman's words might be headed.

"That was fine by me," Norma went on. "Because I really didn't want to leave. You see, during my investigation, I met Jack." The last word came out on a sigh, and she cast a loving glance toward the man hovering near the coatrack.

"When he found out you would be arriving today, and that you and I were supposed to leave together on today's evening train, he asked me to marry him. Just like that!" Norma snapped her fingers and laughed. Peeling the glove off her left hand, she held it up so Ellie could see the glittering band on her third finger. "We got married last night. Jack routed a preacher out of bed, and the poor man performed the ceremony right in his parlor."

She pressed the ring to her lips and announced, "Norma Brooks is no more. I'm now Mrs. Jack Lawson."

"Congratulations." The word fell from Ellie's lips like a stone while her mind tried to make sense of the bombshell Norma had just dropped. It took her a moment to collect her thoughts and realize the other woman was still speaking.

"I should have let the main office know, but it all happened so fast. By the time I got the wire telling me to meet you, you were already on your way. So I decided to wait and let you know when you arrived."

"Are you saying your husband is coming with us?" And how would they explain a third person if he went along?

"No, I'm giving up the detective life for good."

Ellie's heart hammered against her chest. "You mean, after the Arizona job."

Norma's perfect lips formed a delicate pout. "I know it's an awful thing to do, leaving you high and dry like this. I hope you can forgive me."

Ellie studied Norma's expression and sighed. Seeing the other woman's unadulterated joy, how could she not find it in her heart to wish her happiness? "Of course," she said, hoping her smile looked genuine.

Norma drew Ellie into a quick hug. "Thank you. I knew you had a kind face the moment I laid eyes on you. Now, I really must run." She gestured toward her new groom, who stood checking his watch with a look of consternation.

"Our train leaves in less than an hour. We're going to New York for our honeymoon!"

She caught Ellie's hands in hers. "Do me a favor and let the home office know, will you? I should do it myself, but there's no time. If you'll just tell them the basic facts, I'll fill them in on the rest in a few days."

Ellie nodded dumbly, and Norma flashed a radiant smile. "You're a dear. I wish we could have gotten to know each other better." She brushed a kiss on Ellie's cheek and hurried off to join her husband.

Ellie stood in the dim lobby, wondering why she seemed fated to play the role of abandoned underling over and over again. Feeling the need to regain her equilibrium, she wandered back to the overstuffed chair and sat down again.

"Excuse me, miss."

Ellie looked up to see the desk clerk's priggish sneer. "It is against the policy of the Imperial Hotel to allow unescorted young women to loiter in the lobby. If you are not a guest, I'm afraid you'll have to leave. Now."

A wave of heat suffused Ellie's face, and she glared at the odious man. Gathering up her reticule, she dragged the door open and left the lobby in a daze.

What now? Despite Norma's optimistic attitude, Ellie didn't share the other woman's assurance of her future employment. She had been a last resort on the mission, hardly anyone's first choice. Without any training, there would be no reason for the Pinkertons to keep her on. They might not even feel obligated to fund her way back to Chicago.

Tears scalded Ellie's eyes, and she swiped them away before they could roll down her cheeks. Would she want to go back even if they did? Nothing waited for her but bitter cold and likely starvation in Chicago . . . or anywhere.

Her steps dragged as she moved to cross the street and make her way back toward Union Depot. With every step, her pace grew slower, and her eyes blurred. An angry shout brought her to her senses, and she realized she had stopped in the middle of Pershing Road, right in the path of a smart-looking carriage. Appalled at her lack of attention, Ellie hastened to the other side of the street and heaved herself up onto the boardwalk in front of the telegraph office.

The sight of the Western Union sign reminded her of her promise to wire the home office with news of Norma's sudden marriage. She might be on the brink of ruin, but she took pride in being a woman of her word. Lifting her chin and trying to stifle her tears, she marched into the brick building.

"I want to send a wire to Chicago."

The bored-looking clerk pushed a form and a pencil across the counter to her.

Ellie rolled the pencil between her fingers, trying to decide how to word the message that would mean the end of her short-lived career. Was there a way she could phrase it that would make the Pinkertons more likely to keep her on? After all, they still needed to send someone to take up the investigation in Arizona, and she had already been briefed on the situation.

As she pondered the possibilities, a daring idea entered her mind. What if she went ahead as Lavinia Stewart? Gates and Fleming had given her the basic details of the case. How hard could it be for a well-to-do widow to pose a few questions here and there without raising suspicion? Maybe Jessie wasn't as necessary as they thought.

Before she could change her mind, she gripped the pencil and scribbled a brief message to the code name and address Gates and Fleming had given her:

Henry Jeffers
112 Elm Street
Chicago, Illinois

Met Jessie. Leaving for Arizona as planned.

Lavinia

Ellie reviewed the words quickly. Maybe they didn't spell out the whole truth, but they weren't an out-and-out lie, either. She had met Norma, and she was leaving as planned. In a day or two, Norma would surely send them a wire of her own, but by then she hoped it would be too late to summon Ellie back.

She read the words once more and slid the paper back across the counter to the telegraph clerk.

❧ 6 ❧

"Pickford. All out!" The hoarse cry jarred Ellie out of her light doze, and she pushed the canvas window covering aside to verify that the stagecoach had, indeed, reached journey's end. Outside, the sun shone warm from a deliciously clear blue sky, throwing the dusty streets and buildings of Pickford, Arizona Territory, into sharp relief.

The driver swung open the door and moved a wooden block into place, then held out a hand to his gray-haired passenger. "Here you are, ma'am, safe and sound. You watch your step now."

Ellie found his caution more than an empty courtesy the moment she started to get to her feet and discovered that her limbs refused to move. She felt the heat rise in her cheeks as she scooted forward on the seat and tried once again to force her travel-stiffened legs to hold her upright.

The driver offered a look of sympathy. "Just

68

take your time, ma'am. All that jostling along the way can take its toll on anybody. Give yourself a minute or two to loosen up."

Jostling was far too mild a term to describe the unending jarring she had suffered in the six hours since leaving the train in Benson and boarding this infernal contraption. It was a wonder every bit of Lavinia's padding hadn't shaken loose and fallen onto the stagecoach floor. Trying not to let her mortification show, Ellie nodded and mentally counted to three, then reached for the driver with one hand and shoved herself off the seat with the other. The driver tightened his hold and stepped back, using Ellie's momentum to pull her to her feet.

Ellie stood doubled over in the tight confines of the coach's interior and commanded her legs to bear her weight, wishing the other passengers had disembarked first so as not to witness her awkward exit. After a few moments, strength returned to her lower limbs, and she eased herself down to the block and then to the street.

With the driver keeping a protective hold on her elbow, Ellie took a few tentative steps and breathed a sigh of relief when she found she was able to remain upright of her own accord.

Nodding her thanks to the driver, she tottered several paces away and pulled the dusty veil from her face, trying to get her bearings. Having read her share of Ned Buntline novels, she'd expected a rustic setting, but *rustic* didn't begin to describe Pickford. She scanned the roughhewn structures along the main street in vain to find any edifice rising higher than two stories.

Only a few blocks away, the line of buildings ended abruptly, and the road opened onto . . . nothing. Ellie caught her breath as her gaze traveled on and on, taking in what seemed like miles of tawny, brush-covered desert. Behind that lay a backdrop of craggy, brown mountains. She had seen drawings of sand dunes in books, but these resembled them only in their basic shape. The deep folds and jutting peaks didn't have the softness of sand. Instead, they appeared harsh, unforgiving.

Ellie shivered in spite of the midday warmth and tried to ignore the panic that welled up within her. She'd known better than to expect the comforts of city life in the far-flung reaches of the West. She had wanted adventure, hadn't she? Well, there it was, right in front of her. If only it wasn't quite so intimidating.

Visiting new places wasn't such an adventure in itself. She'd done plenty of traveling with Magdalena, after all. But this was the Wild West, not an eastern city. And always before, her duties had been laid out for her. This was the first time she had found herself completely on her own.

Moreover, the sense of openness, the vast expanse of sky—the immensity of it all—made

Ellie feel like a tiny, insignificant speck. And she didn't like the feeling one bit.

She pivoted slowly, taking in the street lined with clapboard buildings and the emptiness beyond. A solitary mule tied to a rail outside a building bearing the sign *Johnson's Mercantile* pawed at the ground, sending puffs of yellow dust into the air.

Ellie dragged in a quivering breath. It all seemed so barren, so raw. Would the people in this wild place match their surroundings? A tendril of fear trailed up her spine. Chicago had its share of rough-and-tumble politicians, shoulder-strikers, and the like, but there still existed some underlying vestige of law and order. What was she doing, thinking she could represent civilized behavior in this untamed place? Before she could help herself, her throat tightened, and a tear started to make its way down her cheek.

Ellie dashed the offending drop away with the back of her gloved hand. She had no time to indulge in self-pity. She had sought this position —wangled her way into it, in fact. And she had made the lengthy journey little the worse for wear, save for her stiff joints and sore body. They hadn't been held up by bandits or attacked by Indians. Lifting her chin, she strode back toward the stagecoach.

After two steps, she came to an abrupt halt. What was she thinking, marching along like a young woman when she was supposed to be a widow of mature years?

She glanced around to see if anyone had taken notice of her nimble movements. When she found no one paying her the slightest attention, she ducked her head slightly and moved forward again, this time at Lavinia's more halting pace.

Better. Much better. Ellie congratulated herself as she approached a man she took to be the station agent, who was taking the luggage handed to him by the driver and stacking it on the boardwalk.

He straightened and touched his hat as Ellie drew near. "Afternoon, ma'am. Which of this lot is yours?"

Ellie pointed out her trunk and the costume hamper, and the man separated them from the rest. "Want me to send it over to the hotel?"

Ellie spoke decisively, in her best Lavinia voice. "Not the hotel. I'm staying on in Pickford. I've made arrangements for a house here."

The agent's wiry eyebrows soared toward his hairline. He glanced around, taking in the other passengers. "Did your husband travel with you?"

"No, I came alone." Ellie allowed her head to droop. "I'm a widow, you see."

The station agent tugged at the brim of his hat. "Sorry to hear that, ma'am. Where's your house? I'll have your things taken there right away."

"It's on the corner of Charles and Second." Ellie recited the location from memory, thankful that Fleming and Gates had assumed responsibility for arranging that detail and hadn't left her to scout out lodging on her own.

The man brightened. "The Cooper place. I know it well. I'll have the boys take your things right over and show you where it is." He whistled, and two teenage boys appeared from the adjacent building.

A snippet of her briefing jogged Ellie's memory. "I need to send a telegram first."

"That's no problem. They'll deliver your luggage while you're sending your wire."

"But . . . I don't have the key with me," Ellie stammered. "I'm supposed to get it from the banker."

"Don't give it a second thought. I'll send one of the boys to get it." His rugged face softened at Ellie's surprise. "I guess we do things a little different out here than you're used to back east. Don't worry, we'll take good care of you."

Such a casual way of doing things. Further confirmation, as if she had needed it, that she had left the East behind. Ellie swallowed back her astonishment and forced a smile. "Thank you, sir. That's very kind of you."

The interior of the telegraph office the agent pointed out to her appeared to be a duplicate of the one in Kansas City—small, dark, and manned by a clerk who looked as though he were half asleep. Ellie stepped up to the counter and cleared her throat. "I'd like to send a wire, please."

The clerk yawned and scratched at his receding hairline before sliding a form and pencil over to her. "Here you are." His mouth gaped in mid-yawn when he looked up.

Ellie nodded her thanks and gripped the pencil between her fingers. The Pinkertons had instructed her to have Norma wire the home office upon arrival so they would know their team of operatives was in place.

She had spent the three-day trip from Kansas City mulling over the wording of her message. The Pinkertons had surely heard about Norma's hasty marriage by now, and she could only imagine the uproar when they learned their newest recruit had ventured off on a solo mission.

This message, therefore, would be crucial to her future. She needed to send a communication that would inspire confidence in the home office and assure them she was capable of handling the job on her own. Rather than launching into a lengthy explanation and pleas for forgiveness, she decided to opt for something brief and optimistic.

Using the coded phrases she'd worked out with Fleming and Gates prior to her departure, she began to write:

Arrived safely this afternoon. Will begin looking at investment possibilities straightaway.

Lavinia

She looked over what she had written and crossed out *this afternoon*. Chewing on her lower lip, she reviewed the message again. Yes, that ought to do it.

She smiled at the clerk, who was now staring at her with ill-concealed curiosity. Ellie could hardly blame him for his display of poor manners. Sitting in a backwater town with nothing to do but listen to the clacking of the telegraph key must make any departure from the norm a welcome distraction.

The telegrapher's pale blue eyes lit up when Ellie met his gaze, and his lips parted to reveal several gaps in his teeth. "Just passing through, Miss . . . Miz . . . ?"

"It's Mrs. Stewart. No, I'll be staying here for a while. I need to let my cousin back in Chicago know I got here safe and sound."

The gap-toothed grin widened. "Amos Crawford, at your service. Always happy to see a new face." He leaned forward over the counter. "Especially when it's one as pretty as yours."

Ellie's jaw sagged. Had he just complimented her looks? Of all the times she had yearned to hear flattery from some man's lips, it finally came from someone old enough to be her father . . . or her grandfather. While she was made up as a woman of advancing years, no less.

Before she could formulate a suitable reply, he turned to pull a slip of yellow paper from one of the pigeonholes over his desk. "Stewart, did you say? This must be for you."

Ellie glanced at the telegram he placed in her hand. Sure enough, it was addressed to Lavinia Stewart and/or Jessie Monroe. She unfolded the paper and read the brief message with a growing sense of dismay.

AWAITING NEWS OF SAFE ARRIVAL STOP WIRED FUNDS TO LOCAL BANK STOP ACCOUNT OPENED IN BOTH YOUR NAMES STOP

COUSIN HENRY

Both names? Ellie's fingers lost their grip, and the paper fluttered to the floor. Apparently Norma hadn't contacted the home office yet, and they weren't aware of the change in her status.

The telegrapher scuttled around to scoop up the message and return it to her. "Sounds like your cousin's worried about you two ladies traveling out here by yourselves."

Ellie nodded, her mind racing. Of course, he had taken down the message. He knew two women were expected. Now what?

She crumpled the form she had just filled out and tucked the wad of paper inside her reticule. "Could I have another, please? I'm afraid I've made a mess of this one."

Taking the new paper, she tried to collect her

whirling thoughts sufficiently to compose a message that would give enough information without causing undue alarm.

Arrived safely. Jessie delayed. Will begin investigating opportunities straightaway.

Lavinia

It wasn't perfect, but it was the best she could improvise at a moment's notice.

She paid the fee and watched while the telegrapher tapped out the words. After the final click, she bade him good day and turned toward the exit. Just before she reached the door, she realized she had no idea where to go next.

Ellie turned back and pushed her spectacles higher on her nose. "Could you direct me to the Cooper place?"

"That where you're staying?" The clerk nodded as if making a mental note. "Sure. When you leave here, turn left and follow Grant Street until you get to Second. Then turn right. After you cross Douglas, the next street you come to will be Charles. You can't miss it, but if you'll give me a second to put things to rights, I'd be glad to escort you."

Ellie stifled a gasp. "No, thank you. I'm sure I'll be able to find it on my own."

As she turned to leave, he called out, "It's

kinda chilly out there. Are you going to be warm enough in just that light shawl?"

"I'll be fine, thank you." Ellie ended the conversation by stepping out into the brilliant blue afternoon. Chilly? She shook her head. People in Arizona had no idea what cold was.

She followed the telegrapher's directions, strolling west along Grant. After three days on the train and half a day spent jouncing along in the stagecoach, it felt marvelous to stretch her limbs, as much as Lavinia's leg wrappings would allow.

For once, she appreciated the need to shorten her stride and take her time. The slower pace of an older woman gave ample opportunity to observe close at hand the terrain she had been viewing through the stagecoach windows. Everything, from the rough-cut lumber that made up buildings and boardwalks to the gray-green cactus studding the surrounding hills, seemed to warn her to keep her distance. And over everything lay a coating of dust.

With her mind distracted by the scene in front of her, Ellie's heel caught on the uneven board-walk, and she scrambled to get her footing. Disaster averted, she continued toward her house, reminding herself to quit gawking and keep a closer watch on where she was walking.

When she turned right off of Grant Street onto Second, her heart sank at the sight of a row of dwellings that looked as though they'd been slapped together from cast-off lumber and sheets of canvas. Lavinia and Jessie were supposed to be ladies of some substance. Surely the Pinkertons wouldn't have chosen to house them in a hovel.

The next block featured somewhat larger shacks that appeared to be made of mud bricks.

Ellie shuddered. She had slept in some odd places during her travels with Magdalena but never in anything that resembled these decrepit dwellings. She stopped on the edge of the street, wondering if one of these was to be her new home. Unbidden tears pooled in her eyes, blurring her vision.

"Mrs. Stewart? Over here."

Ellie blinked the tears away and looked ahead to see one of the delivery boys waving from the end of the street. Behind him stood a small white clapboard house with a neat shake roof. With as much haste as the leg wrappings would allow, Ellie closed the distance between them, arriving just as the second young man jumped off the front porch.

"This is the Cooper place? I mean, my new home?"

Both youths tipped their hats. "Yes, ma'am," the taller one said. "I think you'll be comfortable. I'm sure glad they found someone to live here. It's too nice a house to have it just sit empty and—"

A scowl darkened his face. "Shoo!" he bellowed

in the direction of a small lilac shrub under the front window. "Get out of there!"

Ellie clutched at her throat. What sort of creature was lurking there in the bushes?

The lilac swayed, and a skinny towheaded boy about ten years of age emerged. "What's the matter? I wasn't doin' nothin'."

"Nothing except peekin' in the windows." The delivery boy pointed toward a little wooden house across the road. "Get on home. And don't be bothering Mrs. Stewart. She's a lady, and she doesn't need any pestering from you."

The youngster puffed out his chest but decided to abandon his show of bravado when the delivery boy started after him. He scurried to the house across the street, where he took a wide stance and glared at them all.

Ellie's protector shook his head. "Sorry about that, ma'am. That Taylor kid is always up to some kind of mischief. You'd better keep an eye out for him."

Without missing a beat, he added, "We laid on a fire for you. All you have to do is light it."

Ellie shook her head and dug in her reticule to pull out a few coins for each one. Be it ever so humble, it appeared she was home.

7

Ellie took a deep breath and mounted the three steps to the porch that spanned the front of the house. Deep red curtains covered the windows, and a climbing rose twined its way up one of the porch supports. A pair of wooden rocking chairs invited her to sit and rest. Someone had obviously spent time and effort in making this place a home.

She bent over and plucked one of the rose leaves, still shiny and green even in the middle of winter. She tried to imagine sitting on the porch in the spring months, enjoying the desert breeze and the scent of rose blossoms. What color would they be?

She shook herself out of her reverie. If the investigation went as planned, she wouldn't be around long enough to see the roses bloom.

The front door swung open with a slight creak of the hinges. Ellie stepped inside and couldn't hold back a smile at the charming scene before her. The parlor took up half the width of the house, with good-sized windows on the west and south walls. She pulled the curtains back, letting sunlight spill into the room.

A small pedestal dining table divided the space between the kitchen and the parlor, where a tufted sofa sat in the center of an oval braided rug, flanked by a matching side chair on the right and an upholstered armchair on the left. A round marble-top table holding an ornate oil lamp separated the sofa and armchair. Ellie ran her fingertips over the delicate etching on the lamp's cranberry glass globe, feeling a surge of delight. What a perfect dollhouse of a place.

Peering through the doorway that opened off the opposite side of the kitchen, she saw a neat bedroom, complete with walnut dressing table, matching wardrobe, and a cozy bed with an iron headboard painted white and ornamented with rosettes, vines, and leaves. Her trunk and the costume hamper stood at the foot of the bed. A quick glance into the remaining room to the left of the parlor showed her a smaller bedroom, furnished in similar fashion. A smile touched her lips. Lavinia and Jessie would each have their own room.

The house was set up just the way Ellie would have arranged a snug home of her own. The Pinkertons really did think of everything, and this was yet another indication of their efficiency.

Which meant they would expect her to be equally efficient in her efforts to identify the silver thieves.

Her elation faded as the thought brought her back to her purpose for being in Pickford. She had succeeded in her efforts to find a job to sustain her and escape the bitter Chicago winter.

Now she must perform equally well in carrying out what she'd been hired to do.

But first . . .

Ellie darted toward the front of the house, slowing her steps as she opened the door and stepped out onto the porch. Those rocking chairs and the springlike temperatures were simply too inviting to pass up. Besides, in building a credible character, actions were just as important as appearance. It would be perfectly in character for Lavinia to sit and enjoy a few moments of quietude after her long journey.

She settled into the chair nearest the front door and shut her eyes as the creak of the rocker settled into a steady rhythm, letting the sun's soothing heat seep into her bones. What a blessing after Chicago's brutal winter. The thought made her eyelids spring open again. A blessing? Had the God she had ignored for so long been listening to her prayers after all?

The moment the question crossed her mind, a glow spread within her that rivaled the warmth of the Arizona sunshine. The rocker ceased its motion while she sat transfixed. Could it be true? After all the years since she'd turned her back on God, was it possible He still cared? Maybe she ought to dig her long-neglected Bible out of her trunk and start reading it again.

A rustle near the front window pulled her from her reverie, and she slanted a stern look at the lilac bush. "All right, young man, I'm onto you. You might as well quit your skulking and come out of there right now."

Silence followed; then a moment later the branches parted, and her towheaded neighbor emerged.

"What were you doing in there?"

"Nothin'." The boy twisted his lips into a sullen pout and drew a line in the dirt with the toe of his scruffy shoe.

"Oh, I think you can do better than that." Ellie reached out and patted the seat on the chair next to hers. "Why don't you come up here and sit with me for a spell?"

The boy shot her a startled glance. "Why?"

Why indeed? She was in Pickford to solve a crime, not reform young hoodlums. On the other hand, if she befriended the lad, he might be less likely to lurk under her front window.

"I like to get acquainted with my neighbors," she answered in a noncommittal tone. She waited until he scooted back on the seat of the rocker, his feet barely making contact with the porch floor-boards. "What's your name?"

"Billy Taylor."

"I'm pleased to meet you, Billy. I'm Mrs. Stewart." She leaned forward. "Now, tell me, what is it you find so fascinating about me? Surely you have more constructive things to do than sneak around my house."

"Nah." Billy's shoes made trails in the dust on the porch as he rocked back and forth. "No one wants me hangin' around much."

Considering the behavior she had witnessed so far, she could understand why. "Then perhaps you need a hobby, something you can pursue on your own. What do you like to do?"

A wide grin lit Billy's face. "I like finding out things about people. I'm really good at that. I might even be a spy when I grow up. I'd make a fine one, don't you think?"

"Hmm." Ellie chose not to comment on that. "How about this, then? Do you think you could do your spying somewhere besides my front yard?"

The light in Billy's eyes dimmed. "Yeah, I guess." He slipped out of the rocker without further comment and shuffled across the street to his house.

Ellie watched him go, feeling an unaccountable tightness in her throat. A ray from the afternoon sun caught her squarely in the eye, reminding her that the day was marching on. Time to get to work.

Back inside her bedroom, she surveyed her appearance in the oval mirror over her dressing table, finding it surprisingly presentable after the rigors of traveling. Smoothing the wrinkles out of her dress as best she could, she checked to make sure the gray wig was fastened securely and straightened her wide-brimmed hat. She was ready to begin.

But how? Ellie stared at Lavinia's reflection. The idea of investigating sounded simple enough, but she had no clue what steps were actually involved in accomplishing the task. If only Fleming and Gates had given her more details than the bare information she needed in order to serve as "window dressing."

Question the suspects. Wasn't that what the fictional detectives she'd read about would do? Surely that would be a promising place to start. But she had to locate the suspects first. How was she supposed to do that? On her journey west, she'd envisioned herself asking clever questions of the people in town. Now that she had arrived, she could see she would have to revise her thinking. The people of Pickford seemed to know everyone else's business. If she wandered around asking questions of every individual she encountered, the whole town would know about it by nightfall. Hardly a good way to keep from drawing attention to herself.

Instead of Chicago, where neighbors could be virtual strangers, Pickford reminded her of the tight-knit theatrical community, where gossip whispered in one ear would find its way to everyone else in the company in short order.

Ellie sighed. She'd told the Pinkertons she was resourceful; now she had to prove it.

She pulled her notes from her reticule and spread them on the dining table, then sat down to study them. Miners, business owners, ranchers. She tucked her lower lip between her teeth. That information was a start, but she had no idea how to go about contacting them.

With a low moan, she rested her forehead on the heel of her hand. Her situation was becoming more complicated every moment. Would it be appropriate for an older lady to go around asking questions of rough miners and saloonkeepers? How could she possibly learn anything if she had to observe from a distance? Ellie gritted her teeth and slapped her hand on the table. How could Norma abandon her?

She needed to calm down. There had to be a way. . . . She had no training in being a detective, but she'd spent her life around the theater. The situation in Pickford, filled with nefarious thieves, eccentric characters, and an exotic setting, was a drama of its own, one in which she now found herself enmeshed. Could she somehow use the things she did know to her advantage? After all, she had seen plenty of performances on stage. She knew how a play should be structured.

"If this were a play," she murmured, "what would happen next?" She pushed her chair away from the table and paced the length of the parlor.

"Act one, scene one: the crime is committed. Act one, scene two: the detective arrives and . . .

and . . ." Her steps lagged, and she stopped dead in the middle of the braided rug. Try as she might, not a single idea came to mind.

Her brief surge of hope sputtered and died like a moth flying into a footlight. She resumed her seat at the table and went back to her list of possible suspects. She didn't know where to find these people, but surely someone in Pickford did. Hadn't she already seen evidence that the townsfolk seemed to know the details of each other's lives?

Hope began to flicker again, and Ellie grinned. Here was one instance when being Lavinia would pay off. Elderly ladies were expected to take an interest in other people's business. She gathered up her reticule and headed for the front door.

Johnson's Mercantile smelled of leather, tobacco, and a pungent odor Ellie couldn't identify. She moved past baskets of vegetables and headed toward the fancy-goods section near the rear of the store. Passing a rack holding reins and bridles, she spotted a scruffy-looking man who looked like he'd just crawled out of a hole in the ground. Ellie wrinkled her nose. Apparently the disheveled customer was the source of the unidentifiable smell. She edged around him and made her way to the back.

Ellie eyed the assortment of shoppers and gave a satisfied nod. Two young ladies fingered a variety of notions at a table in the dry-goods area. At the long counter, a sharp-faced woman in an outlandishly feathered hat ticked off the items on her list, insisting to the harried storekeeper that her baking powder had to be the Czar brand, and none other.

A tall, muscular, sandy-haired man dressed in a dark wool jacket and canvas-duck pants carried a keg of nails to the counter and set it down with a thud beside a stack of items Ellie couldn't name. Another man—a cowboy, judging from his large spurs and heeled boots—stood in the ready-made-clothing section looking through a stack of shirts.

Ellie smiled. She had chosen the location for her first foray well. The variety of people she saw represented a fair cross-section of the local citizenry.

Where to begin? The mercantile owner would be a likely source of information, but the frazzled-looking man was still taking orders from the woman with the feathered hat. One of the men might be able to tell her where to find the miners, but how could Lavinia approach him right out of the blue?

The women, then. Ellie made her way to a section of the store devoted to fancy goods and approached a plump woman of about Lavinia's age. "Good afternoon. The storekeeper appears to be occupied. Could you tell me where I might find some picture hooks?"

"I'd guess they would be over there with the curtain rods and such." The woman pointed toward an area on the other side of the store without taking her eyes off Ellie.

"Thank you." Ellie sighed and shook her head. "Setting up housekeeping is always such a trial, don't you think?"

"Oh?" The other woman's eyes gleamed.

Ellie smothered a grin, recognizing a kindred inquisitive spirit.

"I'm Althea Baldwin. You've just arrived in town?"

Ellie nodded. "My name is Lavinia Stewart. I'm staying over on Second Street. In the Cooper place."

"Well, what do you know? Welcome to Pickford." Her new acquaintance set down the set of stamped-muslin pillow shams she'd been looking at and peered past Ellie. "That's a rather small house. How large is your family?"

"It's just me, I'm afraid—at least for the moment. I've been widowed for several years, but I expect my niece to join me later."

"You too?" Althea clucked in sympathy. "It's been nearly five years for me. It's bitterly hard, especially at first, but we must press on, mustn't we?"

Ellie nodded, not knowing what to say. She was merely playing a role, but this woman had to live out that sad truth. She looked around the store, wondering what stories the lives of the others there would tell. "Pickford seems to have quite a variety of people."

"That we do." Althea nodded, seeming fully as eager to impart information as Ellie was to collect it. She tilted her head toward the woman at the counter and lowered her voice. "That's Irene Peabody. She's the banker's wife and the most important woman in town. She'll tell you so herself."

She gestured over Ellie's shoulder. "The cowboy over there looking at shirts is Shiloh Hooper. He rides for the Circle J ranch."

So she'd been right. Feeling a bit smug at her accurate assessment, Ellie looked him over carefully, taking in the wiry frame, the high-crowned hat, and the heavy gun belt.

"And over there . . ." Althea turned back toward the counter and pointed at the man waiting alongside his keg of nails. "That's Steven Pierce. He owns the Redemption Mine." She drew close and nudged Ellie in the ribs with her elbow. "He's a handsome thing, isn't he? Makes me wish I was thirty years younger."

Ellie pressed her gloved fingertips against her lips. She gave what she hoped looked like an empathetic smile while her mind whirled with the information she'd just gleaned. Steven Pierce was one of the names on the letter the Pinkertons had received. One of the miners whose request for help had summoned her to Arizona.

Her gaze sharpened as she studied the easy way he leaned against the counter. It was almost like a sign from above. Surely he was meant to be her first official contact. She watched as the banker's wife sniped at the young boy who helped her carry her purchases outside and Steven Pierce conferred with the shopkeeper and handed over payment for his supplies. Hoisting the keg of nails onto his shoulder, he nodded to the store owner and headed toward the door.

She couldn't let him get away. Ellie took a step forward, then drew up short. She couldn't just walk up and start a conversation with a total stranger. She cast about for inspiration and noticed a loose floorboard halfway along the aisle between them.

Ellie caught her breath and pointed toward a table holding crockery and glassware. "Look at that display of dishes," she said to Althea. "I never expected to see something as fine as that way out here."

Stepping as lively as Lavinia was able, she hurried over toward the display on a course that would intersect with the uneven floorboard. Just before she reached the miner, she pretended to stumble, staggering right into his path. In one lithe movement, he swung the keg down to the floor and reached out to catch her before she fell.

"Oh my goodness!" As her rescuer set her

upright, Ellie adjusted her hat and peered up at him. "Thank you, young man. I would have taken a terrible tumble if you hadn't come to my aid."

Deep grooves bracketed Mr. Pierce's mouth when he smiled in a way that made her wish she was back in his arms again. She stared up into eyes the deep brown of Arbuckle's coffee and felt her heart take off like a racehorse.

His smile turned to a look of concern. "Ma'am, are you all right?"

Ellie collected herself and pulled back into character. Seeing her chance to keep him talking, she reached out and laid her hand on his sleeve. "I do feel a little unstable," she said, realizing her statement was the absolute truth. The room seemed to swirl about them in a way that threatened to make her queasy.

Mr. Pierce looked around. "Do you want me to get you a chair?"

"No, no. Just let me lean on you for a moment. . . . That is, if you don't mind."

"Not at all." Those beautiful brown eyes mirrored his relief. "Take your time until you're sure you've fully recovered."

Over his shoulder Ellie could see Althea Baldwin watching them. When their gazes connected, the woman waggled her eyebrows and gave Ellie a knowing wink.

Ellie felt her cheeks flush and shifted her focus back to the miner. "Gracious, we haven't even been introduced. I'm Mrs. Lavinia Stewart. I've just arrived from Chicago, and—"

The door swung open on its hinges and crashed into the wall. Ellie jumped and turned to see an unshaven man in a battered bowler hat stumble inside. Tears streaked the dirt on his stubbly cheeks as he clasped his hands to his chest. "Somebody shot Fatima!"

8

Ellie gasped and pressed her hands against her throat. The only sound in the room was that of the unkempt man's ragged breath as he sent puffs of alcohol-laden fumes into the air. Ellie waved one hand in front of her nose as discreetly as she could and sent a glance from Steven Pierce to the cowboy to the storekeeper, wondering who would move first.

To her astonishment, everyone went back to what they'd been doing as though nothing had happened, save for the cowboy, who glanced up with a mild show of interest. "Where'd they hit her this time?"

Ellie stared, aghast. Why didn't someone move? She had heard lurid tales of the cheapness of life in the Wild West, but could anyone really be that callous? She straightened her shoulders and raised her voice. "Has a doctor been summoned?"

"There's no need for that."

Ellie looked up at Steven Pierce, feeling a stab of disappointment that took her by surprise.

When he spoke next, it wasn't to her but to the inebriated man. "Take it easy, Lester. It's just one more hole. A little dab of paint, and she'll be fine."

Ellie backed away. Reminding herself to stay in character, she put her hand to her lips when what she really wanted to do was grab his shirtfront with both hands and shake the stuffing out of Steven Pierce . . . and everyone else in the store. Not a soul was paying the least bit of attention to the tragedy. *What is wrong with these people?*

The cowboy took a two-bit piece from his vest pocket and tossed it to the sobbing man. "Here. Why don't you head on over to the Last Chance and drown your sorrows?"

Ellie pushed her glasses up on her nose and gave the handsome miner beside her a severe look. "How can you possibly dismiss an injured woman with nothing more than a wave of the hand?"

His beguiling smile dissolved. "I apologize. I realize how that must sound to a newcomer. It's just that Fatima isn't . . . well, she isn't really . . ."

Ellie drew herself up. "Please don't tell me it's because she's a foreigner."

His eyes widened. Then, to her astonishment, he chuckled.

Ellie narrowed her eyes. "I fail to find anything funny about this, Mr. Pierce."

The smile faded from his lips, and he glanced around the store. "I'll try to explain it to you, but it might be best if we step outside. May I escort you to wherever you're going next?"

Ellie nodded, too stunned to say anything more. Her first afternoon in Arizona was starting to take on the character of a dream, and a bad one at that. Mr. Pierce set the keg of nails next to the counter and called to the store owner, "I'll be back for these later, Walter." He tucked Ellie's hand into the crook of his arm and led her to the door.

Once outside, he asked, "Where exactly are we heading?"

Ellie pointed to the right. "The corner of Charles and Second. The old—"

"Oh, the Cooper place."

Ellie fought the impulse to roll her eyes. "I believe you were going to explain everyone's inexplicable reaction to the shooting of an unfortunate woman."

"She isn't a woman. Not exactly, I mean . . ." Pierce's voice trailed off, and his face colored.

Ellie lifted her eyebrows and spoke in a crisp tone. "Mr. Pierce, she may or may not be a lady, but surely there can't be any question about her status as a woman."

Her companion rubbed the back of his neck with his free hand, looking as though he would rather be anywhere else. "Well, she is a woman, but she's only a painting."

Ellie stopped dead in the middle of the boardwalk. "Are you trying to tell me that man was sobbing his heart out about damage to a painting?" As the words sunk in, she added, "And what connection does he have to this Fatima, anyway? He hardly seems the type to own a piece of artwork."

Mr. Pierce's color deepened. "He doesn't own her . . . it. She hangs on the wall in a local establishment."

The pieces fell into place. "By establishment, I assume you mean a saloon?"

He nodded. "The Palace. Some of the boys have become somewhat infatuated with her. She's rather, ah . . . Rubenesque." His face was now the color of a dark red brick.

"I see. But why would anyone shoot a painting?"

"It probably wasn't intentional. Sometimes things get a little lively at the Palace, and one of the fellows lets loose with his pistol. When they did this time . . ."

"Poor Fatima was a casualty?"

"I'm afraid so."

"Does this happen often?"

One corner of Pierce's lips twitched. "I believe this latest bullet hole brings the count up to nine."

"Oh my." She decided to take pity on him and

changed the subject. "I was visiting with Mrs. Baldwin in the mercantile. She said you're a miner?"

"A mine owner, actually." He squared his shoulders and stood straighter. "I staked the claim for the Redemption two years ago."

Ellie leaped straight at the opening he'd given her. "Then it's quite fortuitous, the two of us meeting like this. Providential, you might say."

"Oh? How so?"

She squeezed his arm, noting again the firmness of his biceps. "Meeting someone like you is the very reason I came out west."

His step faltered, and he shot her a sidelong glance. "Really?"

Idiot! Ellie felt the heat of a flush on her cheeks. What better way to send the poor man running than to make him think an older woman had set her cap for him? She couldn't afford to lose the chance to strike up an acquaintance with a key player in her little drama.

"I am looking for an opportunity to invest in a profitable venture," she explained. "When I heard about Arizona's silver mines, the possibilities seemed worthy of investigation."

A smile tugged at the corner of Steven's mouth. "Do you always research potential investments in person?"

Ellie nodded, improvising according to the background she had created for Lavinia. "My

98

late husband was a great believer in the personal touch. Besides, it's time for me to make a fresh start. I've been widowed for nearly three years, and I need a change. Making a trip out west seemed just the thing to pull me out of my doldrums."

She lifted her eyes to the horizon, where fingers of gold and crimson had begun to weave their way across the sky. "I look at it as a grand adventure. I might even decide to stay on permanently."

Steven smothered a grin. Despite her age, Lavinia Stewart showed spunk aplenty. How seriously should he take her talk of making a fresh start in Pickford? Was she in earnest about investing in his mine? He decided to probe a little. "So you're interested in mining?"

"I'm interested in making money, Mr. Pierce. My husband was both a shrewd investor and a good teacher. I believe I learned his lessons well."

Steven's step faltered. "You don't mean to say you ventured out here on your own?"

"I'm afraid so." A look of frustration crossed her face. "I intended to travel out here with my niece. We left Chicago together, but she was delayed along the way."

Steven looked with new respect at the diminutive woman walking beside him. She might remind him of one of the faded roses his mother used to press between the pages of her Bible, but apparently she possessed more grit than met the eye.

He had heard stories of intrepid women like Tombstone's Nellie Cashman, who once carried loads of potatoes and limes by dogsled to save a group of miners in British Columbia suffering from scurvy. Tales like that never failed to inspire his admiration, but he never expected to come across the same spirit of adventure in a woman of advancing years.

A new thought struck him. He had been asking God to show him a way to keep his business going. Maybe his prayers were being answered. And wouldn't it be just like God to send the answer in such an unusual package?

The heaven-sent response to his prayer was looking up at him with unconcealed interest. "I don't believe in buying a pig in a poke, Mr. Pierce. If I am going to sink my money into this venture, I want to know all about it."

"That's good business practice. I'll be happy to tell you whatever you'd like to know."

Mrs. Stewart's smile shone like a beacon. "Wonderful. Now, tell me all about silver mining. Don't leave anything out."

She couldn't have picked a topic he'd rather hold forth on. From Fourth Street to Second, he talked about ore and veins and the assayed value per ton, watching Mrs. Stewart's face to see if she seemed to be following. She nodded intelligently, throwing in probing questions from time to time.

He bit back a grin and tried not to let his elation show. This was it—he could feel it. He was going to be given the chance to infuse much-needed capital into the Redemption and keep it going after all. *Thank you, Lord.*

As they neared the north end of Second Street, her steps slowed a bit. "What about the actual shipments of the silver to wherever it is you send it? How do you manage to keep it secure?"

Steven felt like he'd just stepped off a cliff. She'd asked the one question he'd hoped wouldn't arise. He opened his mouth, then clamped his lips together, knowing his words could impact her decision. He needed to choose them carefully.

With all his heart, he wanted to gloss over the recent losses and focus on the mine's potential. All he had to do was describe his alliance with the other mine owners and the security precautions they had taken, conveniently omitting the losses they had incurred and the fact that they had been forced to call in the Pinkertons. He could do that easily enough. She had no reason to doubt his word, and he already sensed a rapport between them. All it would take was a few well-chosen half-truths, and she'd be ready to hand over the money that would ensure the Redemption's future.

He looked down at her softly weathered face, and the words froze on his lips. Regardless of what it might cost him, he couldn't violate the woman's trust—or his own standards of integrity.

"I'd like to tell you everything is going well in that department, but the truth is, we've been having problems lately. Not just me, but all the mine owners in the area." They reached the front porch, with Steven knowing his chances of rescue were slipping away with every step he took.

Mrs. Stewart stopped abruptly at the top of the porch steps and aimed a stern look at a lilac bush. "I see you in there, young man. You'd best be getting home now."

Steven eyed his companion with concern until he saw Billy Taylor climb out of the bush, looking more disgruntled than abashed.

"There now." Mrs. Stewart gestured to a pair of wooden rocking chairs. "I believe we'll be able to continue our conversation without fear of being overheard."

Smothering a grin, Steven settled her in one of the chairs, then took the other himself and began outlining his troubles.

She watched him closely but didn't speak again until he had finished. Steven braced himself, waiting for her to thank him for escorting her home and send him on his way. Instead, she tilted her head to one side like a curious wren. "In my experience, nothing worthwhile ever comes without a struggle. I'm sure if we put our heads together, we can come up with some way to thwart these villains."

Her calm statement rocked him. Had he really heard her use the word *we,* as though she was already a partner?

An inspiration popped into his mind, one he felt sure would please the Lord far more than his earlier inclination to compromise the truth. "Would you like to attend church with me on Sunday morning? We could talk more about the mine—and your part in it—afterward. Perhaps over lunch?"

Mrs. Stewart looked up at him with every evidence of delight. "What a lovely idea. I shall look forward to Sunday."

With that arranged, he walked back to his office with a lighter heart than he'd had in days. He managed to keep to a sedate pace, although what he really wanted to do was kick up his heels and shout loud hosannas.

Maybe he hadn't muffed his opportunity after all.

After a light dinner of cheese, crackers, and canned peaches found in her partially stocked kitchen cupboard—the Pinkertons had overlooked no detail in smoothing the transition into her new dwelling—Ellie craved nothing more than to crawl into her cozy bed and surrender her head to the inviting pillow. But she had one more duty to fulfill before she succumbed to her need for sleep.

As part of her brief training, both Pinkerton men had stressed the necessity of making thorough notes on a daily basis.

"During an investigation," Fleming had intoned, "it's easy to forget details. Even though you won't be leading this operation, you need to keep track of everything you see and hear. It could be that some snippet of conversation, some small particle of information will be just the thing that's needed to tie all the pieces together."

Ellie eyed the bed with longing. Assuring herself that a few hours' sleep wouldn't erase important details from her mind, she undressed and shed herself of the tiresome cheek plumpers and leg wrappings, then pulled her flannel nightgown over her head. Getting some much-needed rest might be just the thing to help focus her memory so she could remember even more. Pulling off Lavinia's gray wig, she settled the hairpiece on its stand, then reached for her hairbrush and ran it through her drab brown tresses in long, even strokes, freeing the strands that had been held captive under the wig all day.

Ellie closed her eyes and counted the strokes up to a hundred, longing for the moment she could sink into the mattress. Surely her memory was good enough to remember a few details overnight. . . . Just as it was good enough to remind her she'd never gone to bed without fulfilling all her duties for Magdalena. And wasn't her job in Pickford of even greater importance?

She set the brush back on the dressing table with a weary sigh and pressed the heels of her hands against her eyes. Much as she longed to climb into bed and let the cares of the day roll away, she couldn't afford the luxury of resting—not while she still had work to do.

Time was against her. She had to figure out the particulars of the investigation before the Pinkertons sent somebody else along who would boot her off the case and likewise off their payroll. The realization stiffened her spine. This was no time to give in to the weakness of the flesh. She had to press on.

Not bothering to stifle an enormous yawn, she shuffled out into the parlor and checked to be sure the drapes were drawn tight. It wouldn't do to have some nosy passerby notice a strange young woman wandering around in Lavinia Stewart's house.

Ellie lit the stove under the kettle and heated water for a pot of tea. No telling how long she might be up, and she would need every bit of help she could get to keep going. While waiting for the tea to steep, she gathered pen, ink, and paper from the drop-front desk tucked into the corner between the coatrack and the door to the second bedroom.

The fragrant aroma swirled under her nose as

she took a sip of tea and prepared to write down the names of the people she'd met that day, along with her impressions of them. That much would be easy, although she wasn't sure how it would help her solve the crime. Growing up in the theater, observing people had become a lifelong habit. To become skilled at acting—as her parents had been—one had to watch people and try to understand what made them act the way they did.

Dipping her pen in the inkwell, she started her list, making notes of everyone she had come in contact with—from the stage driver to the station agent to Amos Crawford, the telegraph operator, to Althea Baldwin, the garrulous widow who seemed to know everything about everybody in town.

Then there was Steven Pierce. A slow smile curved Ellie's lips as she remembered his warm brown eyes, the strength of his arm under her fingers, and the attentive way he had treated her.

Because he'd seen her as Lavinia, and not Ellie. Maybe it was just as well he'd met her as an older woman with money to invest, or he never would have noticed her.

The reminder brought her back to the task at hand, and she tried to picture Steven in a villain's role. He, along with the other miners, knew when and how the silver shipments would be made. His spark of interest when she talked of investing made it obvious he would welcome an infusion of cash. Did he need the money enough to acquire it by underhanded means?

Ellie tossed the pen down, sending ink splatters over several sheets of paper. Try as she might, she couldn't picture him in the villain role. She remembered the play of emotions on his face when she asked him about the silver shipments. The obvious struggle when he'd decided to go ahead and tell her the truth about the losses had been real; she felt sure of it. Growing up in the theater, she knew what it was like to exist in a world of constant playacting and make-believe, where people portrayed feigned reactions as a matter of course. But Steven Pierce wasn't a skilled actor . . . was he?

She shoved her chair back and walked to the window. Pushing the drapes aside, she wrapped her arms around herself and peered out into the night. She couldn't allow her emotions to overshadow clear thinking. She was in Pickford to do a job, and part of that job was to suspect everyone, not to play the role of the wide-eyed ingenue. Hadn't that been the reason Fleming and Gates specifically told her not to reveal her identity to any of the miners who had contacted them?

Yanking the drapes shut again, she marched to the table and added Steven's name to her list.

❧ 9 ❧

A mockingbird's cheery trill warbled through the air as Ellie strolled along Grant Street the next morning, doing her best to look like a woman exploring a new community, her mind on making new acquaintances and shopping and not the least bit interested in any criminal activities that might be going on.

She passed McQueen's Cigar Emporium and slowed in front of the Pickford Bakery as if eyeing the confections displayed in the window. Instead of looking at trays of donuts and éclairs, she focused on the reflection in the glass and studied the comings and goings on the street behind her— several matrons with shopping baskets on their arms, a buckboard bound for the livery on Second Street, but nothing that struck her as sinister in any way. On the other hand, how likely was it that dark deeds would be carried out openly on the street in broad daylight?

She blew out an exasperated puff of air and resisted the urge to stomp her foot. Whatever had possessed her to think she was capable of carrying out a criminal investigation on her own?

"Miz Stewart!"

Wrenched from her musing, Ellie turned to see Amos Crawford waving at her from the doorway of the telegraph office.

"A telegram came in for you a few minutes ago. I was just about to send my boy over to your house with it." The telegrapher brandished the half-sheet of paper over his head like someone holding up a trophy.

It had to be from the home office. Bracing herself for whatever grim message it might hold, Ellie angled across the intersection of Fourth and Grant. As she crossed, she saw Althea Baldwin farther along the street, heading her way. Ellie raised her hand and smiled a greeting, whereupon Althea pivoted, marching off in the opposite direction without missing a beat. With no time to ponder the woman's odd behavior, Ellie bore down on Amos Crawford, arm outstretched to receive the missive from Chicago.

Instead of handing it to her, Amos backed into the building, forcing Ellie to follow him inside. Shaping her features into a placid expression, she went in after him, trying not to roll her eyes at his obvious attempt to get her alone. There would be no opportunity to read the communication in private. It was evident the telegrapher wanted the chance to talk it over with her. Either that or he was anxious for more of Lavinia's charming company. Ellie sighed and scanned the paper when he finally handed it over.

DISTRESSED TO LEARN JESSIE DELAYED
STOP IS ALL WELL STOP REPLY POST-
HASTE STOP

COUSIN HENRY

Ellie read the message a second time, then a third. To an outsider, the words would sound neutral enough, but she could practically hear the note of panic rising in Gates's voice.

Amos Crawford cut into her thoughts. "Sounds like your cousin's a mite concerned about you bein' out here on your own."

Ellie nodded absently, her mind still on the flurry of concern her telegram must have stirred up.

"I guess you'll be wantin' to send a reply?"

A noncommittal murmur passed Ellie's lips while her mind churned, trying to muster up a suitable response.

"You can set his mind at ease right now." Amos circled behind the counter and pulled out a form and a pencil. "Let him know there are plenty of people here who'll be happy to watch out for you. We aren't about to let anything happen to a charming lady like yourself."

Something in his tone pulled Ellie's attention away from the telegram. Had she detected a flirtatious note in his voice?

As if reading her thoughts, Amos's face reddened. "Just write out what you want to say."

He leaned forward and lowered his voice to a husky whisper. "I'll throw in a few words for free if you need them."

Dear heaven, all she needed was a suitor on top of her other concerns. Seizing the pencil, Ellie began to write:

Jessie visiting friends.

That was close to the truth, and surely it would make sense to Gates and Fleming once Norma informed them of her honeymoon.

Don't worry about me. Doing well, meeting lots of new people.

Lavinia

There. She hoped that would satisfy both her employers and the inquisitive Amos Crawford. Ellie paid the fee and left without further dialogue, to Amos's obvious disappointment.

Back outside, she prepared to resume her stroll. The station agent stepped out of his office as she passed. He stopped short to avoid a collision. "Mornin', ma'am. Is that niece of yours going to be showing up soon?"

Ellie raised her eyebrows. Was there anything people didn't know about one another in this town? The gossip mill in Pickford rivaled anything she had seen in theater circles. Amos had evidently been spreading the news to his buddy. Yet another reason to keep her identity a secret. Once word of her true mission slipped out, everyone in the area would know about it.

She improvised, choosing her words carefully. "I'm not sure about her arrival date. I believe the friends she's staying with plan to travel to San Diego soon and will drop her off here on their way to the railroad station in Benson."

"Oh. Well, if she changes her mind and decides to come in on the stage, you let me know. I'll be sure she's treated right."

Ellie gave him a gracious nod and went on her way, struggling to maintain an unruffled exterior while her emotions roiled inside. How was she going to get out of the hole she'd dug herself into by promising Jessie's arrival?

She had assured Gates she would have no problem taking on the role of Lavinia and had convinced herself the job would be a great chance to prove her acting ability, but she wasn't in the theater any longer. She had assumed a role, to be sure, and was performing quite well, but this was no play. The story didn't end when the lights went down and the audience went home. The deception she was involved in had to be carried out continuously, and she must never let herself break character for a moment.

She stood on the corner, racking her brain for a way to explain Jessie's continued absence.

Maybe her imaginary niece could contract some illness during her visit with her friends. Yes, that might be the perfect solution. Which disease would suit her purpose best?

"Good morning, ma'am."

Shaken from her woolgathering, Ellie looked up at a square-shouldered man in black broadcloth. His hat tipped down low over penetrating dark eyes that seemed to look right through her.

Ellie flinched in spite of herself. Lowering her gaze to avoid his scrutiny, she noticed the silver star pinned to his vest.

"Why, good morning, Sheriff . . . or is it Marshal?"

Thin lips parted, separating a neatly trimmed mustache and narrow goatee. "Marshal Everett Bascomb, at your service. May I help you across the street?"

Ellie nodded and took his arm, thrilled at the opportunity to make the acquaintance of Pickford's law officer. Mindful of the Pinkertons' admonition that they couldn't vouch for the integrity of the local law, she knew she would have to be cautious about what she said to him. But at least this initial meeting would break the ice and allow them to carry on a conversation. She could decide later how best to fish for information from him.

"I only arrived in Pickford yesterday, but I believe I shall enjoy my stay here very much." Ellie smiled up at him as she had with Steven

Pierce the day before, only to find his attention wasn't focused on her but on a buxom young woman coming out of the mercantile. Ellie cleared her throat and tried again. "It seems a very pleasant town. You evidently do a fine job of keeping the peace."

"Hmm? Oh yes. We have a number of solid citizens . . . as well as enough of the rougher element to keep me busy." He spoke to Ellie, but his gaze was still fastened across the street. As if sensing his interest, the attractive brunette looked his way and smiled.

When they reached the opposite side of Grant Street, the lawman helped Ellie step up onto the boardwalk and tipped his hat. "Pleasure meeting you, Mrs. . . . ?"

"Stewart. Lavinia Stewart. I look forward to—" Ellie's words floated away like the dust motes that hung in the air. The marshal had already covered half the distance between her and his shapely quarry. She watched as he swept off his hat with a courtly bow. The young woman simpered at him, and Bascomb leaned against a lamppost as if settling in for a prolonged conversation.

A group of rough-looking men emerged from an alleyway on the far side of the street. On seeing the marshal, one of them called, "Hey, Bascomb. Over here."

The marshal turned, a frown creasing his forehead. The other men gestured, waving him

114

over, but Bascomb shook his head and turned back to his coquettish companion.

Undeterred, the men renewed their insistence that he join them.

With far more courtesy than he'd shown Lavinia, Bascomb took his leave of the girl and walked across the street.

Could this have anything to do with the case? As casually as she could, Ellie retraced her steps back across Grant Street and meandered along the storefronts at a leisurely pace. The group of men moved a little farther away, stopping in front of G. F. Lemon's Furniture Store. One of them turned slightly, and his gaze met Ellie's. He nudged Bascomb's elbow and nodded in her direction.

Ellie took three steps forward, then hesitated. She could hardly waltz over to the group and plant herself within listening distance. She strained to hear, but they were too far away for her to make out their words.

What now? She couldn't stand there gawking at them, obviously trying to eavesdrop. But where to go?

She glanced around and saw the entrance to the Grand Hotel only a few feet away, on the corner of Grant and Fifth. Without a second thought, she headed straight for it and ducked inside.

"Good morning, ma'am. Can I help you?"

Ellie paused, trying to catch her breath and get her bearings in the dimmer light. A stoop-shouldered man stood behind the counter, eyeing her expectantly. She pulled a lace-edged handkerchief from her sleeve and fanned herself with it. "Actually, I was just feeling a bit weary. I was hoping it might be all right to sit for a few moments and catch my breath. Do you mind?"

With a look of concern on his broad face, the man hurried across the lobby to help her into an overstuffed chair near the window. He hovered solicitously while she settled herself into the cushions. "Would you like a glass of water?"

"Thank you. A drink of water would be lovely." While the desk clerk bustled off on his errand, Ellie drew her first deep breath since being spotted by the rough men outside and looked around at her surroundings. An oak counter stood at the opposite side of the lobby. Two doors, one of which she assumed led to the hotel office, stood behind it. The center of the room was free of furnishings, save for an Oriental rug that covered most of the floor. To one side, a black-and-chrome woodstove gave off a gentle heat. The seating area she occupied filled the space near the broad plate-glass window that faced out on Grant, while a similar arrangement was grouped near the window looking onto Fifth Street.

Ellie's pulse quickened. The fine lace curtains made it easy for her to see what was happening on the street without being seen herself. If she angled her position just so—she took advantage of the desk clerk's absence to scoot her chair a few inches to the right—she had a view of both streets. She leaned back against the comfortable cushion and stared at Bascomb and his companions talking earnestly a few yards away. What a perfect observation post. She couldn't have designed it better herself.

The clerk returned with her water, and Ellie sipped gratefully. "Thank you ever so much. I hate putting you to all that trouble."

"No trouble at all, ma'am. Can I get you anything else?"

"No, I'm feeling much better now. Would it be all right if I sat here a little longer?"

"Take all the time you need. You're welcome to stay as long as you like." His smile brightened his drooping features. "My name's Donald Tidwell, by the way. You just let me know if you need anything."

Ellie smiled back at him. "Thank you, Mr. Tidwell. I'm Lavinia Stewart. I'm pleased to meet you."

He went back to his work behind the counter, and Ellie continued watching the marshal and his companions. The little group was breaking up, Bascomb heading west while the others moved east toward Seventh Street and the saloons beyond.

Whatever they'd been talking about, she had missed it. Ellie let out an unladylike huff. Why hadn't she thought to take up her position in the hotel a few minutes earlier? Even though she couldn't hear their conversation through the glass, she would at least have been able to observe them closely, maybe even read their lips.

"Are you new in town or just passin' through?" The desk clerk's voice broke into her reverie. "I haven't seen you before."

"I'm newly arrived. I've come to Pickford to look into some mining interests."

The clerk's lips rounded, and he seemed suitably impressed. Ellie studied him while pretending to dab at her cheek with her handkerchief. With his stooped shoulders and lanky figure, he looked more suited for an office job back east. At least he was friendly, she thought, remembering the clerk in Kansas City.

She peered out onto Grant Street and then looked toward Fifth, but nothing out of the ordinary caught her eye. Ellie gripped the padded arms of the chair and pushed herself upright, ready to take her leave.

What a shame she had missed her opportunity to do an effective job of spying on Bascomb and his group. The setup of the hotel made it a perfect lookout post. If only she had a reason for returning on a regular basis. "Thank you again for your hospitality. That little rest was just what I needed."

The clerk bobbed his head. "My pleasure,

ma'am. My aunt back in Missouri has a bad knee and can't walk too far at one time. She has to take a breather every so often, just like you. Say, do you want to see something while you're sitting there?"

Without waiting for Ellie's reply, the man pulled a short piece of rope from his pocket and held both ends in one hand. "I'm going to tie a knot in the end of this rope, just by snapping it forward."

Raising his arm as though he was getting ready to crack a whip, he swung his hand down sharply, turning loose of one end of the rope as he did so. When the free end flew forward, Ellie could see that it sported a neatly tied square knot.

She laughed and clapped her hands. "Delightful! I know there's some sort of trick involved, but I have no idea how it was done."

The clerk's face glowed with pleasure. He pulled off his spectacles and polished the round lenses with a cloth he pulled from his pocket. "It's just a little hobby of mine, ma'am. Glad you liked it. Feel free to come in here any time you're walking around town and find you need to sit for a spell. I'd be glad to see you again."

Ellie smiled, trying to hide her elation. "What a thoughtful offer. I expect I'll take you up on that." Before she reached the door, it burst open and a man with a weathered face and wearing a black slouch hat brushed past her. Without so much as a glance in her direction, he strode straight up to the counter.

"What room is Earl Porter in?"

The clerk grew pale. "He isn't here."

The rough-voiced man loomed over the counter, and the clerk backed up several steps. "When he shows up, you tell him I want to see him. He'd better not keep me waiting." He pivoted on his heel and gave Ellie a penetrating stare, as if noticing her for the first time.

She scuttled out of the lobby as quickly as she could manage. Once she reached the boardwalk, she held herself back to a sedate walk instead of giving in to a desire to hitch up her skirts and race headlong toward Charles Street and the sanctuary of her little home.

What had she gotten herself into? The scene she'd just witnessed, brief as it was, had made her skin crawl. Every adventure from the penny dreadfuls she'd read flashed through her mind. This was the Wild West. She couldn't treat her job as some sort of lark. People sometimes ended up dead out in the untamed wilderness.

Two blocks from the hotel and its ill-mannered visitor, she stopped and leaned against the front of Levi Jewelers. She needed a few moments to catch her breath and collect her wits. That horrible man's actions had nothing to do with her. There was no basis for the fear that filled her being.

No one knew who she was or what she was doing in Pickford. She once again blessed the Pinkertons for their admonition not to let anyone know her true identity. As long as she kept up appearances as harmless, nonthreatening Lavinia Stewart, she should be able to continue her investigation unhampered and unharmed.

When her heart settled back into its usual rhythm, she walked on, making a mental note to add the churlish man to her growing list of potential suspects. She supposed she should list the clerk, as well, harmless as he seemed.

At least she had gained one success to her credit, arranging to spend more time at the hotel. She could observe both the clerk and some of the guests up close that way without seeming to take any personal interest in them.

She would keep an eye out for that boorish fellow, too. But she would do that from a distance.

As she mounted the steps to her front porch, Ellie heard the branches of the lilac bush rustle. She cleared her throat, and the rustling subsided. She pulled her key from her reticule and unlocked the front door without further comment, reminding herself to make sure the curtains were drawn tight.

Back in the safety of her snug little house, she bolted the door and closed the curtains, then pulled out her papers and jotted down her morning's observations while they were still fresh in her mind. With that chore out of the way, she went to her bedroom, where she pulled off her wig, arranged it on the wig stand, and ran her fingers through her hair. After that she removed her spectacles, unwound her leg wrappings, pulled out the wax plumpers, and plopped down on the bed.

For the thousandth time, she wished Norma hadn't abandoned her. She needed someone to talk to, someone she could confide in and speak her mind clearly to without having to resort to coded messages. She punched the pillow into a mass of fluffy comfort and propped it against the head-board, then settled back against it, trying to imagine what would be happening now if Norma had come out with her as planned. They might be sipping tea over at the table, comparing notes, assessing what they had learned so far, and deciding what to do next.

What would Norma say if she were here? Ellie had no way of knowing, but she felt sure her senior partner would have made significantly better progress than she had so far. People were nice enough to Lavinia, but they hadn't proven to be founts of information about any nefarious schemes in their midst.

Early afternoon sunlight filtered in through the curtains, throwing the wig and its stand into shadows and creating the illusion that an actual person sat in the room with her. Giving in to the fanciful notion, Ellie tilted her head and addressed the gray wig.

"Lavinia, you're a dear woman, but you aren't

likely to get into the places and talk to the kinds of people who are going to know more about the seamy side of this town. If Norma was here, I'll bet she could figure out a way to let Jessie strike up a conversation with people who'd never take a second glance at a respectable woman like you."

She pushed herself up higher on the pillow. "I hate to say it, but the Pinkertons were right. You're wonderful as a chaperone, but you're entirely *too* respectable to handle Jessie's part of the job."

When she squinted, she could almost imagine the wig nodding.

How could she ever have thought she'd be able to carry out the job on her own? People were civil to Lavinia, but the men who might possess the information she needed wouldn't do more than tip their hat to the gray-haired woman and pass on by. She needed a partner.

And that wasn't likely to happen. It had been hard enough for the Pinkertons to find someone to take on Lavinia's role. She couldn't expect another Jessie to appear out of nowhere. And she didn't dare tell the home office she needed help. She was on probation. If she admitted she couldn't handle her first assignment, they would have no reason to take her seriously.

She stared at the wig. What would Lavinia say if she truly existed? Ellie closed her eyes and waited for inspiration.

"What if you brought in help without asking them for it?"

Ellie jumped. It was almost as if the older woman had actually spoken. As inspiration went, though, that suggestion was sadly lacking. How was she supposed to find help on her own? It would be too dangerous for her to reveal herself to anyone in Pickford.

But the idea, once formed, wouldn't leave her alone. It persisted, hovering around her like a buzzing fly. She had become Lavinia easily enough. Why not become Jessie, as well?

Ellie sat bolt upright, feeling as though someone had set off fireworks in her brain. Could it work?

No, of course not. She was mousy Ellie, the one nobody noticed. It was one thing to transform herself into a middle-aged woman men wouldn't look at twice. Quite another to take on a personality so unlike her own.

Tears stung her eyes. It was a lovely idea, but try to turn herself into a dazzler like Norma . . . ? That would be like making a silk purse out of a sow's ear. It simply couldn't be done.

But she was an actress, wasn't she? This was no time to sell herself short. And there was a red wig in the costume hamper. . . .

Before she could talk herself out of it, Ellie bolted across the room and yanked open the lid to the hamper, where she found the red wig folded neatly in tissue paper about halfway down. She pulled it out and gave it a good shake, eyeing the coppery curls touched with glints of gold. Very much like Norma's hair. With a little touching up, it would be a style and color well suited for catching the attention of any male on the street who had a spark of life in him.

She walked to the mirror and held the red wig up next to her face. Her rising spirits plummeted. The hair was fine, but the features were still Ellie's. It simply wouldn't work.

Or would it? She knew more about makeup than most people. Why, without makeup, Magdalena wasn't nearly as attractive as Norma. Ellie knew full well what the actress had been able to achieve with a few artistic touches.

She looked into the mirror again, studying her features as if they belonged to someone else. The wig's curls would dangle over her forehead and frame the sides of her face, adding a little life to her expression. With renewed hope, she dug through the makeup kit and pulled out an assortment of cosmetics.

Without Lavinia's faded skin and fuller cheeks, she would have an entirely different canvas to work on. Longer lashes, maybe. Darker eyebrows, and a little more color on her cheeks and lips. She put her thoughts into action, applying the makeup with deft strokes. She picked up the wig and tweaked the curls into place, then slipped it on over her hair and stepped back to observe the results of her handiwork.

She caught her breath, trying to reconcile her image of herself with the alluring creature who stared back from the mirror. Norma Brooks—no, an even more self-assured version of Norma—stood before her. Ellie tried a tentative smile, and the tinted lips curled into a teasing grin.

"See?" Lavinia's imaginary voice purred approval. "I knew you could do it."

Ellie didn't bother to concoct a reply. Her mind whirled with the possibilities that opened up before her. How would Jessie walk? She crossed the room with dignified steps. No, that wasn't right. She looked far too prissy. To strike up a conversation with the people she would need to talk to, Jessie couldn't act like a debutante. She rolled her shoulders to ease her tension and tried a looser walk. Still not quite right.

Ellie scrunched her lips to one side, then grinned. Planting one hand on her hip, she strode back across the room with a deliberate flounce. Almost, but not quite. She tried it again, this time with a little less swing of her hips.

Oh yes. That would do. She sashayed back and forth in front of the mirror, feeling more accustomed to her new character with every step. That ought to garner some interest, all right.

She glanced back at the gray wig, wondering if her actions suited a relative of respectable

Lavinia. For that matter, what would Steven Pierce think about Lavinia's niece? Would an upright man like him be pleased or appalled? The thought sobered her. She didn't dare drive him away—he was her link to the miners. But circumspect behavior wouldn't help her connect with many of the other men in town.

She gazed into the mirror again and tilted her head. Maybe she would have to be something of a chameleon, playing a bit of a flirt with men like Bascomb and his ilk while maintaining a more proper front around Steven.

Ellie sighed. It was going to be quite the balancing act.

She imagined Lavinia whispering encouragement. "That it will, my dear. But playing dual roles is nothing new. Magdalena did it in *Twelfth Night*, remember? You're more than capable of carrying it off. You'll see."

Was she? Ellie flopped back on the bed, knocking the red wig askew. Pulling it off, she flung it to one side. What was she thinking? Magdalena had gotten rave reviews for her portrayal of Viola and Cesario, but that was with Ellie's able assistance in costuming and makeup changes backstage . . . not to mention Shakespeare's script, crafted to give her time to make those changes.

Was she crazy to even think of attempting such a thing? That might be the more pertinent question. Trying to decide which character to play and switching between them quickly would be enough to drive anybody over the edge.

Ellie looked over at the dressing table where "Lavinia" stood and buried her face in her hands. She had been carrying on a conversation with a gray wig. Maybe it was already too late to be worrying about her sanity.

10

Ellie tugged her collar into place and tucked an errant strand of brown hair beneath the gray wig, wishing she could put her nerves in order as easily. Would the jet-trimmed basque bodice with its knife-pleated skirt be suitable for Lavinia's first visit to church? It had been years since she'd attended a Sunday morning service, but she assured herself that Steven's assessment of Lavinia as a God-fearing, churchgoing woman was perfectly in character. Besides, it would give her an additional opportunity to meet people in the community. She took one more look in the mirror, checking every detail of her appearance.

A knock sounded at her front door. Ready or not, that was her cue. Slipping into Lavinia's character as smoothly as she had donned the woman's clothes, Ellie opened the door to Steven, resplendent in a black frock coat, white shirt, and string tie. Her breath caught in her throat at the sight of him.

A frown appeared between his eyebrows, and he reached out to cup her elbow with his hand. "Are you all right?"

"Perfectly." Ellie turned to gather up her reticule from a nearby table, hoping the maneuver would mask her emotions and give her a chance to get her breathing under control. There was no arguing the fact that the man was disconcertingly handsome. All the more reason to keep her wits about her.

"A momentary dizziness. That's all. I'm fine now." The first part of her statement was true enough. She hoped the latter part would prove to be true, as well.

He smiled and extended his arm. "In that case, let's be on our way."

Ellie braced herself and rested her fingers in the crook of his arm. Her eyes widened in surprise when she felt a strange tingle. She glanced up, wondering if Steven felt it, too. In contrast to her heightened awareness, he seemed remarkably unaffected.

She fought down a sense of disappointment as they strolled together down Second Street, then turned left on Douglas. What a ninny she was. Lavinia was old enough to be his mother. One could hardly expect him to show her anything other than gentlemanly respect.

"I hope you'll enjoy the service. Pastor Blaylock is a fine preacher, but I'm sure you'll find his style a bit more rustic than what you were accustomed to in Chicago."

"I'm sure it will be lovely." When Steven threw her a quizzical glance, she added, "Inspiring, I mean." She needed to change the subject before he asked about sermons she had heard recently.

Now was as good a time as any to begin laying the groundwork for Jessie's arrival. Before they crossed Fourth Street, Steven halted to let an ore wagon drawn by a team of twenty mules go by. While the heavy wagon rumbled past, Ellie drew a deep breath. "I had some good news. My niece will be arriving soon."

"Your niece?" Steven's surprise was evident in his voice.

"Yes. We traveled west together, but she decided to stop off and visit some friends who have a ranch south of here." Ellie shook her head. "Poor child."

His inquiring look told her he'd taken the bait. Ellie went on as they crossed the street, outlining the story she'd concocted the night before. "She's had a hard time. The poor dear worked as a secretary for a wealthy woman in Chicago and made the mistake of falling in love with her employer's son. When his mother found out, she whisked him off on a grand tour of Europe to prevent him from making an unequal match."

She marveled at the ease with which the words rolled off her tongue. She had already decided to keep the story of Jessie's delayed arrival as close as possible to what she had already told the telegrapher. It would be far easier to stick to one account rather than having to keep track of multiple versions. And she could now appreciate Magdalena's insistence on drawing from her own experiences to round out a character. It was all too easy to relate to being thrown over by an employer who suddenly decamped to the Continent.

Sympathy shone in Steven's eyes. "I'm sorry. That must have been very hard for her."

"She was utterly distraught. I thought a complete change of scenery would do her good, so I invited her to come along." She lowered her voice in a confidential tone. "I've tried to help her see that life is still worth living. I hope you'll extend the same courtesy to her that you have to me."

"Of course. I think it's admirable of you to be so sensitive to her feelings. When will she be arriving?"

As soon as I've had time to perfect her costume and makeup. Aloud, Ellie said, "I'm not certain of the day. Her friends are traveling to San Diego soon, and they plan to bring her to me on their way."

Steven nodded as if making a mental note. "I'll do what I can to make her feel welcome." He stopped and gestured at a building on their left. "Here we are."

Ellie looked up at the unassuming board-and-batten structure on the corner of Douglas and Fourth Street and took in a quick breath. *God, I know I'm here under false pretenses. Please don't let the roof come caving in on me.*

The pungent smell of fresh-cut lumber assailed Ellie's nostrils when they entered the cozy sanctuary. Rows of wooden benches flanked both sides of the center aisle, nearly half of them already filled. Ellie reminded herself to keep from staring. She never would have anticipated such a turnout on a Sunday morning, when she would have expected many of the townspeople to still be in bed, nursing the aftereffects of Saturday night carousing.

People looked up and smiled as Steven escorted her down the aisle to a bench near the front. Several greeted him by name, casting curious looks at his companion. Ellie smiled in return, pleased to recognize several faces. She spotted Althea Baldwin in the third row from the back, and Irene Peabody sat beside her husband on the very front row.

"Mornin', ma'am." Amos Crawford gave one of his gap-toothed smiles when she walked past.

Ellie nodded, trying her best to comport herself as Lavinia would, never allowing herself to forget she was onstage. How would Lavinia, a woman accustomed to attending church on a weekly basis, behave? For the first time, outright panic threatened to seize her, and she struggled to tamp it down. She couldn't afford to lose her concentration and make a mistake.

Steven nodded at a bench on their right, and Ellie slid along to the middle, thankful for the chance to sit down and compose her thoughts. She busied herself smoothing her skirts and settling into place.

From the corner of her eye, she saw Amos rise from his seat two rows back and start forward as if to join them. Before he reached the aisle, the opening notes of a prelude poured forth from a pump organ at the right-hand side of the pulpit, and he sat back down. Ellie assumed an attentive expression and clasped her hands in her lap, grateful to have an excuse not to have to carry on a conversation with the garrulous telegrapher.

While the music played, she took the opportunity to scan the people in the rows ahead of her and across the aisle. After a quick survey, Ellie turned her attention to the front of the sanctuary and studied the man sitting in the chair to the left of the pulpit, attired in clothes similar to Steven's. She assumed he was the minister, although he looked far younger than she'd expected.

As the organ prelude finished, a gangly man rose from the first pew and took his place in the front of the room. "Please stand and join me in singing 'We're Marching to Zion.'" He nodded to the organist, who played an introduction with gusto as the congregation got to their feet. Ellie looked for a hymnal, but there didn't appear to be any at hand.

Her throat tightened. It was one thing to sit and appear to pay rapt attention to all the goings-on, but she'd never dreamed she might need to know the songs by heart, as Lavinia surely would. What was she going to do?

The music leader launched into the first verse, waving his arms like a bandleader marking time. All around her, voices joined in singing about a beautiful city of God. Ellie glanced up at Steven, who sang along in a masculine baritone. He looked down at her and smiled. Ellie beamed back at him, trying to read his lips and form the words as he sang them.

She floundered through the first verse and then the second. By the time the third verse ended, with Ellie finally joining the rest of the group in a rousing "Amen," she was ready to run for the door.

The music leader, seemingly buoyed by the congregation's vigorous rendition of the first hymn, announced the second with even more enthusiasm. Ellie groaned inwardly when the organist struck up the introduction to "Beulah Land" in a lively tempo. She would never be able to bluff her way through this one. She coughed slightly, then pressed her fingers to her throat and gave Steven an apologetic shrug. Singing, she decided, would not be Lavinia's forte.

The singing finally ended, much to Ellie's relief, and the minister rose to take his place behind the pulpit. Knowing she couldn't expect much in such a backwater town, she sat up straight in an effort to make sure she didn't doze off. To her surprise, however, Pastor Blaylock turned out to be an engaging speaker, not talking down to his listeners but sharing what was on his heart as though speaking to a roomful of friends.

"My text today is from Proverbs chapter six." He lifted a well-worn leather volume in his left hand and began to read: " 'These six things doth the Lord hate: yea, seven are an abomination unto him: A proud look, a lying tongue, and hands that shed innocent blood . . .' "

Ellie brightened. If these were things God hated, she must be in better standing with Him than she'd thought. After all, she had never shed innocent blood, and she prided herself on being a truthful person, even when it was to her own disadvantage. More than once she had drawn Magdalena's ire by giving a too-honest opinion of the way she delivered her lines. She turned her attention back to the minister in time to hear him read the last verse of the passage.

" '. . . a false witness that speaketh lies, and he that soweth discord among brethren.' "

Ellie nodded vigorously. She couldn't agree more. Feeling more at ease with each passing moment, she settled into her seat and used the sermon time to stealthily scan the congregation, as she supposed any newcomer to the church might do.

Keeping half her attention on the preacher's comments, she shifted her gaze and examined each face within her range of vision for any sign of shiftiness or guilt. Every person in the sanctuary seemed focused on Pastor Blaylock's discourse on the importance of integrity in the life of a Christian.

Fiddlesticks! She should have known none of these people could be suspects. Would anyone so unethical spend Sunday morning in a church service?

What about you? An inner voice prodded at her. *Aren't you using it as a cover yourself?*

Hmm. The voice had a point. What better way to avert suspicion than to appear upright and guileless? Ellie tucked that thought away for future consideration.

Pastor Blaylock ended his oration with a fervent prayer that God would "move each one of us to examine our own hearts as the psalmist did, asking you, dear Lord, to see if there be any wicked way in us, to shine your light into the darkness of our innermost beings and root out any evil there. And let us give ourselves to you, as the boy in John six gave his loaves and fishes for your use. Let us repent of anything that displeases you and live lives worthy of your calling before we stand before your judgment seat."

A ripple of discomfort trickled its way down Ellie's spine. If only he had left out that last part. The sermon had been far different than the fiery bombast she had expected. Instead, the minister had portrayed God more as a loving father than a disapproving judge. Then he had to go and spoil it all by bringing in the notion of a final judgment. Too bad—she had rather enjoyed his message up to that point.

Ellie gathered up her reticule and stood when Steven and the others did. She moved down the aisle at his side, stopping when he did to greet people and appreciating the fact that he never failed to introduce her to each person he spoke to. Now she had an opening to speak to any of them should she encounter them on the street. If for no other reason than that, she could count her morning well spent.

Pastor Blaylock stood at the back of the sanctuary, shaking hands with each departing parishioner. His face lit up when Ellie approached. "Ah, it's always nice to welcome a new visitor to the house of the Lord."

Ellie took in his smile and the look of sincerity in his eyes. Heavens, he actually meant it. Her own smile widened in response, and she gave his hand a warm squeeze. "Thank you. It's good to be here."

"I hope we'll see you again."

"I'm sure you will," Ellie said, surprised to find she was truly looking forward to her next visit.

When they stepped outside, Steven set his hat on his head and turned to her with an apologetic expression. "I'd planned to discuss the mine with you today, but I'm afraid I'll have to take my leave as soon as I escort you home. A meeting of the mine owners has been called for this afternoon, and I need to hurry to be there on time." A rueful smile twisted his lips. "Since we're meeting at my office, it wouldn't do for me to be late."

Ellie responded with a gracious wave of her hand. "No matter. We can discuss this again at a later time." A sudden idea struck her—being introduced to the other mine owners would be an opportunity she couldn't afford to pass up. "On the other hand, would you think it utterly presumptuous of me to invite myself to your meeting?" She saw the doubt in his eyes and hurried on before he could voice an objection. "It would be such a help to me to get acquainted with some of the other owners and know who else is doing business here. That's something I learned from my late husband."

Steven opened and closed his mouth a couple of times. "I may have misled you by calling it a meeting. It isn't anything formal. We're just getting together to discuss the thefts and try to come up with some new ideas."

Ellie beamed. "All the more reason for me to be there. Since we're standing against a common foe, I ought to get acquainted with our allies, and they with me, don't you think?"

Steven's trapped expression would have been enough to make her withdraw her request if she hadn't been on a mission.

"But what about your lunch, Mrs. Stewart? I wouldn't want you to miss a meal and become faint on my account."

"Piffle, Mr. Pierce. Don't treat me like some china ornament. I may appear fragile, but I assure you I am made of sterner stuff. If you think it necessary, we can stop at one of the eating establishments along the way and ask them to send over a light repast for everyone. Sandwiches, perhaps." She clasped her hands. "It will be like having a picnic."

Steven's eyes took on a glazed look. When he spoke, the words sounded as if they were being choked out of him. "That's very thoughtful of you, Mrs. Stewart. I'm sure everyone will appreciate it."

Ellie kept a sharp eye out as they strolled the length of Fifth Street, watching for anyone who appeared suspicious or out of place. To keep the conversation from lagging, she said, "How nice of you to host this gathering. I take it the others see you as a leader of sorts?"

Steven chuckled. "No, I'm very much the greenhorn of the group. Most of the others have far more mining experience than I do. The reason we're meeting at my office is that it's the quietest place on Sunday. I don't have my men work on the Sabbath as the others do, so we're assured of having privacy."

So he was a man of principle as well as one whose form and features would make any woman swoon. One who acted on his beliefs instead of just giving them lip service. That didn't sound like the kind of man who would covet other men's hard-earned goods.

At Ellie's urging, they stopped at the Beck House on the corner of Fifth and Mill long enough to order lunch for the group, then continued on their way. One block farther south on Fifth Street, the town site came to an abrupt end. Tawny hills studded with gray-green shrubs and spiky cactus rolled out before them to the horizon.

Thinking about trekking across that rough landscape in her good shoes, Ellie paused and looked up at Steven. "I suppose I should have asked before, but where exactly is your mine?"

140

"We're almost there. That's my office." He pointed to a nondescript building some fifty yards ahead.

"Oh, I see. And the mine itself would be . . . ?"

"The work is all done underground. The main entrance is on the other side of the office building. You'll see it in a minute."

Looking beyond the small wooden structure, Ellie could discern similar buildings scattered farther out among the hills, their weathered coloration blending into the landscape so neatly they were hardly discernible at first glance. She indicated them with a nod of her head. "And those?"

"Some of the other mines. Their owners are the ones we're meeting with today." Steven took a firm hold on her elbow and led her along a winding path.

Ellie refrained from asking any more questions, needing all her concentration to keep her footing on the rock-strewn trail.

"It looks like some of them are here already," Steven said.

Ellie spotted a horse tied to a rail next to Steven's office building. As they rounded the corner of the office, she saw three men lounging against the board-and-batten wall and two more squatting in what little shade was offered by a scrubby tree.

"Make that all of them," Steven amended. The

squatting men came to their feet, and all five stared as Ellie and Steven approached.

Steven fished a ring of keys from his pocket and jingled them in his fingers while he faced the group. "Good afternoon, *gentlemen*."

Ellie shot a quick glance at the assembled men when he stressed the last word.

"Allow me to introduce Mrs. Lavinia Stewart from Chicago, recently arrived in Pickford for the purpose of making some investments. She has taken an interest in the Redemption, and she asked to accompany me here today to meet you and learn more about the challenges we're facing."

"Hold on a minute." A round-faced man with bright blue eyes and a red, bulbous nose stepped forward and hooked his thumbs in his front pockets. "You don't mean you told her about . . . you know . . ."

"About the thefts?" Steven didn't back down when the other man flinched and glared at him. "Yes, she's aware of what's been happening to our silver shipments. I know that isn't something we wanted to make public, but I couldn't see any way to get around it, under the circumstances."

The others seemed to share the round-faced man's antagonism. The oldest of the group smoothed back his silver hair with the palm of one hand and faced Ellie directly. "This information is something that must be kept in strict

142

confidence, not passed around town as a frivolous bit of gossip. Do you understand?"

Ellie bristled at his abrupt tone but managed a gracious smile. "Of course."

A man with thick, beetling black eyebrows and one eye that looked off in a different direction than its fellow focused his left eye on Ellie and tipped his hat. "Pleased to meet you, ma'am. I'm Ezra Winslow, owner of the Jubilee." He looked down, frowned, and swatted at his sleeve. A cloud of dust rose into the air. "We wasn't expecting feminine company today, or I would have spruced up a bit."

Ellie extended her hand and clasped his fingers, grateful for the welcome.

"Are you stayin' at the hotel?" Ezra asked.

Ellie smiled. "No, I plan to be in Pickford for some time. I've taken a little house in town—I believe it's known as the Cooper place."

The silver-haired man jerked to attention at the mention of the house. "I'd heard the house had been rented out. You're the one who's staying there?"

"Why, yes," Ellie answered, wondering at his sudden interest. "It's quite comfortable." She turned her attention back to Ezra Winslow, whose face glowed like a western sunset.

"I know where that house is," he said. "You ever need anyone to show you around town, you just let me know. I'll be happy to squire you around."

Ellie smiled and dipped her head, grateful when Steven broke into the conversation.

"Let me introduce the others." He indicated the older man, who measured Ellie with a thoughtful stare. "This is Tom Sullivan. The Constitution Mine is his largest holding, but he actually owns several claims and other properties in the area."

Mr. Sullivan ducked his snowy head in brusque acknowledgment. He reached for the hand Ellie offered but barely brushed her fingers before letting his arm fall back to his side.

Steven motioned toward the remaining men. "And here we have Brady Andrews, Alfred Clay, and Gilbert Owens."

The red-nosed man he identified as Brady Andrews shifted a silver flask from his right hand to his left before reaching for Ellie's outstretched fingers. She caught a whiff of alcohol on his breath when he leaned forward to greet her.

Gilbert Owens followed suit. "Pleased to meet you, ma'am."

Alfred Clay stayed where he was, arms folded tightly across his chest. "I thought this was supposed to be a meeting, not some Sunday school picnic."

Steven's face reddened, but he refrained from commenting. He unlocked the door and waved everyone inside. Ellie studied Alfred Clay as she took the seat Gilbert Owens pulled out for her, imagining what she would write about the surly miner in her notes that night.

Steven turned to address the men, facing squarely toward Alfred Clay. "If Mrs. Stewart is willing to invest in the Redemption, I thought it only fair for her to be apprised of what's been going on."

"The damage is already done. Nothing we can do about it now." Tom Sullivan sent a sour look in Ellie's direction, then leaned back against the desk and rapped his knuckles on its smooth surface. "Let's get started."

He looked at Steven. "Have you heard anything from the Pinkerton Agency?"

Ellie straightened in her chair and laced her fingers together, keeping her gaze on Steven's face.

He shook his head. "Nothing since that letter saying they'd be willing to look into matters here."

"When?" Ezra Winslow asked. "It's been weeks since we got that letter and sent them a deposit."

"A retainer fee," Tom corrected. He stroked his thumb along his chin. "Yes, it does seem like we should have heard something more by now."

Alfred Clay narrowed his eyes. "I've been watching out for an agent. We've got new folks showing up in town all the time, but I haven't spotted anyone who looks like they've been snooping around."

Ellie's mouth went dry, and her breath quickened. She forced herself to take deep, slow breaths. Clay's comment wasn't any reason to get flustered. Her plan was operating smoothly. Everyone expected women of a certain age to be curious. It was obvious from the reactions of the men in this room that no one suspected her of being the Pinkerton operative.

Clay smacked his fist against his denim-clad thigh. "What are we paying them for if they're just going to drag their heels? Every day that goes by means we're losing time, which means we're losing money."

"I have to admit Alfred has a point." Brady Andrews raised the flask to his lips, then caught sight of Ellie watching him and lowered it regretfully. "Just need a little hair of the dog after last night," he muttered. "I'm barely gettin' around today."

Ezra stared at Tom. Or maybe at a spot across the room—Ellie couldn't quite tell which. "What if we hire a bunch of guards, maybe some of those toughs that hang out over in Tombstone?"

Steven snorted. "Come on, Ezra. You know what kind of people they are. They'd be just as likely to steal the shipment themselves."

A chuckle came from Tom Sullivan's direction. "I'd have to agree with that."

Ellie raised a gloved hand. "If I might ask a question?"

Tom looked as if he'd rather eject her from the meeting, but he nodded. "Go ahead."

146

"What has been happening to the ore from the mines while you're waiting for assistance?"

Tom surveyed the other miners before he spoke. "I won't presume to answer for everyone, but I've been sending my silver to the stamp mill as usual. But instead of shipping the ingots to Benson and then on to the New Orleans mint, I've been bringing it back to the Constitution and stock-piling it there."

"Same here," Brady said. "Only I won't be able to afford to pay for the milling much longer. I don't know what I'm gonna do then." The others nodded and murmured assent.

Ellie took a moment to absorb the information. "So you're all on the brink of disaster if the situation isn't resolved soon?"

"That pretty well sums it up," Tom said. "What we need is to find some new investors who will help us ride this thing out." He flattened his lips and looked over at Steven. "It looks like you're one up on the rest of us on that score."

Ellie lowered her gaze and focused on a knot in one of the floorboards. She couldn't let her face give away the fact that Steven wasn't any better off than the rest of them. Despite what he might think, rescue was not at hand, at least not from any financial resources she might offer.

Tom cleared his throat. "I still say the Pinkertons are our best option right now. Let's give them a little more time, instead of acting in haste."

Alfred Clay paced the room like a caged tiger. "How long do you plan on giving 'em? I don't know about you, but I can't sit around on my hands doing nothing."

"None of us can." Gilbert Owens bristled. "You're not the only one losing revenue."

Alfred glared back at him. "It sure seems like I'm the only one who wants to take action instead of watching everything I've worked for come to naught."

Brady Andrews hefted the flask in his hand. "We might as well break this up. We're not gettin' anything done here. Besides, my head's killing me. I need to get something to . . ." He shot a sidelong glance at Ellie. "Eat," he finished lamely.

Ellie offered him a bright smile. "Oh, but there are sandwiches on the way."

Alfred Clay sneered. "I was right. It *is* a Sunday school picnic."

Ellie ignored the remark and fastened a stern look on Brady. "Sandwiches will do you far more good than taking another pull of whatever is in that flask. Really, Mr. Andrews, all of us need to have clear minds if we plan to outwit these hooligans."

Alfred muttered under his breath and strode toward the door. "The rest of you can stay and eat your little dainties if you want. I've had about all of this folderol I can stand." He jerked the door open and stormed out, nearly knocking over a startled delivery boy bearing a heaping tray of sandwiches.

❧ 11 ❧

Ellie tugged a stray reddish-gold curl into place and scrutinized her reflection in the dressing table mirror. With its curly bangs, upswept sides, and the mass of coppery ringlets cascading down her back, the wig she'd chosen to wear as Jessie fit as though it had been made for her. She rearranged one of the ringlets, bringing it forward to drape over her shoulder.

Perfect. Or as close to perfection as she was likely to get. With her costume and makeup in place, she sashayed back and forth in front on the mirror and grinned. Not bad at all. After making her daily rounds as Lavinia, she'd spent the last few evenings working out Jessie's background, developing the mannerisms and speech patterns that would give her a fully rounded personality.

Instead of Ellie's mousy hair and nondescript features, Jessie's bright expression and vivid coloring were more in line with Norma Brooks's appearance—the kind of woman men noticed. She crossed the room once more, swaying her hips as she had seen Magdalena do when she wanted to attract the attention and admiration of any men nearby. The results were simply amazing. The vision in the mirror swayed like a practiced coquette.

Taking up a wide-brimmed hat with a small plume at one side, she pinned it into place, choking back a surge of envy as she did so. What would it feel like to be one of those women who made men take a second glance? She looked in the mirror again to gauge the total effect and sucked in her breath. With any luck, she was about to find out.

She slipped out the front door, breathing deeply of the scents of the desert. Even with the dust that hung heavy in the air, she could still detect the overtones of sagebrush and mesquite. Such a difference from the city smells she'd been accustomed to in Chicago.

"Who are you?"

Ellie gasped and looked around.

Billy Taylor gaped up at her from the edge of the street. "You're not the lady who lives here," he stated firmly. "Where'd you come from?"

Ellie commanded herself to relax. "I'm Mrs. Stewart's niece." This was a perfect opportunity to introduce Jessie to the public. She needed to make the most of it.

"I arrived yesterday," she continued. "And I'll be staying with her from now on." She picked her way down the walk and held out her hand. "I'm Miss Monroe. What's your name?"

"Billy," he answered, ignoring her outstretched hand. That was just as well, she decided, once she glimpsed his grubby fingers.

"Well, Billy, it was good to meet you. I'm sure we'll be seeing each other from time to time."

With that, she gave her ringlets a toss and set off down the street, relishing her renewed freedom of movement. How wonderful to be able to stride along again at her own pace, free of the leg wrappings that dictated Lavinia's age-stiffened movements.

Two blocks later, she reached Grant Street and turned left, ready to strike up a conversation with everyone she met, but the street seemed uncharacteristically empty for that time of morning. Ellie chafed at having her plans hobbled. After all the trouble she'd gone to in fabricating Jessie, it would only seem fair to encounter crowds along the boardwalk when she wanted to introduce her new creation.

Crossing Fourth Street, she smiled when the station agent emerged from the stagecoach office carrying a heavy crate that he set atop a pile of similar boxes already stacked on the boardwalk.

"Good morning," she called.

"Mornin'," he mumbled, barely giving her a glance. But that brief glance proved to be enough. He whipped his head around so quickly

Ellie feared he might do damage to his spine.

Yanking off his hat, he twisted it between his hands. "Brent Howard, at your service."

She nodded demurely and kept her face turned steadfastly ahead while she sauntered past, watching the man from the corner of her eye. He didn't utter another sound, but he studied every swaying movement as she passed. She touched her fingertips to her lips to hide the smile she couldn't quite contain. Success! It was only the first reaction from an adult male to Jessie's initial appearance in town, but it was every bit as gratifying as she'd hoped. So far, so good.

In case he might still be watching, she slowed and studied the signs that hung out over the boardwalk, as if looking for a particular establishment. Two doors down, she turned in at the telegraph office and walked up to the counter.

"Be with you in a minute." Amos Crawford didn't look up as he finished writing a message and handed it to a waiting boy. "Get that to the marshal on the double. And I don't want to hear about you takin' time to stop in the mercantile to buy candy on your way—you hear?"

When the youth scurried out the door, the telegrapher turned back to Ellie. At the sight of her, his eyes bulged like a frog's, and his jaw sagged in a most satisfactory manner. Ellie counted a full fifteen seconds before he recovered enough to speak. "Good . . . morning, miss. Sorry to keep you waiting. What can I . . . do for you?"

"I'd like to send a telegram, please." She gave the bedazzled man a pert wink and watched his Adam's apple bob up and down.

Without a word, he pushed a form and a pencil across the counter, never taking his eyes off her.

Ellie suppressed a desire to burst into giggles at his awestruck expression. "Thank you. I need to let my family know I've arrived safely."

Amos Crawford tilted his head to one side. "But the stage doesn't get in until this afternoon. Where'd you come from?"

A sudden attack of stage fright set Ellie's heart to fluttering, but she commanded herself to exude confidence. Half the battle in being a successful actress was won by making the audience believe the actress *was* the character she portrayed. In order to do that, she had to believe it herself.

She gave her ringlets a toss. "I didn't come on the stage. I arrived yesterday with some people I've been staying with. They were kind enough to make a slight detour to drop me off on their way to catch the train." She held her breath, hoping that version matched the one she'd given him earlier. When he showed no surprise, just nodded his head, she allowed herself to relax again.

Taking the stubby pencil, she wrote down the message she had memorized the night before, a dual-purpose wording that would let the town know of Jessie's arrival and hopefully relieve some of the concerns Fleming and Gates were surely feeling:

Arrived safely. Aunt Lavinia doing well. Looking forward to exploring and meeting new people.

Jessie

There—that should do the trick.

Amos twisted his head to one side in a way that made Ellie feel certain he had plenty of practice reading upside down. His eyes grew round, and a broad grin split his face. "You're Miz Lavinia's niece!"

"That's right." Ellie held back a triumphant grin. Her ploy had worked.

"Did you have a good visit with those friends of yours?"

This time, Ellie couldn't repress her smile. Yet another evidence of the telegrapher staying on top of all the local gossip.

"I should have known it was you," he went on. "You're the spittin' image of your aunt."

"I suppose there is a certain family resemblance." Ellie spoke the words casually enough, but inside she wasn't sure whether to be amused or concerned. Was her disguise so transparent?

"Your eyes are the exact same color as hers," Amos went on. "I'll bet she looked just like you when she was your age."

Ellie took in his dreamy tone and his calf-eyed stare. Who would have thought it? After expecting Jessie to get all the male attention, it seemed Lavinia was the first one with a potential suitor. How funny it would be if the widow Stewart wound up with a line of admirers at her door. Then again . . .

The thought of such a thing actually happening wiped away any trace of amusement. She fervently hoped that wouldn't be the case. It would only add further complications to an already tangled situation.

She slanted a playful look at him. "Why, thank you for saying so. I've always admired Aunt Lavinia's eyes."

As she turned to leave, the telegrapher cleared his throat. "Be sure to tell your aunt hello for me."

Ellie turned right and strolled east down Grant Street, trying to look the part of a newcomer exploring the town. She slowed to admire a high-crowned hat in the dressmaker's window. Sumptuously trimmed with flowers and imitation cherries, it would look striking on Jessie, the deep green ribbon offering a perfect contrast to her red-gold hair. If she'd had resources of her own, she would have marched into the store and bought it on the spot, but the money allotted her by the Pinkertons was meant for necessities, not fripperies. She could just imagine Gates's expression if he knew she was even thinking about such an indulgence.

With a longing look at the lovely confection, she set off again, nodding to other shoppers as they passed.

A tall figure in a black frock coat and red brocade vest made his way along the boardwalk, coming from the direction of the saloon district. Ellie caught her breath when she recognized Marshal Everett Bascomb. He had looked through Lavinia as though she were invisible, but today Ellie was dressed as Jessie. Would she be able to catch his attention now?

His gold watch chain glittered against the deep red brocade as he drew nearer. Several of the people along the boardwalk scooted to one side, giving him a wide berth as he walked past.

Think! There had to be some way she could draw him into a conversation.

Her heart beat faster as he got closer. If she didn't make a move soon, she would lose this opportunity, and who knew when another might come along? It was now or never.

The marshal tipped his broad-brimmed black felt hat as he approached. Ellie opened her mouth to speak, but no words came forth. Her heart sank, knowing she had bungled her chance. In a few more strides, he would be beyond her.

Just as he passed, he swept a cursory glance over her face. His steady gait faltered, and he stopped in the middle of the boardwalk and stared like a poleaxed steer.

Ellie composed her features so as not to let any look of recognition betray her. Jessie hadn't encountered the lawman before. Instead, she fluttered her lashes as she'd seen Magdalena do and let her gaze fall to the street. From the edge of her vision, she could see him sweep off the hat and make a gallant bow.

"Forgive me for staring, ma'am. I thought I knew all the pretty girls in Pickford, but I don't believe I've had the opportunity to make your acquaintance."

Hoping he didn't sense her nervousness, Ellie raised her eyes and stared directly into his. She curved her lips into a cheeky grin. "No, I've only just arrived. I'm staying with my aunt, Mrs. Stewart."

He showed no sign of recognizing the name, but his dark eyes glinted when their gazes met. He stroked one side of his neatly trimmed mustache with his forefinger. "I'm Everett Bascomb, the town marshal." He paused for a moment as if giving her time to be suitably impressed.

Ellie tilted her head and gave him an appraising glance before offering her hand. "I'm pleased to meet you, Marshal. My name is Jessie Monroe."

Bascomb held her fingers several seconds longer than necessary, and Ellie felt gooseflesh prickle up her arm. She withdrew her hand as quickly as she could, resisting the urge to wipe her fingers on her skirt.

He reminded her of a second-rate character actor who toured with Magdalena early in her career—as free with his hands as he was with his compliments. Even the stagehands had seen through him quickly enough. One of them pulled Ellie aside during one of the first stops on the tour. "You watch out for yourself around that one. He's the kind who'd smile at you while he's stealing the gold out of your teeth."

Marshal Everett Bascomb struck her in exactly the same way.

He settled the hat back on his head and swept his arm in a wide arc that encompassed the length of Grant Street. "Why don't I show you around my town? I'd be happy to do all I can to make such a lovely newcomer feel welcome."

"What a wonderful idea. I was just on my way to"—Ellie looked around, seeking inspiration, and spotted the large storefront across the street—"the mercantile. I promised to make a couple of purchases for my aunt."

"Then at least let me escort you that far." Without waiting for her to agree, Bascomb captured her hand and tucked it into the crook of his arm.

Ellie did her best not to flinch at the renewed contact. She gave his arm a squeeze and followed his lead as he stepped down into the dusty street.

"Where do you hail from, Miss Monroe?"

"Chicago." Ellie fought the urge to pull away and kept her lips fixed in an inviting smile. There was absolutely no need for him to lean that close to ask the question.

Bascomb wrapped his fingers more closely around hers. "You must find our Arizona climate a welcome change. The winters get pretty cold back there, don't they?"

"You have no idea." Just the memory of the frigid temperatures she'd left behind made Ellie shiver. Or was it Bascomb's nearness that brought that reaction?

Just before they reached the mercantile, he halted as though struck by a sudden idea. "Would you join me for a slice of pie?" He indicated the restaurant on the opposite end of the block. "Their cook makes a mighty fine peach pie, even if he has to use dried peaches this time of year." He bent his head lower and murmured, "I really am enjoying this conversation. I'd like to extend it a bit so I can get to know you better."

"I'd love to. My errands can wait a little longer." Ellie forced a show of enthusiasm. Here was the opportunity she'd been looking for. She couldn't shirk her duty now.

Despite her best efforts, her attempts at drawing the lawman out on the subject of the silver thefts seemed destined to fail from the start. No matter what line of conversation she pursued, he managed to turn it back to himself and his successful reign as marshal. Before she had finished half her slice of pie, Ellie was ready to scream in frustration. She knotted her left hand into a fist under her napkin and forked another bite of the dried-peach pie into her mouth.

"That's a fascinating story," she said when he paused long enough to take a breath during his glowing account of breaking up a fight at the Palace. She shot a quick glance up at the ceiling as the words left her lips, glad to see the rafters remained in place and no lightning bolts rained down out of the blue after she told such a whopper.

Bascomb's dark gaze bored into hers in far too intimate a way. "I'm glad you think so. It's nice to know someone appreciates my efforts to keep the peace in Pickford."

Ellie choked on her pie and took a quick swallow of water to help wash it down. Leaning forward, she stared at him with what she hoped he would take as rapt admiration. "You've been so generous in showing me the town. I wonder if you might be able to answer a question or two."

His eyes gleamed. "Of course."

"Is it safe for a woman to walk the streets in Pickford alone? My aunt tells me there have been a number of robberies recently—something about silver, I believe. I'm eager to experience every bit of the West that I can, but I must confess, stories like that make me rather nervous."

Bascomb's face tightened. Then a smile stretched his lips, and he reached over to pat her right hand. "Don't you worry your pretty head about that. It has nothing to do with decent folks like you and your aunt. I'm sure you will never cross paths with those lawbreakers, so you have no reason to fret."

Ellie slid her fingers free and drew her hand back to the edge of the table. "Perhaps you're right. But who would do such a terrible thing? I'll feel much better once you've apprehended the criminals. Do you have any idea who they are?"

For a brief moment, his lips twisted as though he'd bitten into a lemon. "I've been tracking down every lead I come across, but I haven't closed in on them yet. But it's nothing for you to be concerned about. It's only a matter of time until I have them behind bars."

Ellie studied his face closely. Did that flicker of emotion signal anger at not being able to catch the thieves, or was it meant to mask his complicity with them? Whatever the reason, the shuttered look in his eyes told her his guard was up. She wasn't likely to gain any more information from him at present, and the realization that she could bring their conversation to an end brought an inexpressible sense of relief.

She pushed her chair away from the table and

folded her napkin beside her plate. "Thank you for the pie and the conversation, Marshal. I feel I know Pickford much better after talking to you."

His self-satisfied expression was back in place. "It was my pleasure, dear lady. I'll make certain this won't be the last conversation we have."

Ellie fluttered her eyelashes and parted her lips in a smile, grateful he didn't seem to realize how she cringed at the thought of having to spend any more time with him.

They parted company at the door, and Ellie strolled into the mercantile alone. She browsed the shelves for a few minutes before purchasing two cans of pork and beans, and some crackers—items she didn't really need. Back outside, she tapped her toe on the boardwalk and eyed the buildings at the east end of town.

She longed to explore the blocks that stretched between her and the saloon district, but she'd told the marshal she needed to take her purchases back home to her aunt. She'd better follow through on that and return to the house, in case he might be watching.

Ellie blew out a puff of frustration strong enough to stir the curls at her brow. Up to that moment, she'd never considered the difficulty of working without a script . . . especially when she didn't know where her audience was located.

She opened her lace-trimmed parasol to keep the noonday sun out of her eyes and started west.

Before she had taken a dozen steps, she heard a voice calling her name and turned to see Amos Crawford trotting across the street, a piece of paper in his hand.

"Glad . . . I spotted you," he puffed. "This just came in." He handed the paper to Ellie.

GLAD ALL IS WELL STOP EAGER TO HEAR YOUR IMPRESSIONS OF PICKFORD AND ANY OPPORTUNITIES YOU AND LAVINIA TURN UP STOP

COUSIN HENRY

Relief flooded through Ellie. Her message seemed to have done the trick of giving the impression she and Norma were working together as planned. A prick of guilt stabbed her, but she pushed it away. Nowhere had she directly said Norma was on the job with her, and it wouldn't hurt for Fleming and Gates to assume so for the time being. The truth would come out soon enough—surely Norma would be contacting the office eventually. In the meantime, it gave her a little more time to continue the investigation and prove her worth.

She spied a dark-coated figure a block farther along Fourth Street. Everett Bascomb touched the brim of his hat and began walking her way. Ellie spun on her heel and set off toward her house as quickly as she could without breaking into a run. The peach pie had whetted her appetite. She might as well make the most of the disruption of her plans and have some lunch.

A quick glance over her shoulder reassured her that Bascomb had given up and turned his steps in another direction. Remembering the feel of his fingers on her hand and the possessive way he'd bent over her, she quickened her steps even more. Suddenly the thought of a hot bath that would let her scrub away every vestige of his touch appealed to her even more than the midday meal.

12

After a brisk scrubbing followed by a hot lunch, Ellie took to the streets again, this time decked out as Lavinia. Despite the mounting pressure to acquire some useful information before the Pinkertons started asking more questions, she didn't want to take a chance on Jessie encountering Marshal Bascomb twice in one day. Once was more than enough.

Brent Howard nodded a greeting when she passed the stage depot, but he didn't stare at her with the interest he'd shown Jessie. Mindful of the admiration Lavinia inspired in Amos Crawford, she hurried past the telegraph office and finally reached the spot where her earlier exploration had been cut short by meeting the marshal.

What next? Her gaze traveled longingly to the east end of town. As Lavinia, she didn't dare cross Seventh Street and enter the saloon district, but getting acquainted with some of the denizens of the seamier part of town might be exactly what was needed to get the information she sought.

Ellie tapped her finger against her cheek. How close could she get without actually crossing the line of demarcation? She surveyed the buildings that sat closest to the invisibie boundary where respectability ended and smiled when she spotted the bank on the corner of Sixth Street.

Situated on the reputable side of town, the bank was still near enough to Seventh Street for the gambling halls and saloons to do business there. It would make perfect sense for Lavinia to lay out her investment plans before the banker and ask the advice of someone who knew the area and its people well. Having connections with people on both sides of town, the banker might make an excellent source of information, if she couched her questions discreetly enough.

She took a firmer grip on her reticule. Yes, the bank would do nicely. She quickened her steps and hurried along, intent on her task. As she neared Fifth Street, she heard a voice hail her. Ellie winced, wondering if Amos Crawford had spotted her after all. Relief spread through her when she looked up to find the desk clerk smiling at her from the doorway of the Grand Hotel.

"Afternoon, Mrs. Stewart. It's nice to see you out and about this fine day."

Ellie bobbed her head, barely slowing her pace.

"My wife is just getting ready to have some tea. I wonder if you'd like to sit for a while and join her."

His wife? She hadn't seen any sign of a woman's presence during her earlier visit. Curiosity warred with frustration at having her plans derailed yet again. After a brief struggle, curiosity won out. "Why, I suppose I could." The man's grateful smile made her decision easy. "Yes, I would enjoy that very much."

She followed him inside. Her mood brightened when she saw a small table set up in the same spot she'd occupied the other day. If she couldn't question the banker, she could at least spend a little more time at her observation post.

"This is my wife, Myra," he said. "Dear, I'd like you to meet Mrs. Stewart."

"Lavinia." Ellie smiled at the frail-looking woman on the serpentine-back settee. She studied her new acquaintance, startled by the transparency of the other woman's skin. She appeared a little younger than Lavinia's supposed age. No wonder her husband thought the two of them would enjoy chatting.

"It's good of you to take the time to stop in."

Myra's voice was as delicate as her appearance. "Donald knows how I crave female companionship after being cooped up in my bedroom for days on end."

"I'm happy to have the opportunity to rest a bit." Ellie smiled and nodded to Donald as he returned with a tea tray and placed it on the table before them. The afternoon might not be lost, after all. Myra seemed eager for a nice long talk. And getting a woman's insight might prove to be of more value than a conversation with the banker. She settled into an overstuffed chair that offered a good view of the street.

When she turned her attention back to her hostess, she tried not to stare at the thin hair, sunken eyes, and bony fingers. Her smile dimmed. She had her own problems, but they seemed trivial compared to the challenges this poor woman faced.

"Would you mind pouring? That teapot is a little heavy for me, I'm afraid."

"I'd be glad to." Ellie poured the golden brew into two cups of delicate bone china. Noticing an array of cookies on the tray, she tucked two on the saucer before she set it on the table next to Myra.

The cup rattled against the saucer when Myra lifted it, and she grimaced. "My strength isn't what it used to be, but I want to make the most of the days I can get out of bed."

"How long have you . . . I mean . . ." Ellie felt her cheeks flame.

Myra smiled, ignoring Ellie's awkwardness. "I've been laid up for several months now. The doctor can't find anything wrong—nothing specific anyway—but my strength seems to be ebbing away a little at a time."

Ellie looked down at her teacup, not knowing what to say.

"I take it one day at a time," Myra went on, as though she hadn't noticed Ellie's discomfort. "I have a good husband to care for me, and the Lord doesn't give us more than we can bear, does He?"

Ellie bit into her cookie so she didn't have to answer. She felt relieved when the door opened and a woman entered, as stout and fresh-faced as Myra was thin and ashen.

"I saw Donald sweeping the boardwalk. He told me you were feeling well enough to be up and around today, so I thought I'd come over and sit with you a mite."

Myra's face lit up. "What fun! It'll be like a regular tea party." She turned to Ellie. "Lavinia, this is my dear friend Gertie Johnson. She and her husband own the mercantile. Gertie, meet my new friend, Lavinia Stewart."

Gertie smiled. "I've heard my husband mention you, Mrs. Stewart."

Myra gestured at the table. "Gertie, would you mind getting another cup for yourself?"

"Not at all. Especially if it means I get to enjoy some of those cookies along with my tea." Gertie winked and disappeared through the door to the dining room. She returned a moment later and plopped down on a dainty balloon-back chair on the other side of the settee. Ellie held her breath when the sturdy woman lowered her substantial bulk onto the delicate seat, but the chair held firm.

Gertie poured her tea and spooned in a teaspoon of sugar, then looked at Ellie. "Are you a guest here at the hotel?"

Ellie stifled a chuckle. Obviously, Gertie was not a woman who minced words. "No, I've rented the Cooper place, and I'm here to look into making investments. My niece joined me recently."

"Two more women in town! Before you know it, we'll have the place civilized." Gertie threw back her head and gave a hearty laugh.

Myra joined in, although her mirth was more subdued. Ellie noticed a sparkle in the frail woman's eye that hadn't been there when she first arrived.

She glanced out the window and sipped her tea while the other women visited, keeping her ear tuned for any tidbits of gossip that might prove helpful. To her disappointment, they focused more on the weather and the new stove the banker's wife recently ordered than anything pertinent to her investigation. It appeared that joining the tea party wasn't going to give her any clues, but she had enjoyed the visit with Myra and Gertie.

"How are things going at the store?" Myra asked.

Gertie set her teacup on her saucer with a clink. "It couldn't be better, to hear Walter tell it. He says he's taking more orders than ever from the mines." A chuckle rumbled from her ample chest. "I'll have to take his word for it. You know what a poor hand I am at keeping the bookwork straight."

Myra pressed her napkin to her lips. "I do indeed."

Ellie pulled her attention away from the window and watched the two women, feeling an unexpected pang of envy for the easy camaraderie they shared. What would it be like to build close attachments in a town like Pickford, where people could simply be friends without the constant bickering and petty jealousy that existed in the world of the theater?

As if sensing her longing to be drawn into their circle, Myra smiled at Ellie and patted a Bible on the cushion beside her. "Would you mind reading a chapter to Gertie and me, Lavinia?"

"I'd be glad to. Where would you like me to start?" Ellie spoke evenly, hoping a calm demeanor would mask her nervousness. She'd started reading a randomly chosen passage in her own Bible every morning, but she was still very much a beginner when it came to locating a specific chapter and verse.

"I've marked the place where I left off," Myra said, earning Ellie's undying gratitude.

Ellie opened the Bible to the marked passage in the book of John, cleared her throat, and began to read. Only a few verses in, she realized she was reading the same story the minister had spoken of on Sunday morning, about how a little boy shared his lunch with Jesus to feed a multitude.

Just when she reached the part where the disciples were picking up the leftover food, Myra set her napkin aside and pressed one hand against her chest. "I'm afraid I've run out of steam. I'd better go lie down."

Gertie pushed herself to her feet, all traces of merriment gone. "Let me help you to bed—or would you rather I get Donald?"

"I'd prefer you did it, if you don't mind. The poor dear works so hard taking care of the hotel and me. I hate to bother him more than necessary."

Gertie wrapped a meaty arm around her friend's shoulders and helped her stand. Beside the hefty woman, Myra looked like a tiny chick under its mother's wing.

Myra smiled at Ellie. "I had hoped we'd have more time to chat. If you'd like to come back, we can continue our visit another day. And feel free to rest here in the lobby whenever you like, whether I'm here or not."

"Thank you. That's very kind." Ellie's throat tightened as she watched Gertie lead Myra to one of the doors behind the desk, which presumably led to Donald and Myra's private quarters.

Wanting to be helpful, she busied herself setting the cups and napkins back on the tray. She didn't know what to do next, so she stood near the window trying to spot anything of interest out on the street, her mind still occupied with the bravery and kindness of one frail woman.

Gertie emerged moments later, closing the door behind her quietly. "I've tucked her in, and she's resting. I believe she was asleep before I even got out of the room, poor dear."

Ellie could see moisture rimming the other woman's lower lids and blinked back tears of her own.

Gertie pulled a handkerchief from her sleeve and used it to swipe her eyes, then blew her nose and tucked the cambric square back into place. "I have to get back to the store. Walter will wonder where I've gone."

Her comment jolted Ellie from thoughts of Myra to her own duties. She hadn't followed through yet on her plan to question the mercantile owner. Seizing the opportunity, she said, "I'll join you. I need to pick up an item or two."

As they crossed the street, she added, "My

niece brought home the canned goods and crackers I needed, but I wanted to see if you had chamomile tea."

"Niece?" Gertie's face lit up. "You wouldn't be talking about that stunning redhead who came in this morning?"

The description of her alter ego brought a warm flush to Ellie's cheeks.

"Now I know who you are." Gertie's broad shoulders shook. "You're the one Amos Crawford has been mooning over."

Ellie stopped short in the middle of the boardwalk. "Mooning? Over me?"

Gertie let out a loud peal of laughter. "I should say so. He comes in at least twice a day, asking if anyone's seen you. And he has a spring in his step I haven't seen before, as if he's a boy again . . . or thinks he is." She winked and dug her elbow into Ellie's ribs. "Just the other day, I caught him eyeing an ivory comb. I knew he wouldn't buy a thing like that for himself, so I asked him who he was thinking of giving it to."

"What did he say?" Ellie asked, captivated by Gertie's tale, in spite of herself.

"He snapped the lid shut and turned as red as . . . as that cabbage over there." Gertie indicated the vegetable in a basket beside the mercantile's door.

Ellie stared at Gertie, not totally comprehending the knowing look the other woman gave her.

Realization dawned. "Wait a minute. Are you suggesting he intended to give that to me?"

Gertie snorted. "Well, he sure wasn't planning on giving it to me."

"I'm hardly the only woman in Pickford," Ellie sputtered. "Surely there are others he might be interested in."

"Maybe, but Amos has never done anything like this in all the time I've known him. It only started since you came to town. I haven't seen a man look that moonstruck since Walter was getting ready to pop the question to me."

Ellie clutched the satin ruffle at the neckline of her dress.

"You know how it is, having been married yourself. And Amos is a good man. You could do a lot worse. You don't want to spend the rest of your days all alone, do you?"

Ellie forced her answer through lips that had suddenly gone dry. "It's too soon to think of that. I still have the memory of my dear Oliver to keep me company."

Gertie gave Ellie another nudge. "Maybe so, but memories can't keep a body warm on a long winter night."

From the heat in her cheeks, Ellie feared they matched the red cabbage in the basket by the door. "Indeed," she muttered. "I'll be sure to keep that in mind."

The bell over the door jangled when they

entered the store, where Walter bent over an assortment of papers scattered across the counter. He straightened at the sound and smiled at Gertie. "There you are. I wondered where you'd gone."

"Myra felt up to having company, so I popped in for a quick visit. And while I was there, I made a new friend." She tilted her head in Ellie's direction. "You've already met Mrs. Stewart, I believe."

Walter acknowledged Ellie's presence with a nod.

Gertie reached for an apron hanging on a hook behind the counter and tied it around her plump midsection. "I didn't mean to leave you short-handed."

"You didn't." Walter scratched the top of his head, leaving wispy strands of hair standing straight up. "There isn't much going on at the moment. I thought I'd catch up on the inventory." He swept up the papers he'd been working on, tapped them on the counter to square the edges, and stowed them out of sight. Resting both arms on the counter, he looked at Ellie. "What do you think about Pickford? Are you getting settled in?"

"I'm enjoying my stay immensely. People have been very helpful, and the weather is certainly nicer than what I'm accustomed to. If things work out businesswise, I wouldn't be averse to making it my permanent home."

"Especially now that you've got someone to keep you company." Gertie snickered. When Ellie's eyes widened, she added, "I meant your niece, not Amos." Still grinning, she turned to her husband. "That was her niece who came in here this morning."

Walter's face brightened. "I can see the resemblance now. She was telling me something about your future plans. What was it . . . ?"

Ellie opened her mouth to repeat what she'd told him that morning, then snapped it shut again. How much should Lavinia know about what Jessie had said?

Good heavens! Keeping her identity under wraps wasn't going to be enough. She would have to exercise constant vigilance to keep track of what Jessie knew that Lavinia didn't, and vice versa.

She closed her eyes and pressed her fingertips to her temples. Maybe she ought to start keeping two sets of notes, one for Jessie and one for Lavinia, to keep everything straight. She felt a touch on her elbow and opened her eyes to find Gertie peering at her, a look of concern crinkling her face.

"Are you all right? You seemed to take a little turn there." She put her arm around Ellie's shoulders and led her to a wooden chair next to a potbellied stove.

Walter disappeared into the back of the store

and returned with a glass of water. "You sure you're all right, Mrs. Stewart?"

Ellie squirmed under the couple's kind ministrations. Letting her mind wander off in all directions was going to get her in trouble. She needed to keep a steady focus if she hoped to carry off her masquerade.

Walter excused himself to go help a man in rough miner's clothing find a pair of boots.

Irene Peabody, the banker's wife, waved imperiously from the notions table. "When I was in here the other day, you had a wide selection of Clark's O.N.T. thread, but now I don't see the color I wanted."

With her back to the woman, Gertie made a face only Ellie could see. "Duty calls. Are you sure you're all right?"

"Don't worry about me. I'll just sit here a few minutes more, if I may."

"Take as long as you want. If you need any-thing, just let me know."

While Gertie tried to find thread in a shade to suit her demanding customer, Ellie took the opportunity to survey the store at leisure. The mercantile's wares were all displayed neatly in their designated sections, and yet . . .

For a business Gertie declared was booming, the store didn't appear to be as busy as one would expect. There wasn't an overabundance of merchandise on the shelves, either, and she spotted a number of empty spaces where it appeared stock hadn't been replenished.

But Gertie said they were taking in some sizable orders, so maybe it wasn't possible to judge the store's prosperity by the amount of merchandise on display.

At a table next to the far wall, a lanky man with a faded red bandanna around his neck sifted through an assortment of spurs. At the other end of the store she saw two of the mine owners she'd met at the meeting, one of them thumbing through a well-worn catalog. Browsers aplenty, but nothing to indicate the store was doing a land-office business.

The bell jingled, and Ellie's heart lurched when Steven Pierce came into view.

Walter emerged from the back at that moment with a pair of boots in his hands. He nodded to Steven. "Be with you in just a minute."

"No rush. I just needed to pick up another spool of that one-inch rope." While the miner checked the fit of the boots, Steven gazed around the store. His eyes sparkled when he saw Ellie. "Mrs. Stewart, how are you this afternoon?"

Ellie rose as quickly as her wrapped limbs would allow and walked over to join him, admiring the way the cut of the jacket comple-mented his manly form. "What a nice surprise. We seem to be making this a regular meeting place."

Steven chuckled. "What did you think about

the owners' meeting? Did it raise any questions in your mind?"

Ellie recognized the hopeful look in his eyes and felt a stab of guilt. He wanted to clear up any doubts she might have so she would feel free to make her potential investment a reality. She wished she really did have the money to ease his worries.

She offered a confident smile. "No, I don't believe so. Everything seemed very straight-forward." She nodded toward the far end of the store and lowered her voice before adding, "Some of the other owners seem like a rather rough-and-tumble lot."

Steven followed her gaze and smiled. "Don't let the external trappings fool you. They may seem a little rough around the edges, but that's more a matter of them blending into the setting—something like a chameleon taking on the color of its surroundings. Tom Sullivan, for instance, has already had a successful business career in San Francisco before moving to Arizona."

He nodded toward the man looking through the catalog. "As far as I know, Ezra is the only one who's had very little education. The others may not have a college degree, but out here, people tend to educate themselves instead of going through formal channels. Why, just the other day, I saw Brady Andrews reading a copy of *Plutarch's Lives*."

Ellie's eyes widened. "Really? I would have imagined he'd be much more interested in the inside of a saloon rather than the inside of a book."

One corner of Steven's mouth quirked up. "I have to admit, each of those would probably hold his interest equally."

Ellie returned his smile, enjoying the warmth as they shared their little joke.

Walter returned from the back room, carrying the spool of rope on his shoulder. He set it down on the counter with a thud. "There you go. Anything else?"

Steven pulled a scrap of paper from his pocket. "I have a list. Just a few odds and ends, but I can get them myself. You don't need to go to the trouble."

Walter shrugged. "Suit yourself, but it isn't like I'm swamped right now." He pulled a rag from under the counter and started dusting the back shelves.

Steven turned his attention back to Ellie. "Are you any nearer to making a decision about your investment?" He cleared his throat. "I don't mean to pressure you. I'm only asking so I'll have a better idea of how to plan for the future."

"It's all right. I quite understand." Ellie injected all the calm she could into her statement while her mind groped for words a real investor might say. What would Lavinia's mythical late husband have advised?

An idea flashed into her mind. "Perhaps it would be a good idea for me to take a look at your mine. Would you be willing to give me a tour?" The words slipped from her mouth without careful thought, but she warmed to the notion as soon as she uttered them. What better way to gain an understanding of what went on in a mine than by actually seeing it herself? The insights gained there might help move her investigation forward.

Steven stared at her. "You want to go down into the mine?"

"Yes! I think that would be a splendid idea, don't you?"

Doubt couldn't have been written more clearly on Steven's face. "It really isn't set up for casual visitors."

Ellie drew herself up and peered at him over the top of her spectacles. "But I'm hardly a casual visitor, am I, Mr. Pierce? After all, if I do decide to invest in the Redemption, we're going to be partners."

"It's rougher than you probably imagine. It isn't any place for a lady."

Ellie pushed the spectacles up higher on her nose and looked Steven squarely in the eye. "Don't think 'lady'—think 'business associate.' "

His Adam's apple bobbed, and she could tell he was weakening.

"It would be impossible for you to be down

there while the mine is in operation. We might be able to arrange something next Sunday, while it's shut down. That is, if you're certain you want to do this."

Ellie glanced away to hide her sense of triumph. Looking back at him, she said, "That would be lovely. We can go there after church. Why don't we stop at the Beck House on the way and have lunch? It'll be my treat."

She imagined Gates grumbling over this expenditure. But surely the Pinkertons would see this as a wise investment in the investigation.

And she certainly wouldn't object to the chance of spending thirty minutes sitting across the table from Steven Pierce and looking into those gorgeous coffee-colored eyes.

Stepping out of the mercantile, Ellie had to halt abruptly in order to avoid a collision with a man in a black slouch hat. Her eyes narrowed when she recognized the unpleasant fellow she'd encountered during her first visit to the hotel. Moving out onto the boardwalk after he passed, she strolled along in the same direction, careful to keep her distance.

The man stopped a little past Fourth Street, where an alleyway opened up next to the Pickford Bakery, and glanced over his shoulder with an air that gave Ellie pause. The action looked positively furtive. What could he be up to? When he ducked into the alley, her curiosity rose another notch.

She moved ahead, chafing at Lavinia's slow pace and hoping she didn't lose sight of her quarry. The corner of the bakery offered a measure of protection as she peeked cautiously into the alley in time to see the man pull what looked to be a slip of paper from a crack in the bakery's wall and bend his head to examine it.

Could this secretive behavior have anything to do with the robberies? Excitement rippled through Ellie.

She watched as he slid his hand into his coat pocket as if tucking the paper away. Excitement turned to elation when she saw the paper flutter to the ground unnoticed.

She waited while he exited the other end of the alley that opened onto Douglas Street. Then she scuttled along the narrow passage to retrieve the paper and read the words printed on one side:

Meet me tonight. Usual place. Nine o'clock.

Aha! Hadn't she felt there was something sinister about that man the first time she'd laid eyes on him? Her instincts had been right on target. He was obviously up to no good.

But while she had just discovered her first clue, the information itself didn't do her a bit of good. Without any idea where the "usual place" might be, she couldn't very well set up any sort of surveillance. Besides, nine o'clock at night was far too late for either Lavinia or Jessie to be walking around town alone.

Ellie stared at the scrap of paper in her hand. A clue at last, but what was she supposed to do with it? She sighed and tucked the note into her reticule, then squared her shoulders. Maybe she couldn't spy on his meeting this time, but she would keep a sharp lookout for him in the future.

Somehow she would manage to find out what he was up to.

❧ 13 ❧

Dusk settled over Pickford, casting deep pockets of shadow across the richly appointed living room. The master of the house picked up a box of matches and selected one from within, flicking its tip against the phosphorus strip. A flare of light danced on the end of the wooden matchstick.

With a quick movement, he lit the wick of the oil lamp on the carved mahogany desk and shook the match out. Turning the wick down to nothing more than a soft glow, he seated himself on the leather chair behind the desk and waited. Listening intently, he heard nothing save for the steady click of the mantel clock. His impatience mounted with every tick.

Finally, the sound he'd been waiting for—a soft scuffle of footsteps on the back porch. He moved toward the door even before the muffled knock sounded and opened it just wide enough to admit his visitor.

"It took you long enough." Peering outside to make certain they hadn't been observed, he closed the door and led the way back to the living room.

"Too many people out and about. I had to wait until it was clear before I could get here without being seen . . . *boss*."

The inflection on the last word made his hackles rise, but he chose to ignore the man's insolence. It wouldn't do to overreact, not when he was so close to reaching his goal. He turned up the lamp, illuminating the other man's stony expression. "Did you find out where Owens is hiding his silver?"

The downturned lips gave answer even before his visitor spoke. "No, he's cagier than I expected. Try as I might, I haven't been able to get a thing out of him or his foreman."

"Keep working on it. We don't have much time. With the Pinkertons likely to show up any day and that Stewart woman snooping around, we may need to move the schedule up a bit."

"I don't know that we have anything to worry about." His quick shrug dismissed the comment as an unnecessary concern. "The Pinkertons haven't shown up yet. Maybe they're spread too thin to spare a man right now. They might not come for a while, maybe not at all. As for the woman . . ." He gave a bark of laughter. "I think you're losing your nerve. Why are you worried about an old biddy like her?"

"She isn't just an old lady, she's a *nosy* old lady. That can mean trouble."

His minion scoffed, ignoring the steely glare that usually brought men into immediate submission. "So she's nosy. What harm can she do?"

"She's been poking into things all over town. Those questions of hers might start people thinking. If they start putting pieces together, someone could figure out what we've been doing."

The other man's smile evaporated. "So what do we do about it?"

Feeling more at ease with his leadership reestablished, he drummed his fingers along the edge of the desk. "She needs to be discouraged from investing in Pierce's mine. Then she'll have no reason to stay here stirring things up."

"How are we going to do that?"

"I already have an idea or two along that line. A good scare ought to go a long way toward convincing her to leave town."

"That might work," his visitor conceded. "On the other hand, it took a lot of nerve for her to come out west in the first place. What if she has more gumption than you give her credit for?"

"In that case, I may do a little snooping of my own." He reached into the center desk drawer and brought out a brass key, dangling it from his fingertips. "I own the house she's living in. The bank handles the rental transactions for me, but I retain a set of keys. I can get in there to look around anytime I like."

"I don't get it. What good will that do?"

He slipped the key into his vest pocket and patted it gently. "Knowledge is power, my friend. She wants to know about mines and robberies. I want to know about her. Everybody has secrets, even snoopy old ladies. I may come across something she doesn't want anyone else to know about."

The taller man raised his eyebrows. "Something that might convince her to leave town before it gets out?"

"Exactly."

"Why go to all that trouble? If you want her to disappear, we can make that happen easy enough. Then there's nothing to worry about unless the Pinkertons show up."

One more reason why he was in charge. He'd always had the ability to think several steps ahead. "That would be the easiest way, but it may not be the best. There's that niece of hers to consider, for one thing. Having her family raise the alarm if she goes missing would only create more problems. We'll try this way first."

"And if that doesn't work?"

A stillness settled over his features. "We've come too far to let one old woman interfere with our plan. If we can't scare her off or persuade her to leave on her own, we'll take whatever measures are necessary."

❦ 14 ❧

Steven wrote the final figure in the column in his ledger and shook his head. His operating costs were eating away what remained of his nest egg with a speed that left his head spinning. He pushed the cloth-bound book away and pinched the bridge of his nose between his thumb and forefinger. If nothing changed, he could hang on a little longer, but just by the skin of his teeth. He felt like someone dangling over a cliff, clinging to the end of a rope and watching it fray before his eyes.

He flipped the cover of the ledger, closing it with a thump. Something had to change, and soon. When he came out west to seek his fortune, he looked on it as a grand adventure. He never expected the weight of responsibility that came along with knowing the livelihood of a dozen men rested squarely on his shoulders.

It looked so promising when I came into this,

Lord. Did I misread your leading and get myself into something you never wanted me to be a part of?

Memories of his father's dire predictions of certain failure rose to haunt him, and he wished he could rid himself of those as easily as he had pushed the ledger aside.

He shoved his chair back and walked to the small window overlooking the mine entrance some fifty feet away. Lavinia Stewart's providential interest in investing in the Redemption had seemed like manna from heaven when she'd first arrived, but she didn't appear to be in any rush to loosen her purse strings and write him a draft.

Steven tried to tamp down the desire to hurry things along in that department, or at least find out where he stood. After all, he only had the promise of her interest. He didn't know the full extent of her financial standing, and he could hardly ask her to sink all her inheritance into his venture.

Maybe touring his mine on Sunday would be just the thing to help them come to some sort of understanding. He sighed and leaned his forehead against the windowpane, still wondering why he'd been foolish enough to acquiesce to her suggestion. A mine was no place for a woman, let alone one well past her youth. He would have to tell his foreman to be sure the workers cleared the debris off the stope when the last shift ended on Saturday. Having her slip on some loose rubble and twist an ankle—or worse, fall and break a limb—was hardly the way to gain the infusion of cash he needed if the mine was going to survive.

Would the tour be enough? Was there anything else he could do that might help move things along? His gaze fell on the ledger, and he felt a knot in the pit of his stomach. Would she want to examine the books, as well? Probably so, since she'd made it plain she wanted to know as much as possible about the mine.

Steven groaned and rubbed his forehead. If Mrs. Stewart had any head for business at all, one look at his current status and remaining assets would be enough to send her packing. He walked back to the desk and opened the ledger again, hoping that by some miracle the figures there would paint a rosier picture than they had when he'd closed it.

They didn't.

If only he could show her last year's figures, before the thefts began, when the income from the ore was increasing his bottom line every week. Those would convince anyone they'd be getting a substantial return on money invested.

He ran his finger along the cloth cover, and his gaze shifted over to the shelf on the opposite wall, where last year's ledger stood tilted against the bookend. A thought stirred within him. *What if . . .*

He crossed the room in three quick strides and pulled the account book down. Returning to his desk, he opened the book and leaned over it, scrutinizing the figures. Yes, they were every bit as promising as he remembered.

What if . . .

If Mrs. Stewart asked to see his figures, why not show her this one instead, letting her see the Redemption's full potential without dwelling on his recent losses? After all, the current figures didn't give a true reflection of the mine's economic possibilities. These robberies couldn't go on forever. Once the thieves were caught and the losses ended, the Redemption would be back in full swing, bringing more than enough income to satisfy them both.

He pictured Lavinia in his mind, seeing her gray hair and faded-rose complexion. She didn't strike him as a person with enough business savvy to demand the most recent accounting. Would she even notice the difference? It wouldn't be misleading her, not really. He'd merely be showing her the true picture of what things would be like as soon as his current problems became a thing of the past. All he would be doing was simplifying matters.

Taking the easy way out? Again?

Steven's train of thought came to a dead stop. He could almost hear his father's disapproving voice echoing through the room, bringing back the memory of the rift that had fractured their relationship. The realization of what he'd been about to do made the bile rise in his throat.

Before that temptation could sway him any longer, he slapped the ledger cover closed and returned the book to its place on the shelf. He wouldn't tamper with the truth. He'd taken that route once before, and look what it had cost him.

When he parted company with his father, he'd vowed to be a man of absolute integrity, and he was going to abide by that, come what may. If his mining business succeeded, it would be because he relied upon the Lord, not on his ability to cover up the truth. Or on Lavinia Stewart's investment.

The door swung open, and Milt Strickland, his foreman, stepped into the room. "You busy?"

"Just finished catching up the books."

Milt raised one eyebrow. "How bad is it?"

"Still hanging on, but just barely."

"Some of the men are wondering if they need to think about moving on. Over to Tombstone, maybe."

"Tell them we're going to meet the payroll. They can count on that. This time, at least."

"That'll take a load off their minds. Things are slowing down a bit because the drills are getting dull. Jake promised he'd have that other lot sharpened by this afternoon. Want me to go pick them up?"

"No, I'll get them. You go let the men know they'll be paid on schedule."

Steven walked the fifty yards to the edge of town and followed Mill Street toward Seventh. As he passed Brady Andrews's house on the corner of Fifth and Mill, he tipped his hat to the slender woman sweeping the front walk.

"Good afternoon, Dora."

Brady's wife set her broom aside and shaded her eyes with one hand, her lips drooping when she recognized him. "Oh, it's you, Steven. I was hoping it might be Brady."

He took in the tightness around her eyes and the corners of her mouth. "Is anything wrong?"

"Everything's wrong." She folded her arms tight against her chest. "I wouldn't say this to just anyone, but you've been a good friend to Brady. With the loss we've taken because of these thefts, it's driving him to the bottle. . . . Even more than usual," she added with a bitter laugh.

The pain in her eyes wrenched at Steven's heart. "I noticed he seemed to be drinking more than before. Is there anything I can do to help?"

Dora Andrews shook her head and blinked rapidly. "It's something we have to work out between the two of us, and I'm afraid of what that's going to mean for our marriage. I've told him we needed to cut our losses and get away from here. Tom Sullivan offered to buy him out, but Brady insists the offer is too low."

A faraway look came into her eyes as she stared out across the cactus-studded hills. "It's breaking my heart to watch him drink himself to death. I can't stay around and watch it happen." She pressed her hand against her lips, and her shoulders began to shake.

Steven shifted uncomfortably. "I wish I knew the answer, Dora. Let me know if there's anything I can do. In the meantime, you know I'll be praying."

"I know, and thank you. You've been a friend to both of us, and I appreciate it." She gave him a watery smile. "If you see him around town, send him home, would you?"

Steven nodded and went on his way, wondering if Brady would take Tom up on his offer. When he reached Seventh Street, he turned left and made his way to the blacksmith's shop at the corner of Grant.

Jake Freeman looked up and grinned when Steven entered the smithy, wrinkling his nose against the sharp smell of coal smoke. "Figured you or Milt would be in today. I got your drill steels ready." He nodded toward a canvas bag in a corner.

"Thanks." Steven picked up the heavy bag by the handles and headed toward the door. "I'll get the others to you in the next day or so." He stepped out of the dimness of the shop and stood for a moment, letting his eyes adjust to the afternoon sunlight.

A girlish laugh trilled from across the street.

Steven blinked his eyes, and a man and woman came into focus. The man stood with his back to Steven, obscuring his view of the fellow's companion, but even from that angle, the light-colored plantation hat he wore tipped at a rakish angle, the natty black frock coat, and the gray, pin-striped trousers proclaimed his occupation as surely as if Steven could see him seated before the green felt of a faro table.

The woman's tinkling laugh sounded again, and Steven shook his head. For the most part, the town's gamblers and their courtesans kept to the saloon district on the east side of Seventh Street. What were they doing out in front of the stationer's shop on the respectable side of town?

As soon as the thought entered his mind, another one followed: *Who are you to look down your nose at them?* He'd lived in the West long enough to know that immorality was common enough in the mining camps, but few women entered that life by choice. More often than not, it was the result of one bad decision leading to another, creating a downward spiral from which there was little chance of escape. He knew well enough how one seemingly insignificant act could set off a chain of events that could change a person's life forever.

Where they stood and talked was none of his business. As he started to turn away, the gambler shifted position, and his companion came into view.

Steven stopped in his tracks as though he'd been caught by a single jack to the forehead. This woman was no denizen of the saloons. The modest neckline and long sleeves of her sapphire blue dress attested to her respectability. A shaft of sun glinted off her coppery ringlets and made her creamy complexion glow like alabaster. What was a radiant creature like that doing talking to a knight of the green cloth?

He heard a sigh at his elbow and turned to see Jake Freeman beside him, a dreamy smile on his rugged face. "She's a real looker, ain't she?"

Steven nodded. "Who is she?"

"Why, she's the niece of your Mrs. Stewart."

Steven whipped his head around to stare at the brawny blacksmith. When had the prospective investor become "his" Mrs. Stewart? He looked back at the couple across the street. So this was the niece she had been expecting.

Jake went on as though unaware of Steven's musing. "She came in and passed the time of day with me while I was finishing up your drills. Sure brightened up the place. I can tell you that." He dug an elbow into Steven's ribs and gave him a wink that set his teeth on edge. "Appears to be just like her aunt—friendly as all get out and interested in everybody."

Steven nodded slowly. "Apparently so." The steels clanked as he shifted the canvas bag to his other hand. He looked at Mrs. Stewart's niece with renewed interest, trying to reconcile this dazzling sight with the woman he'd imagined. He had built up an image in his mind of someone less exuberant, more sedate, drooping from heartache. A plain little daisy, not an exotic orchid.

And he'd expect someone related to Lavinia to exhibit more common sense. Visiting Jake's smithy seemed harmless enough, but what on earth was she doing talking to that gambler? He was hardly the type of person Lavinia Stewart would choose to engage in conversation. Steven shifted his glance farther down the street. She had ventured entirely too close to the saloon district, scarcely a block away. That wouldn't do her reputation any good.

He stepped down off the boardwalk, prepared to rescue her from what must surely be an awkward situation. Halfway across the street he checked himself when another burst of laughter rang out. On closer observation, it seemed she wasn't at all bothered by the man's attentions.

Steven watched the way she chattered away, giving every evidence of enjoying their conversation. Maybe she didn't want to be rescued. He turned on his heel and started back to the Redemption. *Better mind my own business.*

But what about Mrs. Stewart? Would she approve? Steven felt sure she would not. He didn't owe a thing to her young, vivacious niece, but if Lavinia Stewart was willing to trust him with her money, he ought to live up to that same trust when it came to something far more valuable than cash. Her niece was new in town and hadn't had time to learn the lay of the land yet. Coming from what he assumed to be a rather sheltered environment, she might not even be aware of the sordid goings-on that lay east of Seventh Street or the perils of associating with the wrong kind of people.

Steven pivoted and studied the couple. If he saw someone headed toward a cliff, unaware of the sheer drop-off that lay ahead, could he in good conscience walk on by without warning them of their danger? Hardly. This young woman might not know she needed rescuing, but he did.

He strode toward them, wondering how he could accomplish his task without appearing even more of a boor than the gambler. To all indications, the other man's attentions seemed to be welcomed, but he was about to push his way into the conversation uninvited.

He waited to speak until he was only a few steps away from the pair. "Good afternoon."

Caught in midsentence, the redhead started when he spoke and whirled to face him. When their eyes met, she gasped.

"Aren't you Mrs. Stewart's niece?"

The object of his query stared at him like a hunted doe. "Why, yes. Yes, I am." She stretched out her hand, then pulled it back. "But I don't believe I've had the pleasure of making your acquaintance."

The gambler shifted position, edging slightly between Steven and the young woman, assessing Steven with a measured gaze. "I don't believe we've met, either."

Steven took a wide stance and returned the stare. He'd hoped that bringing Mrs. Stewart's name in at the beginning would help take the edge off what could turn out to be a tense situation. He held his hand out to the dandy. "Steven Pierce. I own the Redemption Mine south of town." He hoped Mrs. Stewart had talked to her niece about her interest in becoming his business partner. Maybe hearing his name or the mention of his mine would make a connection in the young woman's mind.

The dandy eyed Steven's hand for a long moment before clasping it in his own. "Quincy Taylor. I'm newly arrived in your fair town." His easy smile didn't quite reach his eyes.

The young lady held her hand out again with a smile that made Steven's heart do flip-flops. "I'm Jessie Monroe. It's a pleasure to meet you, Mr. Pierce. My aunt speaks highly of you."

Encouraged, Steven wrapped his fingers around hers and smiled. "I'm glad to hear that. I hold your aunt in high regard, as well. As a matter of fact, I was thinking about paying her a visit this afternoon." He saw no point in mentioning that the idea had just popped into his head. "If you're heading that way now, I'd be happy to escort you."

"Oh." Jessie's lips parted, and a tinge of pink colored her cheeks. "But I . . ."

Her gaze darted from him to Taylor and back again, obviously reluctant to end her conversation with the card player. "Well, I suppose . . . If you'll excuse me, Mr. Taylor?"

The gambler swept off his hat and bowed. "It has been my pleasure, fair lady. Until we meet again." Without a word to Steven, he turned and walked back toward the tinny piano sounds that wafted across Seventh Street.

"I don't mean to rush you," Steven said as they set off in the opposite direction on Grant. "If you have something else to do, I'd be happy to walk with you while you go about your business."

Jessie gave her head a little shake that set her ringlets dancing. "No, thank you. I believe I've accomplished all I'm going to be able to today."

His mouth went dry when she smiled up at him. From a distance, she was dazzling. Close at hand, he found her simply breathtaking.

"What is it?" she asked, when he continued to stare without saying a word.

"Your eyes." He blurted the words out without thinking. Seeing her startled expression, he explained, "They're a most unusual color. My grandmother had an aquamarine ring that same shade of blue." He paused a moment and added, "Come to think of it, your aunt's eyes are the exact same shade."

Jessie dropped her gaze and looked away. "Yes, I suppose they are. It's a . . . family trait."

They walked another block before he spoke again. "I hope I didn't offend you by interrupting your conversation that way."

Jessie glanced up and gave him a look that made his breath catch in his throat. "Not at all. I had just encountered Mr. Taylor on the street, and we were passing the time of day. I'm sure I'll be able to talk to him again another time."

Steven licked his lips, searching for the right words. "Are you aware of Mr. Taylor's occupation?"

She tilted her head to one side, and a pucker formed between her brows.

"He's a professional gambler. He spends his days—and nights—at the gaming tables. In the saloons." He waited for a shocked reaction that didn't come. If possible, her eyes sparkled even more.

"I know. Isn't it exciting? A real, live gambler! I feel like I truly am experiencing the Wild West."

Steven wanted to warn her that a good many aspects of the Wild West weren't appropriate experiences for a proper young lady. Instead he found himself struck dumb by the impact of her aquamarine gaze.

He swallowed back the intended admonition. He would caution her—or maybe her aunt—another time.

The family resemblance ran to more than eye color, he realized. Jessie was more slender and stood an inch or two taller than Mrs. Stewart, but there were definite similarities in their facial features. All in all, Jessie was a brighter, more vibrant version of her aunt. The thought made him smile. If Lavinia Stewart reminded him of a faded rose, Jessie was that same rose in full, glorious bloom.

He walked on without speaking, content to listen to the lilt of her voice as she described the contrast between Pickford and Chicago. Before he knew it, they had reached the little house at the corner of Charles and Second.

The canvas straps pressed into his fingers, reminding him of his earlier errand. He'd told Jessie he intended to visit her aunt. How short could he make his visit without appearing rude? Milt would have been expecting him and the sharpened drill steels back at the mine long before now.

"I hope I won't be imposing, dropping in like this unannounced."

The sparkle faded from Jessie's eyes, and she averted her glance. Instead of opening the door when they stepped up onto the front porch, she fidgeted, twisting the drawstring of her reticule around her fingers. "Actually, this may not be a good time. . . . Aunt Lavinia was feeling a little tired before I left, and I'm afraid she may be resting."

She pressed her lips together and looked up at him. "Perhaps you could come back another time? I'll let her know so she can be ready for your visit."

Steven felt torn between relief at being able to get back to work without further delay and a sense of loss at having to tear himself away from the captivating Jessie Monroe. "That's fine," he said. "I can talk to her again on Sunday."

Inspiration struck. "Your aunt is coming to tour my mine after church. Would you like to join us?"

Jessie looked confused for a moment, but then she turned her smile on him full force. "What a kind offer, Mr. Pierce. I'll have to see what I can do."

He touched his finger to the brim of his hat and walked away, his mind in a turmoil. He had done his moral duty by freeing her from the clutches of the gambler, but in the process he feared he might have allowed his heart to be ensnared by the beguiling young redhead.

15

"Watch your head. That outcropping over the adit is lower than it looks."

Ellie looked around for the adit—whatever that was—and grazed her head against a large rock that hung out over the sloping walkway leading into the Redemption Mine. She let out a muffled yelp and clapped her right palm against her temple.

Steven sprang to her side. "Are you all right, Mrs. Stewart?"

"I'm fine, thank you. I scarcely felt it." She waved him aside and glanced up at the offending overhang. "Is that what you meant by an adit?"

"Actually, the adit is what you call the entrance." His chagrin was obvious. "I said it without thinking. I should never have expected you to understand mining terminology. I'm so sorry."

"Think nothing of it. Let's press on." Ellie surreptitiously checked her right glove, relieved when she didn't see any blood. She put on a bright smile, trying to appear unfazed by her collision with the unyielding rock. "Why don't you start by teaching me more mining terms? If I'm to have a part in this operation, I ought to learn the jargon."

"That's a good idea. Let's start right where we are. You've already learned about the adit." He offered her a rueful grin as he indicated a pathway leading inside the mine. "This walkway we'll be following is known as a drift. The roof is called the back, the side of the wall is the rib, and the ground is known as the sill."

Ellie nodded, trying to remember every word. While Steven waxed eloquent about the two-foot-long steel spikes he called drill steels that the mining crews hammered into the wall—the rib, she reminded herself—to hold dynamite sticks prior to blasting, she let her gaze wander around the walls of rock, finally coming to rest on the dark cavern that yawned before them. Would she discover anything of value inside?

Steven's brief lecture came to an end, and he looked at her expectantly. "If you're ready to go in?" At Ellie's nod, he took up a lantern hanging from a hook just inside the entrance and lit it with a match from his vest pocket. With a gentlemanly bow, he led her inside.

Ellie trailed behind, pleased to find the descending path wasn't as steep or rocky as she had feared. Nor was the temperature what she'd expected. Instead of a dank clamminess, the air felt dry and surprisingly warm compared to the temperature outside. Somewhat reassured, she stepped out with more confidence, following him along the drift.

"I met your niece the other day."

Ellie caught her breath at the sudden change of topic. "Yes, she told me." Seeing that his attention was focused in front of him, she didn't try to hide the smile that curved her lips at the memory of the way he had looked at Jessie Monroe.

He cleared his throat. "If it isn't too personal a question, may I ask why she didn't accompany us to church this morning?"

Ellie's smile fled as she scrambled for some explanation that would satisfy. The last thing she wanted to do was create a rift between Steven and her mythical niece. "She said she woke with a headache, but I was concerned about her absence myself. I'm sure attending the service would have done her more good than lying in bed, brooding."

Her visits to church had blessed her more than she'd ever expected, showing her a compassionate side to the God she'd thought had abandoned her all those years ago during the dark days of her childhood.

But they were speaking about Jessie, she reminded herself. "I'll see what I can do to encourage her to attend services next Sunday."

Steven tossed a grin over his shoulder. "I'm glad to hear that. I'll look forward to seeing her there."

Ellie returned the smile, hoping her trepidation didn't show. Lavinia and Jessie onstage at the same time? Even Magdalena couldn't manage a feat like that.

Before long, the drift opened up into a roomy open area. Steven stopped in the middle of the cavelike room and held the lantern high to illuminate a sizeable expanse. "This space held a particularly rich vein of ore. As you can see, we've removed most of it. The room it created is called a stope."

The rocky chamber stretched back into the shadows, and Ellie shivered. She had envisioned a tight, cramped working environment, but this place was big . . . almost too big, making her feel dwarfed in comparison. The lantern flickered, and she caught her breath, wondering what they would do if it went out.

On further examination, she noticed the piles of rock that lay in various places around the stope. She started over to examine them. "Is this the ore you get the silver from?"

"Careful." Before she could take another step, Steven caught her by the arm. "You don't want to get too close to that shaft."

Ellie gasped when the lantern threw its light on an inky hole only a couple of yards from her feet. She shrank closer to Steven, vowing it would be the last time she ventured from his side until they reached daylight again.

"That's the base rock. Those black streaks you see are lower quality ore, not worth taking out with the richer silver."

Ellie pivoted, careful not to move from her

position beside Steven. "How do you get it up to the surface?"

"We send it down, not up." Steven laughed at her bewilderment and went on to explain how they dropped the ore down into ore carts at a lower level, where the silver was then taken to the main shaft and dumped into an ore bucket before being hoisted to the surface.

Ellie became so intrigued she almost forgot she was playing a role. "What happens once you get it out?"

"The ore wagons take it to the stamp mill just outside town on the banks of the San Pedro, where the ore is crushed so the silver can be melted down and made into bars before being shipped out."

"Shipped where?"

"We send them to the United States Mint in New Orleans, where they're made into silver dollars." Steven gave a doleful laugh. "When they actually get where they're supposed to go, that is. Our bars only weigh about 80 pounds each. The Tombstone mills cast their silver into 180-pound ingots, which makes it much harder for thieves to carry it off."

"What a clever idea."

"I wish we'd thought of it. It would take considerable time to do the retooling necessary to form the larger ingots, but we may have to go that route ourselves . . . if we can do it before it's too late."

The last words came out as the barest whisper before they floated off into the darkness. Ellie wondered if Steven realized he had spoken them aloud. She looked at him more closely, noticing the tightness around his eyes and the corners of his mouth.

"At the meeting last Sunday, Mr. Sullivan mentioned something about stockpiling your silver until the thieves are captured. Where are you keeping it?"

Steven looked away, then met her eyes again. "At this point, even my workers don't know that. My foreman is the only one besides myself who has that information."

"Quite right." Ellie nodded approval. "That information shouldn't be shared." She took a step to one side, and a fist-sized piece of loose rock rolled under her foot. Her arms flailed wildly, but before she could fall, Steven caught her with one strong arm, wrapping it around her shoulders.

Oh my. Ellie took her time catching her breath, leaning against him longer than strictly necessary.

"Will you be all right if I take my arm away?"

She nodded, calling herself a liar as she did so. The moment his arm left her shoulders, she felt an ache of emptiness.

"Over here is one of the veins we've been working." Steven led her to a wall of fractured rock pockmarked by inch-wide holes. "So far this one is holding strong, so we'll keep on following it until it plays out."

Ellie filed the information away and stared around in the dim light, feeling her chest tighten at the thought of spending long days underground. "How can your men work in such gloomy conditions?"

"They're issued three candles apiece at the beginning of each shift. Quite often, though, the men will have only two or three candles burning in the cavern at any given time." He smiled at her look of disbelief. "I know it seems strange, but it doesn't take long for them to become comfortable working in the dark."

Ellie looked at the blank wall before them. "It appears we've reached the end of our tour." She tried not to let her relief show at the thought of being out from under the earth's oppressive weight.

"I want to show you one more thing." A note of excitement rang in Steven's voice. He led her back the way they had come.

Ellie followed him, comforting herself with the thought that they were at least heading in the right direction, back toward sunlight and the open air.

"I've saved the best for last." Steven guided her to the far side of the stope, which hadn't been visible before. A tunnel opened off of the main room, its mouth braced by sturdy beams.

"We hit this vein a couple of weeks ago, and it's the richest one we've found so far. If we can keep the mine going, there's every reason to expect a huge return for everyone involved."

The meaningful look he gave her made Ellie want to melt right into a puddle at his feet. Maybe she should find another rock to slip on.

"Here, let me show you the new drift and what we've done so far."

With an effort, Ellie pulled her focus back to the job at hand and away from the distractions of Steven Pierce's exhilarating presence. What would Lavinia ask? Probably something about money matters.

Hating herself for holding out false hope, she followed him into the new tunnel. "How much will it take to keep things—"

Without any planning on her part, her foot caught on something, and she started to go down. As quickly as before, Steven gripped her elbow and held her upright. Before she could thank him, a loud crack shattered the stillness of the mine, followed by a grating sound that sent a shock of terror through her.

"Look out!" Steven wrapped his arm around her shoulders and yanked her inside the drift, pulling her tight against his chest.

A rolling crash echoed through the mine. An instant later, the flame in the lantern guttered wildly. Ellie opened her mouth to scream, but

Steven was holding her so tight she could barely breathe, let alone make a sound.

She stood pressed against him in the dimness, choking on the dust that filled the air while her heart pounded like a trip hammer. "Was it a cave-in?"

"Keep your voice down," he whispered. "We don't want to create any vibration that might set off another slide."

"What happened?"

"Give me a few minutes for the dust to settle, and I'll find out. In the meantime, try not to move around."

Ellie had no quarrel with that idea. The steady beat of Steven's heart against her cheek was the only thing keeping her from total panic.

She tipped her head back and saw him gazing down at her, his lips tantalizingly close. A soft sigh escaped her as she tilted her chin up and let her eyelids drift closed.

"Are you all right, Mrs. Stewart?"

Ellie's eyes flew open, and her heart skipped a beat when she saw the alarm etched on Steven's face.

"I'm . . . fine," she managed.

"You're sure?" His look of concern deepened. "For a moment, I thought you were about to faint."

Ellie squeezed her eyes shut again, imagining the scene from Steven's point of view—the older woman nestled against him, her head dropping back, her eyelids closing, her lips parting . . . Mortification gripped her in a chokehold. No wonder he'd thought she'd been suffering from the vapors.

And thank heaven for that! Far less humiliating to be seen as a delicate old woman ready to swoon from the shock of their near catastrophe than to have him realize she'd been on the point of pressing her lips against his. What would he have thought of Lavinia Stewart then? She clenched her teeth to hold back a moan.

She wanted to cry out an objection when she felt him take his arms from around her and move back a step. Opening her eyes again, she dared to look up into Steven's face, shadowed by the settling dust.

"Will you be all right if I leave you for a moment?"

No! "Yes, if you don't go too far."

"I'll only be a step or two away." He moved over to the entrance, and Ellie watched him trace an arc in the air with the light, outlining the doorway. "One of the beams came down," he said in a grim voice.

"Then it wasn't a cave-in?"

"No, it brought a good bit of debris along with it when it fell, but everything is fine. We'll have to climb over a few rocks, but at least it didn't block the exit." Steven reached for her hand and helped her step over the debris; then they made their way out of the mine in silence.

Soon a glimmer of sunlight came into view, and a moment later she stood outdoors again, gulping in great lungfuls of the blessed fresh air.

Steven eyed her with concern. "Are you sure you're all right?"

"Yes." *Except for nearly making an utter fool of myself.* Ellie swallowed to clear the quaver from her voice and added, "I'm a bit shaken. That's all."

He nodded, not looking totally convinced.

She glanced back at the mine entrance and felt a shudder sweep over her. "Are accidents like that a common occurrence?"

"No, they aren't." Steven followed her gaze, his mouth set in a grim line. "I'll have my foreman find out which one of the men is responsible for putting that beam in place. He'll have to answer for his shoddy workmanship."

He turned back to Ellie, hesitation in his eyes. "I had planned to show you my office and go over the books with you, but perhaps this isn't the best time."

Ellie wavered. A good detective would welcome the opportunity to learn as many facts as possible. At the moment, though, she felt less like a detective and more like a frightened child. "I'm afraid you're right. If you don't mind seeing me home, I think I'd better lie down."

• • •

The moment she stepped into the house, Ellie knew something was wrong. She froze just inside the front door, trying to determine what had set her senses on alerts. The curtains were drawn, and the living room furniture looked just as she'd left it. From what she could see from her position by the door, the kitchen appeared to be undisturbed, as well.

She shifted her gaze to the drop-front desk near the second bedroom, and her heart leaped into her throat. The drawers had been closed when she went out—she was sure of it. Now two of them were open slightly. Edging closer, she saw the corners of several papers poking out of the drawer where she kept her notes.

Someone had been in the house. Someone had looked through her notes.

A floorboard creaked in the second bedroom, Ellie clapped one gloved hand over her mouth to stifle a scream. Whoever had rifled through her desk was still there.

Casting a wild glance around the room, Ellie snatched up a parasol propped beside the front door. Holding it over her shoulder like a base-ball bat, she nudged the door open with her toe and prepared to confront the intruder.

A figure was crouched before the window, tugging at the latch. This time Ellie couldn't hold back the scream that rose to her lips. The prowler whirled to face her.

"Billy Taylor!"

The boy backed away until he came up against the wall, eyeing her improvised club.

Seeing the flicker of fear in his eyes, Ellie lowered the weapon and planted her hands on her hips. "What on earth do you think you're doing in my house?"

"Nothin'." His dejected tone spoke of sorrow at being caught rather than remorse for house-breaking.

Ellie's hands tightened on the parasol, and then she set it against the wall, putting temptation out of reach. She folded her arms. "Nothing, indeed. This is far worse than snooping under my window. How did you get in here, anyway? The door was locked."

A triumphant smile lit his face. "The back window wasn't. It doesn't open up very wide, but it was enough to let me slip through."

Ellie made a mental note to make sure she locked all the windows from this point on. "And once you were inside, then what? Did you come to steal from me, or just go through my things? I have a good mind to tell your mother. Or maybe Marshal Bascomb. I bet he could scare some sense into you."

"Go ahead," he retorted. "And I'll tell him what I know about you."

His words brought Ellie up short. "And what would that be?"

"There's really only one of you."

Ellie's knees sagged, and she pressed one hand against her chest. "What are you talking about?"

From his cheeky grin, she suspected her own show of bravado wasn't nearly as effective as Billy's had been. She made an effort to stiffen her trembling knees and tried to bluster her way out. "What makes you say a foolish thing like that?"

"It ain't foolish. Nobody's using this bedroom, for one thing."

"Two people can share a bedroom, you know."

"Yeah, but there's only one hairbrush in the other. And only one set of dishes drying by the sink. Besides, I found her head."

Ellie gasped, then realized he must be referring to the wig stand, now holding Jessie's red curls.

Billy hooked his thumbs in the top of his trousers. "I know what you're up to."

Ellie's mouth went dry. "What do you mean?"

He tilted his head toward the doorway and the desk beyond. "All that stuff you've written down. You're awfully interested in the silver that's gone missing." His eyes took on a knowing light. "You're some kind of detective, aren't you?"

Ellie gave up any pretense of not understanding. "And what if I am?"

"I knew it! Wait'll I tell the other fellas."

"No, you can't do that!" Horror seized Ellie, but then inspiration struck. Billy had aspirations of being a spy. Maybe she could work that interest to her advantage. "How would you like to be a junior detective, Billy?"

The boy's face crinkled. "A what?"

"A junior *Pinkerton* detective. You've already shown remarkable talent for gathering information." She held her breath while she awaited his response.

Billy tilted his head. "What would I have to do?"

"Well . . ." Ellie took a deep breath and improvised as she went along. "You could be my helper and carry out assignments to assist me in this investigation. But you couldn't tell anybody else what you were up to. That's very important. Nobody could know except you and me."

He narrowed his eyes. "How do I know this is the real thing?"

"Wait here." Ellie hurried to her bedroom and rummaged through the wicker hamper. Pulling out a small tray of costume jewelry, she selected a medallion-shaped brooch and carried it back to where Billy was waiting.

"Here's your badge."

His eyes widened in a most satisfactory manner. "For keeps? Can I wear it all the time?"

Ellie nodded. "But you'll have to wear it like this." She bent over and pinned it to the inside of his shirt. "There, now it's official. But to be a good detective, you have to be able to keep a secret. This is just between you and me, understand?"

Billy nodded and puffed out his skinny chest. "So what am I supposed to do first?"

Ellie scrambled for an answer. "Keep your eyes open for any suspicious activity. If you see something I should know about, report to me immediately."

His face glowed. "You can count on me." He threw his shoulders back and stood straighter as he hurried from the house . . . through the front door this time.

A brief nap and a bracing cup of tea went a long way toward restoring her equanimity. Who would have thought that a day that had begun with the intention to educate herself about mining would turn out to bring such peril? A light shudder rippled across her shoulders as her memory replayed the panic that had swept through her when that heavy beam came crashing down. But it was almost worth it to experience the safety she'd felt in the circle of Steven's arms.

Ellie tightened the belt on her wrapper and walked to the desk, where she kept her notes. She had no desire to do any more investigating that evening. Between the incident in the mine and discovering Billy Taylor rifling through her house, she'd already had plenty of adventure for one day. Any work she did on the case that night would be of a more cerebral nature.

Outdoors she could hear the cries of Billy and

his cronies as they whooped and hollered along the road. She checked to make sure her front drapes were pulled tight. The last thing she needed was for any more curious children to spy a brown-haired stranger in Mrs. Stewart's house.

Pulling the papers, pen, and ink from the drawer, she spread them out on the table. She couldn't possibly continue investigating every single person in town. She would have to narrow the field of possibilities.

Ellie scanned the list, looking for names she could consider above suspicion. But how could she possibly determine that?

With a groan, she folded her arms on the table and rested her forehead on them. What was she going to do? Bringing Jessie into the investigation had broadened the scope of her inquiries by allowing her to converse with a wider range of people, but it hadn't done a thing toward helping her focus her efforts. And it hadn't brought Norma's expertise into play. Yes, she had found the note that might be a correspondence between the thieves, but she hadn't seen the man she saw reading it since. Ellie's stomach knotted. If she didn't make significant progress—and soon—how long would the Pinkertons be satisfied with cryptic telegrams?

And how long would it be before she received a wire letting her know that her services were no longer needed?

16

"Got a minute?"

Steven looked up from his desk to see Milt Strickland leaning in the doorway. "Sure. What's on your mind?"

"I want to show you something."

Now what? Mystified, Steven followed his foreman to the mine entrance, hoping he wasn't about to receive more bad news. The abrupt ending to Lavinia Stewart's mine tour the day before left him with little optimism about his financial prospects. Plucky and adventuresome Mrs. Stewart might be, but no woman in her right mind would choose to invest in a venture she probably now viewed as a deathtrap.

He waited while Milt lit a lantern, then led the way down into the mine. "Is everything going all right with that new vein?"

"It's going fine. It didn't take long to clear away the debris and reset the beam. But I've got something else on my mind." They turned toward the new shaft, but instead of entering it, Milt stopped and knelt at the right side of the entry-way. "Take a look at this."

Steven dropped to one knee beside him and watched as Milt moved a fist-sized rock to one side and pointed. The flickering lamplight showed it clearly enough—a slender spike driven into the wooden upright. One end of a thin wire about eighteen inches long was wrapped around the metal shaft.

Steven sat back on his heels. "What on earth?"

Milt pushed himself to his feet and stepped across to the other side of the entryway. "Now look down there."

Steven studied the impassive face of his foreman and did as he was told. Milt obviously intended for him to figure something out for himself. The round end of an eyebolt protruded from the left upright at the same level as the spike on the right.

He stood and rubbed the back of his neck. "Call me thick-headed, but I still don't see what you're getting at."

Milt reached behind a pile of rubble and scooped up a dark object. He held it out to Steven. "That's the wedge that was holding this end of the brace in place."

Steven reached out to take the wedge and noticed several feet of the same thin wire trailing away from the chunk of wood.

Milt traced a line from the top of the doorway down to the eyebolt. "It appears to me this wire was fastened to the wedge and run down here through the bolt, then across to the spike on the other side."

Steven looked from the wedge in his hand to the top of the opening, then down to the eyebolt at his feet and across to the spike, trying to come up with some other explanation than the one that seemed all too obvious. He turned back to face Milt. "You mean—"

"Yeah. It was no accident."

Steven braced one hand against the wall and hefted the wedge in the other hand. Someone meant to bring that beam down. All it would take was a boot catching the wire at the entrance to the tunnel. Like a flash, he remembered Mrs. Stewart stumbling as they entered the shaft, and anger roiled up through him. *Deathtrap* might not be too strong a word to describe the ambush some evil mind had devised. "But who would want to sabotage the Redemption?"

Milt shook his head and glanced toward the mine entrance. "Best we talk about it outside. You don't want one of the men to overhear this and wind up losing your whole crew."

Back in his office, Steven closed the door and stared at Milt. "Okay, I'm asking again: Who would want to sabotage the Redemption?"

Milt shrugged. "Hard to tell. I can't see any reason for it myself, but evidently someone could. Everything was fine in there when we cleared out Saturday night. You were in there with Mrs. Stewart yesterday afternoon, so it had to be set up late Saturday or early Sunday."

Steven groaned. Of all the days, they had to pick the one his would-be investor chose for her tour. He leaned back against one corner of the desk. "It doesn't make sense. Unless it hit a person directly, that beam wouldn't finish anyone off. And the trap they set wasn't big enough to cause a cave-in."

Milt pursed his lips. "Maybe what we ought to be lookin' at is the *why*. Once we get that figured out, we might have a better chance at working out the *who*."

Steven nodded. He knew that question would be gnawing at him day and night until he found an answer.

"We can't wait any longer. We have to do something now!" Steven's palm smacked the polished surface of Tom Sullivan's desk.

Tom pushed his chair back and stared as if having misgivings about Steven's sanity.

Steven couldn't blame him. Bursting into a man's office with wild-eyed demands to take action wasn't the best way to convince anyone to take him seriously. He smoothed his hair back with both hands and waited until his breathing steadied.

Tom rose and circled the desk. "I thought we agreed the Pinkertons were our best option."

Steven caught himself before he whacked the desk again. "Don't you understand? I just finished telling you what happened at the Redemption on

Sunday afternoon. They're not just going after our silver anymore—it's getting personal. What are they going to do, try to pick us off one by one and get the mines for themselves as well as the silver they've already stolen? To make matters worse, Mrs. Stewart was there with me. She could have been killed."

Tom's silvery eyebrows rose toward his hairline. "Your investor? What were you thinking, taking a woman her age underground?"

"You can't call me a worse fool than I've already called myself. I should never have agreed to do it. The point is, nobody is safe while this group is in operation. Think about it, Tom. You could be next."

Tom's head drew back, and his chest heaved. "All right, you've convinced me. What do you think we should do?"

"I've already questioned Brent Howard and Amos Crawford. Both of them swear they never let anything slip about our plans to ship the silver."

Tom studied him closely. "And you believe them?"

"At this point, it's hard to know who to believe."

Tom nodded. "It's sad, but that's probably a wise attitude to take. Who do you plan to question next?"

"I thought I'd go into the mercantile and the saloons and try to get people talking, see if anyone has been spending more money than they should."

Tom reached for his hat. "Sounds like a good plan. I'll go with you."

Thirty minutes later, they left the mercantile with no more information than they had when they entered.

"Do you have time to make the rounds of the saloons with me?" Steven asked. Getting a nod from his companion, he started east on Grant Street.

"What about Bascomb?" Tom asked as they strode along. "Do you think he might be on the take?"

Steven slowed, wrinkling his nose against the sharp smell of coal smoke emanating from the smithy across the road. Even though he disliked Bascomb on principle, especially after witnessing the attention he paid Jessie, he didn't want to cast suspicion on anyone without solid evidence.

"I'm not sure—" he began.

A familiar laugh made him jerk his head to the right in time to see Jessie step out of the smithy, followed by Jake Freeman. The dark-haired blacksmith said something, but they were too far away to hear what he said. Jessie let out another tinkling laugh and waggled her fingers in farewell as she sashayed west along the opposite side of the street. Jake followed her every movement with an utterly smitten expression on his face.

"You were saying . . . ?" Tom prompted.

"What?"

Tom followed his gaze and chuckled. "She's quite a looker, isn't she? Ah, youth."

"That was a complete waste," Tom grumbled after they'd visited every saloon Pickford had to offer. "If we don't figure something out soon, I may have to pack it in and start over again at that new silver strike in New Mexico."

Steven let out a huff of frustration. "I don't know which way to turn next. I guess the best we can do is keep our guard up at all times."

Tom grunted assent, then glanced across the street with an intensity that directed Steven's attention toward the Cosmopolitan Bar, where Alfred Clay and Gilbert Owens were entering through the swinging doors.

"What's the matter?"

Tom yanked his gaze away. "Nothing, I suppose. It just seems like an odd time of day to see the two of them going into a saloon."

One corner of Steven's mouth quirked up. "If they'd been following us this morning, they could say the same thing. Maybe they're trying to find some answers, too."

"Maybe." Tom's brow furrowed. "On the other hand . . ."

Steven looked at him questioningly.

"Alfred and Gilbert were the ones who resisted my suggestion that we stockpile our silver together."

Steven stopped dead in the middle of the boardwalk. "What are you saying?"

"It probably doesn't mean anything. But it makes me wonder why they don't want any of us knowing how much silver they have." Tom's expression grew somber. "I'm afraid you're right. At a time like this, we can't afford to trust anyone."

17

"Good morning, Mrs. Stewart." Gertie Johnson's broad face beamed as she waved across the sanctuary.

Ellie ducked her head in greeting and moved along to her usual spot in the third row. From the corner of her eye, she caught sight of Steven entering the building as she settled into her seat. Turning back toward the front of the room, she focused her attention on the cross that hung on the front wall.

"Good morning."

Ellie allowed herself to look startled when Steven appeared at the end of her pew. She gave him a pleasant smile.

His fingers worked around the brim of the hat he held in his hands. "Do you mind if I sit with you?"

"Of course not." Ellie felt her smile broaden until it reached ridiculous proportions, and she tried to compose her features before he noticed. She pressed her fingers to her throat, willing herself to breathe. What was the unsettling effect this man had on her? She still hadn't gotten over the memory of his strong arms wrapped around her—or rather, Lavinia—a week before.

Steven hesitated and looked around the sanctuary. "Is your niece sitting with you? I wouldn't want to take her place."

It cost Ellie an effort, but she managed to keep her smile intact. "She's a little under the weather this morning, so she decided to stay home." She watched a shadow of disappointment flicker across his face and braced herself for a spate of questions.

"I'm sorry to hear she isn't feeling well. Please pass along my wishes for a speedy recovery."

Ellie drew a sigh of relief when he slid onto the bench beside her without further comment. His query about Jessie brought up another issue she hadn't taken into consideration. The more people got to know both Lavinia and Jessie, the more they expected to see the two of them together. That was clear enough now, but she hadn't thought that part through when she'd first hatched her scheme to bring Jessie on board.

Lavinia's age gave her a built-in excuse—an older lady could always call on some physical ailment to keep her under wraps when the need arose—but she would have to come up with equally plausible excuses whenever she had to explain Jessie's absence. Her being conveniently ill whenever her absence needed to be explained away wasn't going to work for much longer.

The music leader stood to begin the service, curtailing the possibility of more awkward questions. Ellie rose with the others and joined in the singing more smoothly than she had on her first visit. The hymns were becoming more familiar with every passing week.

So were the sermons, she realized when Pastor Blaylock directed the congregation to turn to the eleventh chapter of Proverbs and started off on yet another discourse on the importance of living a life of integrity.

Again? Ellie folded her arms and glared at the minister over the top of her spectacles. If the man was going to keep his flock's attention, he simply had to come up with fresh material. During her Bible readings, she had rediscovered a number of stories she remembered from her childhood, stories of slaying giants and miracles in the wilderness. Why didn't he use some of those?

Without moving her head, she stole a peek at the people sitting ahead of her and on the opposite side of the aisle. Every face wore an expression of interest. Ellie narrowed her eyes. What was wrong with these people? Didn't they tire of a steady diet of the same topic over and over again? Did they really need these constant reminders?

Take her own situation, for instance. She had plenty of acquaintance with letting truth rule in her life. Wasn't she in Pickford for that very reason, to bring evildoers to justice by ferreting out the truth? She sniffed her displeasure.

Steven turned to look at her, and Ellie felt the heat rise in her cheeks. Pulling her handkerchief from the pleated cuff at her wrist, she used it to dab at her nose, hoping he would mistake her irritation for hay fever. Tamping down her annoyance, she squared her shoulders and focused her attention on the minister with the same polite interest Lavinia Stewart would give him.

If she existed.

By the time the sermon wound to a close, Ellie felt as if she had been listening to Pastor Blaylock's sermon for an eternity. At long last, he bowed his head for the final prayer, and Ellie joined the rest of the congregation with an amen that might have sounded a bit too heartfelt. She rose with alacrity, prepared to exit the sanctuary as quickly as decency would allow.

Steven, however, had other plans. It seemed every person in the church wanted to speak to him, and he showed no sign of being in any hurry to leave. Finally they made their way to the door, where she shook Pastor Blaylock's hand before stepping out into a crisp, sunny day. Escape at last! She wasn't sure she could continue coming every week if it meant listening to the same topic over and over again.

She joined Steven at the edge of the boardwalk, suddenly feeling nervous at the thought of what she should say if he asked to accompany her home and she was forced to find a way to keep him from entering the house.

"Hellooo!"

Ellie whirled at the piercing call behind her and found herself face-to-face with Althea Baldwin.

"Good morning, good morning!" The older woman fairly crackled with energy. "Someone pointed out your niece to me this week, and I hoped I might be able to speak with her this morning."

"I'm afraid she wasn't able to make it today. She isn't feeling well." This time the words didn't roll off Ellie's tongue as easily as they usually did. She hoped Pastor Blaylock's admonishments about telling the truth weren't going to impair her ability to maintain her roles. "But I'm sure you'll see her again around town." That, at least, was the truth. Or something close to it.

"I expect I will, but I needed to talk to you, as well. You can relay the message to your niece for me." Althea Baldwin's chins wobbled as she bobbed her head enthusiastically. "The ladies of the church are forming a theatrical group. Strictly an amateur undertaking, you understand, but we've made arrangements to hold performances in Pickford Hall, and we hope our efforts will bring a bit of culture to the community."

Ellie nodded, her pulse quickening despite knowing it would be prudent to hide any connection with the theater.

"In order to succeed, we're asking for the cooperation of all the ladies in town. May I count on your participation, and your niece's, as well?" Mrs. Baldwin tilted her head to one side and pursed her lips. "If she is able to act at all, I'd be willing to offer her a starring role. Those stunning looks of hers would surely draw a crowd."

A chance to perform before an audience? How she wished she could. "It sounds like a wonderful idea, but I'm afraid we may not be able to take part." When the other woman's face fell, Ellie hastened to add, "I'll discuss it with my niece and let you know."

"Very well, but I do hope you'll be able to participate. The more the merrier, you know." Without warning, the smile slid from Althea's face, and she stared over Ellie's right shoulder.

Ellie spun round, wondering if some sort of danger was afoot, but the only person she saw looking in their direction was Amos Crawford. When she looked back, Althea had already turned and hurried off to assault another unsuspecting churchgoer. Shaking her head, Ellie turned to find Steven regarding her with a smile.

"You're not too eager for Jessie to have that starring role?"

Ellie ducked her head to hide the tears that stung her eyes. Steven mustn't guess that his words cut closer to home than he could ever dream. It seemed like only yesterday that the opportunity to appear onstage before an audience, no matter how small, would have been the answer to her fondest wish. But now she was already playing the role of a lifetime, one where the slightest blunder could cost her far more than a bad review.

Steven chuckled at Lavinia's embarrassment. It seemed clear she wasn't the type to seek the limelight—one more thing he found endearing about the woman. An idea stirred in his mind. "Would you like to have lunch with me?"

Lavinia raised her face to his, and he could see traces of color on her faded cheeks.

"I'm sorry," he said. "Of course you'll need to go back home and tend to your niece." He wanted to kick himself for blurting the invitation out without thinking about her responsibilities at home.

"No, that isn't it." Spots of pink deepened in her cheeks. "What I mean to say is, Jessie isn't really ill, you see. It's more a matter of not sleeping well. She's subject to that from time to time. When I went in to see her this morning, she told me she'd barely closed her eyes all night. More than anything, she wanted to be left alone. She said she might sleep until well into the afternoon."

"I see." Steven wondered if this sleeplessness was a common occurrence or if it was a sign of Jessie's distress over her broken romance.

Lavinia tilted her head back and looked straight into his eyes with the air of one who had just made a decision. "Actually, I'm afraid I've misled you a bit. There's something I'd like to discuss, and I'd be pleased to do that over lunch, if your invitation is still open."

A low murmur of conversation punctuated by the soft clink of silverware filled the dining area of the Beck House. Steven placed their orders, wondering what Mrs. Stewart wanted to talk about. Had she decided not to invest in the Redemption after all? He tried to hold back his curiosity while he watched his companion take her time stirring cream into her coffee and slicing her roast beef into bite-sized bits.

Finally she laid her knife and fork across the edge of her plate and laced her gloved fingers together. Her gaze flickered to the side for a moment before she met his eyes. "I'm afraid I've made a grave error in regard to Jessie."

Steven drew back slightly. He had braced himself for the possibility of seeing his hope of financial support evaporate, but he never expected her to confide in him about a family matter. He took a long sip of iced tea, studying her while he tried to cover his confusion. Her chin was set in a determined line, and her hands were clenched so tightly together he could see the shape of each knuckle through the fabric of her gloves.

Compassion won out over confusion. The poor woman had no family in Pickford other than Jessie. If she trusted him as one she could turn to in her dilemma, he would help her in any way he could. He rested his arms on the table and leaned forward, giving her an encouraging smile. "Go on."

She drew in a deep breath before she spoke. "When you asked me why she didn't accompany me to church, I told you she stayed home because she didn't feel well, wasn't sleeping well . . ."

Steven drew his brows together, wondering what she could be leading up to.

She watched him carefully as she spoke. "That isn't exactly the case. You see, Jessie and I have had a bit of an . . . altercation."

"Oh?" He pursed his lips, trying to decide how far he should delve into a family matter. "Just a minor disagreement, I hope?"

Lavinia's lower lip trembled. "It's more serious than that, I fear. I learned that Jessie has been making forays into an area of town I simply can't approve of. She's been visiting some of the establishments east of Seventh Street."

Steven sucked in a quick breath. "She hasn't just been talking about it? She's actually been going there?"

Lavinia nodded, her face lined with sorrow. "I've warned her that such actions aren't good for a young lady's reputation—"

"Not to mention her safety," Steven put in, his temper rising. "Forgive me for interrupting, but I've warned her about that part of town myself. I can understand why she might not listen to someone who's little more than a stranger, but to disregard the counsel of her own aunt . . ."

"I quite agree." Lavinia raised her head, and he could see the tense lines etched around her eyes and lips, a testament to the concern she harbored for her wayward niece. "But Jessie doesn't see it that way. She's determined to make the most of her 'Wild West adventure,' as she terms it, and she was quite upset by my admonition. So much so that she refuses to accompany me anywhere."

Steven stared at her. "I had no idea."

"And that is why she wasn't in church. Jessie doesn't want to be seen with me."

Steven picked up his fork and stabbed at a bit of steak. He simply couldn't make head nor tail of Miss Jessie Monroe. More than once, he'd seen her flitting around town like a bright butterfly, striking up conversations with everyone she met. Hardly the behavior of someone heartsick over a broken romance. Just the other day, he'd seen her walking arm in arm with Marshal Bascomb, throwing her head back and laughing as though he'd made the wittiest comment she'd heard all year.

Not possible, since he knew for a fact Bascomb didn't have enough wits to come in out of the rain.

The day he met her, she'd been talking to that gambler in a manner that was altogether too familiar, to Steven's way of thinking. But when he escorted her back to the house she shared with her aunt, she'd seemed different. Softer, somehow. While she hadn't accepted his caution about consorting with the gambler and his ilk, he couldn't imagine her acting in the defiant manner Lavinia described. She almost seemed like two different people.

So which one was the real Jessie?

Lavinia cleared her throat gently, pulling him away from his baffled musings. "I'm afraid I've ruined your meal, Mr. Pierce. Let's talk about something else—the problems you're facing, for instance. Who do you think is behind the silver thefts?"

"Huh?" The abrupt change of topic brought him back to the moment with a jolt. He blinked hard, trying to regroup his thoughts.

"I honestly don't know. I've racked my brain

trying to figure it out, but I haven't gotten anywhere." He hated to make that admission, hoping it wouldn't diminish him in her eyes and jeopardize their future partnership.

"What about the other mine owners we met with? Do they have any ideas?"

Steven shook his head. "There are plenty of ideas floating around, but none that I think have merit."

"Why don't you tell me about the people they suspect? Sometimes talking a situation through helps me think more clearly. It might help you, too." Her eyes lost their sadness and took on a sparkle of interest. "Maybe we can figure this out together."

"I'd like to think it was that simple. If it were, though, we would have collared the culprits by now." Steven lowered his voice. "To tell you the truth, I placed a lot of hope in getting help from the Pinkertons."

Lavinia looked down at the piece of biscuit she was crumbling between her fingers. "You still haven't heard from them?"

He pushed a bit of potato around his plate with his fork. "I can understand them wanting to find the best agent to deal with this, but I have to admit I'm not as optimistic as I was before. We sent them a deposit some time ago, so you'd think someone would have shown up by now."

"I'm sure they're working on it. Don't give up."

"I won't." He managed a crooked smile. "Not yet, anyway." Pulling his watch from his pocket, he checked the time and called the waitress over to settle their bill. "I hate to hurry off like this, but I need to check on one of my men. He's been laid up for several days, and I want to make sure his family has everything they need."

A shadow of disappointment dimmed the light in Lavinia's eyes. "There's no need to apologize. It's kind of you to show such care for your men. Don't bother walking me home. It's a lovely afternoon, and I'll be fine on my own."

"No, I'll be glad to see you home first."

Steven helped her out of her chair and led her outside, his thoughts torn between pondering his own dilemma and concern about the rift between Lavinia and her niece. Their falling-out obviously distressed the older woman, and he respected her determination to take a firm stance in spite of Jessie's obstinate attitude. Excursions into the seamy side of town held perils a well-brought-up young lady couldn't possibly imagine. Was there any way he could intercede to bring about an understanding between the two?

He pondered the captivating mystery that was Jessie Monroe while they walked up Fifth and turned on Grant. A block later, a young lad came barreling out of the telegrapher's office and ran straight into Lavinia.

Steven caught her and set her upright, then

snagged the youngster by the shirt collar. "Hold on there. Where do you think you're going in such a hurry?"

The boy squirmed under Steven's grasp. "Lemme go. I've got a telegram to deliver."

"That can wait until you've apologized to this lady for nearly knocking her down."

"Sorry," the boy mumbled.

Steven gave the lad's collar a little shake. "I think you can do better than that."

The boy looked up, embarrassment staining his cheeks a dark red. "I really am, ma'am. Sorry, that is. If I'd seen you, I never would've run into you." His forehead crinkled. "I didn't hurt you, did I?"

"No," Lavinia assured him with a smile. "You just knocked the wind out of me for a bit."

"I'm glad. I wouldn't have wanted to hurt you. I was just in a rush because Mr. Crawford told me to get this to Mrs. Stewart in a hurry."

"Mrs. Stewart?"

"Yes'm. She's a new lady in town." He glanced over his shoulder and lowered his voice to a whisper. "If you ask me, I think Mr. Crawford's kind of sweet on her."

Steven saw the way Lavinia's face stiffened before she held out her hand.

"Well, I can save you the trouble of running all the way to my house. I'm Mrs. Stewart."

"Really? That's great. Here you go, and I'll make sure I don't run into you like that again."

Lips pursed, Lavinia opened the paper and scanned the brief message. The color drained from her face. She folded the paper again and tucked it into her reticule without comment.

Steven touched her arm. "Is it bad news?"

"No, not at all." Her voice wobbled, and her smile seemed forced. "Just a message from our family in Chicago. It seems we'll be having a visit from one of my cousins very soon."

18

Ellie stood in the shadows outside the Palace Saloon, feeling the pulse in her throat pound out a tempo as rapid as that of the tinny music that filtered out past the batwing doors.

A shout of raucous laughter burst forth, loud enough to drown out the off-key piano for a few brief seconds. Ellie's heart picked up its pace. What was she thinking, venturing east of Seventh Street after sundown and preparing to enter a den of vice?

She spun around, ready to flee back to the safety of her cozy little house, when a thought stopped her in her tracks. She had exhausted every means she could think of to elicit helpful information from the upstanding citizens of Pickford. It was time to look in less respectable places. Getting acquainted with the habitués of the Palace might be her only chance to move forward on the case. She couldn't allow herself to give in to fear. If she backed down now, she might never regain enough nerve to try this again.

Besides, she wouldn't be entering the Palace as anxious Ellie Moore. She would walk through those swinging doors as Jessie Monroe—woman of spunk and daring.

Pulling herself into the role, she patted her coppery ringlets into place, pushed through the doors, and walked inside.

The piano music broke off the instant she set foot inside the smoky interior, and the hum of conversation ended as if on cue. The cloying smell of alcohol permeated the room. Ellie fought down the urge to run away as fast as her feet would carry her and scanned the room.

Over at the gaming tables, two groups of poker players sat looking at her as though frozen. Letting her gaze sweep over the rest of the crowd, she saw expressions of stunned disbelief on every face. She recognized several from her jaunts around town, wiry miners she had seen from a distance but hadn't spoken to. Jake Freeman, the blacksmith, showed none of his usual friendliness, avoiding her eyes as though embarrassed to see her there. One or two men recovered from their surprise enough to stare at her boldly, and Ellie averted her gaze.

She pulled her reticule tight against her and twisted its drawstring between her fingers. She had been an idiot to come. Her heart leaped into her throat when a man detached himself from the crowd and stepped forward. Her panic ebbed only slightly when she recognized Marshal Everett Bascomb.

The dapper lawman doffed his broad-brimmed hat and bowed with a flourish. "Welcome, fair lady. Such beauty has seldom been seen within these walls."

Her little drama had begun. Ellie put one hand on her hip and gave him the most flirtatious look she could muster. "Good evening, Marshal. What a pleasure to find you here."

A satisfied gleam lit Bascomb's eyes. He turned in a slow circle, surveying the room. Everyone else went back to their business, resuming their conversations in hushed tones and casting furtive looks in Ellie's direction.

"You're the last person I would have expected to see in this establishment. What brings you here?" Bascomb drew nearer, close enough for Ellie to smell the alcohol on his breath.

She shifted position slightly, trying not to let her distaste show. As she turned, an enormous painting on the opposite wall came into view. Ellie let out a startled yip and stared at the vast expanse of female flesh, marred here and there by an occasional bullet hole. She spun on her heel, turning her back on the appalling sight.

Bascomb gave her an amused smile. "I gather you don't approve of our Fatima?"

Fatima? Ellie's mind raced while she struggled to regain control. This was the painting whose fate the drunken miner had been lamenting on the day of her arrival in Pickford.

She shuddered, trying to erase the image from her mind. What was the word Steven had used to describe the painting? Rubenesque—that was it. And his description had been right on target. She couldn't imagine a more accurate summation of the lady's all-too-evident charms.

She darted a quick glance around the room to see if anyone else had noticed her embarrassment. No one met her eyes, but she spotted a number of other holes in the walls that must have been made by rowdy patrons shooting off their pistols. Apparently the Palace had a boisterous clientele, making it exactly the kind of place Jessie needed to visit in order to further the investigation.

She forced a smile to her lips and met Bascomb's eyes. "I've led far too sheltered a life. I'm ready to see more of the world and have a few adventures."

Bascomb's lips widened, revealing a row of teeth in a wolfish grin. "I admire your spirit. What kind of adventure were you looking for?"

Not the kind he meant. Ellie felt sure of that. She shrugged one shoulder and tried to think of a way to respond that wouldn't make the situation worse. Her goal in going to the Palace had been to strike up a conversation with some of the town's rougher element, but she couldn't hope to accomplish that if the lawman insisted on sticking to her like a burr.

She tilted her head and wrinkled her nose at him. "Maybe I wanted to see if a Wild West saloon would live up to the reputation it's been given in the dime novels."

"Ah, I see." The lawman leaned a bit closer and spoke in a suggestive undertone. "Things are pretty calm this evening. If excitement is what you're after, why don't you come back here with me on a Saturday night, when—"

"There you are, hangin' around the bar again. I shoulda known."

Ellie spun around to see a man stagger toward them and recognized him as one of the mine owners she'd met. Holding aloft a bottle half filled with an amber liquid, he swayed across the floor until he stood face-to-face with Bascomb.

"How d'you expect to catch those thieves if you spend your time chasin' skirts? No wonder you haven't found 'em yet, when you're too busy makin' eyes at this redheaded floozy."

Floozy? Ellie sucked in her breath, trying to decide whether to shrink away in mortification or give the rude fellow a piece of her mind.

Bascomb shouldered the man to one side and

sent him stumbling into a table. "You're drunk, Andrews. Don't talk to me again until you're sober enough to tell the difference between a lady and a saloon girl."

Brady Andrews. The mine owner who had seemed so fond of his flask during the meeting she attended with Steven.

"What good would it do to talk to you? You haven't turned up one clue in all this time." He pulled a swig from the bottle and wiped his mouth with the back of his hand. "We don't need you, anyway. We've got Pinkertons comin'."

Bascomb's hands balled into fists, and Ellie saw his face tighten. "What kind of nonsense is that? More of the whiskey talking?"

Brady Andrews pushed away from the table and tottered back toward the marshal, one hand raised as though taking an oath. "Gospel truth. We told 'em what was going on, and they're sending somebody out."

Ellie's heart stopped. The mine owners had been adamant that no one outside their circle should know they'd summoned the Pinkertons. What could he be thinking? He wasn't thinking, she reminded herself. Not in his inebriated condition.

Bascomb's jaw worked. "When?"

"Who knows?" Brady made a wide gesture with the arm holding the bottle, sending an arc of whiskey through the air.

Ellie scuttled backward a few steps to keep

the liquor from splattering her skirt and took refuge in a shadowy corner.

"We wrote to 'em weeks ago." Brady slurred the words but spoke in a voice loud enough to catch the attention of everyone in the place. "Oughta be here any day now."

Bascomb stepped forward and caught a wad of Brady's shirtfront with his left hand. "What do you mean bringing those snooping Pinks into my town?" He drew his right elbow back, fist poised to crash into Brady's jaw. "Why, I ought to—"

"Hold it, Bascomb."

Ellie whirled at the sound of Steven's voice and saw him push his way between the two men. Her mind reeled. Where had he come from? The lazy swing of the batwing doors gave the only clue to his sudden appearance.

"Easy now," he said to the lawman in a placating voice. "He's so drunk he wouldn't feel it anyway. Might as well save yourself a set of scraped knuckles."

Bascomb's chest heaved as he stared at Steven with blazing eyes. Then he lowered his arm to his side, shoving Brady away from himself at the same time. "Are you a party to this cockeyed plan, Pierce? I don't want any stinking Pinkertons in my town."

Brady staggered, and Steven moved to wrap a supportive arm around the other man's shoulders.

"Let me take him home. That's what I came here to do. His wife's worried about him."

"She'll have more to worry about if he keeps mouthing off." Bascomb tugged at the sleeves of his coat and stalked toward the bar without another glance at Ellie.

Steven turned toward Brady. "Come on. Let's get you home." Steadying his friend, he started toward the door.

Ellie slid farther back into the shadows, hoping to avoid his notice. Too late. The shocked look on his face when he spotted her could have easily passed for Macbeth catching sight of Banquo's ghost.

His arm slipped from Brady's shoulders. The tipsy man wobbled for a moment, then sank gently to the floor, still clutching the bottle. Holding it to his chest like a precious treasure, he closed his eyes, and a soft snore emanated from his lips.

"What are you doing here?" Steven stepped over his snoring friend and fixed Ellie with a fierce scowl. "Miss Monroe, this is no place for a lady."

For once in Ellie's life, words failed her completely. "I was . . . I only . . ." She cleared her throat and tried again. "I wanted to see what a Western saloon was really like," she said, trying to recapture Jessie's spunky attitude.

Steven's nostrils flared. "Well, now you've seen it. If you have no respect for your own reputation, you might at least consider how this is going to reflect on your aunt. I'm taking you home right now."

"What about your friend?" Ellie almost succeeded in keeping a quaver out of her voice.

Steven hesitated a moment, then he bent over and slipped his hands under Brady's shoulders, dragging the recumbent form across the floor toward the far wall, where he deposited him under an empty table before he turned to stride back to Ellie.

With a baleful stare, he gripped her elbow and marched her toward the door like an angry father escorting an unruly child. "He'll be asleep for a while. I'll come back and get him once I've delivered you to your aunt."

Before they reached the exit, the batwing doors swung open, and a shiny-faced man lurched inside, brandishing a large pistol.

Before Ellie could react, Steven shoved her against the wall and shielded her with his body.

"Congratulate me, fellas," the newcomer roared. "I just discovered a new vein, and it looks every bit as rich as that new strike they're talkin' about in New Mexico!" A burst of gunshots followed.

Ellie clapped her hands to her ears to protect them from the deafening crash. The moment the shooting ceased, Steven propelled her out the door. She had only time enough for a fleeting glance back over her shoulder, revealing that Fatima now sported a new bullet hole.

❧ **19** ❧

Ellie readjusted the gray wig and slipped the cheek plumpers into place, then checked herself in the dressing table mirror for the tenth time. She couldn't afford a single flaw when she made her appearance at the stage depot. Reassured, in that regard at least, she picked up the telegram, now creased from a dozen readings since she'd received it on Sunday.

COUSIN TED ARRIVING ON TUESDAY STAGE STOP HE LOOKS FORWARD TO A NICE VISIT WITH BOTH OF YOU STOP
                                                          HENRY

Ellie read the words aloud, hoping she could somehow inject new meaning into the message. No such luck. The ominous note had held the same threat every time she'd gone over it. She pulled on her gloves and took a sip of the mint tea she'd brewed earlier in hopes of calming her stomach. So far, it hadn't worked.

Her foot tapped out a staccato beat on the kitchen floor. Although Cousin Ted was a new character in her little drama, the fact the telegram came from "Henry" confirmed that the telegram had come from the home office. Who was this new relative, and what did his coming to Pickford mean?

Were Fleming and Gates about to pull her off the case? How could she blame them if they did? They'd thought they were sending two operatives to Arizona, one of them a seasoned professional. Instead of that, they wound up with one rank amateur trying to pull the wool over the eyes of her employers as well as everyone in Pickford.

She set down the teacup and swiped at her eyes. If only they'd given her more time. Surely even experienced operatives needed a while to carry out their undercover work. With another week or two to ask probing questions and assess reactions to them, she might glean enough information to ferret out the culprits and ensure future employment for herself.

Frustrated, she picked up the teacup and brought it to the sink. Who was she kidding? She'd carried on conversations, both as Lavinia and Jessie, with anyone in town who would give her the time of day, and what had she learned so far? That Gertie loved to gossip, that Bascomb had an undeservedly high opinion of himself, that Amos Crawford had fallen head over heels for Lavinia . . .

And that being around Steven Pierce turned both her brain and her heart to mush.

As far as the robberies, though? Nothing. Either

the thieves had no connection to Pickford, or she was an utter failure as a detective. She only hoped the Pinkertons would let her keep the money they had deposited for her use in the Pickford bank. It might help her get by until she found another position.

And if she didn't? She didn't want to contemplate what that would mean for her future. There would be plenty of time for that later.

Acting on that gloomy thought, she lifted her parasol from the rack near the door and reached for her reticule on a nearby table. The stage wasn't scheduled to arrive for forty-five minutes, but waiting at the station, where she might stumble upon a clue, seemed wiser than waiting in solitude at home. Locking the front door behind her, she drew a fortifying breath and set forth to meet her new cousin.

Just as she turned onto Grant, she remembered a slim volume of poems she planned to loan Myra. She hesitated, wondering if she should wait to do it another time. But if things didn't go well with "Cousin Ted," she might not get another chance to see the woman. With a weary sigh, she turned around and trudged back to her house.

The moment her feet crossed the threshold, she once again sensed something amiss. A quick glance at the desk and its misaligned drawers confirmed her suspicions. Billy Taylor had struck again.

How? She remembered locking the front door only minutes before. A quick check assured her all the windows were locked. The back door, however, wasn't latched. That solved the mystery of how Billy had entered, but how could she have overlooked something so important?

The thought nagged at her as she grabbed the book, locked both doors, and turned down Second Street once again. If she couldn't remember such simple precautions, maybe she had no business remaining in the Pinkertons' employ.

A flash of movement caught her eye, and she saw Billy slipping around a corner in his best Junior Pinkerton mode.

"Stop right there, Billy Taylor!"

The boy skidded to a halt and trotted toward her with a bright smile. His sunny look faded when he saw her expression. "What's the matter? Wasn't I bein' sneaky enough?"

"I think you've been entirely too sneaky. Didn't you give me your word you wouldn't go in my house without permission again?"

Billy's eyes rounded. "Yes'm. And I haven't."

Ellie crossed her arms and glared down at him. "Don't go spinning any of your yarns, young man. Someone was in my house just a few minutes ago, going through my desk, and we both know who that was."

The boy opened his mouth to protest, but Ellie

cut him off. "I've been patient with you, Billy. But any more of your mischief, and I'll have to take stronger action. Understand?" Without waiting for him to reply, she pivoted and went on her way.

After delivering the book to Donald, who promised to pass it along to his wife, Ellie turned her steps toward the stage depot. On the opposite side of the street, she spotted a figure in a slouch hat. She took a second look and caught her breath.

She hadn't been mistaken—it was the man who had acted in such a surly manner at the hotel. The man who'd dropped that mysterious note. She watched as he approached the bakery and almost let out a whoop when he repeated his earlier actions of looking over his shoulder before ducking into the adjacent alleyway.

Ellie tried not to let her excitement show as she crossed the street, paused in front of the bakery as though looking for something in her reticule, and ventured a glance around the corner of the building.

Sure enough, there he was, in the very act of slipping a note into the secret hiding place. She waited until he went out the other end of the alley and hastened to the crack in the wall.

Slipping her fingers inside, she held back a cry of triumph when her fingers encountered a scrap of paper. Pulling it out, she unfolded it with trembling hands and read the brief message:

Seven o'clock tonight. Behind Pickford Hall.

A slow smile curved Ellie's lips. Finally, a real lead and a chance to prove her worth to the Pinkertons!

She tucked the paper back into its hiding place and returned to the boardwalk, trying to control her elation. Maybe this would be her opportunity to see the hidden face behind the silver thefts at last.

Ellie fidgeted outside the depot. How would she know this alleged cousin when she saw him? Fleming and Gates could hardly have given a description in their telegram, but it would have been nice to know who she was supposed to be meeting. Unable to stand still, she paced the width of the boardwalk and hoped her show of nervous energy looked more like anticipation rather than the agitation she felt.

For the dozenth time, she adjusted her sleeves, tugged at her gloves, and pushed her spectacles back into place. She had chosen to dress as Lavinia for this little family reunion, reasoning that Gates and Fleming had only seen her in this disguise and wouldn't have known how to describe Jessie. Assuming they believed "Jessie" was actually there in Pickford.

A dusty cowboy stepped down, followed by a young couple who looked to have come straight from the East and a jaunty-looking man in a bowler hat. The man turned a slow circle on the boardwalk, and his face lit up when he spotted Ellie.

"Cousin Lavinia!" He spread his arms wide and approached her with a broad smile.

"Dear Theodore!" Ellie stepped into the circle of his embrace and returned his hug. "How long has it been?"

"It seems like forever. I can't remember the last time I saw you." The twinkle in his eye would have put Ellie at ease if not for the suspicion that he was there to drive her into the ranks of the unemployed. "Where is this cozy little cottage Henry told me about?"

Ellie picked up on the cue. "Just a few blocks away. It's an easy walk, even for me."

"Let me deal with my luggage first. I plan to take a room at the hotel, since Henry says there's only enough sleeping space for you and Jessie at your house." He gave Ellie a penetrating look she chose to ignore.

"That's very thoughtful of you. I'm sure the station agent would be glad to keep an eye on it for you." She waited while he made arrangements, grateful for his tact in not trying to foist his presence on her overnight.

When he was ready, she tucked her hand into

the crook of his arm, and they set off toward Second Street. "I hope your travels have given you a hearty appetite. I have a pot of stew simmering on the stove, made just the way you always liked it. How is dear Matilda? Has she recovered from that bout of pleurisy?"

The spurious Cousin Ted spoke gravely, although Ellie detected the flicker of a smile. "She's doing splendidly. Back to her usual robust health, I'm glad to say."

Ellie prattled away about other imaginary relatives all the way to her house. Ted fielded her questions with ease, seeming to enjoy the improvisation.

As they neared the corner of Second, Ted tilted his head toward her. "And how is Jessie adapting to life in the Wild West?"

Ellie's step faltered enough to pull them both slightly off balance. "Jessie? She's . . . well, she's . . ."

"Never mind." Ted patted her hand and they continued on. "I'll ask her myself."

Ellie caught a glimpse of Billy Taylor and his cronies skulking behind a rain barrel as she led Ted up the front steps. Raising her voice slightly, she replied, "She's been looking forward to seeing you. You're the first relative to visit us in our new home."

Ted followed her gaze and gave an almost imperceptible nod. "It isn't every day I get a jump on the rest of the family like this. They're all eager to hear the news of your adventures out here."

Ellie fumbled for her key, inserted it into the lock, let them inside, and closed the door. Out of the public view, she abandoned Lavinia's round-shouldered stoop and pulled her shoulders back, eyeing Ted warily. Now what?

He removed his bowler hat, revealing salt-and-pepper hair thinning on the top. He hung the hat with care on the coatrack near the door. "So, Miss Moore, what's going on?"

Ellie reminded herself to breathe. "I'm not sure what you mean."

Ted turned to face her, all traces of the genial visitor gone. "Your wires have created quite a stir back at headquarters. We know Norma Brooks never came out here. It's obvious that no one with any experience is running this investigation. So that leads to my next question: Who is out here with you?"

"No one."

His bushy gray eyebrows drew together. "Come, Miss Moore. You wired the office to say that Jessie had arrived, yet now you insist you're acting on your own. It's little wonder the home office pulled me off my own investigation in Denver and sent me here to find out what is going on." He took two steps toward her, and his eyebrows lowered. "I'm asking you one more time—who are you working with?"

Ellie pressed her lips together to stop their trembling. Now that the time had come to confess, words failed her. How could she explain an idea that seemed so simple at its inception but had turned into a quagmire of confusion?

She waved her arm toward the armchair. "Would you wait here, please? I'll be back in a few minutes."

Ted raised one eyebrow but did as she asked. She noticed that he moved the chair so it put him in a direct line between her and the front door, presumably in case she decided to make a break for it.

Feeling a little like a suspect herself, Ellie walked into her bedroom with as much dignity as she could muster. Once inside, she moved like a whirlwind, pulling off Lavinia's charcoal gray dress and tossing it on the bed. Off came the gray wig, the spectacles, and the leg wraps, and out came the plumpers.

Yanking Jessie's sapphire blue princess dress from the wardrobe, she pulled it on, utilizing every quick-change technique she had learned working backstage. Next she wiped "Lavinia" from her face with cold cream and with a few deft strokes applied Jessie's makeup. Finally, she lifted the red wig from its stand and pulled it on over her own drab locks.

She took a last look at the image in her mirror and adjusted the curls in her bangs. Smoothing the skirt of the dress with her hands, she walked toward the parlor, ready to give the performance of her life.

And Ellie couldn't have hoped for a more satisfactory reaction from her visitor. The moment she stepped into the parlor, Ted's mouth fell open, and he started bolt upright.

"Norma? But I thought . . ."

Ellie shook her head and allowed a small smile to play across her lips.

He bent forward and eyed her closely. "All right, you aren't Norma, but you look remarkably like her. Who are you?"

Ellie allowed her shoulders to droop and walked over to him using Lavinia's stiff gait. "Why, Cousin Theodore, have I changed so much in such a short time?"

Ted's mouth worked, but no words came forth. He pulled a handkerchief from his pocket without taking his eyes off Ellie and used it to mop his forehead. "My stars! They told me you had some theatrical experience, but I never dreamed . . ."

"The stew is ready. Shall I dish it up?" Without waiting for an answer, Ellie straightened again and sashayed toward the kitchen, adding a Jessie-esque swish to her walk. Best to keep him off balance as much as possible.

In spite of her attempts to appear casual, Ellie spoke little during dinner, asking only if Ted would like her to refill his bowl with more of the savory stew. He accepted her offer without hesitation, but she couldn't tell whether his quick agreement boded well for her or not.

When he'd spooned up the last bit of the rich liquid, Ted pushed his chair back from the table and sat regarding Ellie thoughtfully. "Would you care to explain to me what's going on?"

The moment of truth had arrived. Ellie blotted her lips with her napkin and faced him squarely. "It isn't hard to explain what started it all. . . . I needed this job. Without it, I would have starved to death on the streets of Chicago. It's as simple as that."

She eyed him closely but couldn't discern what thoughts were running through his mind. "I went to Kansas City as directed, but then I met Norma and found out she'd gotten married and had no intention of taking on this case.

"I didn't know what else to do, so I decided to come out here as planned and conduct the investigation on my own. I didn't intend to mislead anyone with those telegrams." Remembering Pastor Blaylock's favorite topic, she swallowed and offered a clarification. "Not much, anyway. I just wanted to have time to get my bearings and decide what to do next. I really couldn't go into much detail, since anything I sent to the home office would be repeated around Pickford before nightfall."

She waited for some response from Ted, but

he remained silent. "Then I realized I needed Norma's character in addition to Lavinia. Sending that wire saying Jessie had arrived was more to let the people in town know to expect a new arrival than to deceive anyone in Chicago."

She raised her chin and looked Ted straight in the eye, willing herself not to flinch under his scrutiny.

His voice held only curiosity when he spoke. "What progress have you made so far?"

Ellie was tempted to amplify what she'd learned but decided to make a clean breast of things instead. When Ted took over the investigation, he would need to know the facts—sparse as they were—so he could clean up the mess she had made. She owed that much to Steven and the other mine owners.

What about the note she found in the bakery wall? She opened her mouth to tell Ted of her discovery, then clamped her lips together. She wouldn't mention that now. The note was her ace in the hole, her chance to show what she could do on her own. There was no point in letting him in on it too early so he could step in and steal her thunder.

"To be perfectly honest, I haven't gotten very far. I've struck up conversations with as many people in town as I could, but no one seems to have any ideas about the robberies or who might be involved."

"And no one seems curious about why you've been asking these questions?" Ted studied her intently. "You don't think you've raised any suspicions?"

"No," she said slowly. "At least none that I can tell. But I have noticed a difference between the way people respond to Lavinia and Jessie. When I'm playing Lavinia, I have to be more careful about the way I put things. Most people expect older ladies to be inquisitive about what goes on around them, but I have to make sure I don't push too hard."

Ted nodded. "Go on."

"But when Jessie talks to men around town, there isn't any need to press them for information. Once I get them started talking, they fall all over themselves trying to keep the conversation going."

Ted covered his mouth with his hand as if wiping away a smile. "That's one reason Norma was so effective. Men get so dazzled by a pretty face that they forget to think. They don't even realize how much they've let slip. It sounds like you're using your looks to good advantage." His voice held a note of approval.

Jessie's good looks. Ellie made a silent correction. Her own appearance wouldn't garner more than a quick glance and passing hello, if that.

Ted steepled his fingers and tapped the tips of

his forefingers together. "It sounds as if you've made a good start, but quite often you'll get more information from approaching people by a more indirect route."

Ellie willed herself to breathe. His response wasn't at all what she'd expected. When was he going to tell her to pack her bags and leave?

"It's a little like piecing together a puzzle," he said, sounding more like a teacher than a detective. "Each person may have only a single scrap of useful information, but when you take everything you've learned and fit it together, a bigger picture starts to emerge."

Ellie leaned forward, intrigued by his lecture in spite of her nerves. "For instance?"

"Have you noticed anyone who has more money than they should have? Or some person or group who tends to be highly secretive?"

Ellie shook her head. "I've kept those things in mind, but I haven't found anyone who fits that description. Other than the storekeeper, whose wife tells me their business is prospering although the inventory on their shelves is thin, I haven't found anything to indicate that anyone local might be involved. I think we may be on the wrong track altogether, and the robbers have moved on."

Ted pondered her statement, then shook his head. "If there had only been one robbery, I'd be inclined to agree with you, but multiple robberies imply someone staying in the area, someone who takes pains to hide their involvement. From everything I've heard about this case, these thefts aren't done on the spur of the moment. They have a substantial amount of planning behind them. I'd say they're being orchestrated by someone with a long-term plan, someone who's adept at maintaining an upright public profile while pulling strings behind the scenes."

"That makes a lot of sense," Ellie admitted. Why hadn't she been able to see that on her own? It sounded so simple when Ted laid it out like that. That was the very reason they needed someone on the job who had experience, instead of a rank amateur like herself. She only hoped her blundering wouldn't cost Steven and the other miners dearly in the long run.

Ted drummed his fingers on the table and glanced out the window. "We still have a bit of daylight left. Let's take a walk."

His abrupt suggestion startled Ellie, but she rose when he did and made a few adjustments to her disguise, pulled a shawl from the coatrack, and followed him outside.

To her surprise, he led the way west on Charles Street instead of heading back into town. In a few moments they had left the buildings behind and entered a path that led through a thicket of mesquite and cottonwoods. "Where are we going?"

"I noticed the line of trees from the stage as

we neared town. Out here, a mass of trees like that means water, most likely a river."

Ellie's uneasiness returned full force. What did he have in mind? Ted seemed to take no notice of her discomfort but made his way through the grove as calmly as though they were taking a walk in the park.

She judged they'd walked about half a mile before they reached the banks of the San Pedro where it made a wide curve. From this point, the stamp mill was far out of sight, its incessant pounding muffled.

Ted nodded his approval. "Perfect. An easy walk from town, but far enough away that people won't take note of the noise." He reached into his right pants pocket and drew out a small revolver. "Have you ever handled one of these?"

Ellie eyed the little weapon with distaste. "Only as a stage prop."

"Then it's time you did. Here, let me demonstrate." He raised his arm and took aim at a driftwood log twenty feet away.

Ellie jumped and clapped her hands to her ears when the crack of the gun shattered the evening quiet.

"Now it's your turn." Ignoring her reluctance, Ted showed her how to load the cylinder, cock the hammer, aim, and fire.

The lesson continued until Ellie lost her aversion to the weapon and it felt more at home in her hands. At last, Ted seemed satisfied. "You're no expert marksman, but you could use it to take care of yourself if you ever needed to. Let's head back now."

She handed the gun to Ted, and they walked back to the house in silence, Ellie trying to make sense of the afternoon's events. Had she passed muster with Cousin Ted? Why would he have taken the time to teach her to shoot if he planned to send her packing?

When they stepped into her parlor, he held out the pistol. "Keep this handy." When Ellie started to protest, he pressed the revolver into her hand. "I have more. You may not need to use it, and I hope you never do. But if a situation arises where you're up against the wall, I'll feel better knowing you're prepared."

"But I—"

A knock at the front door cut her off.

"Are you expecting anyone?"

Ellie shook her head. She looked at the gun in her hand, then glanced around the room for a hiding place. Spotting the desk, she darted over to it long enough to yank open the drop front and slip the pistol inside before hanging her shawl back on its hook and opening the door.

Amos Crawford stood on the front porch, a nosegay of desert wildflowers in his hands. Ellie stared at him, openmouthed.

The telegrapher's face turned a deep pink.

"I've come to call on Miz Lavinia. Is she in?"

Ellie heard a snort of laughter, quickly muffled, from Ted's direction and shot him a quick glare. "I'm afraid she's lying down. She . . . had a bit of a dizzy spell, probably brought on by the excitement at seeing her favorite cousin again." She reached out to take the flowers.

Amos's face fell, but he kept a firm grip on the small bouquet. "Are you sure she can't come out? I'd be happy to wait as long as she needs to make herself presentable."

"I'm sorry," Ellie said firmly. "I think it's better that she rest."

The stubborn set of Amos's jaw told her he didn't intend to take no for an answer. "I'd appreciate it if you'd ask her."

Ellie couldn't very well shut the door in his face, tempting as she found the idea. "All right, I'll check with her. Wait here, please." She darted another glare at Ted when she passed him. He hadn't done a thing to help her out at all.

In the temporary sanctuary of Lavinia's bedroom, she stood with her back to the door, her thoughts racing. How on earth was she going to get rid of the man? She looked at the gray wig on the stand and the charcoal dress that lay across the bed. Should she reappear as Lavinia and accept the flowers?

No, there simply wasn't enough time to change her makeup again. Even if there was, transforming herself into Lavinia didn't seem a good idea at that point. No telling how long it would take to convince the love-struck man to go away.

She knotted her hands into fists and pressed her knuckles against her temples. *Think!* The idea of a double identity that had seemed so brilliant at first now struck her as the most foolhardy scheme anyone had ever proposed. It was simply impossible to bring two roles to life onstage at the same time.

But she wasn't onstage at the moment. . . .

A sudden idea struck her. Pitching her voice so it would carry through the door and out into the parlor, she said, "Aunt Lavinia? Are you awake?"

Switching to Lavinia's quavering tone, she answered. "What is it, dear?"

Ellie grinned, warming to her new ploy. "Mr. Crawford came to call. He brought you flowers. Are you able to come talk to him?"

She sat on the side of the bed, bringing forth a creak from the bedsprings, and let out a pitiful moan. "Oh, dear me. My poor head is still swimming. Thank him for me, will you? And would you put the flowers in some water so I can enjoy them in here?"

"Of course." Ellie stepped back into the parlor, closing the bedroom door with a decisive click. "I'm sorry, she says—"

"I heard." Amos surrendered the flowers. "Tell

her I hope she feels better soon, and I'll see her around town before long."

"I'll do that." She shut the door behind him and sagged against it. A soft, pattering noise caught her attention, and she turned to see Ted applauding gently.

"That was quite a performance, Miss Moore. The stage lost out when you decided to become a detective instead of an actress."

The moan Ellie uttered wasn't contrived this time. "I feel sorry for misleading the poor man. I never intended anything like this to happen."

Ted gave her a sympathetic smile and shrugged. "It comes with the job, I'm afraid. You get used to it after a time. Besides," he added with a twinkle in his eye, "Lavinia really *was* in the bedroom, if that makes you feel any better."

To Ellie's surprise, he walked across to the coatrack and retrieved his hat. "I've enjoyed our time together thoroughly, but it's getting late."

"You're going back to Denver?" She tried not to let too much relief show in her voice.

His eyes twinkled as though he knew exactly how she felt. "No, just back to the hotel. It's been a long day, and I'm ready for a good night's sleep. You and I need to meet again tomorrow. You have a lot to learn besides how to shoot a pistol."

Ellie tried one last time. "But your investigation . . ."

"It will have to wait a few more days. In the

271

meantime, I need to send my report to Gates and Fleming and see what they want to do." He opened the front door and turned back to face her. "Meet me at the hotel for breakfast. We'll continue your lessons then." With a jaunty tip of his hat, he strode off into the evening.

Ellie watched him leave, feeling her spirits soar one moment, then plummet the next. Ted's mention of further training gave her hope he wasn't ready to give up on her yet, but the home office would have to make the final decision. What would Gates and Fleming think when they learned the truth about what she'd done? And what sort of telegram could Ted send without drawing Amos's attention?

She locked the front door and sank onto the sofa. In spite of her worst fears, her performance had turned out to be a rousing success. She had received unexpected acclaim from a seasoned operative and managed to pull the wool over Amos Crawford's eyes. She ought to be celebrating a giddy triumph. So why did she feel more like crying?

It must be her jangled nerves. They had been frazzled ever since she received word of Ted's impending arrival. But the day wasn't over yet. She still had to spy on the secret meeting behind Pickford Hall. Once she'd unmasked the criminals, she would have ample reason to celebrate.

Ellie lurked—there was no other word for it—behind the rear staircase leading down from the second floor of Pickford Hall, thankful for the charcoal dress and gray wig that let her blend into the shadows. The moon's pale glow gave enough light to illuminate the scene, but it didn't extend to her little pocket of darkness. Peering out between the stair treads, she congratulated herself. The arrangement couldn't be more perfect for spying. She felt sure Billy Taylor would approve.

The crunch of footsteps announced the arrival of one of the conspirators. Ellie ducked farther back under the stairs and watched as the man she'd followed earlier that day entered the open area behind the building. The constant glances he cast around him betrayed his tension.

Ellie's mouth went dry. Maybe the gang was planning another raid against the miners. If so, she would be in an ideal position to overhear all the details. She willed her heart to slow its pace. She needed to be able to concentrate on catching every word.

A second set of footsteps approached from the direction of Charles Street, hesitantly at first, then pattering quickly across the hard-packed ground. Ellie held her breath and watched in disbelief as a young woman came into view and ran across the lot to throw her arms around the man's neck.

"I'm sorry I'm late." Her breathy apology

floated to Ellie's ears. "Daddy kept us at the dinner table until I thought I'd scream."

Her companion made no reply but lowered his head and planted a long, hard kiss on her lips.

Ellie gasped, and the couple sprang apart.

The man peered into the shadows, quickly locating the staircase as the only place of concealment. He crossed the distance in a few quick strides. Reaching out, he grasped Ellie's arm and dragged her out into the moonlight.

"You!" His hard expression spoke volumes more than the single word he uttered.

Unable to find her voice, Ellie stared open-mouthed, flicking her gaze between him and his companion, who she now recognized as the buxom brunette she'd seen flirting on the street with Marshal Bascomb not long after her arrival.

He tightened his grip. "What are you doing here?"

Ellie scrambled for something, anything, to explain her presence. "I was out for an evening stroll," she faltered. "I heard someone coming but couldn't tell who it was, so I ducked out of the way, thinking you'd pass on by. I never intended to intrude on your . . . um . . ."

She tried to withdraw her arm, but his hold remained firm.

The girl walked over to them. "Let her go. She looks scared." She turned to Ellie. "You won't tell anyone, will you? We're not really doing anything wrong. It's just that my father doesn't approve. He thinks there's too much difference in our ages." She looked up at the man with an adoring smile. "But Daddy's wrong. We'll make him see it one of these days, won't we?"

The man's angry scowl melted into a somewhat softer expression. He released Ellie with a show of reluctance, managing to give her a tiny shove as he did so. "You've seen all you need to tonight. It's time you got back home—where you'll be safe."

Ellie didn't need further urging to convince her to comply. Spinning on her heel, she made her way home at as fast a clip as Lavinia could manage, berating herself with every step. Her big break in solving the mystery had turned out to be a huge mistake, and an embarrassing one at that.

The only consolation she could find in the whole humiliating mess was that she hadn't told Ted about her plans.

❧ 20 ❧

A soft tap sounded on the back window. Setting aside the assay reports he'd been studying, the man walked swiftly to the rear door and opened it long enough to admit his henchman before closing it softly against the evening gloom.

The new arrival pushed his hat farther back on his head. "I got your message. You wanted to see me?"

A quick nod. "We need to talk."

The other man's eyes sparked with an eager light. "You got into the house?"

A grimace tugged at his lips and forehead, but he stiffened his features before his discomfort could show. This wasn't the way he'd planned to start the conversation. "I got in," he said in a flat voice. He glanced down at his hands, then back up in time to see a slow smirk spread across his visitor's face.

"Don't tell me you got caught?"

Rage boiled up inside. How dare a subordinate take on such an arrogant tone? The man was an underling, a tool, nothing more. He'd never been one to put up with a superior attitude from any employee. He clenched his hands, then forced them to relax, telling himself their association would soon be at an end.

He took a moment longer to tamp down his irritation before going on in his usual confident manner. "I watched her leave the house. She spends hours wandering around town, so I naturally assumed I'd have plenty of time."

The smirk widened. "So what happened? Did the niece catch you?"

He narrowed his eyes and sent a venomous look at his minion. "I'm not a fool. I went up the front steps and knocked on the door to make sure no one was home. There was no answer, so I slipped around to the back and used my key to get inside."

The other man hooked his thumbs in his waistband. "And?"

He held back the urge to use his fist to wipe the sneer off his visitor's face and raked one hand through his hair instead. "I planned to go through the desk first. I'd just opened the first drawer when I heard her coming back up the front steps. I barely had time to shut the drawer and get out the back way without being seen. I didn't even have a chance to lock the door behind me."

A slow hiss of air escaped through his visitor's teeth. "Nobody saw you?"

"No. There was no one out and about on that side of the house. I came home through the alleys."

"When are you going to try again?"

"I'm not. That was too close for comfort. Now some cousin is visiting them, and no telling how long he's going to stay. At this point, I'm willing to put your plan into operation, with some modifications."

The tall man raised his eyebrows. "With the cousin here in town? I thought the idea was to keep her family from getting involved."

"You aren't going to make her disappear, just put her out of commission. Make it look like an accident." He clipped the words out and eyed the other steadily. "Her family will be too distraught to think about looking into her business dealings. And . . . poof!" He waved his hands like a stage magician. "All those pesky questions will go away."

The second man nodded slowly, then with increasing assurance. "All right, I'll handle it. When and how?"

He arched one eyebrow. "I'll leave the 'how' up to you. Take care of it the first chance you get."

After another round of asking questions everywhere he could think of, Steven was ready to concede that the art of detection was best left to experts. Not only had his probing borne no fruit other than curious looks and raised eyebrows, but he wondered if the criminals were laughing at his amateurish efforts.

Pondering his lack of progress, he left the business district behind and walked out past the west end of town, where buildings gave way to the desert. He'd been looking for someone with a sudden flush of money, but perhaps these robbers were shrewder than run-of-the-mill thugs. What if they were hoarding the silver before making their next move, whatever that might be?

He felt the need to talk it over with someone, but Tom was unavailable that afternoon, and after the older man's cautions about Alfred and Gilbert, Steven no longer felt comfortable confiding in the other mine owners.

But there was someone always available to help bear his burdens. Somewhat sheepishly, Steven turned his steps toward the San Pedro, ready to lay his cares at the feet of the one he should have turned to in the first place.

The riverbank had often provided a quiet spot when he needed to think . . . or pray. He followed the familiar path through the thicket of mesquite and cottonwoods, and the words started pouring forth even before the river came in sight. "Lord, you know my father expects me to fail, and it looks like that's exactly what's going to happen unless you intervene and show me how to—"

A sharp sound split the air. *Was that a gunshot?* Standing motionless, he stood listening, but the only sound he heard was the steady thump of the stamp mill in the distance.

His eye caught movement up ahead. Stealthily, he stepped behind the trunk of a mesquite tree. Footsteps rustled the leaves along the pathway, and Steven drew farther back into the shadows, watching as a figure dressed in sapphire blue came into view—Jessie. He stepped forward and called a greeting.

She let out a squeak and clutched her reticule against herself.

In spite of the strain of their last meeting, Steven couldn't hold back the smile that spread across his face. "I didn't expect to see you here."

She offered a hesitant smile, as if the picture of

him marching her out of the Palace was fresh in her mind, as well. "I could say the same thing. But it's a pleasant surprise."

Afternoon sunlight filtered through the bare branches, dappling her copper curls. Steven's breath caught in his throat at the sight. "I was heading for one of my favorite spots, out there where the river curves. It's a good place to sit and sort things out." Acting on impulse, he added, "Would you like to join me?" To his delight, she nodded and turned to walk with him.

Moments later, he cut off the path and led the way over to a fallen cottonwood log on the bank. "This makes a nice bench to sit on and watch the river go by." He pulled his handkerchief from his pocket and spread it on the log, giving Jessie a place to sit. He held her elbow as she settled into place, then sat beside her.

When she looked at him, her gaze held none of the brash expression he'd come to expect. "You said you wanted to come here to think. You have a lot on your mind?"

He looked deep into those aquamarine eyes. "Everything's falling apart, and there doesn't seem to be anything I can do about it. The silver is in the mine, ready for the taking, but we can't ship it for fear of having more stolen. I came out west planning to show my family I could do something that mattered and make a place for myself in the world. But now . . ." Feeling his throat tighten, he bowed his head and looked down at his boots.

Without speaking, she reached over and placed her slim fingers on his hand. The light touch sent a flush of warmth throughout his entire body.

"I can't imagine why anyone would think you don't matter."

He gave a bitter laugh. "You don't know my father."

Jessie arched her delicate eyebrows and gave him a questioning look.

What was it about this woman? Only a few days before, he'd been admonishing her about her behavior, and today he was ready to open his heart to her.

"Several years ago, a college friend asked me to take the blame for something he'd done. It seemed a trivial thing at the time, but he stood to lose a great deal if the truth came out. Wanting to help my friend, I agreed to do as he asked."

A tiny pucker appeared between her brows. "That seems a terribly small thing to create a rift between you and your father. We all make mistakes, and you were very young."

"Young and foolish." Digging his heel into the soft earth at their feet, he felt the pain of the past wash over him afresh. "We don't always realize what impact our actions will have. I never dreamed at the time that this would become a defining moment in my friend's life. Getting away with this misdeed seemed to give him the idea

he could always find a way of escaping conse-
quences, that he could do whatever he wanted
and never be called to account."

The soft gurgle of water flowing over rocks
filled the silence before he went on. "That attitude
carried over into every part of his life—his
friendships, his business practices, his marriage
—until it wound up ruining them all."

Jessie increased the pressure of her fingers on
the back of his hand. "But those choices were his,
not yours."

"His father didn't see it that way. When my
friend's business crumbled and his marriage
failed, the whole story finally came out. His father
was devastated. Instead of blaming his son, he
held me responsible, said what I had done all
those years before showed a lack of moral
strength that brought about the downfall of his
son. And he may have been right. If I had just
stood up to my friend, insisted he take responsibility for his own actions, it might have turned out
quite differently."

"You don't know that," Jessie said. "I think
you're being far too hard on yourself."

"My father wouldn't agree with you. When he
learned what I had done, he berated me for my
lack of integrity. He called me every kind of
irresponsible fool and said I would never amount
to anything."

"What happened then?" she asked quietly.

"I took the inheritance my grandmother left me and came out west determined to do two things. One was to make my mark in the world. The other was that I would never intentionally tell a falsehood again, no matter how inconsequential it might seem."

He looked at Jessie, hoping to see approbation in her eyes. Instead, she stared into the distance with a troubled expression.

To cover the awkward silence, he said, "I'm sorry. Here I've been rattling on about myself. I've enjoyed getting acquainted with your aunt, but I'd like to know more about you." He smiled, trying to lighten the mood. "For one thing, I hope your relationship with your parents is better than mine."

To his dismay, Jessie's face crumpled. The bleakness in her eyes tore at his heart.

"I don't have parents—not anymore. They died in an accident when I was young."

Steven turned his hand and wrapped his fingers around hers. "I'm sorry. Did you have to go live with relatives?"

The quick shake of her head was almost indiscernible. "No, there wasn't anyone. Friends of my parents took me in—people they'd worked with."

Steven drew back, startled. "What about your aunt?"

Jessie pulled her hand away and wrapped it

around her reticule. "She . . . she and my parents had been estranged for some time. It's only recently that we've regained contact."

She scrambled to her feet. "I had no idea it was getting so late. Our cousin is coming for dinner, so I need to get back to the house."

He started to rise. "Let me escort you."

"No, don't bother. You needed some time alone. I can make my way back on my own." With that, she hurried toward the path, dabbing at her eyes with her fingertips.

She disappeared into the trees a moment later, and Steven listened until her footfalls faded and silence reigned again.

Did she realize how much of herself she had revealed in those few sentences? Steven picked up a chunk of wood lying at his feet and turned it between his fingers, deep in thought. In the short time he'd known Jessie, he'd seen her shift from charming conversationalist to reckless thrillseeker to sympathetic listener. But never once had he suspected she'd experienced such tragedy. Maybe that explained the contradictions in her manner.

He'd assumed her relationship with Lavinia was one of long standing, but obviously that wasn't the case. Did that explain the tension between them? Maybe Jessie harbored some resentment about not being reared by her family after her parents' death.

He stood and flung the chunk of wood into the flowing water below and watched it float downstream. Jessie had seemed different today. Softer, more open than he'd ever seen her before. He felt like he'd gotten a glimpse of the woman beneath the saucy exterior for the first time. And he felt drawn to what he saw, no doubt about it.

But then there was the way she behaved around Bascomb and Jake—not to mention her foray into the Palace. He didn't want to let his heart become ensnared by a woman who was wrong for him.

Today, though, she'd exhibited some of Lavinia's compassion and gentleness. How wonderful it would be if Jessie's zest for life and Lavinia's finer qualities could be found in the same woman. If that were the case, he could easily lose himself in those blue-green eyes forever.

❧ 21 ❧

Ellie pushed her spectacles higher on her nose as she turned left on Grant Street and wondered what Ted had in store for her that morning. Over the past four days, he had put her through her paces, not only repeating her shooting lessons by the river, but training her in various techniques of observation, ways to ask leading questions, and the finer points of shadowing a suspect.

At first the exercises proved stimulating, but as time wore on, she felt increasingly overwhelmed by the need to remember everything she'd learned. What could be left? She couldn't imagine, but she had no doubt Ted would have more information to impart. The man seemed to be a never-ending fount of knowledge in the craft of detection, one who was willing to share his wisdom freely.

And that offered her a ray of hope. Surely he wouldn't invest so much time with her if he planned to recommend her dismissal. But he remained closemouthed about his intentions every time she broached the subject.

When she reached the hotel lobby, she found Ted leaning against the counter watching Donald retrieve a rope from the floor.

Ted waved her over. "You have to see this."

Donald's face glowed as his audience doubled. Handing the rope to Ellie, he said, "Pass the rope under the arm of this chair, then cross the ends over the top."

Mystified, Ellie did as directed.

Donald placed his wrists on top of the rope. "Now tie my hands together. Pull the knot as tight as you can."

Ellie threw a questioning glance Ted's way but received only an amused smile in response. Still puzzled, she tied a secure knot, then stepped back.

Donald turned to Ted. "Would you cover my hands with that towel?"

No sooner had Ted complied than Donald pulled his hands free, picked up the towel, and folded it over his arm.

Ellie stared, openmouthed. "However did you manage that?"

Donald gave a small bow. "A magician never reveals his secrets."

She turned to Ted, who merely chuckled. "It's amazing how much a person can do with a little sleight of hand." He lowered his eyelid in a conspiratorial wink.

Ellie held back a smile. He was a nice man. However things turned out, she couldn't complain about Ted's treatment of her. He had shown her nothing but kindness and respect.

The lobby opened, and a couple approached the counter. While Donald moved to register his new guests, Ellie looked up at Ted, trying to appear more enthusiastic than she felt. "What do you have planned for us today?"

"Today, dear cousin, I must take my leave." Ted reached down and picked up a carpetbag Ellie hadn't noticed earlier.

"You're going? Now?"

Ted broke into a low chuckle at her surprise. "Yes, it's high time I was getting back to Denver." He crooked his elbow at her. "Would you care to stroll to the depot with me?"

Ellie took his arm, so nervous she could scarcely breathe. "Have you sent in your final report?" she asked in a low voice.

"Not yet. I will send it in Benson, before boarding the train—away from prying eyes." He nodded and set off in the direction of the depot.

Not a word about her needing to start looking for new employment? Mustering up her courage, Ellie tugged him to a stop and faced him directly. "What will you tell them?"

Crinkles formed at the corners of Ted's eyes. "If anyone had told me before I came here about this scheme you've cooked up, I would have said it was a recipe for disaster."

Ellie drew a deep breath and braced herself for the worst.

"I'm still not convinced your plan will work, but one thing I am sure of . . . if anyone can pull it off, you're the one to do it."

Ellie clung to his arm, afraid her legs might give way. "Then you aren't taking me off the case?"

"I will recommend they give you more time. We all needed a while to learn the ropes. You've already done a good job establishing yourself with the townspeople. Now that you have a better idea of how to carry out an investigation, I have a feeling you'll do fine."

They reached the depot, where the stage stood waiting, and Ted handed his carpetbag to the driver. Drawing her away from listening ears, he added, "If you carry it off successfully, this should be a great coup for you. It will rock them back on their heels in Chicago."

Tears blurred Ellie's vision, and she blinked them away. "I can't thank you enough—"

He dismissed her gratitude with a wave of his hand and led her back toward the stage, where he bent to give her a hug. "Good-bye, dear Lavinia. I can't remember when I've had a more pleasant visit."

Ellie recovered enough to call out to him as he climbed into the stagecoach. "Have a safe journey, Theodore. And give my best to the family." She waved her handkerchief until the coach was out of sight, then squared her shoulders. She had been given a second chance. It was time to prove herself.

Ellie pushed open the door of the Grand Hotel and stepped inside the lobby for the second time that day. "Hello again."

Donald looked up from polishing a brass sconce near the doorway to the dining room. "Mornin', Mrs. Stewart. Good to have you back." He took a second look at her and crossed the lobby and reached out as if to brush something off her collar. "What have we here?" Withdrawing his hand, he held up a gold piece before palming it and returning it to his pocket.

Ellie stared in astonishment, then burst out laughing. "What a wonderful trick! You're very clever with your hands, Donald. If only money would really materialize out of thin air like that."

She peered around, disappointed not to see any sign of Myra. "How is your wife today?"

Donald shook his head and tucked the dust-cloth into his back pocket. "Not so well, I'm afraid. She has good moments from time to time, but on the whole she seems to be getting weaker."

"I'm so sorry." At a loss for anything more comforting to say, Ellie gave him a solicitous pat on the shoulder. Up close, she could see the fine worry lines that creased his forehead. "I guess she isn't up to coming out for a visit?"

"She's sleeping right now. Has been doing that more and more. She's enjoying that book you dropped off, though. She reads it whenever she's awake. Says it helps her pass the time and gives her something pleasant to think about."

"I'm glad. I hope she regains some strength soon." Ellie paused a moment. "Do you mind if I sit here and knit awhile? After having my cousin around the last few days, and with Jessie out most of the day, my house seems too quiet right now."

Donald pulled out the dustrag again and flicked it over an already spotless spindle-leg table. "Make yourself at home. I'll be puttering around here, so let me know if you need anything."

"Thank you." On impulse she decided to ask for something that would greatly assist her surveillance. "Mr. Tidwell, the breeze is lovely. Would you mind if I opened this window?"

"Not a problem, the lobby could use a little fresh air. Let me get that for you."

As he raised the window, Ellie repositioned one of the upholstered chairs to give herself the widest viewing angle possible. "Thank you. I do enjoy watching people pass by." True enough, but not for the reason he might think.

She settled herself in the chair, feeling a quiver of anticipation. After her haphazard attempts at sleuthing, the thought of putting Ted's advice into practice exhilarated her. The one bit of counsel she chose not to accept was his admonition to carry the gun with her. That she simply could not bring herself to do.

After talking it over with Ted, she had decided to let her characters work in shifts. Lavinia would take the morning hours, letting her use her observation post at the hotel to best advantage. She would save Jessie's appearances for the afternoons and evenings, when those involved in Pickford's seamier side would be more likely to be available to talk with the younger woman.

She set her knitting bag at her feet and pulled out the tan scarf she'd started the night before. She slipped the soft yarn from one needle to the other, grateful for the simple pattern that let her fingers work without much thought on her part while she focused the bulk of her attention on the goings-on outside.

Keeping Ted's lessons in mind, she kept a close watch on the passersby, alert for any suspicious activity or anyone who looked more prosperous than they should. Three matrons entered and exited the mercantile. Ellie scrunched her lips and shook her head. Everything about them looked quite normal.

A couple of miners made their way back from the saloon district, talking about a new singer who graced the stage at the Palace. They didn't seem to be plotting anything other than their own degradation. And they certainly gave no appearance of having an abundance of cash. If they did, they would surely have been able to afford clothes with fewer holes and look like they'd bathed sometime within recent memory.

Ellie sighed and turned her knitting to begin a new row. Ted had warned her that surveillance required patient vigilance, but he hadn't mentioned how utterly tedious it could become. Her fingers found a hole where she had dropped a stitch, and she bent her head to go back and correct her mistake.

She jumped when the hotel door banged opened, and she looked up to see the man whose tryst she'd interrupted stride into the lobby. Ellie averted her face, wishing she could make herself invisible.

He glanced her way, and she caught sight of piercing dark eyes that regarded her with distaste. She swallowed hard and avoided his gaze until he moved beyond her field of vision.

A flicker of movement caught Ellie's eye when he rapped on the desk. Looking up, she noticed the mirror that hung near the door to the street, giving her a clear view of the desk and the man standing there as Donald came out of the dining room and joined him. Keeping her head bent toward her knitting, Ellie surreptitiously slanted her eyes upward and watched the reflection.

"I need to talk to you," the visitor said.

Donald wiped his hands on the dish towel he carried. "Sure. What's on your mind?"

"Not here." Ellie saw the new arrival jerk his head in her direction, then motion toward the office. After a quick glance her way, Donald nodded, and the two men walked into the other room and closed the door.

Why was he so anxious for them to talk where they couldn't be overheard? Ellie felt the hairs at the back of her neck stand up. She turned in her chair to look directly toward the desk and saw that the door hadn't latched and still stood open a crack. She tried to rein in her mounting excitement.

It might be nothing. Again.

On the other hand, after weeks of fruitless effort, she couldn't afford to ignore any suspicious activity. She needed to check it out.

But how? She couldn't just get out of her chair and sneak over to eavesdrop. What possible reason could she give if someone came in and found her with her ear pressed against the crack in the door?

She looked down at her knitting and smiled. No one could blame her for retrieving a ball of yarn that slipped off her lap and rolled across the room. She picked up the tan ball and let it slide off her palm. It bounced on the floor and rolled all of three feet before it came to a stop. Ellie grimaced and leaned over to retrieve it.

Checking to make sure no one stood outside to witness her little subterfuge, she reeled off a few yards of yarn, then gave the ball a good toss. This time it bounced all the way across the lobby, coming to rest mere inches from the desk. Much better.

"Oh, bother." Ellie pushed herself out of her chair and walked slowly across the room, keeping up the role of frustrated knitter, even if she had no one in the audience.

She stooped stiffly to pick up the yarn, shaking even more coils loose as she did so, then stood and began to rewind the loose yarn, all the while straining to hear what was going on behind the office door.

". . . need you one more time." That was the other man's harsh rasp.

Ellie's hands froze, and she forced them into motion again.

"I don't think that's going to be possible." She could hear the tremor in Donald's voice when he answered. "I have my wife to think of. I can't afford to be part of this any longer."

"You can't afford not to. How would your wife get along without you?"

A long pause followed, during which Ellie hardly dared to breathe.

"When?" Donald asked.

"At the next full moon." The other man gave a contemptuous snort. "That'll give you a little time to work up some courage."

It sounded like the brief conversation was coming to an end, which meant she'd better be sitting down again. Ellie scurried back to her chair, reaching it just as the men reentered the lobby. Both stopped short when they saw her on her feet.

Ellie held up the ball of yarn, indicating the trailing strands. "Clumsy me. I'm getting more butterfingered all the time."

The dark-eyed man cocked his head slightly and gave her a thoughtful look before turning back to Donald. "Don't forget."

He eyed Ellie on his way out, and the hostility in his gaze made her blood run cold.

She resumed her seat and finished winding her yarn with trembling fingers. Did what she just heard have anything to do with the thefts, or did it pertain to something else entirely? She had no difficulty believing Donald's visitor capable of any kind of evil, but surely not Donald. His easygoing personality aside, he simply didn't seem to have the kind of gumption needed to take part in a robbery. Why would he be involved in such a thing? And what was supposed to occur at the full moon?

She picked up the scarf and tried to continue knitting but gave it up for a loss when she made more mistakes than progress. It wasn't likely she would learn anything more at the hotel. Might as well move on. Maybe she could ask Gertie some carefully worded questions that might tell her more about the kind of man Donald really was.

Putting her yarn and needles away, she gathered up her knitting bag and turned to Donald with a bright attitude she was far from feeling. "I don't want to wear out my welcome. I'll be on my way for now. Please tell Myra I said hello, and I hope to see her again soon."

Donald looked at her with eyes that reminded her of a mournful hound dog. "Come back whenever you can, Mrs. Stewart. You're always welcome here."

Ellie started toward the door but then turned back, unable to contain her curiosity. "Who was that odious man? He's a thoroughly unpleasant sort."

"His name's Marvin Long. He's a shift foreman out at the Busted Shovel. Don't you worry about him, though, Mrs. Stewart. He just likes to throw his weight around. It makes him feel important."

Ellie nodded and left, her mind in a whirl. That was the second time she'd seen Marvin Long at the hotel. What business did he have there? More importantly, what kind of hold did he have over Donald?

Hoping to glean a hint from Gertie, she glanced quickly to her right and left along Grant Street. The only movement was a team of horses plodding toward her pulling a buckboard at a sleepy pace. They were still a block away, leaving her plenty of time to cross.

She stepped into the street and headed toward the mercantile, her mind on what she'd overheard. Gertie liked to talk. How could she get her to talk about Donald, or Long, or both without giving away the reason for her interest?

A shrill whinny caught her attention. Ellie looked up, horrified to see the horses bolting into a dead run, heading straight toward her.

The driver's face was a mask of fear. "Get out of the way!" he shouted.

Ellie knew she ought to run, but she couldn't seem to convince her legs to agree. *God, help me!*

A pair of strong arms wrapped around her from

behind and jerked her off her feet, then tossed her to one side, where she landed like a rag doll in a heap.

She lay still, fighting to catch her breath. Time seemed to slow down as the crushing hooves pounded past. Through the cloud of dust they raised, Ellie saw her rescuer fall to the ground and then, thankfully, roll to his feet again. He turned, and she recognized Jake Freeman, the blacksmith.

"Let me help you up." The smith extended a work-worn hand. "Take your time. You want to check first to make sure nothing is broken."

Ellie moved her limbs gently and found that her fingers and toes, arms and legs all appeared to be functioning. Then she clapped her hands to her head. Had her wig slipped? To her relief, it seemed to have remained in place despite her tumble. She patted her sides, making sure her padding was still where it belonged. A quick swipe of her tongue assured her that the plumpers remained firmly tucked in her cheeks.

Thus reassured, she took Freeman's proffered hand and eased herself upright.

The mercantile door flew open. "Lavinia, is that you?" Gertie rushed from the store, wringing her hands. "Land sakes, what happened?"

"I'm not sure." At a loss for an explanation, Ellie turned to Jake Freeman.

The blacksmith's eyes blazed. "I can't tell you a

reason, but I'm going to have some words with Clifford Watson. He nearly ran her down, the crazy halfwit." He spat into the dusty street, then wiped his mouth on his sleeve. "That's the stupidest stunt I've seen in a long time. He was bringin' his buckboard in to have me do some repairs on it, but any fool knows better than to be running horses right through the middle of town like that."

He pulled off his hat and swatted the dust from his pant legs. "If you'll excuse me, I aim to go give Clifford a piece of my mind." As he stalked across the street to his shop, his determined gait told Ellie that Clifford Watson was about to receive the tongue-lashing of a lifetime.

Gertie wrapped her sturdy arm around Ellie's shoulders and started clucking like a mother hen. "Come on inside, where we can brush you off proper. You're absolutely covered with dust. I'll have Walter put some water on for tea to soothe your nerves. Why, you could have been killed!"

Ellie allowed herself to be led away without resistance. She had been heading to the mercantile anyway. Spending time with Gertie fussing over her would give her ample opportunity to ask the questions she'd been formulating—as soon as she could remember what they were.

Just as soon as her body quit shaking.

❧ 22 ❧

"Good day, Miss Monroe." Marshal Everett Bascomb tipped his hat and looked at Ellie with an appreciative gleam in his eyes.

"Good day to you, Marshal. Where are you going this fine afternoon?" Ellie smiled up at the lawman and fell into step beside him, trying not to limp. Being tossed to the ground like a sack of potatoes that morning had left her limbs stiff and sore.

"I'm waiting to see who comes in on the afternoon stage. After that, I'm heading down to the Palace to sit in on a faro game."

Ellie formed her lips into a pout. "What a shame. I was hoping we'd have time for a nice chat." She stepped off the boardwalk when they crossed the street and tried not to wince.

Two cups of Gertie's bracing black tea had helped her regain a measure of composure, enough so that she had managed to totter back home, where she divested herself of Lavinia's trappings and tried to calm her jangled nerves. After a belated lunch, she redressed as Jessie and went back into town.

Tempting though it was to remain in the house the rest of the day, the success of her eavesdropping at the hotel spurred her on. She couldn't shirk following up on it to see if she could find any connection between Marvin Long's comment about the full moon and the silver thefts. It might turn out to be nothing more than an odd coincidence, but she needed to know one way or another. Ellie hoped it would turn out to be a false lead. As much as she wanted to catch the thieves, the thought of Myra's husband involved in felonious activity left her heartsick.

As it turned out, she encountered the marshal as soon as she reached the downtown area. Much as the thought of spending time in his presence sickened her, she couldn't pass up the opportunity.

Bascomb's lips curved up at the corner. "Why don't you come along to the Palace with me? You could sit beside me and be my lucky charm." He lowered one eyelid in a slow, suggestive wink. "You could even sit on my lap, if you'd like."

As nauseating as his proposal was, Ellie found it even more repugnant to have to act as though his improper behavior didn't bother her. She batted her eyes and gave his arm a playful swat. "What a scoundrel to even suggest such a thing."

His easy laugh showed he hadn't taken offense at her rebuff. "It doesn't hurt to ask. Nothing ventured, nothing gained."

Ellie forced herself to laugh along with him, fighting the urge to slap that vulgar leer right off his face. If not for her need to gain information pertinent to the case, she would have stomped off and left him behind in a cloud of dust.

As they strolled past the marshal's office, she waved at the assortment of Wanted flyers posted on the outside wall. "Maybe you ought to skip the faro game, Marshal, and spend more time on catching some of these criminals. Why, look! This one offers a reward of five hundred dollars for the capture of a band of stage robbers. Surely that would be a more certain thing than playing cards."

A look of disgust replaced the jovial expression on Bascomb's face. With a sweep of his arm, he snatched the flyer off the wall and crumpled it between his hands. "Lousy good-for-nothings!"

What had sparked that explosion? "Those outlaws? Did they do something to you personally?"

Bascomb shook the wrinkled paper at her and jabbed his finger at a wavy line of large print at the top of the page. Ellie glanced first at the picture of three men wanted for stage robbery, then sucked in her breath when she read the words he indicated: Pinkerton National Detective Agency.

She looked up, suddenly wary. "You have something against the Pinkertons?"

"Bah! They call themselves detectives. Thieving rats is more like it. They come sticking their noses in where they have no business and getting all the glory for themselves. But once all the excitement dies down, they've run back to their hole and don't have to worry about what's involved in keeping order day in and day out."

She tried to think of some response that would pacify him. "Goodness. If that's the way they operate, I can see why you aren't one of their admirers."

Instead of calming him, her remark seemed to inflame him even more. His face turned dark red, and thick veins stood out in his neck. "Not by a long shot. And now that bunch of mine owners have come up with the bright idea of bringing them in to investigate those robberies we've had." He twisted the flyer between his hands as if he wanted to wring someone's neck. The paper ripped in two, and the pieces fluttered down to the ground.

Ellie stared at him, her heart pounding like a stamp mill. She had seen—and thoroughly disliked—the way the marshal fancied himself as a ladies' man, but she would take that over this darker side of his personality any day. Once again, she blessed Gates and Fleming for warning her not to let anyone in Pickford know her identity or for whom she was working. More than ever, she was willing to believe what the men had told her about not assuming that the law in these parts was above suspicion.

While Bascomb ranted, Ellie glanced around, noting that his tirade was drawing curious glances from others on the street. She started to speak, then thought better of it. She had plenty of experience with actors flying into a rage when someone else was given a role they thought belonged to them. Best to let him wind down of his own accord and not say anything else to fuel the flames of his anger.

He went on raging, leaning over until he stood nose to nose with Ellie. "Do I look like some kind of incompetent?" he roared. "Do I?"

"Not at all." Ellie's voice came out in a squeak, and she took a step backward.

Bascomb stopped as though he'd been doused with a bucket of water. He shook his head and looked at her, as if recognizing her distress for the first time. The mask of anger vanished like mist in sunlight, and his contorted features resumed their usual genial expression. "My apologies, Miss Monroe. I'm afraid I let my feelings get the better of me."

Unsure of what to say, Ellie settled for nodding. She looked over the marshal's shoulder and found sudden inspiration for changing the subject. "Look, here comes the stage."

In an instant, Bascomb's attention turned to the depot across the street. He watched intently as the stagecoach drew to a stop in front and four men got off. His focus centered on a short man in a loud checkered suit. "I don't know that fellow," Bascomb muttered.

Ellie watched the driver hand a large case down to the passenger. "That looks like a sample case. He must be a drummer of some kind."

"Maybe. Or maybe he's the one the Pinkertons sent out. They like to try to disguise themselves. Think they're so smart that no one will notice." Bascomb's face darkened again. "But this time they've got a surprise coming. I'm on to this one." Without another word he set off across the street, ready to accost the hapless salesman.

Ellie recognized her cue to exit the scene. She spun on her heel to put her thought into action, and a smile curved her lips when she saw Steven bearing down on her from the direction of the blacksmith's shop. It wasn't until he drew closer that she noticed the set look on his face.

"I need to talk to you."

His abrupt tone caught Ellie off guard. Had she just gone from one angry man to another? She shot a quick glance over her shoulder to where Bascomb seemed to be interrogating the new arrival. "Can we talk while we walk?"

Without waiting for a reply, she set off toward the mercantile, walking quickly to put as much distance as possible between herself and the irate marshal. Steven joined her without a word. She could see the muscles in his jaw bunch as he marched along.

Just past the corner, he stepped off the board-walk and drew her into the alleyway between the dressmaker's shop and the mercantile. Without preamble, he blurted out, "How is your aunt?"

Given his brusque manner, that question was the last thing Ellie had been expecting. "She's shaken and sore but as well as can be expected under the circumstances." Her voice trailed off in a quaver when she finished.

Steven seemed to notice her unease and softened his tone. "I'm sorry. Learning she'd nearly been run down must have come as a shock to you. I'm sure you must be rattled, as well."

More than he knew. Ellie lifted her chin and tried not to think about the way her left leg throbbed and how sore her arms were where the smithy grabbed her before throwing her to safety. She fully expected a bumper crop of bruises to blossom by morning.

"I'm not sure how to say this. There's something I feel your aunt should know, but I don't want to alarm her, especially after what she's been through today."

Ellie's hand flew to her throat. "What has happened? Another robbery?"

"I wish it were that simple." Steven paused a moment as if searching for the right words. "I've been talking to Jake Freeman. He told me about pinning Clifford Watson's ears back after he let that team run away. Clifford swears those old horses of his are the laziest pair around. He didn't think they had that kind of life left in them, said they acted like they'd been stung by a hornet. When Jake helped unharness them, he checked the horses over to see if he could find anything to explain them acting up like that. He found a good-sized welt on the flank of the near-hand horse."

Ellie nodded, trying to appear attentive while her gaze roamed over Steven's rugged features. This was the first time she'd been with him since their unexpected meeting at the river. If she hadn't let her emotions get the better of her and hurried off so abruptly, she felt sure their time together would have ended much differently. Perhaps with a stroll along the river beneath the arching canopy of cottonwood branches. She even dared to imagine him taking her in his arms.

Her heart beat faster at the mere thought.

She traced his lips with her gaze and realized Steven had quit talking and was looking at her as if expecting a response. What had he been saying? She ran her mind back over the last words she remembered hearing. "Oh yes, the welt on the horse's flank. So it was a stinging insect of some sort?"

Steven looked at her with the same expression one would use in dealing with a backward child. "This is February. Do you see any bees or wasps flying around?"

Ellie shook her head, feeling every bit the dullard he evidently thought she was.

"Jake checked the welt closely. It was tender—the horse flinched when he touched it. But he couldn't find a stinger or anything else to account for it." A ridge formed between his eyebrows.

Ellie tried hard to keep her attention focused on the topic at hand, but it was hard to do when her mind kept wandering. What would it feel like to rub those creases from his forehead? He'd lost her, at any rate. She hadn't the slightest idea what he'd been getting at. Still, she ought to make some effort at keeping up her end of the conversation. "So the horse is all right?"

Steven shook his head. "All Jake could think of was that the welt looked like something you'd see as the result of a whiplash, or maybe a rock flung from a slingshot. But Clifford swears he never picked up a whip, and Jake believes him.

"So do I, for that matter. Clifford doesn't have any more get-up-and-go than his horses do. He'd not be likely to hurry them along that way, especially not in the middle of town when he'd almost reached Jake's shop."

A feeling of foreboding crowded out the delight of imagining what it would be like for Steven's lips to touch hers. The contrast jarred her, something like the way Juliet would have felt if she'd toppled off her balcony, plummeting past Romeo to land on the cobblestones below.

"You're saying it was a prank? Some urchin with a slingshot caused that accident? Why, I could have been . . . I could have lost my aunt."

"I don't think—"

"Which boy was it? Billy Taylor?" The more she remembered the fear and danger of that moment, the more her anger grew. "That sounds like something he might do. Do you think it was him?" If it was within her power, Ellie would have been glad to rain fire down on the little wretch. "I'll tell his mother. No, better yet, I'll wring his scrawny neck myself."

"Jessie." She felt a gentle pressure on her shoulder. Through the mist of rage that shrouded her vision, she realized Steven was squeezing her arm.

"What?" With an effort, Ellie reined in her ire and pulled herself back to the moment.

"I don't think it was a childish prank." Steven stared at her intently, as if waiting to see whether his words would sink in.

"Then what . . . ? Who . . . ?"

"It could have been done intentionally."

Steven had her full attention now.

"What I'm trying to say is, there's a possibility that someone deliberately spooked those horses in an attempt to run your aunt Lavinia down."

Ellie gaped at him. A tendril of dread coiled its way up her spine. "That's ridiculous! Why would anyone do such a thing?"

"I'm not sure, but it may not be the first time they've tried." His lips pressed together. "Did your aunt tell you about the collapse in the mine?"

She nodded her head.

"My foreman discovered that was no accident, either. At first I assumed it was an attack directed at me, that somebody wanted me out of the way so they could get their hands on the Redemption. I never dreamed anyone might be trying to harm Lavinia until this happened today and I started putting the pieces together."

"You mean . . . you're saying someone is trying to kill . . ." Ellie's vision closed in around the edges, as if she were looking down a long, dark tunnel. Her knees buckled, and she began to sway.

She heard Steven say something, but his words were distorted, as if coming from a great distance. His hand slid past her shoulder and circled around her back, catching her before she could slump to the ground. She leaned against him as he half led, half carried her to the bench in front of the dressmaker's shop.

The irony of the situation didn't escape her in spite of her hazy thoughts. Only moments before she had been longing for Steven to take her in his embrace. And now she rested in the circle of his arms, but she was too numb to fully appreciate the experience.

He let her sink onto the bench and steadied her with one hand while he fanned her with the other. Keeping a firm grip on her arm, he knelt down beside her, his face mere inches from hers. "I guess I should have broken the news to you a bit more gently."

His breath grazed her cheek, jolting Ellie back to awareness as effectively as if he'd waved smelling salts under her nose. She looked deep into his eyes, feeling as though she were being drawn into their deep brown pools.

The crease between his eyebrows deepened. "Are you all right?"

Ellie nodded. The numbness was definitely fading now, leaving her all too aware of the warmth of his touch. Every nerve ending in her arm tingled.

A warm smile curved his full lips. "I'm glad, Jessie. Really glad."

"Me too." The simple statement was truer than he could imagine. It was worth that kind of shock to experience this closeness and see the tender concern in his face. She longed to admit to every deception, every lie, so nothing stood between them and they could start anew.

I'm the Pinkerton agent you sent for. I'm here to find the men who have been stealing your silver. The words trembled on her lips, ready to spill forth and end the secrecy. It was time he learned the truth.

Much of the reason for keeping her identity secret was to protect her from those who would want to thwart her efforts. But Steven was not one of those evildoers. She knew it in her heart. He was the soul of integrity through and through. She should tell him. They could work together to find the robbers and bring them to justice. And then . . .

And then . . . what?

The tenderness she saw in Steven's eyes was for Jessie Monroe, not for Ellie Moore. What would he do if she stood before him as herself? If Jessie's wig and makeup were gone, and he saw her as just plain Ellie?

She knew the answer to that question. Jessie dazzled everyone who met her—Steven included. But he wouldn't look twice at mousy Ellie Moore.

The harsh truth struck her like a blast of icy air off Lake Michigan. She was in Pickford because she had a job to do. And finishing that job would save Steven's mine. That was what counted, not her romantic fantasies. She needed to keep her focus where it mattered.

Once she solved the case, her future with the Pinkerton Agency would be secured. She would investigate more cases and solve more crimes. She might even build a brilliant career as their premier woman detective.

But she would never find someone who made her feel the way Steven did. He smiled again, and Ellie's heart wrenched.

"Should we tell your aunt about my suspicions?

I don't want to frighten her, but it's important that she keep her guard up."

"But why?"

He leaned back, as if confused by her question. "Why?"

"Yes, why would anyone try to hurt her?" She thought she knew the answer but was curious about what he saw as the reason for the attacks.

"Well, I'm afraid it is because of her interest in investing in my mine—and she does ask a lot of questions. I'll talk to her soon about spreading word around town that she is no longer interested in investing in the Redemption, but I thought it best you talk to her first."

Ellie bobbed her head. "Yes, that makes sense. I'll be sure to let her know."

Steven's smile stretched into a rueful grin. "It's probably best that you have her sit down before you break the news. I'm sure you'll do a better job than I did." The light in his eyes faded, and the grin slid from his face. "I'm not entirely sure that you're safe, either."

Ellie's mouth sagged open.

"It's something we probably have to face. They might not believe she has changed her mind and could try to get to Lavinia through you." Steven stroked her cheek with his thumb, sending a delicious wave of warmth surging through her. "I don't think I could bear it if anything happened to you," he whispered.

Her throat constricted. "I'll try to be careful. I'll do everything I can think of to keep myself safe. I promise."

"There may be more than one way you need to guard yourself." Steven looked down and cleared his throat, then resumed eye contact. "I was just talking with Jake Freeman. With all the times you've stopped by the smithy, he's convinced you've set your cap for him."

Ellie caught her breath. "You don't mean it."

"I do. More importantly, Jake does. He's already spinning daydreams and building castles in the air about a future together. Not only that, but I noticed you talking with Marshal Bascomb when I came up. It isn't the first time I've seen you chatting with him . . . and others around town who are no better than he is."

His words doused the warmth in her veins like a splash of cold water.

"I'm sure you don't know what kind of man he is, or the sort of reputation he and those other men have. But reputation is a precious thing, and I don't want to see you get yourself into a situation that would tarnish yours. So while you're making promises, would you also promise me you'll be more careful about where you spend your time and who you talk to?" Steven's dark eyes gazed into hers with an intensity that left her breathless.

She ran the tip of her tongue across lips that felt as dry as sandpaper. "I . . . can't do that."

Steven drew back as if she'd slapped him. "What?"

Ellie rose quickly, bringing a stab of protest from her stiff muscles and knocking Steven off balance. "I said I can't make that promise."

Steven scrambled to his feet and loomed over her, standing so close she took a step back. "I don't understand."

He advanced a step, and Ellie moved back again, coming up hard against the front wall of the dressmaker's shop. The sharp nubs of the rough-cut boards jabbed into her shoulder blades.

He reached out his hand but drew it back before he touched her. "I thought there was something between us, Jessie. Was I wrong?"

No! The denial reverberated through Ellie's brain as she struggled to keep her outward composure. She hated being the cause of the pain she could see etched on his face. But those were Ellie's emotions. Jessie had to be a stronger person.

She grasped for words, knowing that any explanation she might make wouldn't satisfy. "I want to experience the West. I know these men are a little rough around the edges, but it's the only opportunity I may ever have to meet the kind of people I've only read about."

Steven stared at her as though she'd lost her mind. "Don't you understand? These men aren't gentlemen. I don't want to see you hurt . . . maybe even ruined."

Ellie averted her gaze and looked past him. Farther down the boardwalk, a couple stared at the spectacle she and Steven were creating. A lanky cowboy strolled past, a knowing smirk on his face.

She steeled herself and met his eyes again. "Don't worry about me. I can take care of myself."

The anguish in his eyes was no match for the misery in her heart. With all her being, she longed to reach out, cup his cheek in her hand, and tell him how she truly felt. But that wasn't possible. Feeling a profound sense of loss, she turned and started to walk away.

Quick as lightning, Steven's hand shot out and gripped her arm. He spun her back to face him. "That isn't good enough, Jessie. We need to talk about this."

Ellie put her hands up to catch her balance, and they came up hard against Steven's chest. She could feel his heartbeat through the fabric of his broadcloth shirt, pressed flat under her splayed fingers. Everything around them faded away. The only thing she was aware of at the moment was the man standing over her, filling her senses and drawing her ever closer.

She felt his hand pressing against the small of her back. He dipped his head lower. Ellie watched his lips draw nearer, felt his breath flutter her lashes. Her eyes drooped halfway closed.

"Jessie." His soft murmur sent renewed heat flooding through her veins.

A harsher sound pierced her consciousness. Ellie pulled back, suddenly aware that she had been about to let Steven kiss her right out on the boardwalk. In broad daylight, no less. A flush of embarrassment scorched her cheeks, but a quick glance reassured her that no one seemed to be paying the slightest attention to them. As the strident clanging continued, she realized people were shouting, running west along Grant Street.

She looked up at Steven. His face had lost its ardor, replaced by a chiseled sternness. Dread clutched at her with cold talons. "What is it?"

Steven's mouth set in a grim line. "That's the bell at the Redemption hoist works. It means there's a fire."

❧ 23 ❧

"A fire at your mine?" Even as Ellie spoke, her mind registered that couldn't be the case. People weren't running south of town, where the Redemption was located. Instead, they seemed to be converging at a point farther west on Grant.

"There." Steven pointed to the plume of black smoke spiraling upward. "The hotel." He set off at a dead run, with Ellie at his heels. Moments later, they joined the crowd of townspeople, some staring, some shouting, all showing a devastating awareness of what could happen if the fire got out of hand.

Six men wheeled a hose cart down the middle of the street. "Come on, boys!" their leader shouted. "Let's get the pump going."

A man tossed a bucket to Steven, who hurried off to join the bucket brigade forming at a nearby horse trough. As he ran, he yelled back over his shoulder, "Stay back! This is going to be dangerous."

Ellie couldn't have moved if she'd wanted to. She stood transfixed, her horrified gaze focused on the cloud of smoke pouring out of the hotel's front windows. The fear she'd felt once before when standing outside a burning building threatened to engulf her even as the flames began licking along the eaves.

Once again she was a helpless child standing on a Chicago street, held back by a policeman's strong arms while she watched the flames devour the theater where her parents were trapped inside.

"I got more buckets." The man carrying them bumped into her as he ran past. Ellie did a quick sidestep to maintain her balance, and the movement jolted her back to the present.

The powerless feeling remained, though. How well she remembered the raw terror of the night her world came down around her in a heap of blazing timbers, leaving her an orphan, dependent on her parents' theater associates to take her in.

Was anyone still inside the hotel? As the question popped into her mind, the paralyzing fear fell away, and the urgency of the moment galvanized her into action.

Ellie gathered up her skirts and ran to the man barking orders near the hose cart. "Did they all escape?" When he paid her no mind, she grabbed his arm and shook it. "Did everybody get out?"

He barely gave her a glance. "I don't know, lady. We're trying our best to keep this thing contained. If it takes off like that fire did in Tombstone last summer, we could lose this whole section of town."

Ellie looked around frantically for someone else to ask. No one paid her the least bit of mind. They were all scrambling to save the hotel and the adjacent buildings.

A knot of people moved. Beyond them, she spied two men dragging Donald Tidwell across the street. After propping him up against a hitching post, they ran back to join the others fighting the fire.

Ellie sprinted across the street, dodging a falling ember as she ran. She could hear Donald's racking coughs over the tumult of the crowd. When she reached him, she fell to her knees at his side. "Donald, are you all right? Where's Myra?"

Another fit of coughing seized him. Ellie waited

for agonizingly long seconds until the spasm ended. Donald looked up at her blankly, his head lolling to one side. Seizing both his arms, Ellie bent over him and repeated the question: "Where is Myra?"

Grief darkened his eyes. "I tried. So help me, I tried, but it was too late. I couldn't get to her." He bent over double, his body convulsed this time by sobs.

Ellie caught sight of a woman hurrying past. Seizing the woman by the sleeve, she pointed to Donald. "This man needs help. Go get the doctor. Hurry!" Without waiting to see if her command had been obeyed, she dashed off toward the hotel.

Heat from the flames pushed against her as she drew near, and a stocky man blocked her way. "Get back! Get back. You're too close."

"But someone is still inside!"

The man's face paled, and he looked over his shoulder at the twisting flames. He turned back to Ellie and shook his head. "It's too far gone for anyone to go inside now. It won't help to send someone else in there to die."

He gave her a little push. "Go on, now. You need to get back to where it's safe."

Ellie stumbled backward, her eyes fixed on the burning building. The memory seared in her mind from long ago threatened to overpower her once more.

"Not Myra."

The words seemed to bolster her courage. No, not Myra. It wasn't going to happen again, not if she had anything to say about it. She wasn't a frightened little girl anymore. She was a grown woman, with a will of her own.

She studied the scene with a critical eye. Most of the smoke seemed to be confined to the front of the hotel, while the back appeared to be relatively clear. Myra's bedroom was somewhere in the back.

Maybe, just maybe . . .

"Please, God," she breathed as she dashed around the corner to the alleyway that ran behind the hotel.

Which room? She had never seen the hotel from the rear before.

She ran up to a small window near the west end and peeked inside. A sink, a stove, a set of cupboards. Obviously the kitchen.

She backed away, trying to picture the layout of the hotel in her mind. If that was the kitchen, the window next to it probably belonged to the office. And if that was the case, the one to the right might be the bedroom.

Ellie rushed over to it and cupped her hands against the glass. Her calculations were correct. Inside she could see the bed, its rumpled sheets pushed to one side, as though someone had scrambled out of it in a hurry. She stood on her tiptoes and gasped when she saw Myra's frail body lying on the floor.

Gripping the bottom of the sash, she shoved it upward until it gave way. Then she hopped up on the sill and swung her legs inside the room. "Myra?"

A sob of relief escaped her when the other woman turned her head at the sound of Ellie's voice.

"Donald. I need to find him."

"He's already outside, waiting for you." Ellie looked toward the door. For the time being, the air inside the bedroom was relatively clear, but she could see smoke seeping in underneath and around the top. "Do you have any guests? Is anyone else inside?"

Myra shook her head. "The last one checked out this morning." She looked at Ellie as if registering her appearance for the first time. "Do I know you?"

"Of course you do. I'm—" Ellie bit back the words. Today she was Jessie, a woman Myra had never seen before. "I'm Lavinia Stewart's niece."

Without giving the other woman a chance to reply, she added, "Let's get you out of here. Can you stand if I help you?"

Myra made feeble attempts to push herself off the floor, but in the end Ellie had to wrap her arms around the fragile woman from behind and bodily drag her toward the window.

She took in a deep breath and immediately choked. It was getting harder to breathe, and she felt herself getting weaker. Another glance at the door showed the smoke increasing. The door itself was now smoldering.

Ellie leaned against the sill, longing to gulp in a breath of clean air. But that would have to wait. She had to get Myra out first.

But how? The bottom of the sill was above Ellie's waist. Under normal circumstances she probably would have no problem lifting Myra's light frame up over the window ledge and out to the alley, but now it seemed an insurmountable task.

The smoke grew denser, reducing her breathing to shallow gasps. Ellie tightened her hold on Myra and heaved upward. She only managed to raise her an inch or two. Not nearly enough.

Keeping her arm tight around Myra's waist, Ellie leaned out the window and looked down the alleyway. "Help." She intended it to be a scream, but the words came out in a dull croak.

A muffled thump sounded behind her. Ellie whipped her head around. The door had popped open, admitting a scorching wave of heat. Through the smoke that filled the room, she could see flames dancing their way inside, licking up the walls to the ceiling.

Time was running out, and no rescue was at hand. Ellie took a fresh grip on Myra. "You've got to help me. We can do this if we work together."

"I . . . can't." Myra's breath came in a series of

weak little puffs. "Don't have . . . the strength. Go on. Bless you for . . . trying, but it's time . . . to save yourself."

No. Ellie gave her a little shake. "I'm not leaving you. Here, hold on to the ledge a moment. Please!"

Before Myra's tenuous grasp gave out, Ellie swung herself up on the sill, sitting half in, half out of the window. Turning back around, she reached under Myra's arms and laced her fingers behind Myra's back. Holding the other woman tightly against her, Ellie breathed a prayer and flung herself backward.

For a sickening moment, she didn't know if her gambit would work. Then as gravity took over, her leverage increased, until both of them dropped out the window and landed on the hard-packed ground.

A loud roar sounded from inside the room, and a plume of flames whooshed out the window above them.

Ellie lay with Myra's weight atop her, trying to get a breath. They weren't home free yet. The heat was so intense it was almost unbearable.

She felt a vibration thrumming along the ground, and a voice called out, "Over here, boys. I need a hand."

Strong arms reached down and lifted Myra. Freed of the other woman's weight, Ellie rolled to her side and sucked in a ragged breath of air, then another one. Mindful of the need to flee, she scrambled to her hands and knees and pushed herself to her feet.

The man holding Myra yelled above the roar of the flames. "We have to get out of here! No telling how quick that wall's going to come down!"

Ellie nodded. "I can walk. Get her over to her husband. The doctor should be there helping him now."

The man ran off, and Ellie staggered across the alley. Air. She needed air.

She leaned against the back wall of the neighboring building for support as she stumbled toward the corner, trying to make her stinging eyes focus through the billowing smoke.

"Jessie!"

Her heart leaped at the sound of Steven's voice. She gathered the strength to totter forward a few more steps. The next moment, he appeared through the haze. He opened his arms, and Ellie fell into them, unable to do more than let him sweep her up and carry her away from the inferno.

Ellie felt her head bounce against his shoulder as he dashed past the bucket brigade and the men wielding the town's only fire hose. Not until he reached a point far enough removed from the fire that the air tasted blessedly clear did he stop and stand, chest heaving from exertion.

He didn't seem any more ready to put Ellie down than she was to be set on her own two feet again. His arms made a sweet haven after her ordeal, one she wished she never had to leave.

"How did you know I needed you?"

He rested his cheek against the top of her head. "I didn't. I saw one of the men carrying Myra out and ran to lend a hand. He told me there was someone else back there. When I saw it was you . . ." His voice thickened and trailed off.

The next moment, he set Ellie back on her feet and turned her to face him. "What on earth were you doing back there? You could have been killed."

Ellie clutched at his shoulders to steady herself. "Donald told me his wife was still inside. I had to get her out."

Steven goggled at her as if she'd taken leave of her senses. "You didn't think to get help? Send someone else?"

"I tried, but no one would pay any attention to me. There wasn't time to wait for someone to listen."

Steven's mouth twisted. He traced her cheeks with his fingers and cradled her face in his hands. "It was a brave thing you did, but it could have turned out so differently." He rested his forehead against hers, and his voice dropped to a rough whisper. "I could have lost you."

Ellie pressed her palms over his hands, and her eyes welled with tears. "I know, but I had to try."

Steven straightened and stared at her with a

look of wonder. "Do you even know Myra?"

"It doesn't matter." Ellie swallowed back a sob. "No one deserves to die like that. No one."

A shout from the street made them both wheel around. The crowd in front of the hotel scrambled back as the walls collapsed, sending up a shower of sparks.

A hoarse cry went up. "Look out! It's going to take the furniture store next!"

Steven looked down at her. "I've got to help. If we don't get this stopped, we could lose the whole town." Concern crinkled his brow. "Can you get home by yourself?"

Ellie bobbed her head. "I can manage. Don't worry."

His lips lifted in a crooked smile. "Don't give me any more reason to worry, all right?" He leaned down to brush a light kiss across her lips before he turned and ran back to join the effort to contain the fire.

She watched him go, her fingertips pressed against the spot where his lips had grazed hers. She saw him grab one side of the hose cart and help push it into place farther along the street, his cotton shirt straining across the muscles of his back. Smoke streaked his shirt, his hands, his face, and a thick lock of sandy brown hair tumbled down over his eyes. At that moment, he was the most heroic man she'd ever seen.

And he cared about her. She'd felt it the moment

he swept her into his arms, heard it in his voice when he talked about losing her. With one look, one word, one touch from her, he could be hers.

If she were Jessie Monroe.

A sob rose in her throat, choking her even more than the smoke. She turned to leave, needing more than anything to get back to the safety of her home, where she could sort out her maelstrom of emotions away from the tumult on the street. Away from Steven's distracting presence.

Away from the mess she had created for herself.

It took far longer than Ellie could have imagined to rid herself of the acrid stench of smoke. Her first bath washed away enough soot to let her tend to Jessie's accoutrements and clothing without leaving smudges on every surface she touched.

Now she soaked in her second bath of the evening, luxuriating in the pleasant fragrance of the lavender-scented bath salts she'd added to the blissfully hot water. The carefully washed red wig, its curls wrapped in soft rag strips, sat on its stand. The dark green grosgrain walking dress and her undergarments had been consigned to a reeking pile outside the back door. Much as she liked the gown, she didn't have the time or inclination to launder it until a whiff of it wouldn't remind her of her foray into the burning hotel.

She stepped from the tub and toweled herself dry. With her hair still damp and loose about her shoulders, she donned a warm wrapper and pulled out her notes about the case. After everything that had happened—the "accidents," the fire, and those intoxicating moments with Steven—she felt an urgency to refocus her thinking and get back on a firm footing in regard to the investigation.

How would the loss of the hotel impact her ability to watch the comings and goings around town, since its demise meant the end of her favorite observation post? As soon as the thought crossed her mind, she felt ashamed of herself. Donald and Myra had lost far more than she. She no longer had a surveillance point, but the ruin of the hotel had taken away their home, their livelihood, and very nearly their lives.

Thoughts of the Tidwells brought back the memory of being in the lobby of the Grand Hotel—had it been only that morning?—and her unpleasant encounter with Marvin Long. Ellie leaned back in her chair and stared at the opposite wall, wondering for the dozenth time what Long had meant by his brusque demand to Donald regarding the full moon.

When was the next full moon, anyway? She jotted a note to find out. It was imperative to know how long she had before the unknown event occurred.

The more she puzzled over Marvin Long's comment, the more confused she felt. Ellie leaned her elbows on the table and ran her fingers through her damp hair. Try as she might, she couldn't begin to guess what the date might signify. Was something scheduled to happen then? Surely not another silver shipment—Lavinia would have heard of it. Or was there something Donald was supposed to do?

With all her heart, she hoped it would turn out to be something innocuous. But Long's voice had been so threatening, so full of menace. Remembering his hostile tone, Ellie couldn't believe for one minute that it—whatever "it" happened to be—could be connected with any innocent activity.

But casting Donald in the role of a villain? That was equally hard to imagine, although who knew better than she how easily one could live out a charade that masked reality? It seemed unfair to suspect Donald of wrongdoing after he had just endured a tragedy.

Ellie pressed the heels of her hands against her eyes. Just because the man had suffered a disaster didn't mean he wasn't guilty of treachery. As the Pinkertons had emphasized, no one was above suspicion.

A thought sprang into her mind, and she sat bolt upright. Had the fire been set deliberately? Could it have been a warning of some kind to bring Donald into line and make sure he went along with Marvin Long's plans, whatever they were?

Much as she wanted to reject the notion out of

hand, she couldn't. There had been too many suspicious happenings of late—the supposed accident in the mine, the runaway horses. If these miscreants would stoop to violent methods to keep an elderly lady from learning the truth, maybe this fire signaled another of their actions, this one meant to coerce Donald into doing as he was told.

Remembering Marvin Long's appearance, Ellie shuddered. As hard as she found it to accept that Donald was connected with the villains, she didn't have the slightest difficulty believing Long capable of any sort of wrongdoing.

A new thought chilled her. She had spent a significant amount of time in the hotel lobby as Lavinia. Had the fire been another "accident" meant to stop Lavinia's prying? And worse . . . if that was the case, was she to blame for Donald and Myra's trouble?

The mere possibility was enough to make her want to run home as fast as she could . . . if she had a home of her own to run to. Ellie shoved the papers away with a low cry and buried her face in her arms. She couldn't bear to spend another moment on this bewildering mystery.

Besides, she had another mystery to solve, one just as puzzling as this one, but much more personal: Who was she?

Since the day she presented herself at the Pinkerton office as Lavinia, she had become a chameleon of sorts, switching from Lavinia's character to Jessie's and back again with ease . . . most of the time.

But in the process, she had lost her own identity. In the time she had been in Pickford, Cousin Ted was the only person she'd talked to as herself. And even then, he had seen her only as Lavinia or Jessie . . . never as Ellie.

Which led back to the question that plagued her: Who was she? Not the successful stage actress she'd dreamed of becoming—although at the moment she was playing roles in a way that would put any theater performer to shame.

She certainly wasn't Jessie Monroe, vibrant, vivacious, and desirable. Ellie's hands knotted into fists, thinking of the way Steven's eyes lit up when he looked at Jessie. Could he ever look at her . . . at Ellie . . . with that same kind of hunger in his eyes? She might be plain as a post on the outside, but inside, she carried the same fire that made Jessie the woman he wanted to claim as his own. Would he ever see that, see her and love her for who she really was?

But who was she?

Ellie slipped to the floor, kneeling beside the chair with her face pressed against the wooden seat. Truths she'd learned in the time spent reading her grandmother's Bible since arriving in Pickford came back to her. "God, your Word says you know me, inside and out. And even if I'm confused, you can make sense of this."

A wisp of peace, as indistinct as a tendril of smoke, wafted through her spirit.

Clinging to the sprig of hope it brought, she wrapped her arms around the chair as though it would somehow help her hold on to the presence of the Almighty.

"What is it you want from me?" she whispered. "I'm only Ellie. I have so little to offer you."

Just like that boy in the Bible story with the loaves and the fishes. The peace increased, bringing along with it a tingle of excitement.

"He gave you all he had. Is that what I'm supposed to do? All I have is myself."

The sprig of hope sprouted and blossomed, twining through her like a tendril of pure joy.

"Is that it? Is that all?" Ellie loosened her grip on the chair to wipe away the tears that streamed from her eyes.

"All right, Lord. If that's what you want, I give you myself. I'm yours."

24

"Would you like a slice of pie, Miss Monroe?"

Ellie pulled her gaze away from the passersby on Grant Street and looked up at George Parker, proprietor of the Mother Lode Restaurant. "No, thank you. After that delicious pork roast, I don't believe I could eat another bite."

Parker beamed. "My wife fussed over that roast all afternoon. I kept telling her it smelled good enough to eat. And sure enough, it is." He dropped a conspiratorial wink. "I sneaked a bite of it just after she pulled it from the oven, but don't let her know. How about another cup of tea to finish out your meal?"

"That would be lovely." While he headed to the kitchen, Ellie shifted her chair to stretch out her aching muscles—and change her viewing angle a bit. Her mood sobered when she spotted the charred ruins of the Grand Hotel directly across the street.

She thought again of what would have happened if she hadn't gotten there in time to pull Myra from the building, and she shuddered. Losing the hotel had been bad enough, but the results could have been far, far worse.

Today she was testing out the Mother Lode as her new outpost. It didn't have the range of view she'd gotten used to at the Grand, and she couldn't sit there for hours on end as she'd done in the hotel lobby, but looking out on Pickford's main street while lingering over a meal was much better than loitering on one of the benches scattered along the boardwalk in full view of everyone who passed by.

George Parker set the fresh cup of tea on the

table before her. "I'm surprised to see you eating alone. Where is your aunt today?"

Ellie took a sip of tea and blotted her lips with her napkin. How long would she be able to carry out this subterfuge?

"She's still rather sore after yesterday's accident with Mr. Watson's horses. She didn't feel up to having anything more than a bowl of clear broth this evening. I was in the mood for something more substantial, but the thought of fixing a whole meal just for myself seemed a bit daunting, so I decided to have my dinner here instead." She took another sip of the fragrant tea and smiled up at him. "It was a good choice."

Parker beamed. "You're welcome here anytime. My wife is the best cook this side of El Paso, if I do say so myself." Instead of going back to the kitchen, he lingered beside Ellie's table and shuffled his feet. "I just want you to know the wife and I think it was mighty brave, what you did yesterday when you pulled Myra Tidwell out of the hotel."

She felt a warm flush stain her cheeks and tried to wave the compliment away. "Anyone would have done the same thing."

"Maybe. But you're the one who did."

Ellie avoided his gaze and traced the rim of the teacup with her fingertip. She didn't feel like a heroine, especially after spending the previous night tormented by the possibility that the blaze might have been set on her account.

Not knowing whether she really wanted an answer to her question, she asked, "Do they have any idea what caused the fire?"

Parker shook his head dolefully. "It turns out it was Donald who started it."

Ellie set her cup down and blinked, certain she must have misheard him. "Mr. Tidwell?"

"Yep." Parker wiped his hands on the towel draped over his shoulder. "Myra had been having one of her bad days, and Donald had about run himself off his feet taking care of her. He stoked up the fire in the stove in the lobby and went out to sweep the boardwalk.

"But they figure he must not have gotten the stove door closed properly. Once the fire got going and the wood started popping, it would have shot sparks out onto the rug. From there it caught some of the chairs and kept on going. Once it got hold of the drapes, it was all over."

Ellie pressed her hand against her lips.

"Donald was out there sweeping at the west end of the building when someone yelled to him that there was smoke coming out the doors. He tried to get back inside to get Myra, but the flames were too much for him. If a couple of the men hadn't dragged him out, he would've died trying to save her. As it was, with all the smoke he took in, it was a pretty near thing."

Parker scrubbed his hand across his eyes as if to

wipe away the memory. "Doc said he's going to be okay, but he was in quite a state until he learned you'd gotten Myra out safe."

"And they're sure that's how it started?" Ellie forced the words out past the tears that clogged her throat.

Parker grunted an affirmation. "That poor woman's been through so much. God sure was watching out for you, gettin' you both out safe like that. You ought to stop over at Doc's and talk to them. I know they'd both like to thank you."

Ellie nodded absently, relief at knowing the fire couldn't be laid at her door mingling with grief for Donald and Myra. A new thought popped into her mind. "They've lost their home. Where will they go once they're back on their feet?"

He shrugged. "That's anybody's guess." When Ellie frowned, he added, "Donald didn't own the hotel, he just managed it. The owner lives in Tucson. He's coming over later in the week to check things out and see if he wants to rebuild. Even if he does, Donald isn't sure he'll have a job, once his boss finds out Donald's negligence was responsible for losing the—"

His voice trailed off, and his eyes bulged, staring out the window at a point beyond Ellie's right shoulder.

She whirled around in her chair in time to see a bareheaded man stagger down the middle of

337

Grant Street. One hand clutched his head, the other gripped a dust-covered slouch hat.

"That's the foreman from the Busted Shovel," Parker said at the same instant Ellie recognized Marvin Long, the man she'd encountered twice in the hotel lobby and once in the alley behind Pickford Hall.

Without another word, Parker bolted out the door. Ellie fished in her reticule, tossed the payment for her meal on the table, and hurried out to join the small crowd that had already gathered and was shouting questions.

"What happened?"

"How bad are you hurt?"

Long placed a hand to the bloody wound on his head. He swayed but shook off the hands that reached out to steady him. He cast a wild glance around the group of onlookers. "Where's Mr. Clay? I've got to find him."

A wide-eyed man pointed down the street. "I saw him go into the smithy a little while ago. I'll go get him." He returned moments later with Alfred Clay on his heels.

"What's going on?"

"They got your silver, boss."

Ellie sucked in her breath and darted a glance at Alfred Clay, whose face drained of color at the news.

"What?" The mine owner looked as though his knees might buckle any second.

"I was comin' out of the mine when three of 'em jumped me. Someone must have told them you were keeping your bullion in that old side shaft."

Ellie felt a hand clutch her elbow and turned to see Gertie standing next to her. "What's going on?" the older woman panted.

"Someone just robbed one of the mines." Ellie kept her answer brief and turned her attention back to the scene playing out before them.

Beside her, Gertie *tsk*ed her disapproval. "Those varmints are getting more brazen all the time."

Ellie nodded agreement but didn't take her eyes off the action in front of her. She studied the faces of the onlookers, looking for a flicker of knowledge, any sign of guilt.

Alfred Clay pulled out a bandanna and mopped his brow. "They took all of it?"

Long slowly shook his head. "I don't think they were expecting me to be there. It must have thrown their plans off kilter when I put up a fight. It looks to me like they only got away with a box or two. The rest is safe for now, but I wanted you to know right away."

"Three of them, you say." Clay had regained command of himself, his face set like granite. "Did you recognize any of them?"

"Sorry, boss. They were wearing masks."

"Which way did they go?"

"I didn't see them leave." Marvin Long stared down at his feet, as if embarrassed by the admission. "One of them clouted me over the head before they left, and it took a few minutes before I could see straight again."

Alfred Clay looked around the group. "I need some men to help me track them down. Who's with me?"

Four men stepped forward, and the grim-faced mine owner nodded his thanks. "This thieving has gone on long enough. It's time we put an end to it." He jerked his head toward Marvin Long. "You get on over to Doc's and have him check you over."

Long started to turn away, then looked back over his shoulder. "Boss, I'm thinkin' we need to move the rest of the silver someplace safer, if you get my drift."

Clay stared at him, then gave a quick nod. "Good idea. You can help me in the morning. You did a good job, Long. You'll have a bonus coming on payday."

Marvin Long ducked his head in acknowledgment and made his way toward Sixth Street, where the doctor had his office.

Alfred Clay and his group of volunteers hurried off, men on a mission. The rest of the group dispersed, leaving Ellie and Gertie standing on the edge of the street.

Gertie's outraged expression reminded Ellie of a hen ruffling her feathers. "What's this world coming to? If that no-account Bascomb was worth his salt, he'd find whoever's responsible and drag them in. They ought to be locked up until they're old and gray. And that's exactly what would happen if I had anything to say . . ."

Gertie's voice took on a note of concern. "Honey, are you all right? Your eyes look a little glassy."

Ellie blinked and pulled her focus back to Gertie. "No, I'm fine." She forced her lips to curve. "Really."

Gertie eyed her skeptically. "Here I've gone rattling along, never giving a moment's thought to how you must be feeling after all you and your aunt went through yesterday." She looked around as if expecting to see Lavinia. "Where is she, anyway? I would have expected her to be right in the thick of doin's like this."

Ellie seized the opportunity to make a graceful exit. "I left her resting at home. I really ought to get back and see how she's doing."

A flicker of disappointment flashed in Gertie's eyes, but she smiled and nodded. "You're probably right. Give her my best and let her know I'm praying for you both."

"Thank you. I'll tell her." Ellie took her leave, grateful for the promise of prayer. She needed all the help she could get. And with Gertie praying for both Lavinia and Jessie, that ought to count as a double dose.

She turned her steps toward home, realizing for the first time it was far later than she'd planned to be out. The sun had already dipped below the horizon, and shadows deepened all around. Inky blackness formed between the pools of light cast by the few gas lamps along the storefronts.

Ellie watched Gertie go back into the mercantile. After the flurry of activity a few moments before, it seemed strange to be the only person on the street, apart from the lamplighter moving from one gas lamp to another at the far end of Grant.

Feeling suddenly isolated, she almost called out after Gertie but caught herself. She wasn't a child with a fear of the dark. Her house lay only a few blocks away. It was time to be moving along.

She made her way slowly from one pool of light to the next, taking advantage of her unexpected solitude to let her mind go back to the aftermath of Marvin Long's announcement of the theft.

Letting the scene play through her mind once more, she felt again the shock Long's words had caused. Gertie had been right. It seemed the thieves became bolder by the day, striking right at Alfred Clay's mine instead of lying in wait for a shipment to pass along the road.

She passed the dressmaker's shop and stepped off the boardwalk to cross Fourth Street. What did it mean? Was this a sign they were growing more desperate? That hardly made sense, though. Why would desperation enter into their actions? They could hardly have gone through all the silver they had stolen already.

She frowned when she recalled something Marvin Long said.

How had the thieves known Alfred Clay was storing his silver in a side shaft at the Busted Shovel? He had mentioned something along that line at the meeting she attended as Lavinia, but the fact couldn't have been common knowledge.

Considering he was attacked, it seemed her suspicions about Marvin Long were unfounded, but could someone else in Clay's employ be helping the thieves . . . or be one of them himself?

How could she find out? Ellie went back over the scene again, searching for anything—a word, a reaction, a gesture—that might give her a clue.

As she crossed Third Street, something niggled at the back of her mind. She thought through the scene once more, line by line, but instead of focusing on the words, she concentrated on picturing Marvin Long's stance, his demeanor, his dramatic gestures.

Dramatic. That was the word for it. The exaggerated stagger, the hand clasped to his head like a tragic hero.

Her steps faltered, and she came to a halt in front of Wilson's Gun Shop. For a moment she no longer stood on the dusty boardwalk in Arizona, but backstage at the Orpheum during a production of *Much Ado About Nothing*, watching Roland Lockwood as Claudio being told he'd caused Hero's death.

Lockwood had played up the role to the hilt, so much so that titters spread throughout the audience. It hadn't take long for word to get around about his overacting, about his chewing the scenery. Magdalena had been furious about her play receiving attention for all the wrong reasons and prodded the director to convince the actor to tone down his portrayal. Eventually the titters—and Magdalena's ire—died down, and life got back on its usual track.

The next moment she found herself back in Pickford, staring into the gloom. She glanced around and shivered. Best to be getting home, where she could mull over her odd feeling of displacement to her heart's content.

She stepped out briskly, hurrying from one pool of light to the next. What had sparked that memory of Lockwood's ham-fisted overacting? Was there any connection between that and the action she had just witnessed?

Ellie mentally compared the two scenes side by side. A giggle escaped her lips when she recognized the similarity: Marvin Long's mannerisms and tone of voice had been near duplicates of Roland Lockwood's. From one point of view, his actions were well suited to the situation. From another, they seemed more fitting of a stage performance. Her mind must have made the connection between them without conscious thought on her part.

Her footsteps echoed on the wooden walk while her eyes strained ahead through the murky darkness. Just past Levi Jewelers, where the shadows lay deepest, she felt a strong arm encircle her waist, pinning her arms to her sides and yanking her off her feet.

Ellie caught her breath, but before she could let out a scream, a rough hand clapped over her mouth, stifling her outcry. The next moment, she was pulled into the narrow gap between the buildings.

Her feet flailed wildly as she thrashed around, trying to get purchase on the ground. One heel managed to connect with her captor's shin, bringing forth a muffled grunt and a low curse. The arm around her tightened, pulling her up so close against his muscular chest she could scarcely breathe.

She winced when the hand over her mouth pulled her head back and a whiskered cheek scraped the tender skin of her neck. Hot breath slid down the side of her neck, and a hoarse voice hissed in her ear. "Stop your fightin'. Any more of that, and the next move you make could be your last. Understand?"

Caught up in her struggle for breath, Ellie managed a quick nod. Her vision began to go gray at the edges, and she feared she might faint. With all her might, she strove to stay awake. If she lost consciousness, there was no telling what this fiend might do to her.

He eased his grip enough to let her feet rest on the ground once more, but kept his hand over her mouth, with the back of her head pressed tightly against his chest. With the constriction on her lungs lessened somewhat, Ellie drew in as much breath as she could. It helped a little—her vision began to clear—but she couldn't suck in the deep gulps of oxygen her body craved.

She had no idea what the man had in mind and no intention of staying around to find out. There was no one to help her. If she was going to get away, it would have to be through her own efforts.

Ellie tensed her muscles, not sure what she could do but wanting to be ready to take advantage of any opportunity her captor might give her.

The taut arm jerked back, squeezing the air out of her and threatening to plunge her into blackness. Then the pressure eased again, allowing life-giving air back into her starving lungs.

"Settle down. I only want to give you a message, but it'd be just as easy for me to snap your neck, if you give me a reason to."

Ellie forced her muscles to relax. There was no help for it. The only thing she could do was take him at his word and hope he meant what he said.

"That's better." The smell of stale alcohol drifted past her nose when he spoke.

She wanted to jerk her head away but forced herself to stand still. The calloused hand clamped across her mouth was reminder enough of what he promised to do if she didn't cooperate.

"Ready to listen?"

The tiny nod she gave seemed to satisfy him.

"That nosy aunt of yours has been snooping around in things that don't concern her. You tell her she'd better mind her own business and quit asking questions. She's already had two warnings, but she doesn't seem to be catching on. Maybe she needs something more direct, so this time we're telling her straight out: If she doesn't steer clear and mind her own business, she's going to have more to worry about than her own safety."

The prickly whiskers grazed her neck again as his chin nuzzled her ear. "Ask her how she's going to feel if something bad happens to her favorite niece."

A scream rose in Ellie's throat. She tried to swallow it back, but a faint whimper escaped her lips.

The man chuckled. "That's more like it. Now you're going to go home and give your aunt the message like a good girl. Right?"

Ellie bobbed her head again and tried to keep her knees from buckling.

The restraining hands moved quickly from her mouth and waist to grip her upper arms. Before she could react, they shoved her hard.

She flew forward in the darkness, landing on

all fours. Her knees skidded along the rough ground, and she felt a sting where pebbles scored her palms.

Ellie rolled over and pushed herself to her feet, ready to fend off another attack, but no one was there. The alleyway lay shrouded in silence, except for her labored breathing and the sound of boots pounding away between the buildings in the direction of Douglas Street.

Ellie grimaced as she dabbed iodine on her palm where the skin had been scraped raw by the unforgiving pebbles. The cuts, while sore, were fairly clean. They would heal quickly in the dry desert air. More quickly than she expected her ragged emotions to heal.

After a long, hot soak in her bathtub, she still didn't feel clean. Getting rid of the memory of her assault would take longer than doing away with the smoke from the fire. She touched the raw spot on her neck, wishing she could wash away the feeling of the bristly whiskers against her chafed skin.

When Gates and Fleming had warned her of danger during her briefing in Chicago, she'd brushed it off as the type of admonition a concerned uncle would give to a niece heading off into a new situation. But now their concern for her well-being seemed altogether warranted.

Ever since her arrival in Pickford, she had lamented her slow progress on the investigation. Evidently, some of Lavinia's questions had struck closer to home than she'd thought.

The reality of her recent brushes with danger shocked her through and through. Finding herself in imminent danger in real life was far different than living it vicariously through a character in a novel or play.

A play . . . Her mind jumped back to the comparison she'd made earlier of the scene from *Much Ado* and the one she'd seen on the streets of Pickford that evening.

Ellie shook her head. What was it about Marvin Long's account of the robbery that bothered her so?

She bent to scoop up the dress she had been wearing. If she could have her way, she would never touch it again, let alone wear it and bring back the memory of what she had just been through. But after throwing away the smoke-damaged dress the day before, that wasn't an option. Her limited wardrobe didn't give her the luxury of disposing of a second one.

Holding the dress at arm's length, she examined it for any tears it might have gotten when she fell. Her gaze fastened on what appeared to be a splotch of blood on the right sleeve.

Why hadn't she noticed a cut on her arm before? Ellie pulled up the sleeve of her wrapper.

A discoloration on her arm where her assailant had held her in his grip told her another bruise would likely be forthcoming, but she couldn't find a spot where the skin had been broken.

Mystified, she looked more closely at the dress. Turning it over, she saw another streak of blood on the back of the collar.

She let the dress fall to the floor and hurried to her dressing table. Letting the wrapper slip down over her shoulders, she picked up her hand mirror and held it up so she could check her neck and back.

Nothing. Not even the beginnings of a bruise.

Ellie pulled the wrapper back up over her shoulders. Picking up the dress again, she carried it over to the armchair and held it up under the light of the cranberry-glass oil lamp. The stains looked like blood, all right. They must have come from her attacker.

Holding this evidence of his contact in her hands made her feel as if he'd invaded her home with his presence. She felt the bile rise in her throat. Swallowing it back, she forced herself to examine the spot more closely.

She hadn't injured him. Much as she'd wanted to, he hadn't given her the chance. But he'd been hurt somehow. The thought gave her immense satisfaction.

Ellie studied the bloodstains again, giving particular attention to their location. The one on her sleeve must have come from his hand, and the one at her collar from his face.

A vision of Marvin Long staggering into the street flashed into her mind. She remembered the way he'd held his left hand against his bleeding head. Her attacker had used his left hand to hold her against him.

But Marvin Long had gone to the doctor, hadn't he?

Not necessarily.

Ellie swallowed hard as a succession of thoughts raced through her mind with startling clarity. She'd seen Long go off in the direction of the doctor's office, but that was no guarantee he had actually gone in to see the physician.

She closed her eyes, straining to remember every detail of the way she'd been grabbed and manhandled. She hadn't been able to see a thing, but she'd heard him clearly enough. Could that grating voice belong to Marvin Long?

But that would make him one of the robbers, or at least in league with them. It didn't make sense that they would attack one of their own.

She recalled the strength of the arms that had held her in the alley. Her assailant hadn't shown the signs of weakness Long displayed out on the street. He certainly hadn't acted like a man dazed from losing a significant amount of blood.

Acting. The word teased at her mind. Once again, she saw herself backstage at the theater, watching one of the actors apply theatrical blood to a simulated wound before he staggered onstage.

Just the way Marvin Long had staggered into the middle of Grant Street.

Ellie held the dress up closer to the lamp's etched-glass globe. A slight sheen on the stain reflected in the lamplight.

Real blood didn't shine after it dried on fabric. Ellie had pricked her fingers with a sewing needle often enough to be sure of that.

What could it be, then? Harold Stiller, the Orpheum's stage manager, had a favorite recipe for concocting stage blood, a mixture of sugar syrup and berry juice. Sugar would glisten like that when it dried.

Ellie raised the fabric to her lips, then lowered it back into her lap. The very thought of tasting blood—particularly Marvin Long's—sent a wave of nausea through her.

But it wasn't blood. She was positive of that.
Almost.

She stretched the fabric between her fingers. Whatever made that offensive stain, it was up to her to determine what it was. She was a detective, and detectives sometimes had to perform unsavory tasks in order to discover the truth.

Besides, hadn't she promised God she would give Him all of herself? That meant every bit of her belonged to Him.

Including her queasy stomach.

Once again, she lifted the dress. This time she dabbed the tip of her tongue against the spot and smacked her lips together, trying to identify the taste.

She'd been wrong. The stain on her dress wasn't Harold Stiller's blend of sugar syrup and berry juice after all.

It was raspberry jam.

She lowered the dress again, her mind in a whirl. If those splotches had been made by Marvin Long, then he had indeed been acting, and she'd been duped, just like any gullible theater audience.

But why? The question wouldn't leave her alone.

Now that she had thought things through, she had no problem once again believing Long to be one of the robbers, but why the act? What purpose could it serve?

Ellie didn't have the answer, but she knew she would have to keep an eye on him from that moment on.

And she was equally certain of one other thing—never again would she leave the house without the pistol Cousin Ted had given her.

❦ 25 ❧

Ellie slipped out of the dark gray dress and sat on the edge of her bed to unwrap the cloth strips from around her legs. A paisley-print frock in creamy yellow lay draped across the bed, ready for her to assume her second role of the day. When she got up to hang Lavinia's dress in the wardrobe, she tottered a little, as if old age truly was creeping up on her. Grasping the bedpost to steady herself, she removed the gray wig and prepared to transform herself into Jessie.

Maybe the weariness shouldn't come as a surprise, she thought as she pulled out the cheek plumpers. After Marvin Long's warning, she hadn't asked questions of anyone—she would save the inquiries for Jessie, whose questions for some reason did not concern the thieves—but she had spent the morning in a state of constant awareness, noting every detail of her surroundings and each person she saw around town. That was enough to wear down the sturdiest constitution.

She settled the red wig on her head, dabbed a bit of color on her cheeks, and slipped into the paisley dress. A memory stirred of helping Magdalena into the dress months before, bringing with it a wistful longing for days gone by. How she would welcome the chance to be back in

Chicago again, dealing with what she used to consider the hardships of theater life.

A hollow laugh escaped her lips. The girl she used to be had no idea what hardship meant.

But if she had remained in Chicago, she never would have met Steven.

But that was of no consequence at the moment. She didn't have time to act like a love-struck schoolgirl. Not while menace loomed on the horizon. And the best way to overcome that peril was to identify the gang members and notify the Pinkertons so they could call in the authorities and break up the ring.

She went to the kitchen, where she foraged in the cupboard for food and decided on a quick snack of tea, cheese, and crackers. No time for a proper meal. She could get something more at the Mother Lode if her hunger became too great.

During the morning's foray through town as Lavinia, she thought through the previous night's performance yet again and reached a conclusion. Marvin Long was very probably a member of the gang, but he wasn't the leader. Nothing about his actions spoke of him as being the author of the current drama, only a character playing out his lines as written.

Ellie carried a cup of tea to the table and sipped at it while she nibbled on her cheese and crackers. In that case, in addition to keeping a watchful eye on Long, she also had to watch for someone higher up in the organization. The thieves' hold on the mine owners of Pickford had gone on far too long. She needed to bring it to an end, and it had to be done soon. The sense of imminent peril, along with harboring suspicions about everyone she met, was eating her alive.

The only person she trusted was Steven, and now, more than ever, she couldn't tell him what had happened. If these criminals would go to such lengths to keep a sweet-tempered old lady from asking questions, what would they do to stop a robust man bent on saving his business?

The possibilities made her shiver.

No, if she planned to help Steven—and herself—she would have to keep her own counsel and play out the role she'd been given.

She swallowed the last drops of tea and swept the cracker crumbs off the table. Lavinia hadn't been able to discover anything of note. She would see what Jessie could turn up.

By dinnertime, Ellie's steps were flagging, along with her spirits. Despite an afternoon of carefully guided conversations, she hadn't been able to turn up one scrap of useful information. Nor had she seen any sign of Marvin Long, though she kept a constant watch for him.

Time was getting short, and she knew it was getting more and more foolish to keep asking questions—she had no way of knowing when she might ask the wrong question of the wrong person. She felt as though she were watching the final grains of sand slip through to the bottom of an hourglass.

Walking west on Grant, she crossed to the south side of the street at the corner of Third. She couldn't bear to retrace her steps over the same spot where she'd been assaulted the night before. Mildly embarrassed by her squeamishness, she continued on, squinting into the rays of the setting sun.

She hated to go home with nothing accomplished. It felt too much like giving up. Her intuition told her to linger awhile, that she would have a better chance of noting things of significance after darkness settled over the town.

But she couldn't afford to stay out after dark. Not again. Whether as Jessie or Lavinia, the risks were too great. Even the weight of the pistol in her reticule didn't offer enough sense of security to offset her fears.

Ellie reached Second Street and turned right. How she wished Norma hadn't found the love of her life until after their job had been completed. She needed another person for companionship, for counsel, and to guard her back.

She needed help, it was as simple as that, but she had no one to turn to. If she asked Steven to watch Marvin Long, he would be sure to ask why. And what could she tell him?

"Bang! Bang! I got you!"

Ellie shrieked and spun around to see Billy Taylor behind her, his finger pointed at her midsection in imitation of a pistol. Without thinking, her hand shot out, catching his ear between her thumb and forefinger.

"Owww!" His yowl of protest sounded like a cat who'd gotten its tail under a rocker. "What are you doing? Lemme go!"

"What am I doing? What do you think *you're* doing, sneaking up on people and scaring the daylights out of them? I ought to drag you home and give your mother a piece of my mind. What can she be thinking of, letting you stay outside so late?"

The boy tried to pull away, but her grip on his ear held him fast. He jutted out his chin and glared up at her. "It isn't all that late. Ma always lets me play outside after supper. She says it gives her peace of mind."

Ellie could well believe it.

And the news didn't really come as any surprise to her. On many an evening, she had seen Billy and his buddies playing outside long after she would have expected their mothers to have called them inside. Shouldn't they be concerned about what their children were doing? There was no telling what they could be getting into, running all over town like that.

In the dark.

Unnoticed.

With no one paying them any mind.

Ellie tilted her head and regarded the lad thoughtfully. "If I turn loose of your ear, will you stay here and not run off?"

Billy drew his brows together in a fierce scowl. "Why should I?"

Ellie released the pressure of her fingers a smidgen, but not so much that she couldn't nab him again if he made a move to run off. "How would you like another detecting job?"

The offer held him in place even more effectively than her fingers had. He stared up at her with a look of awe. "What do I get to do? Shoot someone for real?"

"Heavens, no!" Her voice came out in a squeal, far louder than she intended. She looked around and lowered her voice. "Nothing like that. I just want you to keep an eye on someone for me. Do you think you can do that?"

Billy shrugged. "Sure. I'm good at watching people, especially when they don't think I'm around. Who do you want me to spy on?"

Ellie eyed him, wondering if she'd just taken leave of her senses. "Do you know Marvin Long? He's—"

"The one who got beat up at the Busted Shovel yesterday? Sure, I know him." Billy's face darkened. "He doesn't like kids much. He caught me pokin' around the mine office one day and threatened to box my ears if he ever saw me there again."

A look of doubt spread over his features. "You just want me to watch him? That's all?"

"That's all," Ellie said firmly.

"Why? Are you sweet on him or something?"

Ellie bit back another yelp. "Not at all. I just want you to let me know if you see him doing anything suspicious."

Billy wrinkled his nose. "Like what?"

Ellie cast about for some explanation vague enough to cover all the possibilities but not so specific it would give her true purpose away. "Like if you see him somewhere he isn't supposed to be. Trying to get into a locked building —anything like that."

The boy's face lit up. "You *are* sweet on him. You want me to make sure he isn't visiting some other girl, right?"

Ellie resisted the urge to pick him up by his collar and give him a good shake. "Don't worry about why I want to know. The only thing you need to remember is to let me know if you see him sneaking around or doing something he shouldn't. And make sure no one sees you, especially him."

She held out her hand. "What do you say?"

Billy crossed his arms. "What's in it for me?"

Ellie bit back the sharp retort that sprang to her lips, saying instead, "A detective who does an extra-good job deserves a bonus. What would you say to a nickel for any information you can bring me about Mr. Long?"

Billy stared at her for a long moment, then spit in his palm and clasped it against hers. "A whole nickel? Lady, you got yourself a deal."

26

"Thanks for getting to these drills so quickly, Jake. I'll be back in a couple of days for the next set." Steven hefted the canvas satchel of sharpened steels in one hand and set off toward the Redemption. Normally he would have spent a few minutes chatting with the blacksmith, but the other man's interest in Jessie made it difficult for him to make pleasant conversation.

Sunlight glinted in a brilliant blue sky, brightening his mood. In spite of all his troubles of late, days like this made him glad to be alive. Just before he turned down Sixth, he spotted a familiar figure two blocks down the street. He pulled up short and grinned.

True to form, Lavinia Stewart was out making her morning rounds. Steven's admiration for the woman soared. Narrowly escaping the collapse in his mine, nearly being trampled by a team of horses, then learning those events might have been aimed specifically at her—all that was enough to send most easterners into hiding . . . or running for the nearest train station. But not his Mrs. Stewart.

He was going to do everything he could to keep her out of the line of fire, including spreading the word she was no longer considering investing in his mine, but she had come west in search of adventure, and she was proving herself up to the challenge.

Steven tugged at the brim of his hat and turned his steps toward her. He crossed the street with an easy stride, angling his course to meet her where she was admiring a gown with an abundance of pleats and lace in the dressmaker's window.

"Good morning."

Mrs. Stewart jumped and whirled around. For a fleeting moment Steven saw a flash of panic in her eyes and immediately regretted startling her. Considering all that had transpired in recent days, it probably hadn't been the wisest thing to do.

The look of alarm fled as quickly as it appeared, replaced by her usual placid smile. "Good morning to you, Mr. Pierce. I'm just out enjoying the morning air."

"I had a couple of errands to run." Steven lifted the satchel in his hand, then set it at his feet. He pushed his hat back on his head and moistened his lips. "I haven't seen Jessie around town since the fire. Is she doing all right?"

Mrs. Stewart shifted a quick glance to her right, then met his gaze again. "She's been out and about every day. You must have missed her."

Steven's lips tightened. "I must have." He spoke the words in a noncommittal tone that belied the tension he felt.

Had Jessie been avoiding him? Their last contact had been the brush of his lips against hers just before he raced back to fight the fire. At that time it had seemed like the right thing to do, but he'd wondered ever since if he'd crossed an invisible line and pushed too far, too quickly.

He shoved his hands into his front pockets. "Do you have any idea where I might find her now? I stopped by the house a little while ago, but no one answered when I knocked."

"Oh dear." Mrs. Stewart fanned herself with her hand. "I suppose she may have been resting, or . . . otherwise occupied."

Heat flamed in Steven's cheeks. He needed to drop that line of questioning before he embarrassed either one of them any further. He cleared his throat. "Maybe I should talk to you, then. Would you mind relaying a question to her?"

"No, not at all."

"I just learned there's a theatrical company touring the territory. They'll be performing at Pickford Hall on Friday night, and I wondered if Jessie might like to accompany me."

Mrs. Stewart's mouth rounded in a way that

reminded him of Jessie's expression when surprised. He hastened to add, "I didn't mean to exclude you. If you'd like to join us, I'd be pleased to escort you both."

For the first time since he'd met her, Lavinia Stewart seemed at a loss for words. Her mouth opened and closed without making a sound, and her blue-green eyes darted back and forth as though seeking an answer from an unseen source.

Finally she looked straight at him and drew a deep breath. "I don't believe I will be able to attend, but I'm sure my niece would welcome the opportunity to spend the evening with you."

The day seemed to brighten even more. Steven tried to rein in his spiraling spirits before they got out of hand. "I'm glad to hear that. Do you think I should consult Jessie herself, though, just to make sure?"

Mrs. Stewart's smile softened. "I know my niece very well, Mr. Pierce. I'm certain she'll be happy to go to the theater with you, and I hope the two of you will have a lovely time together."

Steven wanted to drive his fist into the air and let out a loud whoop. Instead, he contented himself with saying, "I'll be looking forward to it. It isn't often we get a troupe from Chicago in our neck of the woods. Would you please tell her I'll come by to pick her up at seven?"

With a tip of his hat, he picked up his satchel and made his way back to the Redemption. Even the weight of the heavy drill steels couldn't keep him from feeling as if he were walking on air.

Ellie turned back to the dressmaker's window and watched the reflection of Steven's retreating back in the glass. *Chicago?* What had she done? Maybe she should call him back and tell him she'd made a mistake. It would be foolish to take the chance of running into someone she knew.

She tossed her anxiety aside with a petulant shrug. No one in Chicago had ever seen her as Jessie, so she was in no danger of being exposed. There was no reason at all to avoid going.

Except for the possible damage to her heart.

On the other hand, if her heart was going to be broken anyway, how much more broken could it be? This was not some amateur group thrown together by Althea Baldwin and her church ladies. An evening at Pickford Hall would bring her into contact with the professional theater again. And with Steven as her escort, what could be better?

She studied her reflection and gave a little nod. She would do it. Once she moved on to other investigations, she would still have the memory of one perfect evening to cherish. Tucking that bittersweet knowledge away, she started walking toward the mercantile.

"Miz Stewart!"

Oh no. Ellie closed her eyes. When she opened

them, she saw Amos Crawford trotting across the street toward her.

She forced her lips into what she hoped would pass as a smile. "Good morning, Mr. Crawford."

"Mornin', ma'am. I need to talk to you."

Ellie peered at him curiously. Something about him seemed different this morning. After a moment, she realized what it was. For once, the telegrapher wasn't looking at her with calf-eyed longing.

Intrigued at the change in spite of herself, she nodded. "Go on."

Amos swallowed and ran his finger around his collar. "About those flowers I brought you."

Ellie's defenses went up again, and she edged half a step to the right. "Yes, they were lovely. Thank you so much for your thoughtfulness."

Amos looked down at the boardwalk and shuffled his feet. "It's kind of a funny thing. You're never going to believe it."

For someone about to tell a humorous story, he seemed remarkably ill at ease. He looked more like an accused criminal about to spill out a confession.

"It seems Miz Baldwin—Althea—got wind of me bringing them to you." Amos smoothed the top of his balding head with one hand.

"Yes?" With an effort, Ellie refrained from tapping her foot. The man seemed to be going in circles and was not getting anywhere.

"Well, it turns out she's had her eye on me for a

long time." He pushed out his chest and pulled in his stomach a fraction of an inch. "Sort of an infatuation, you might call it."

Ellie blinked. She had met Althea only a few times, but she had always seemed like a woman in full possession of her faculties. "Do tell."

"Yes, ma'am, that's the gospel truth. When she heard about me bringing you those flowers, it lit a fire under her, so to speak, and she started in to wooing me."

"Wooing?"

"That's right. Before I knew it, she was bringing me cakes and pies, asking me over for Sunday dinner." A dreamy look came over his face, and he smacked his lips. "My, that woman can cook."

His smile faded, and he looked at Ellie again. "I want to tell you straight out that I've proposed and Althea has accepted me. We're going to get married at the end of the month."

Ellie's mind reeled at the news. "How nice for you. My congratulations to you both."

Amos reached out and touched her shoulder briefly. "You don't have to put up a brave front, Miz Stewart. I'm afraid I may have given you false hopes, and I want you to know I feel bad about it."

Relief made Ellie's knees weak. "Oh no. Don't give it another—"

"No, a man's gotta take responsibility for his actions, and I intend to own up to mine. I just don't want you to think I'm the kind of man who's only interested in flittin' from flower to flower and breakin' hearts. I am—"

Ellie cut off the flow of words with a wave of her hand. "Mr. Crawford, I can truthfully say I would never take you for that type of scoundrel. You and Mrs. Baldwin have my blessing, and I wish only the best for your future together."

His Adam's apple bobbed up and down. "That's mighty fine of you, ma'am. Mighty fine. I always knew you were the kind of woman a man would be lucky to have beside him."

His eyes took on a wistful gleam. "When I think of what might have been . . . maybe I—"

"No." Ellie injected the word with all the firmness at her command. "Put those thoughts out of your mind, Mr. Crawford. Make it a clean break. You owe it to yourself and your future bride."

Over his shoulder, she could see the subject of their conversation walking toward the telegraph office, a covered tray in her hands. "Look! There she is now."

Amos turned, and his face lit up. "She's bringin' me lunch. What a woman." With the spryness of a much younger man, he loped across the street toward his lady love, apparently consigning Lavinia to the past forever.

Thank heaven. Ellie watched the pair greet each other and go inside the office.

At least one romance had gone right in Pickford.

✣ 27 ✣

" 'Cheviot—my husband—my own old love—if the devotion of a lifetime can atone for the misery of the last few days, it is yours, with every wifely sentiment of pride, gratitude, admiration, and love.' "

" 'My own! My own! Tender blossom of my budding hopes! Star of my life! Essence of happiness! Tree upon which the fruit of my heart is growing! My Past, my Present, my To Come!' "

Thunderous applause roared from the seats of Pickford Hall as Cheviot embraced Miss Treherne, Minnie comforted Belvawney, Angus offered solace to Maggie, and the final curtain rang down on the evening's performance of W.S. Gilbert's *Engaged*. The clamor swelled to an even greater volume, and the red velvet curtains rose again, allowing the members of the company to bask in the adulation of the audience once more.

Ellie joined in, swallowing back emotions that threatened to consume her. From the moment she and Steven had entered the lobby, she'd felt as though she'd been swept back in time. The hush of anticipation as the curtain rose, carrying the audience away from reality and into a world of make-believe, the lines spoken with perfect timing, even the sounds of the actors' feet treading the boards—all of it combined to draw her back into her old life, where she had spent so many hours hovering in the wings.

Steven leaned over and whispered, "They did a fine job, didn't they?"

Ellie nodded, unable to speak past the lump that blocked her throat.

Steven's lips curved up in the smile that never failed to send a tingle shooting through her. "I take it you enjoyed the performance?"

More than he knew.

Ellie nodded again and dashed a bit of moisture from her eyes. Let him think it was a rush of feeling brought on by the performance. For one evening, she had been back at the Orpheum, experiencing the sights and sounds she knew so well.

Steven rose and helped her to her feet, keeping her close to his side as they joined the crowd making their way back toward the exit. Bending down, he murmured into her ear, "We have another treat in store. The cast promised to greet the audience out in the lobby."

Ellie gave him a watery smile. She only hoped she could bear up under more reminders of what she had left behind. It wouldn't do to break down in front of Steven and the rest of the town.

When they reached the lobby, they found members of the troupe stationed at various points around the open area. "Is there any particular player you'd like to speak to?"

Ellie found her voice at last. "You decide. Whoever you choose will be fine with me."

He scanned the room, focusing on a spot where the knot of people wasn't quite so thick. "How about over here?"

He led her to a group surrounding Estelle Renault, who played the role of Maggie MacFarlane.

Ellie watched the young actress greet the awestruck citizens of Pickford with grace and charm, showing none of the condescension Magdalena had often displayed. She seemed genuinely happy to meet members of her public and receive their acclaim.

When it was their turn, Steven cupped his hand under Ellie's elbow and stepped forward. "Thank you for your performance, Miss Renault. We enjoyed it thoroughly."

The actress dipped her head in acknowledgment. When she turned to Ellie, a quizzical look spread over her face, and she tilted her head. "Don't I know you?"

Ellie's smile froze. "I . . . don't believe so."

Estelle's lips pursed in a charming moue. "Are you positive? I can't put my finger on when or where, but I'm quite sure I've seen you before."

Steven chuckled. "She's from Chicago. Maybe your paths crossed back there."

The room seemed to spin around Ellie, and

she cast her mind back. Had she met Estelle Renault before? And if so, where? When?

The actress tapped one finger against her lips and studied Ellie again. Then her face lit up. "It's your eyes—that beautiful shade of turquoise. I once played in a theater with an actress whose assistant had eyes of that very same hue."

The missing piece in Ellie's memory snapped into place. Of course! The young woman had once played Mary Melrose, cousin to Magdalena's character, Violet, in a production of Henry James Byron's *Our Boys*. Her path and Ellie's had barely crossed, as Magdalena deemed herself too important to hobnob with the lesser players. And once compliments started filtering in about Estelle's beauty and talent, Magdalena made sure she never played the Orpheum again. No wonder Ellie hadn't recognized her right away.

She forced a light laugh. "I'm afraid I've never been on the stage."

Estelle chuckled along with her. "Now that I look at you more closely, I know you couldn't be the same person I was thinking of. The eyes are right, but she was a much plainer woman than you."

Ellie absorbed the dagger to her heart with as much composure as she could muster.

"It's a very unusual eye color, though," Estelle said. "No wonder it brought back memories."

"I'll certainly agree that they're beautiful eyes."

Steven's tender glance threatened to undo Ellie completely. "Her aunt's eyes are that same color, too. Maybe it isn't as uncommon a shade as one would think."

"Really?" The actress arched her eyebrows.

"Yes," Ellie said. "It's something of a family trait."

Steven chuckled. "You never know. This other woman might turn out to be a long-lost relative. You may have more family in Chicago than you realize." After exchanging a few more comments with Estelle Renault, they took their leave and walked out into the crisp night air.

They strolled a block before Steven spoke. "I hope you enjoyed this evening as much as I did."

"More than you can imagine. It will always be one of my most cherished memories."

"I'm glad. I wanted tonight to be special." He opened his mouth as if to say more, then gave a barely perceptible shake of his head, and they continued on in silence.

Ellie matched her steps to his unhurried gait, wishing she could do something to prolong their time together. She longed to rest her head against his shoulder, to feel his arm wrap around her in response and hold her close, but she held herself in check. It was one thing to enjoy the moment, quite another to build up expectations in his mind that could never be realized.

She cast about for something to say. "It's hard

to believe we can see our way so clearly. It's almost as light as daylight outside."

Steven drew her arm closer to him. "There's nothing like taking a stroll with your special girl by the light of the full moon."

"Full . . ." Ellie stopped in her tracks and pivoted around to look behind them, where an enormous silvery disk hung suspended in the eastern sky.

"Yes, a full moon." Laughter bubbled in Steven's voice. "Surely you've heard of those in Chicago?"

Ellie stared at the shimmering sphere. "But when I asked Gertie, she said . . . I thought it wasn't supposed to be full until tomorrow night."

Steven stepped closer and traced her chin with his forefinger. "I'm rather glad Gertie was wrong. It puts the finishing touch on a wonderful evening."

A furrow appeared between his brows. "You're shivering. Did you just take a chill? Come on, let's keep moving."

They resumed their stroll down Douglas Street. Ellie's feet moved along steadily of their own accord while her mind raced, trying to reclaim the shattered pieces of her perfect evening.

How could Gertie have gotten the day wrong? No, she couldn't blame her friend. She should have checked the date herself.

In any case, this was the night she'd been waiting for, the night of high significance, according to what she'd overheard from Marvin Long. And instead of being on the alert, she'd spent the last few hours enjoying the company of the man she . . .

No. There was no point in pursuing that line of thought. Suffice it to say she had squandered precious time when she should have been on the lookout for . . . whatever was supposed to happen.

She took a deep breath and tried to calm herself. Maybe she hadn't missed it, after all. The moon wasn't even high overhead yet.

And Billy Taylor was on watch. As keen as the boy was to earn his nickel, she felt sure he would be steadfastly on the lookout. That knowledge let her relax enough to lean on Steven's arm again.

He covered her hand with his own. "Better?"

She nodded. For the moment, at least.

Much too soon, they reached her porch, mounted the steps, and stood before the front door. The night wrapped around them like a velvet blanket, the only sources of light the moon and the dim glow from the small lamp she'd left burning in the parlor.

Steven shifted from one foot to the other, suddenly seeming ill at ease. With a pang, Ellie realized what this meant. He would be saying his good-byes in a moment, and this dream of a night would be over.

She closed her eyes to squeeze back the tears that threatened. Her Cinderella moment had ended. It was time to go back to reality. The best she could hope for was to let their magical evening end on a good note, leaving them both with a memory they could treasure for the rest of their days.

Twisting her hands together, she lifted her chin and opened her eyes to look up at Steven. To her astonishment, his whole demeanor had changed in that brief moment. Instead of the self-assured man who'd escorted her to Pickford Hall, a nervous schoolboy stood before her.

He shuffled his feet and cleared his throat once, then twice. With a bashful smile, he reached for her right hand with both of his. "There's something I need to ask you."

Something in his expression made her mouth go dry at the exact moment her heart picked up its tempo. Her intuition warned her where this conversation was leading. She had to do something, say something to stop him. Her lips moved, but no words came out.

Steven captured her fingers in his hands and looked at her with a light shining in his eyes that put the moon to shame.

Ellie felt her heart soar and break at the same moment.

"Jessie, we haven't known each other very long, but I think my soul recognized you the first day we met."

Ellie's free hand crept to her throat.

"I've been waiting for someone like you all my life," he said.

Footsteps pattered along the dirt on Second Street.

"If you are willing . . ."

The running feet grew nearer, now pounding up Ellie's walk.

". . . I would like to begin courting—"

"Miss Monroe!"

Ellie's hand dropped from her throat, and she turned to face Billy Taylor, not sure whether she wanted to hug him or throttle him.

"I followed him! I followed him! Do I get my nickel now?"

Cut off in midsentence, Steven glared at the boy.

Ellie caught her breath. "You followed him? Where?"

Steven swiveled his glare to her. "Jessie?"

Ellie held up her hand, cutting him off again as Billy replied, "He was walkin' along Grant like he'd just come from one of the saloons, but then he cut south and headed out of town."

Steven spread his hands and looked at her and Billy as if they'd both lost their minds. "Could someone explain to me—"

"Do you have any idea where he was going?"

Billy gave her a cheeky grin. "Better than an idea. I followed him there."

Ellie gripped his shoulders. "Followed him

outside of town? Didn't I tell you to be careful?"

The boy's grin widened. "With all this moonlight, I didn't even have to stay close to see where he was going. He went straight out to the Constitution."

Steven clutched at his hair. "What are you two talking about?"

Ellie waved him to silence, her mind racing. What would the foreman of the Busted Shovel be doing at the Constitution Mine so late at night?

Only one thing came to mind. She'd been certain the robbers were planning something big, and this had to be it. They were going to rob Tom Sullivan, just as they'd tried to rob Alfred Clay's mine.

She opened her reticule and fished inside for a nickel. "Good job, Billy. That's exactly what I needed to know."

"That isn't all I saw. There was somebody else following him."

"Who?"

"Mr. Tidwell from the hotel . . . or what used to be the hotel."

Donald Tidwell? The news sent a cold shock through Ellie, followed by a rush of white-hot anger. "Are you sure?"

"Sure as I'm standing here." Billy held out his hand, palm up.

Ellie let the nickel slip from her fingers and

dug in her reticule again. "Here's a dime, five cents for each man you saw. Now go home and stay inside."

"A dime?" With a whoop, Billy snagged the coin and raced toward his house.

Ellie turned to face Steven, who stared at her with a combination of hurt and confusion.

"You're paying that boy to follow people? I don't understand."

"I know." A shaft of agony pierced Ellie's heart. She brushed her fingertips across his right cheek. "I can't expect you to. And I don't have time to explain right now."

He leaned forward and clasped her hands. "Jessie, dear . . ."

She pulled her hands away. "Don't call me that."

Steven straightened as if she'd slapped him. "I'm sorry. Maybe that was presumptuous of me."

Ellie shook her head violently and choked back a sob. "I'm not who you think I am."

She looked at him through a film of tears and tried to keep her voice steady. "My name is Ellie Moore, not Jessie Monroe. I was sent here by the Pinkerton Agency to find out who is behind the silver thefts." She pressed her lips together, hating herself for causing the pain she saw in his eyes.

She stretched out her hand again, then let it fall to her side. "I have to go now. I'm sorry. So very sorry." With that, she spun around and ran down the steps into the night.

Steven stood as though he'd been turned to stone and watched Jessie disappear into the darkness.

What just happened? Their evening had been going so well—perfectly, he'd thought. As far as he could tell, everything had been falling into place to begin a courtship with Jessie. Whatever happened to the Redemption, he harbored the hope that she was going to be a part of his future, and in the end, that was all that mattered.

Then the bottom had fallen out of his carefully laid plans. He felt as if he'd just seen his life caught up in a whirlwind.

He swung his head from side to side like a punch-drunk boxer, trying to make sense of what he'd just heard. So Jessie had been paying her neighbor's boy to spy on some of the local townspeople? That was hard enough to fathom, even without her cryptic parting statements.

If he couldn't make heads or tails of it, maybe Lavinia could. He reached the door in two short strides and gave it a sharp rap. There was no answer.

She must not have heard him. He raised his hand again, ready to knock hard enough to rattle the door loose from its hinges, when a thought stopped him. It was late. Was she still awake?

Cupping his hands against the window, he peered into the parlor, where the low-burning oil lamp cast a dim glow around the room. No sign of movement, no indication that anyone stirred inside the house. Apparently, Lavinia had already retired.

Another parting comment filtered into his muddled thoughts. Had he understood correctly? Had Jessie really told him she was the Pinkerton agent?

And that led to another question: Had Lavinia been duped into coming to Pickford? Did she know her niece's true purpose in coming to Arizona was to investigate the silver thefts?

If that was the case . . . His progression of thought knocked the wind right out of him.

If that was the case, then it followed that Marvin Long and Donald Tidwell had something to do with the robberies.

Which meant he'd just let the woman he hoped to eventually make his wife go haring off after a couple of criminals in the dark.

He leaped from the porch and set off toward the Constitution. Pinkerton or not, he loved her. They could sort the rest of it out later.

Right now, he knew only one thing—he had to go after her and do everything in his power to keep her safe.

28

Ellie hitched her skirts a little higher as she sped down Second Street. Steven couldn't have looked more stunned if she'd hit him between the eyes with a two-by-four.

But this was no time to dwell on the ruination of their evening. She needed to concentrate all her attention on the job before her.

Once again, she experienced the stab of betrayal she'd felt on hearing the news of Donald Tidwell's treachery. She'd wanted to believe him innocent, had balked at even considering him as a suspect. Yet when all was said and done, he turned out to be every bit as guilty as she'd feared.

What could have possessed him to get involved with this dastardly gang? He had a solid standing in the community and a wife who depended on him. In turning his back on what was good and honest, he had let down Myra, the citizens of Pickford, and himself.

Ellie rounded the corner at Grant Street at a dead run, trying to push back the dark cloud of rage. She needed to keep her mind clear for the task ahead. She had no intention of bearding the thieves in their den—Gates and Fleming had been adamant about that. Her job was merely to identify the criminals and send word posthaste to the home office, who would notify the U.S. marshal in Tucson.

All she had to do was trail Marvin Long and Donald to the Constitution, make certain what they were up to, then slip back into town, where she would rout out Amos Crawford and have him send a wire to the Pinkertons.

A sense of exhilaration lent wings to her feet. It was almost over. She was coming down to the wire on her first investigation, almost ready to cross the finish line. By the time the night was over, her part would be completed, and she'd be free to return to Chicago, leaving constant quick changes, runaway horses, and amorous telegraphers behind.

A pang of anguish caused her steps to falter. There would be other things she'd leave behind, as well. Steven . . . and a part of her heart.

Ellie paused to get her bearings when she reached Mill Street. From that point on, her journey would take her across open country. Slowing her pace, she picked her way across the rough terrain in the moonlight, finding comfort in the reminder of the pistol in her reticule as it thumped against her side. She chafed at her slowness, but she didn't dare risk turning her ankle—or worse, being seen—not when she was this close to her goal.

The scent of greasewood and creosote filled

the night air. Spotting a clump of cactus, she skirted to the left to avoid its needlelike spines, then forged on, straining to detect any motion ahead of her and stopping every few yards to listen for footsteps. The only sound she heard was the soft scuff of her own padded footfalls.

Fifty feet ahead, something glinted in the silver light. Ellie froze, every sense alert. She stood rooted to the spot, hardly daring to breathe.

She waited an agonizingly long moment before she allowed herself to relax. It must have been her imagination.

She'd just lifted her foot to take a step forward when she saw it again, a brief flicker of movement. Every muscle in her body tensed.

Peering intently, Ellie made out the form of a man crouched next to a scrubby bush. She hesitated, not knowing what to do. She hadn't planned on playing a nighttime game of cat and mouse.

What should her next move be? She'd intended only to identify the perpetrators and confirm their activities. She daren't allow herself to be spotted. But it was vital to ascertain who she was looking at and find out what he was up to.

Ellie glanced to her right, where a large mesquite tree offered cover and a better viewing angle. If she could move over there, she might be able to see well enough to recognize her quarry. Scarcely daring to breathe, she drifted in that direction a few inches at a time, testing every step before putting her weight down.

Once in the shelter of the mesquite, she pressed against the trunk, trying to blend into its shadow. As she hoped, the viewing angle was much better from that vantage point. She leaned forward, willing the man to turn her way.

As if in response, he shifted position, and she saw his face clearly. An icy sickness coiled in the pit of her stomach.

She was looking straight at Donald Tidwell.

Despite Billy Taylor's report, a small part of her had still harbored the hope that the boy had been wrong. Faced with the truth, Ellie found it impossible to keep her anger in check.

Stepping out from the shelter of the mesquite, she covered the distance between them with long strides, not bothering to take care with her footsteps. Just before she reached him, Donald jumped to his feet and whirled to face her.

"Miss Monroe? What are you doing here?"

The shock in his face would have drawn her sympathy under other circumstances. Instead, Ellie gave full vent to her wrath. "How could you be a part of this? I trusted you. *Myra* trusted you!"

She drew in a shuddering breath and let it out on an angry sob. "How could you betray her like this?"

He peered past Ellie as if expecting someone else to appear. Then his face lost its look of a cornered animal and took on a crafty smile. "What are you talking about? Can't a man take a walk in the moonlight without being accused of something?"

Ellie shook her head. "Don't try to talk your way out of this. I know you're in league with the robbers who've been stealing the mine owners blind. I . . . my aunt . . . overheard your plans to get together at the full moon. I didn't want to believe it . . . but here you are."

Donald's attempt at bluster crumbled. "You don't understand." He started walking toward her.

"Don't take another step." Ellie reached inside her reticule and drew out her pistol. Holding it in both hands, she pointed it at Donald, hoping he didn't notice the way it trembled in her grip. "You can say anything you need to from right there."

He stood like a statue and stared at the gun in her hands. "I won't move an inch. Would you mind lowering that thing so it doesn't go off by accident?"

Ellie shook her head slowly. "I trusted you once and found out I was wrong. I won't make that mistake twice. Now, tell me what it is I don't understand."

A tear trickled down Donald's cheek, glistening in the moonlight. "It was all for Myra. I can't stand to see her so sick, but there's nothing any of the docs out here can do for her. She needs to go someplace where she can get better treatment, but I don't have the money to take her."

Moved in spite of herself, Ellie allowed the pistol to droop slightly.

"They promised me a share of the silver if I helped them. I knew it was wrong, but it was the only way I knew to get Myra the help she needs."

Ellie renewed her grip on the gun and brought the barrel back up level. "That's a touching story, but it hardly explains what you're doing here tonight."

Donald stretched out his hands. "I came here to tell them I wanted out. I'm not going to claim my share."

His hands trembled even more than Ellie's. "There's got to be a better way. I used to be a praying man. What I need to do is get back on my knees and see if God will forgive me, or at least make a way to help Myra—one that's honorable."

Ellie wavered a moment, then slipped the pistol back in her reticule. It hadn't been an act, she was sure of it. Every word Donald spoke rang true. She felt a tug of compassion as she looked at the broken man before her. "I believe you."

Donald had made mistakes, certainly, but in the end he wanted to clear his name and make amends. Surely that ought to count for something. And in this contrite mood, she felt sure he'd be willing to give her all the information she and the Pinkertons needed.

She pulled the ties of her reticule shut and took

a step toward Donald. "Why don't you come back to town with me? Maybe I can help you sort this out."

He wiped his sleeve across his face. "If you can help me get rid of this load of guilt I've been carrying, I'll tell you everything I know."

The scrape of boots on gravel cut across his last words, followed by a metallic click Ellie recognized as the sound of a gun hammer slipping into place.

Behind her, a grating voice spoke from the shadows. "I don't think so."

Steven pounded down Second Street following the direction Jessie had taken. There was no point trying to catch up with her. He'd lost too much time with his dithering for that.

The Taylor kid said he'd followed Long out to the Constitution. Jessie would most likely get there by going through town to Fifth, as if heading to the Redemption. But he knew a shortcut.

Taking Second all the way to the south end of town, he cut across country toward the area where the mine headquarters was located. He topped a low rise and paused to catch his breath and scan the terrain before him.

A hundred yards ahead, he caught a hint of movement. Straining his eyes, he could make out Jessie's slender figure in the moonlight, along with two stockier forms. She must have caught up with Long and Tidwell. The thought chilled him.

He cupped his hands around his mouth but stopped himself before he shouted her name. Had she caught up with the two men, or had they ambushed her? One of the men moved, and the glint of moonlight on the barrel of a gun gave him his answer.

"No, Lord! Don't let anything happen to her."

He patted the pockets of his frock coat and growled in frustration. Of course he didn't have a pistol with him. He'd set out for Pickford Hall hoping to begin a courtship, not preparing for mayhem.

Steven looked around wildly. There was no time to get help. No time to retrieve a gun from his office. Throwing all thought of his own safety aside, he raced down the hill. The only weapons he had at his disposal were himself and the most fervent prayers he'd ever uttered.

"Please, God, let that be enough."

The rasping voice spoke again. "What you're going to do, Miss Monroe, is drop that bag and walk over there by Tidwell."

Ellie let her reticule slip through numb fingers and forced her legs to carry her next to Donald. Even before she turned around, she knew who that grating voice belonged to.

Keeping a watchful eye—and a pistol that dwarfed her own—trained on them both, Marvin Long squatted down long enough to scoop up her reticule and loop the strings around his gun belt.

Donald stepped forward. "Glad you showed up. I was on my way to meet up with you when she held me up."

"Nice try, Tidwell, but I heard the whole thing." Long waved his gun to the side. "Now both of you walk ahead of me. No, not to the office," he added when Donald started toward the wooden building twenty yards to their left. "We're going down into the mine."

A lighted lantern hung from a hook inside the mine entrance. Marvin Long picked it up with his left hand, then nodded to Donald and Ellie. "Keep moving."

Ellie stumbled along behind Donald as Long brought up the rear. Once again, the warmth of the air inside the mine came as a surprising contrast to the cooler temperature outside. She took a deep breath, trying to overcome the feeling the walls might close in around her at any moment. Bits of rubble lay scattered across the walkway, making it hard to find her footing.

How deep were they going? With every step she took, Ellie felt less certain she would ever see the surface again. A sense of panic threatened to close off her airway, and she struggled to breathe. She had to keep her wits about her if she hoped to survive this nightmare.

She had to do something, take some kind of action. But what?

She eyed Donald, trudging along in front of her with his head bowed. She couldn't count on him. And the man behind her held a gun, one she felt sure he wouldn't hesitate to use if given the slightest provocation.

The narrow path opened into a large stope. "Bear to the right," Long ordered.

Ellie and her fellow prisoner complied. They rounded a corner, where light filtered through a small opening near the floor.

"Through there."

Ellie's knees locked. Surely he wasn't serious. "How?"

"Get down on your knees and crawl. Tidwell, show her how it's done."

Donald dropped on all fours as if he possessed no will of his own and proceeded to squeeze through the narrow hole.

Long prodded Ellie in the back with the barrel of his gun. "Your turn."

Ellie lowered herself to her hands and knees. *Dear God, what have I gotten myself into?* It was one thing to walk upright through the mine's dark corridors, but this felt more like entering a grave—her own.

She gathered up her skirt so it wouldn't tangle around her legs. Gravel bit into her tender palms as she planted one hand ahead of the other, crawling toward the light.

Emerging from the short tunnel, she blinked in

the sudden brightness. She scrambled to her feet and started to brush the dust off the skirt of the blue-gray silk gown she had chosen for the evening. Her hand froze when a noise caught her attention, and she realized she and Donald weren't alone. Half a dozen lanterns hung around a cavernous room, and four or five men stood staring at them.

Misery engulfed Donald's face. "I'm sorry I got you into this, Miss Monroe. It's poor payment for what you did for my wife."

One of the men set down the crate he'd been carrying. The thump echoed throughout the cavern. "For the love of . . . What's she doing here?" He straightened, bringing his face fully into the lantern's glow.

Ellie's head buzzed. "Jake Freeman?"

The muscular blacksmith avoided her glance as he dusted his hands against his pant legs and stalked over to stand nose to nose with Donald. "I asked you a question, Tidwell. What were you thinking of, bringing her in here?"

"It wasn't me. It was Long's idea."

The rest of the men moved nearer, eyeing Ellie and Donald closely.

Jake shoved his hat back off his forehead and planted his hands on his hips. "Long? I don't see him anywhere. What's going on?"

The sound of cloth scraping against rock came from the passage Ellie had just come through.

Donald gestured toward the hole. "I don't know what took him so long. There he is now."

A figure emerged from the tunnel, but the face she saw was not that of Marvin Long. She watched in horror as Steven crawled out of the opening and stood.

🎐 29 🎐

Ellie watched Steven close the distance between them, feeling as though she'd been caught up in a bad dream. When he put his arm around her shoulders, she stiffened and pulled away from the man she thought she knew.

Marvin Long clambered through the passageway and joined the group. Donald Tidwell and Jake Freeman were men she'd trusted. Men she now knew were part of the band of thieves. As much as she didn't want to believe it of them, her mind accepted that truth.

But Steven?

Long's face wore a grim expression. He looked around the group, then called out, "Hey, boss. We've got visitors."

Footsteps crunched on gravel, drawing Ellie's attention to a formation of rock near the other end of the massive room. A moment later, a man stepped into the light.

Ellie's knees gave way, and she sagged against Steven.

His arm tightened around her, pulling her close. She heard him draw in a sharp breath. "So you're a part of this? I have to admit I didn't see that coming."

Tom Sullivan smiled, his silver hair gleaming in the lamplight. "Not just a part. It's been my operation all along. Sorry you had to find out this way."

Ellie's head swiveled from Steven to Tom and back again. She leaned close to Steven and whispered, "So you aren't one of them?"

He drew back, and she saw a flash of sorrow in his eyes before he pulled her close to his side again.

"No," he murmured. "The only reason I'm here is to protect you."

Tom's laughter bounced off the limestone walls. "You planned to play the hero, eh? Too bad it didn't turn out that way." He turned to the watching men. "Go ahead with what you were doing. We need to get this silver moved out."

He took a stance a few feet in front of Steven and Ellie. "You have to admit, it's been a good plan."

Steven looked around at the stacks of crates waiting to be moved. "I understand that you had a plan." His calm tone belied the tension Ellie felt quivering through him. "What I don't understand is why. The Constitution is a good mine, and it's doing well. Why resort to this?"

A paternal smile creased Tom's face. "You think small, Steven. Great men think big, and I intend to be a great man in this territory. We're moving toward statehood, and I plan to be governor someday, maybe even a U.S. senator.

"Who knows?" The gleam in Tom's eyes turned Ellie's veins to ice. "The White House may even be in my future."

As he talked, the other men carried crates from the room, returning empty-handed to repeat the process in a way that reminded Ellie of a line of worker ants.

Steven watched the crates of silver disappear into the darkness. "But stealing from the other mine owners? From men you called your friends?"

Tom shook his head. "A political career takes capital. More than the Constitution is likely to produce in my lifetime."

He leaned against an outcropping of rock. "Things are changing in the territory, and quickly. I needed a way to amass wealth in a hurry. Once a man's position is established, nobody questions where it came from."

Steven's hands knotted. "You've put together quite a little enterprise."

Three men appeared and lifted the last of the crates, disappearing once again into the cavernous depths. As they left, they carried the remaining lanterns with them, leaving only two sitting on the floor near Marvin Long's feet.

Tom indicated the departing men with a nod. "I couldn't do it on my own. As you can see, I have men from the other mines who provided information and helped stage the robberies. As for Donald, here . . ."

A frown crossed Tom's face. "Donald, why are you just standing there instead of helping?"

Long's lips curled in a sneer. "He's a turncoat, boss. He was gettin' ready to snitch on us."

Tom's brows lifted. "Oh? That's a shame. Ah, well, that just means more for the rest of us to divide."

Marvin Long snickered.

Ellie found her voice. "What about Mr. Freeman?" In spite of the evidence of her own eyes, she still hoped that somehow he hadn't entered this den of thieves of his own free will.

"I can guess what Jake's contribution was," Steven said in a stone-cold voice. "You've had him melting the ingots down and recasting them to hide the silver's origins. Am I right?"

Tom chuckled. "Good guess. Yes, our friend Jake has been quite busy during his evening hours."

"Now what?" Steven looked mad enough to spit nails. "How can you expect to get away with this?"

Tom pushed away from the outcropping and shrugged. "The men are dividing up the shares right now. The others will take theirs and head out for parts unknown. I'll stay here, ready to greet my political destiny . . . and no one will be the wiser."

Steven scoffed. "You don't think anyone is going to question so many people disappearing, all in the same night?"

Tom chuckled again. "I've dropped a few hints here and there about a new silver strike over in New Mexico. You know how mining towns are. Word of a new strike gets around, and people leave in droves.

"Speaking of disappearing"—Tom gestured to Marvin Long—"why don't you bring our guests along to the other end?"

Picking up one of the lanterns, he walked over to the passageway and reached up to a two-by-six protruding from the supporting timbers.

"Are you familiar with mining operations, Miss Monroe? Boards like this are messengers of a sort. If one drops down, it indicates there has been a shift in the rock. Sort of a warning that a cave-in might be imminent."

He gave the board a hard pull and stepped back as a shower of rocks and dirt cascaded to the floor, blocking the exit back to the mine. He pulled a handkerchief from his pocket and used it to cover his mouth as clouds of dust billowed up.

When the dust settled he continued. "Your aunt almost met her end in a similar collapse, but she didn't seem to get the message. It's a pity you seem to have inherited her lack of caution." He motioned them around to the other side of the rock formation.

Tom led the way, holding his lantern aloft to light their path. Steven and Ellie followed, with Donald behind them. Marvin Long brought up the rear, carrying the second lantern in one hand and his gun in the other.

"What is this?" Steven asked after a few yards. "It isn't one of your mine shafts."

"It's a natural cave." Tom sounded as nonchalant as if they were discussing the weather. "We discovered it by chance when we followed a vein this direction and broke through. I had a feeling it would come in handy someday. It opens up on the other side of the hill, well away from town. There's nothing at all to connect it with me or my mine."

Ellie took comfort from Steven's presence as they walked on. To keep hysteria from overtaking her, she concentrated on the rock shapes that cast weird shadows in the light from the moving lanterns. They passed one oddly shaped column after another, their path winding around until she had no idea how far they had come, or from what direction.

An eerie formation rose on her right, reminding her of a troll from one of the Grimm brothers' fairy tales.

Another appeared, this one in the shape of a large rabbit. Ellie felt her tension ease a fraction and kept her mind focused on her whimsy.

Ahead on their left, Tom's lantern illuminated a massive pillar of rock. As they passed, Ellie decided it bore a marked resemblance to Althea Baldwin's profile.

Their route twisted and turned until it finally opened up into a smaller version of the cavern they had been in before.

"Here is where we must part." Tom turned and pulled a small revolver from his jacket pocket. "Marvin, I believe we have some rope a little farther down the tunnel. Would you be so kind?" He leveled the gun at his three captives while Long hurried off.

"You're going to tie us up and leave us here?" Ellie's voice sounded reedy and thin, even to her own ears. "How will we find our way out?"

Steven turned to her, his eyes filled with a grim sadness. "He doesn't mean for us to leave. We know too much."

Dread washed over Ellie in a wave. "But there are people in town who will miss us."

Steven looked back at Tom. "She's right. I already have a profitable mine. I'm not likely to go off chasing rainbows like the others."

Marvin Long trotted back carrying several lengths of hemp rope. At a nod from Tom, he pulled Donald's hands behind his back and wrapped the rope around his wrists.

Tom watched him bind the hotel clerk's hands and feet with an expression of approval, then turned his attention back to Steven.

"No, your tale will be much more romantic than that. You'll be going after something worth even more than gold. I'll let it be known that you came to me and asked me to buy your mine while you and Miss Monroe eloped to San Francisco. I'll make sure a note to that effect is found on your desk tomorrow morning."

Long moved over to Steven. Ellie flinched at his grimace when his bonds were yanked tight.

She shrank away when Long's rough hands reached for hers, but he pulled them behind her back with the same strength she remembered from the assault in the alley. She looked straight at Steven, trying to convey a silent question. Wasn't there anything they could do?

His bleak expression was answer enough.

Tom checked to make sure all the ropes were tight, then he and Long picked up the lanterns and started toward the exit. They hadn't gone more than a few steps when Tom stopped suddenly and turned back.

"Good-bye, Miss Monroe. It's a shame your visit to Pickford had to end this way. And don't expect your aunt to sound an alarm about your disappearance. Once I leave here, I'm going to pay her a visit and stop her snooping once and for all."

With that, he walked away down the tunnel, taking Marvin Long and their only source of light with him.

Fear clutched at Ellie with a clammy hand when the darkness closed in around them. Rustling sounds emanated from the locations where the men lay bound, but she couldn't see a thing in the inky blackness.

"Jessie?" Steven's voice calmed her, even in their dire predicament. "I'm wedged between two rocks, and I can't move very far. See if you can scoot over here. Maybe I can work your knots loose."

She inched her way toward the sound of his voice. Before she had gone more than a foot or two, her skirt snagged on a protrusion of some kind, bringing her to an abrupt halt. "I can't move any farther," she cried. "What are we going to do?"

No sooner had she spoken than she heard a scratching sound, followed by the bright flare of a match. Blinking against the light, she saw Donald standing in front of her, his hands and feet free. While she looked on in astonishment, he pulled a candle from his pocket and lit the wick.

"How did you do that?" she gasped.

In the candlelight, Donald's smile took on a

sinister gleam. "Let's just say I learned a lot practicing those rope tricks." He looked down at her and Steven. "You're both nice people, but if I let you go, you'll turn me in."

Steven eyed him steadily. "That would mean adding murder to what you've already done."

"You're going to leave us here?" Ellie felt her last hope drain away. "No, Donald. You can't."

He took two steps back, and then his shoulders slumped. "You're right, I can't." With a few deft movements, he untied the rope holding Ellie's hands, then moved to release Steven, as well.

Ellie shook her hands free and reached to undo the knots binding her ankles. Yanking her skirt free of the jutting rock, she scrambled over to Steven. Just as she reached him, a muffled *whump* filled the room, followed by an ominous rumble.

The candle flickered wildly. Ellie pressed close to Steven. "What was that?"

"Dynamite." He whipped a bandanna from his pocket and handed it to her as a cloud of dust rolled into the room. "Here, put this around your face. I think they've just dropped the ceiling on the exit."

He tugged his shirt up over his mouth and nose. Behind him, Ellie saw Donald do the same. Long minutes later, the air cleared enough to let them breathe without too much difficulty.

Ellie pulled the handkerchief from her face. "What do we do now?"

"Let's check that exit. This is one time I hope I'm wrong." Steven held out his hand to Donald, who reluctantly surrendered the candle. Steven cupped his hand around the flame. "Thank goodness that blast of air didn't snuff it out."

No one spoke as Steven led the way in the direction Tom and Marvin Long had taken. By Ellie's estimation, they walked about a hundred feet before reaching a forbidding pile of rocks and dirt.

Steven surveyed the rubble. His grim expression did nothing to allay Ellie's mounting terror. "How bad is it?" she asked.

"There's no way to know, but it was a large explosion—we'll never be able to dig our way out."

Her breath came in ragged puffs. "Are you saying they've won? We're going to die down here?"

Steven pressed his lips against her forehead. "Don't give up hope. We aren't done for yet."

"What have you got in mind?" Donald was making an obvious attempt to look brave, but the thread of panic in his voice echoed the fear in Ellie's heart.

"We need to get back to the other end. There isn't as much debris there. We can move it with our hands."

Donald eyed the candle. "How long do you reckon that light's going to last?"

Steven grimaced, as if he wished the other man

403

hadn't raised the question. "A new candle will last about an hour and a half."

Something in his voice set off a warning bell in Ellie's mind. "Is that a new one?"

Steven hesitated, then shook his head. "It's already burned about a third of the way down."

Ellie made a rapid calculation. "So that means we have an hour of light left?"

"We would, if we were sitting still, but we're going to be on the move. I'd give it thirty minutes. Forty, at the outside."

Donald's voice rose half an octave. "It'll take us half that long just to walk back . . . and that's if we can go straight there without getting turned around."

"In that case, we'd better get moving," Steven said. "The important thing is to get there. If we have to, we can go on digging in the dark."

If his remark was meant to be encouraging, it failed miserably. The panic Ellie had tried to hold at bay ever since being captured by Marvin Long tore through her like a monster's claws.

She wanted to say something courageous to reassure Steven she wouldn't be a burden and could accept her fate as calmly as he seemed to, but her throat felt as though a giant had wrapped his hand around her windpipe. She couldn't have spoken even if she could find the right words.

Lord, I read that you always watch over your people. I sure hope you're watching right now.

Steven stepped out with a confidence Ellie hoped was well-founded. Their route from the mine through the cave had followed so many twists and turns, she didn't see how anyone could find his way back through that maze.

They marched along single file, the crunch of footsteps on the cave floor the only sound marking their passage. Ten minutes later, Steven stopped.

"What is it?" Ellie's voice sounded unnaturally loud in the echoing gloom.

"We've gone this way before. I recognize that column over there." He held the candle high, indicating a limestone pillar.

Donald's voice reached an even higher note. "You mean we've been going around in circles?"

"I'm afraid so."

Ellie's gaze fastened on the dwindling candle. According to Steven's reckoning, they had twenty minutes left, no more than thirty. How could they ever find their way back in the dark?

They couldn't.

The knowledge hit her like a blow, and she clenched her lips together to hold back a moan. She looked around at the eerie formations, wondering what it would be like to be stranded in the darkness with those otherworldly shapes for company.

Donald raised another thought. "We could wander around in circles in this cave for a year. . . . Except we won't last anywhere near that long."

Steven's mouth tightened. "How about keeping your thoughts to yourself, unless you have something helpful to say?"

"What about footprints?" Donald persisted. "Aren't there any we can follow?"

"None that are clear enough to show me which direction to take." Steven wiped his free hand across his brow, then set off along a narrow path to their right. "Let's try this way."

"Wait!" Ellie held her ground.

Steven turned. "What is it? We don't have time to waste."

"That's the wrong way." She pointed to the left. "Bring the candle over here."

Steven complied, impatience showing in every movement. "What makes you think this is the right one?"

Ellie swept her arm out in a triumphant gesture. "Althea told me. See?"

Steven and Donald exchanged glances, and then Steven rested his hand on her shoulder. "Mrs. Baldwin isn't here, Jessie. It's easy to let your imagination run away with you in a place like this."

"I am not hallucinating." Grabbing Steven's hand that held the candle, she raised it higher. "Look at that rock over there. It looks like Althea Baldwin's profile. See?"

"Okay," Steven said slowly.

She wanted to shake him.

"Don't you understand? I noticed her before, when Tom led us through here. She was staring the way we came from then, so all we have to do is follow her nose to the mine."

Steven whooped and gave her a hug that nearly squeezed the breath out of her. "Good for you, Jessie. Let's go!"

Ellie allowed a ray of hope to rise within her for the first time since the explosion blocked their exit from the cave. Maybe God was going to get them out, after all.

The men seemed to catch her optimism and moved along more quickly. Ellie's elation grew as she noticed other familiar formations. There was the big rabbit, and farther along, the fearsome troll.

Just beyond the troll, Steven halted again.

Ellie trod upon his heels before she realized he'd stopped. "Now what?"

"I need something I can set this candle on." He held out the stub of wax, burning ominously low between his fingers. "It's getting too hot to carry in my hand."

Ellie stared at their rapidly diminishing source of light and voiced the thought she was sure must be on Steven's mind, as well. "We're not going to make it back to the mine entrance, are we?"

He gave her a quick squeeze, then broke off a

thin, flat slab of rock jutting out from the cave wall. "We know we're on the right track, thanks to you. We'll go as far as we can in the light. When the candle burns out, we'll take it one step at a time. It'll take us longer, but we can feel our way there as long as we know we're heading the right direction."

Behind them, Donald cleared his throat. "Maybe we won't have to."

❧ 30 ❧

Ellie and Steven spun around to see Donald staring at a spindly formation that looked like a cluster of jackstraws.

"What do you mean?" Steven demanded.

Donald reached out his hand. "Can I see the candle for a minute?"

Steven stepped to his side and raised his improvised candleholder. "Why don't you show me what it is you want us to look at?"

Donald indicated a point beyond the feeble gleam. "We can get out that way. If we hurry, we can make it before we lose our light."

Steven eyed him skeptically. "What makes you so sure there's a way out?"

"I don't have time to explain. Do you want to stand here arguing or get out while we still can?" Donald stood up as straight as his round shoulders would allow, and his voice held an assertive tone Ellie hadn't heard before.

Steven turned toward her, looking as surprised as she felt by Donald's sudden show of confidence. "What do you think?"

She looked from the flickering candle flame to the newfound assurance on Donald's face. "Let's try it."

Steven handed the candle to Donald and let the older man take the lead past the jackstraws and into the unknown. Their path zigzagged upward before it led them to a dark opening in the cave wall.

Ellie scrambled after the men, struggling to commit each twist and turn in the path to memory. If Donald's promised exit failed, perhaps they could still find their way back in the dark.

"Through here." Donald held the light for them to pass through the fissure and into a small room. A wooden ladder leaned against one wall, leading to another hole in the ceiling.

Steven stared around him. "What is this place? It can't be part of another mine."

Donald ignored the question and held the candle out to Steven. "I'll go up first. You can hand the candle up to me once I reach the top."

Steven kept his hands at his sides. "I have a better idea. Why don't I go up first, and you hand me the candle?"

Donald accepted Steven's suggestion without argument. "Fine. You go on ahead."

Steven clambered up the ladder and disappeared over the edge of the hole. The next moment, his hand reached back over the opening. "All right, I'm up. Give me the candle."

Donald handed him the rock with its precious blob of wax. Ellie saw the light move around before Steven's head popped over the edge again. "It's all right. Come on up."

Donald helped her step onto the first rung of the ladder. Clutching the ladder with one hand and her voluminous skirts with the other, she made her way up as quickly as the yards of fabric would allow. Once at the top, Steven pulled her the rest of the way over the ledge. Donald followed an instant later.

Steven held the candle up. "You want to tell us where we are?"

The dim glow illuminated another small room containing a broken chair, several pieces of tattered luggage, and a heap of empty crates. Blackened timbers hung from the ceiling at a crazy angle, and an acrid stench permeated the air.

The pungent smell and the sight of the timbers stirred Ellie's memory. She gasped and turned to look at Donald. "The hotel?"

He gave a short nod. "What's left of it. This is the storeroom in the basement."

Steven walked over to a charred set of stairs

that slid to one side the moment he laid his hand on one of the steps. "We're not going to make it up that way."

Donald gestured toward the hole in the floor. "Give me a hand with this ladder."

Steven handed the candle to Ellie. She held it while the two men hauled the ladder up through the floor, unable to tear her focus from its sputtering flame.

Steven set the ladder in what remained of the stairwell and shook it to make sure it was secure. He turned to Ellie with a broad smile just as the candle flickered and died.

Ellie sucked in a panicked breath, then realized she could still make out Steven's form through the gloom. Looking up, she saw moonlight filtering in through the latticework of charred beams.

Thank you, God.

She wanted to grab Steven's hands and spin around in a jubilant dance, but that would have to wait. They weren't out of danger yet.

They ascended the ladder in the same order as before. Steven cautioned her to keep her head low when she reached the top. "Be careful up here. Some of the walls have already fallen, and the rest could go at any minute."

Once out of the storeroom, they made their way across the rubble and ash that littered the main floor of the hotel, testing every step along the way.

They didn't reach the street outside a moment

too soon for Ellie. That section of Grant Street lay deserted in the waning moonlight, with distant sounds of laughter and tinny piano music drifting in from the east.

The silver glow showed clear evidence of their rugged trek. Smudges of charcoal streaked both men's faces, and clumps of gray, powdery ash clung to clothing already coated with dust from the mine.

They looked as if they'd just climbed out of a grave. Ellie felt sure she looked rather like Banquo's ghost herself. But at that moment, only one thing mattered.

"We're alive," she said softly.

Steven responded with a triumphant smile, which faded the next instant. "Come on." He grabbed her hand and started in the direction of Second Street. "We have to make sure your aunt is all right."

"That won't be necessary."

He stopped short and stared at her as though she were crazy. "What are you talking about? You heard what Tom said."

"There isn't any Lavinia."

"You mean she really isn't your aunt. But what does that matter? Whoever she is, she's in danger, and we have to help."

Ellie dug in her heels and stood firm. "I mean there is no Lavinia Stewart, period. No Jessie, no Lavinia, just me."

She watched him struggle to work out what she meant, recognizing the moment he understood her double deception.

"What's going to happen to me?" Donald's voice broke the uncomfortable silence. "I finally got up the nerve to call it quits tonight, but that doesn't take away the wrong of what I've done. But I can't bear the thought of them taking me away from Myra. Who'll take care of her if I'm not around?"

"That isn't for me to decide," Steven said. "But I'd say your decision to quit them and the way you helped us escape ought to count for something. I'll be glad to put in a good word for you with Judge Spicer. If you're willing to testify against the others, that should go in your favor, as well."

Donald clasped his hands together. "I'll tell them everything I know. The devil led me down the wrong path, but I've learned my lesson."

"In that case, let's go wake up Marshal Bascomb. We've got some thieves to catch."

"Bascomb?" Ellie stiffened at the mention of the lawman's name. "What makes you think we can trust him?"

Steven's teeth gleamed in the moonlight, and his smile told Ellie he was recovering from the double blow he'd received. "Under ordinary circumstances, I'd share your doubts. However, I happen to know that Tom Sullivan did everything he could to block Bascomb's appointment as

413

marshal. Believe me, there is no love lost between those two. Bascomb will go after Tom like a cat after a mouse."

"Tom didn't act alone," Ellie said. "What about the others?"

Steven chuckled. "Unless I'm sadly mistaken, Tom will turn on the rest of his gang and sing like a canary. Especially if he thinks it will make him look better in the judge's eyes."

He slipped his arm around her and pulled her close to his side. "This nightmare is finally over. Do you want to go with Donald and me while we talk to Bascomb, or would you rather I see you home first?"

No sooner had he spoken the words than his expression changed. He loosened his arm and drew back, looking at Ellie as if trying to bring her into focus. "Wait a minute. What you said earlier . . ."

Ellie's mouth went dry.

"*You're* the Pinkerton agent?"

"Yes." The word came out as a barely audible sigh.

He moved away another step, sending her fragile hope plummeting again. "In that case, I guess this is your show now. You have even more right to get the law involved than I do."

Ellie stared at him across what seemed like a great chasm, although only a few feet separated them.

Steven was right. The case was over, the mystery solved. She had finished the job she had come to do.

His nightmare had finally ended.

And hers had begun.

❦ 31 ❦

Steven stood beside his foreman and watched a small procession of heavily loaded wagons start off toward Benson, flanked by a contingent of armed men.

Milt Strickland tipped his hat down over his eyes to block the noonday sun. "Do you think they'll have any trouble getting through this time, boss?"

"I think we're past our problems on that score." Steven looked around at the other mine owners assembled nearby. The hope on their faces reflected his own. "But I know I'll breathe easier once I'm sure it's on the train bound for New Orleans."

They watched a few minutes more, then turned back toward the mine. It didn't take them long to reach the south edge of town and walk to the Redemption.

Steven stopped at the door to his office while Milt headed for the mine entrance. "Make sure the men know we won't be scrimping on supplies anymore. I'll be ordering new drill steels and stocking up on plenty of candles and dynamite before the day is out. We ought to be back up to full production in no time."

Milt grinned. "It'll be good to see things get back to normal."

Steven went inside his office, where a stack of paperwork awaited him. He sank into his chair, ignoring the pile of papers on his desk, and pinched the bridge of his nose between his thumb and forefinger. "Normal" had a nice sound to it. It was a shame he wasn't sure what that meant anymore.

Nothing had seemed normal since the silver thefts began. Since financial troubles started keeping him awake at night.

Since Jessie Monroe walked into his life and turned it upside down.

He shoved the papers to one side and rested his forehead on the heels of his hands. If the weeks of frustration and worry seemed chaotic, the past two days had turned his life into a whirl-wind with Steven caught squarely in its vortex. Jessie's revelation about being a Pinkerton agent had been stunning enough, but her insistence that she wasn't even the woman he knew as Jessie Monroe had knocked the props right out from under him.

Did it matter if she used a different name? "*A*

rose by any other name . . ." The line from Shakespeare brought a slight smile to his lips. Why did she seem to think the use of an alias amounted to so much? She had already stolen his heart. What she called herself didn't make one bit of difference to him.

Pushing away from the desk, he got to his feet and paced the office floor. If only he could talk to her, he knew they could work out whatever problems she thought existed between them. But he hadn't seen a trace of her since the night of their narrow escape.

He paused at the window and looked back toward Pickford. After filling Bascomb in on what had happened, he'd escorted Jessie home before setting out with the lawman to confront Tom Sullivan. True to his prediction, the gang's ringleader named every one of his confederates in an attempt to ingratiate himself with the law. Several others had already been caught, Marvin Long among them, and Bascomb expected to have the rest in custody within the week.

Recovering the silver and knowing his financial troubles were over should have left him riding high on elation instead of fighting the sense of emptiness that gnawed at him.

In between parceling the silver out to the rightful owners and arranging for it to be shipped to New Orleans, he'd gone to the house at the corner of Charles and Second to straighten things

417

out. But no one responded to his knocks on the door, or to the heavy hammering he'd employed when polite taps didn't work.

And that left him with a new worry. Jessie—Ellie, he reminded himself—planned to go back to Chicago. Had she already left, without a word of good-bye? When he approached Brent Howard, the station agent told him she hadn't left town on the stage. So where could she be?

Steven pounded his fist against the wall, wishing the pain in his knuckles could take away the ache in his heart. He had his silver back, but she was gone. After all was said and done, it astonished him how little the recovery of the silver mattered in comparison to losing the woman he loved.

Another thought occurred to him, one that filled him with dread. She had shown herself to be a highly skilled actress, convincing him and everyone else in Pickford she was a high-spirited young woman—and an aged woman—rather than a skilled detective.

Had the connection between them been a part of the act, as well?

She had avoided him after the fire, when he'd brushed her lips with his. Now it seemed she was avoiding him again. A sick feeling settled in the pit of his stomach. Maybe her attraction to him had been an act.

Pulling his wayward emotions under control, he

returned to his desk and squared the papers into a neat pile. He looked at the top sheet and reached for his pen. It was time to stop acting like an infatuated schoolboy.

Ellie looked around the parlor of her little house, ticking items off her mental checklist. Had she missed anything? Her trunk sat open near the front door, with the wicker costume hamper alongside. The hamper and its contents had served her well during her stay in Pickford. There were still more items in its depths that she hadn't had occasion to use yet, but they might come in handy in her future cases.

After her telegram informing the Pinkertons that the gang of robbers had been identified and the leader was already in the custody of the law, a flurry of jubilant wires ensued, giving Amos Crawford enough fodder to keep the town gossip mill churning away for the next six months.

Along with their hearty congratulations, Gates and Fleming made it clear that her future employment was assured for as long as she wanted to remain with the agency. Ellie's lips twisted in a wry smile. At least she had that bittersweet victory for comfort.

She had packed her bags and tidied the house in preparation for catching the afternoon stage to Benson. There she would board the train for Chicago, where—judging from Fleming's response

—she could expect a hero's welcome when she reached the home office.

Her time in Pickford had taught her one important thing. On future cases, she would be sure to keep her affections firmly under control. From this day forth, she would focus every bit of her attention on the case at hand and not let herself get caught up in the people involved. Losing Steven was the most painful thing she'd ever had to endure. Her heart would never bear that a second time.

She picked up her Bible from the marble-top table and laid it in the open trunk with care. Then she shut the lid and fastened the latch. One good thing that had come out of this tumultuous period in her life—her renewed relationship with God. No matter what she faced in the future, He would be there to strengthen her.

And wrestle with her from time to time when her will didn't agree with His.

After the bouts they'd already had over the past day and a half, she felt sympathy for what Jacob must have gone through, grappling with that angel. As exhausted as she'd been when she arrived home in the wee hours following the ordeal in the cave, she found herself unable to sleep. Instead, she'd divided her time between making preparations for her departure and spending time on her knees, thanking God for leading her to the thieves.

For getting them out of the cave without mishap. For the capture of Tom Sullivan and most of his gang.

She'd thought her outpouring of thanks would have been sufficient for the Almighty, but no—apparently there was something else He wanted of her, and that was when their wrestling match had commenced in earnest. After hours of arguing—and losing—her case, she rose from her knees, as stiff as Lavinia had ever been, knowing what she had to do.

It wasn't enough that she'd brought Tom Sullivan's thieving days to an end. Now it seemed God had one more thing for her to accomplish before she left Pickford. She had to make her peace with Steven Pierce. And not as Jessie or Lavinia this time.

Ellie still didn't understand that part of the Lord's directive, but she suspected it had something to do with the importance of integrity that Pastor Blaylock kept harping on. She supposed it only made sense. Going about in disguise seemed perfectly reasonable when it came to carrying out an investigation. She didn't sense the Lord taking any exception to that.

The point where she'd gotten herself into trouble was when she let her character become entangled with Steven. She had played with fire, and they'd both been burned. She had no right to trifle with his emotions that way.

The man had fallen in love with a woman who didn't exist. It was only right that she face him and try to make amends before she left. Much as she dreaded shattering his image of beautiful Jessie, he deserved to know the truth. Even if that meant seeing the disappointment in his eyes when he beheld her as herself.

She walked back into her bedroom and checked her appearance in the dressing table mirror. It seemed odd to see her own bland features looking back at her instead of Lavinia's or Jessie's. She poked at her mousy brown hair, wishing there was something she could do to make it more like Jessie's copper ringlets.

Ellie wrinkled her nose at the reflection. Her features were regular enough, but they held nothing of Jessie's sparkle and verve. She pinched her cheeks to bring out a bit of color and watched the pink tinge fade almost as quickly as it appeared. A sigh escaped her lips. She would just have to go the way she was.

She walked out to the front porch and shut the door behind her, ready to step out onto the streets of Pickford as Ellie Moore for the very first time.

Walking down Second to Grant at a leisurely pace, she nodded to people as she passed by. Most of them returned her greeting, but they were nods of politeness rather than recognition, accompanied by the mild curiosity shown toward any newcomer.

Ellie stopped when she reached the south edge of town and gazed out over the desert, remembering the way it had looked bathed in moonlight during her pursuit of Marvin Long two nights before. Then the moon's glow had softened the landscape, but today the view was stark and barren in the noonday sun.

She picked up her pace as she walked the now familiar path to the mine office. She had timed her visit carefully, allowing herself just long enough for her revelation to Steven before making a hasty exit in time to catch the stage. There was no point in prolonging the agony for either of them.

At the door to Steven's office, she paused with her hand on the door latch and looked over toward the Constitution. God had delivered the three of them from what seemed like certain death in the cave, just as He had delivered Daniel from the lions' den. She hoped the Lord was still in a delivering mood today. At the moment, facing Steven seemed a lot more worrisome than confronting a group of hungry lions.

He looked up when she entered. Before she could say a word, he sprang to his feet and circled around his desk.

The nearness of him made her catch her breath. Squaring her shoulders, she lifted her chin and stepped toward him, extending her hand. She felt the familiar tingle run up her arm when he clasped her fingers. "I thought it was time we were properly introduced. My name is Ellie Moore."

Instead of releasing her, he tightened his grip and sandwiched her hand between both of his while he stared into her eyes. A look of wonder spread across his face, and his lips curved up in a slow smile. "Ellie Moore. That's a beautiful name."

Ellie tugged at her hand, but his fingers only increased their pressure. She stared back at him and frowned. Had the man taken leave of his senses?

He pulled on her hand, drawing her closer to him. His eyes wandered over her face as though taking inventory of every feature. "I like Ellie. It fits you even better than Jessie did."

She felt as if she'd just stepped off into a mine shaft. "You couldn't possibly have recognized me. How did you know?"

Steven raised one hand and traced his finger along her brow. "Those eyes, those amazing eyes. I'd know them anywhere."

Lord, why are you making this so hard? Ellie bit her lip. She was doing all she could to be obedient. She'd think the Lord would at least meet her halfway.

If she was going to complete her mission, she needed to keep her distance. Standing so close to Steven was throwing her senses into a muddle. Pulling her hand free, she moved away from him toward the desk.

He closed the distance between them with one easy stride.

Ellie sidestepped, putting the desk between them. If he kept on looking at her with that burning gaze, she was going to forget why she was there.

She caught a quick breath and tried to maintain her focus. "I came here to apologize . . . and say good-bye."

"Apologize for what?" He advanced to the left side of the desk.

Ellie retreated three steps to her right. "For deceiving you. For not letting you know who I really am."

"It was part of your job. I know that now. I'll admit it took me a while to understand that, but you were only using an assumed name. That was just a pretense to help your investigation. You weren't misleading me about who you really are. You're part Lavinia, part Jessie, and totally wonderful."

He leaned across the desk and reached out as if to touch her cheek. "It's like I tried to tell you the other night. Something in my soul seemed to recognize you the moment we met."

Ellie backed up again and bumped against the office wall. Her breath came out in a sob. "How can you say that? I don't look a thing like her . . . like Jessie. You can't possibly know who I am."

"You're wrong. And I can prove it." Rounding the desk, he took her by the arm and led her to the window. "Look out there. What do you see?"

Ellie twisted around to look up at him over her shoulder. "What do I see? You mean the clouds? The sky? The mountains?"

He pressed closer to her, his sleeve brushing her cheek when he pointed at the rolling landscape before them. "Right out there in front of us. Tell me what you see."

Ellie turned back to the window, more mystified than ever. "Dirt. Trees. Shrubs. Cactus. Is that what you mean?"

His voice held a smile when he spoke. "Let me tell you what a miner sees. Over there is an outcropping of quartz. To me, that indicates an uplift that has probably caused a fault line under the surface. And that could be a sign that precious metals are present."

He took her shoulders with a light touch and turned her to face him. "A trained eye knows how to look below the surface to see the treasure that lies beneath." He gazed at her with an intensity that made her shiver. "Do you know what I see when I look at you?"

Tears brimmed her eyes, and she shook her head wordlessly, afraid of what he was about to say.

He leaned so close that his breath caressed her cheek. "When I look at you, I see your determination, your selflessness. I see a person willing to put herself at risk for people she doesn't even know."

His hand cupped her chin and lifted it so that she stared straight into his eyes. "I see the beauty of your character—and it takes my breath away."

Ellie listened in disbelief. Could this be happening? For her—for Ellie—this time? Her entire body began to tremble.

Steven took her right hand and cradled it against his chest. "Don't go back to Chicago, Ellie. Not right away, at least. I have a feeling God has something special in store for the two of us, and I can't bear the thought of letting that slip away."

She couldn't hold her tears back one moment longer. They spilled down her cheeks, and her shoulders shook with sobs. "I can't believe . . . I never thought . . ." She covered her face with her left hand and tried to regain her composure. "I'm sorry. I just can't find the words."

She heard the scrape of Steven's boot against the plank floor. The next moment, his arms wrapped about her and pulled her close. "Stay in Pickford, Ellie. Give us a chance to find out if we're meant for each other. I think I already know the answer, but I want to give you time to be sure."

She flung her arms around his neck and let her kiss answer for her. His arms tightened as his lips pressed against hers. When she could breathe again, she looked up at him and gave a shaky laugh. "Just in case I didn't make myself clear, that was a yes."

Steven pulled back and gazed down at her, his eyes full of laughter. "I rather thought it might be."

She squealed as he tightened his arms about her and whirled her around the office. "What are you doing?"

"Celebrating the beginning of something wonderful." He set her down on the floor again and rested his forehead against hers, his breath teasing at her cheek. "With all the uncertainties the future may hold, one thing I'm certain of— life with you will never be dull."

AUTHOR NOTE

Dear Reader:

As a third-generation Arizonan, my love for this state and its history is deeply rooted, first through countless hours of listening to stories told at family gatherings about the "old days," and later through my own explorations along any number of highways and byways. As newlyweds, my husband and I lived in Sierra Vista, which became our base for making weekend forays, including my first visit to Tombstone. What an experience to walk the streets made famous by Old West figures such as Wyatt Earp and Doc Holliday! That fascination with Tombstone and the surrounding area stayed with me over the years, and I was thrilled to share my enthusiasm for that corner of Arizona by using it as the background for Ellie's adventures.

I'm often asked if my books are set in real places, and the answer varies. Sometimes an actual town provides the perfect location, but other times the story demands a special setting all its own. *Love in Disguise* is one of those books. You won't find Pickford on any map of Arizona, but in my imagination it's alive and thriving only a few miles away from Tombstone along the San Pedro River. I took the liberty of borrowing some elements from Tombstone—the mines located just outside the town and the layout of some of the streets—then rearranged them to suit this story. Oh, and there's the portrait of Fatima. That painting—complete with numerous bullet holes—hangs in Tombstone's Bird Cage Saloon. I invited Fatima to put in a guest appearance in my book, and she didn't seem to mind.

Like most of you, I wear a number of hats as I go through my daily life. I'm a pastor's wife, homeschool mom, grandma, writer, church pianist, Sunday school teacher, women's Bible study leader, co-director of our local historical society . . . The list goes on and on. Like Ellie, I sometimes feel I'm constantly switching from one role to another. If I don't watch out, it's easy to forget who I really am. How grateful I am that my true identity doesn't have to be defined by my success—or lack of it—in any of those areas, but in my relationship to the King of kings!

Thank you for taking time to read this book. Wherever you go and whatever you do, may you find your true identity and purpose in Him!

Carol
Philippians 4:4

ABOUT THE AUTHOR

Author of nearly 30 novels and novellas, **CAROL COX** has an abiding love for history and romance, especially when it's set in her native Southwest. As a third-generation Arizonan, she takes a keen interest in the Old West and hopes to make it live again in the hearts of her readers. A pastor's wife, Carol lives with her husband and daughter in northern Arizona, where the deer and the antelope really do play—within view of the family's front porch.

To learn more about Carol, please visit her at:

Her Web site: *www.AuthorCarolCox.com*
Her blog: *www.AuthorCarolCox.com/journal*
Facebook: *www.facebook.com/carol.cox*
Twitter: *www.twitter.com/authorcarolcox*

Center Point Large Print
600 Brooks Road / PO Box 1
Thorndike ME 04986-0001 USA

(207) 568-3717

US & Canada:
1 800 929-9108
www.centerpointlargeprint.com